PRAISE FOR THE NOVEL

I come from a family descended from Gabriel Renville (Ti Wakaŋ, Sacred Lodge), a Sisituŋwaŋ headman who helped to resolve the U.S.-Dakota War of 1862. But among my people that conflict never ended. It still divides us today. We were once a strong, spiritual people. We need reminders of who we really are and where we come from. *Beneath the Same Stars* helps us reexamine our own history and identity. Will that create some positive change among us? I hope so, for the sake of our children, most of all.

> —DARLENE RENVILLE PIPEBOY
> Independent Dakota scholar and elder

This is a sensitive portrait of a complicated woman caught in the politically and culturally fraught conflict that led to the U.S.-Dakota War. It both reflects the prejudices and divisiveness of that time and offers bridges to help heal the rifts between and within the communities that continue to be affected by the events of 1862 and their aftermath. The novel turns historical figures into living, breathing embodiments of the conflict, making tangible both the historical events and the contemporary impact of those events on all the affected communities. It raises questions and concerns of substance rather than trying to resolve them and is a constructive contribution to the dialogue we continue to need.

> —CAROL CHOMSKY
> Professor, University of Minnesota Law School,
> and author of "The United States-Dakota War
> Trials: A Study in Military Injustice"

Beneath the Same Stars weaves feeling and concern into the tragic landscape of the U.S.-Dakota Conflict. Readers are taken on a journey beyond history-book headlines and into the world of a woman who, despite confusion and weakness, dares to care. The story has echoes for today—it invites us all to acknowledge and appreciate cultural differences despite the ever-present social anxiety directing us not to.

—JIM GREEN
Former director, Institute for Dakota Studies,
Sisseton Wahpeton Tribal College, and current
co-director, Center for Indigenous Teaching,
Sinte Gleska University

This novel, whose title beautifully expresses the ongoing relevance of the so-called "past," should be widely read and discussed in schools and communities. Through impressive research and powerful storytelling, Cole-Dai contextualizes one of this country's most tragic histories exceptionally well. *Beneath the Same Stars* is a significant contribution to the literature of cross-cultural understanding.

—CHARLES L. WOODARD
Distinguished Professor Emeritus, South Dakota
State University, and author of *Ancestral Voice:
Conversations with N. Scott Momaday*

BENEATH THE SAME STARS

A Novel of the 1862 U.S.-Dakota War

PHYLLIS COLE-DAI

ONE SKY PRESS

BENEATH THE SAME STARS. Copyright © 2018 by Phyllis Cole-Dai.

For information write to the publisher: One Sky Press, 46855 200th St., Bruce SD 57220-5210.

Visit the author's website at www.phylliscoledai.com.

Cover Design by www.e-booklaunch.com.
Printed in the United States of America.
Beneath the Same Stars / Phyllis Cole-Dai—1st ed.
ISBN 978-0692154151

Mitakuyeowasina wićoye waśte

To the healing of the peoples,
all my relatives

ACKNOWLEDGMENTS

A multitude of people assisted me in the creation of this book, most of them without even realizing. I can't possibly name them all or cite every way they helped me. But I wish to lift up certain people for special thanks.

I'm indebted to the published writings of Gary Clayton Anderson, Walt Bachman, Mary Hawker Bakeman, Scott Berg, Elijah Blackthunder, Clifford Canku, Carol Chomsky, Linda M. Clemmons, Ella Deloria, Mark Diedrich, Craig Howe, John Isch, Norma Johnson, Elden Lawrence (in special remembrance), Roy Meyer, Corinne Monjeau-Marz, June Namias, David Nichols, Larry O'Connor, Muriel Pronovost, Antona M. Richardson, Michael Simon, Virginia Driving Hawk Sneve, Delphine Red Shirt, Gwen Westerman, Bruce White, Waziyatawin Angela Wilson, Mary Lethert Wingerd, Alan Woolworth, Kathryn Zabelle Derounian-Stodola and Carrie Reber Zeman. Anderson and Woolworth's *Through Dakota Eyes: Narrative Accounts of the Minnesota Indian War of 1862* was indispensable.

I'm grateful for the expert assistance of Marie-Pierre Baggett, Dusty Beaulieu, Terri Dinesen, Betty Dols, Sandee Geshick, Peter Boulay, Bernice Hoffman, Craig Howe, Franky Jackson, Mark Kratochvil, Harvey Markowitz, Virginia Meyer, Darlene Renville Pipeboy, Deanna Stands, James Star Comes Out, Daniel W. Stowell, Brian Szott, J.B. Weston, and various staff at the following institutions: Blue Earth County (MN) Historical Society; Brookings (SD) Public Library (Betsy Lenning); Minnesota Historical Society; North Kingstown (RI) Free Library; Briggs Library, South Dakota State University; Ramsey County (MN) Historical Society (Elizabeth Rosenberg); Scott County (MN) Historical Society; South Dakota State Archives (Virginia Hanson); and South Dakota Art Museum (Jodi Lundgren, Lisa Scholten).

I have no words to adequately thank the remarkable friends who served as critical readers for various drafts of my manuscript and who were such insightful companions throughout my research and writing. I bow in appreciation to the generosity and expertise of Jordan Curnutt,

Ruth Harper, Sarah Hernandez, Darlene Renville Pipeboy, Ruby Wilson and Chuck Woodard.

Also helping to shore me up by their encouragement, hospitality and/or sharing of wisdom were Carl Kline, Julia Eagles and Abby Finis, Mavis Gehant, the Todd and Ann Hampson family, Mary Alice Haug, Franky Jackson, Faith Spotted Eagle, Jim Wilson, my friends in Stand for Peace, and my parents Carol and Lynn Cole.

To Ruby Wilson: Our weekly sack lunches were welcome escapes from my tempest-pot of work. Thank you for your patient and attentive listening, your astute observations, and your gentle reminders to take more breaks. I treasure your presence in my life.

I bow in gratitude to my husband Jihong Cole-Dai, who always believes in my projects, no matter how demanding, so much so that they seem to belong to us both; and to our son Nathan, full of heart and light, who likes to look over my shoulder as I write, even as I like to look over his. I love you both.

Finally, I bow to the life-givers who have gone before.

TO THE READER

Beneath the Same Stars is based on the life of Sarah Wakefield, a white doctor's wife who was caught up in the U.S.-Dakota War of 1862. That conflict, obscured in national memory by the concurrent Civil War, saw a faction of the Dakota nation (i.e., "the eastern Sioux") rise up against American government workers, traders, settlers and troops in south-western Minnesota. Though lasting only six weeks, from August 18 to September 23, it was pivotal in the history of this continent.

I wrote this novel because I was fascinated by the people involved and by their shared history. I wanted to bear witness to them, create empathy for them, and facilitate greater understanding of the complex world they inhabited. I also wrote because I'm troubled by how some of the uglier dynamics of their nineteenth-century world are still with us, contributing to much suffering. I wanted to shine a light on those dynamics, spark discussion of them, and help promote wise changes in the status quo.

Stories can be good medicine for what ails us. That's why we bother to tell them. They delve beneath jockeying facts and opinions to help us fathom one another and ourselves. They can nudge us toward the difficult reparation of wrongs, long recovery from woundedness and trauma, and the prevention of additional injury.

I offer this story with a good heart for the healing of the peoples. In the hard work of repair, we have much yet to do.

NOTES ON LANGUAGE

This novel's nomenclature for tribal peoples conforms to nineteenth-century parlance. Indian characters identify themselves as Dakota instead of Sioux. Their aboriginal name means *friend* or *ally*, whereas Sioux, a name assigned by a traditional enemy, the Anishinaabeg, appears to derive from a word meaning *little snakes*. Euro-American characters, meanwhile, refer to Dakotas as Sioux, to Anishinaabeg as Chippewas, and to Ho-Chunks as Winnebagos.

Dakota characters belong to one of four tribal subdivisions, listed here by their anglicized names: the Mdewakantonwans and Wahpekutes, collectively referred to as the Lower Sioux; and the Sissetons and Wahpetons, known as the Upper Sioux.

In writing Dakota words I relied heavily (as did Sarah) on the *Grammar and Dictionary of the Dakota Language* (1852), compiled by the Presbyterian missionary Stephen Riggs. His was the only published Dakota orthography in use during the mid-nineteenth century. I'm indebted as well to several contemporary Dakota speakers who lent their expertise to this project. Foremost among them is Darlene Renville Pipeboy, a Sisseton elder. For your reference I've included a Dakota glossary in the back of the book.

Every Dakota person of Sarah's acquaintance had multiple names. For example, her protector Ćaske, *First Son* (a birth order name), was also Wićaŋḣpi Waśtedaŋpi, *He Who Is Liked By The Stars* (a given name). In writing the novel I generally privileged the names Sarah used for individual Indians in her captivity narrative, entitled *Six Weeks in the Sioux Teepees*. Learn more about her narrative and the factual underpinnings of this novel in the Author's Afterword.

Sioux Outbreak, Sioux Uprising, Little Crow's War, Dakota Conflict ... over the years this six-week period of hostilities has acquired a variety of names. I tend to call it the U.S.-Dakota War of 1862, a recent term that more clearly identifies the parties involved. However, within the novel you will hear language of the period.

I was reluctant to give voice to the racial, ethnic and religious slurs commonly employed in Sarah's day. While whitewashing the language—and with it, the history—of any historical period is risky, I resorted to such pejoratives only when necessary for the sake of story-truth.

BENEATH THE SAME STARS

I

❧ I ❧

JUNE 9, 1861

"*HERE IS* where I'm to live? *This* is where you've brought me?"

Sarah steps off the sternwheeler's deck onto planking, her only bridge to land. Ahead of her, three-year-old James skitters down the boards to the sandy bank where John has dropped their bags. Nellie is fussing in the crook of John's arm. The girl always fusses when he's got her. Even a baby can tell when she's not wanted; when she has been born other than what she should have been.

Sarah stands motionless on the planking, peering through the fringe of her frayed parasol at the hundreds of Sioux on the riverbank, wrapped in blankets of every color. They're making a study of the freight and live-stock. Of the disembarked passengers, laboring up the steep footpath to the heights. Of *her*, the last white woman off the boat. They don't look happy. Hereabouts, Indians aren't wanted either.

She lifts her skirts and inches down the soft boards, not trusting their warp beneath her weight. Three days ago, in Shakopee, she and John had loaded onto the *Jeanette Roberts* what was left of their earthly possessions. Then the boat snaked up the Minnesota, putting in at a string of Valley towns. After the German settlement of New Ulm, the world of whites receded. All that remained was the infernal river. It refused to run straight. Sometimes, to make a mile, it zigzagged fifteen. The bow of the boat was forever sweeping around another bend. She despaired of ever reaching the end almost as much as she dreaded getting there. At last, on this godfor-saken Sunday, she has been spat out upon dry land, like Jonah from the whale. She can scrape up no words for this wild country, where her skin is ten shades too pale and her hard-won sophistication worth less than a leaky teakettle. The only sign of white civilization is a blacksmith's shop.

The planking ends in mud and a swarm of black flies. "Here, John? *Truly?*"

"No, not here." He helps her to shore. "The rest, we go by wagon."

"A reservation's no place to rear children! It's no place to take a proper wife!"

"Sarah, I've *told* you—we won't be here long." Nellie is fighting him, starting to squall.

"But I didn't traipse clear across the country to live like this!"

"The last Sioux agent is building himself a mansion. Three stories, nineteen rooms, two pianos. There's no reason I shouldn't fare as well, even as physician. Thomas all but said so. Wouldn't you like to have a piano again?"

She hides beneath the meager shelter of her parasol. She has no objection to the Sioux, really. Why, in Shakopee, she used to trade with them in the streets. On occasion she would drive the carriage out from town to visit the women at Tiŋta Otoŋwe, the village of chief Śakpe. She would even welcome the Indians who appeared unannounced at her house, always when John wasn't home. She would turn from the stove or look up from her ironing to find herself watched. She could have locked the house against them, but they were never hostile, and she learned not to be afraid. She gave them potatoes and turnips from the cellar. She applied salve to their sores and administered whatever powders and tinctures she dared to pilfer from John's medicine cabinet. She let them page through her books and plunk keys on her piano. Her parlor still had one, then. "Wopida," they would say, before vanishing. "You're welcome," she would say.

But she hasn't seen an Indian in better than two years. Not since the treaty-signing in '58, when the U.S. government agreed to pay the eastern Sioux tribes fifty years of annuities and provisions in exchange for their old hunting grounds. Soon after, Śakpe's people retreated onto a sliver of reservation along the upper Minnesota. Tiŋta Otoŋwe fell into gentle ruin, overrun by vines, inhabited by ghosts.

Now John has brought her here, to that very reservation, to raise her babies. To actually *live* among the Indians, in God knows what kind of house and conditions, remote from any white town.

"I can't do it! I *won't* do it! Take me home!"

"Christ." He shoves a wailing Nellie into her ribs, yanks away her parasol, collapses the canopy, spanks the handle beneath his arm. "For the *last time*"—he leans toward her ear, lowers the menace in his voice—"I'll be making a thousand dollars a year. *More,* under the table. After everything we've lost, you *know* what that will mean. So, let's be getting on with it, shall we?" He straightens, adjusting his crooked pince-nez.

Soothing Nellie, she casts a look at the column of new government men plodding up the hill with their kin. Thomas is in the lead with Henrietta and their two youngsters, almost out of sight in the trees. Friends they might be, but he, more than anyone, is to blame for this. A change in Presidents, and suddenly he isn't Mister but "Major" Galbraith, Indian agent, in charge of all the Sioux in Minnesota. Laughable. What he knows about Indians wouldn't fill his whiskey glass. She could say the same about John, not to mention his brother J.B. and every other Mason whom Thomas has named to plum reservation posts. Empty glasses, all of them.

John collects his medical bag and their valise. "*Shall* we?" he says again.

"What about the rest of our things?"

"Don't be fretting, my pet. Sioux will cart them up the bluff. If they steal so much as a hairpin, Thomas will have their hides."

With a sigh she holds out her free hand to James. "Ready, little man?"

She tows him into line behind George Gleason, another Masonic Brother. He's singing to himself, like always. His pup Sadie, riding his shoulder, paws at the pheasant feather in his hat.

"One term," she calls to John behind her, Nellie cooing at her neck. "As soon as Mr. Lincoln's finished, I'm going home. With or without you."

A HALF-MILE STRAIGHT UP FROM THE LANDING, SHE TOPS THE HILL, BEADS OF perspiration rolling down her face and limbs. She pauses for breath. Ahead, an array of buildings squats on the prairie, hundreds of feet above the Minnesota.

"Mama"—James tugs at her arm—"are we there yet?"

"Welcome to Redwood!" A burly, red-faced man seizes John's medical bag and starts pumping his hand. "You must be Wakefield. I'm Philander Humphrey, physician here at the Lower Agency. You'll be staying with us tonight. Wife's waiting, this way...."

John crouches low for James to climb on his shoulders. "Good of you, Humphrey."

"House rules: No liquor, no tobacco, no cards. And I'll have no talk of slavery. I'm a man of principle."

Up the lane they meet a couple of Indians in settler dress. Humphrey nods them a greeting. Once they're past, he spits. "Some of Hinman's converts. He has an Episcopal meetinghouse to the east of here. Papist, if you ask me."

"How many Indians do you have here, Doctor?"

"A couple thousand, Missus. Where you'll be, on the upper reservation, at least twice that many, but they live further out from the Agency than our Indians."

"So"—bouncing Nellie to relieve the ache in her arm—"four thousand of *them*, and how many of *us?*"

"Can't say for certain. Fewer than here at Redwood. We're about a hundred, if you count the dogs."

Despite being the headquarters of the Lower Sioux reservation, the Agency town looks smaller than Exeter, her tiny home village in Rhode Island. A boardinghouse, mess house, barns, stables, storehouses and various employee dwellings center on a green called "Council Square." A trading post, Humphrey tells them, is within a short walk across the ravine.

Most of the government buildings are neat and sturdy, their white paint weathering to gray. But the agent's quarters is a lopsided two-story cabin. This is where Thomas will reside when duty summons him from the Upper Agency. She conceals a smile in Nellie's curls. Such impressive lodging for a "Major." If the cabin doesn't topple over first, J.B. will also be quartered there, as deputy agent. He's yet to arrive from Blue Earth City.

"Dr. Humphrey"—she pries Nellie's fingers from her nose—"do you and your wife have children?"

"Why, yes, God's blessed us with three."

"And do you feel safe, living here?"

"Don't worry your pretty head, Missus. The Sioux up your way are mostly farmers and mission Indians, all pretty docile. The Devil's been beaten out of them by now. But in case of trouble, Fort Ridgley isn't far off."

Weak reassurance. On the way here, the *Jeanette Roberts* landed below Fort Ridgley to offload military freight and a few troops. While the crew resupplied the boat with wood for the boilers, she and John ventured up the gentle bluff with other passengers to tour the garrison. Ridgley afforded a fine view of the Minnesota Valley, to be sure, but it stood in the open on wind-blown prairie, with neither palisades nor earthworks for protection. Manned by a ragtag force—a couple hundred men at most, with sway-backed mules—it was a fort in nothing but name.

AT DAWN THE NEXT DAY THEY SET OUT IN A TRAIN OF SEVEN WAGONS FOR THE Upper Sioux Agency, also called Yellow Medicine, thirty miles to the northwest. Behind Sarah's buckboard rolls a freight wagon laden with chests under canvas. They're said to contain $160,000 in gold coin, the upcoming annuity payment for the Sisseton and Wahpeton tribes—the Upper Sioux, as they're known.

She cares little about annuities, rations and what-not, but from nervousness about the gold and the chance of ambush, she cleaves to her babies. When the train trundles through the village of chief Little Crow, several miles above Redwood, Indians converge for a glimpse of their "new white Father." She covers James and Nellie with a blanket on the floor as Thomas waves his hat from the lead wagon. "Not one wiggle or peep," she warns, "till Mama says so!"

The wagon train is beyond the last village on the lower reservation when she throws back the blanket. "Look, children!" She pulls her babies up. "Isn't it beautiful?" The sky is the color of her boy's bluest marble. On either side of the rutted road, wildflowers wave in the tallgrass, tossed by wind. The vegetation sways to the reach of the horizon, displaying subtle shifts in shape and color, as though the land itself were breathing.

LOW GRAY CLOUDS ADVANCE FROM THE WEST ACROSS THE LUMINOUS DOME of sky.

"A storm brewing?" she asks John.

"I doubt it. Smoke from a prairie fire, perhaps."

Little by little the sky darkens to slate. Only when overtaken by shadow do they see the clouds for what they are: vast legions of passenger pigeons, a mighty Mississippi of wings.

The men shoot for sport as the wagons move north, competing for kills. George Gleason, with a single shot, plugs seventeen birds. It's a full hour before the last pigeons pass over. The dead are left to rot where they dropped.

MIDDAY, THEIR BUCKBOARD IS BOGGED DOWN IN MIRE. DRENCHED IN SWEAT, Sarah helps offload trunks, crates and barrels, slipping and sliding in mud, smacking at mosquitoes and black flies. This is the fourth time one of the wagons has stuck fast in a slough. The length of the government road wants for bridges.

Once the buckboard is empty, the teamster enlists all hands in the train to dig at the sunken wheels, to strain at the push. "On three!" he cries.

Sarah throws her weight against the wagon. She's a big woman; bigger than John beside her, bigger than every man in their company.

"Again, on three!"

Knee-deep in slop, they grunt and heave. Grunt and heave.

"Again!"

The wagon nudges forward, rocks back.

"And *again!*"

This time they groan the wagon into a roll and propel it to drier ground. Dripping mud, Sarah raises a delirious cheer. Henrietta Galbraith and the other women moan over their ruined dresses.

"But look"—Sarah smears her fingers down her cheeks—"beauty mud, like Cleopatra!" She dissolves into a fit of laughter.

John attacks his mud-flecked spectacles with his kerchief. "Lost her senses in the sun," he says to Gleason, beside him.

THE PRAIRIE SHIMMERS LIKE A MIRAGE; A GREAT LAKE OF RIPPLING GRASS, tinted violet with bluejoint. Last hour they met a freight wagon headed down from Yellow Medicine. Otherwise, except for a slew of jackrabbits and an occasional Sioux, the rough road has been deserted.

Their teamster points out Joseph Brown's mansion across the river. Built of pink granite, the house has a full-length veranda along each of its three stories. Somewhere inside its nineteen rooms are two pianos, doubtless exquisite.

"What did I tell you?" John says, in her ear.

"The Major's door is always open," the teamster tells the wagon. "His missus is part Sioux. Indians are right neighborly, that way. If we wasn't hauling gold, we'd stop, let you see the place, get out of the sun a spell."

Finally, from the brow of a bald hill—an old Indian burial mound, their teamster says—they spy the Upper Agency. Even at this distance, it's a grand statement of power. The formidable buildings dominate a bluff-top, resembling a fort without a stockade. Most are flying Stars & Stripes from their windows, a gesture of welcome.

Shortly after three o'clock they enter a Sioux village in the valley of the Yellow Medicine, just below Agency Hill. A thin haze of smoke wraps the grove of trees. Women bend over cookfires outside lodges made of bark.

Men lounge alongside the river, some playing wooden flutes, with only casual looks toward their train. The scene is peaceful as a painting, reminding Sarah of Tiŋta Otoŋwe. But her heart swells into her throat. Her prior contact with the Sioux will count for little, here.

ATOP AGENCY HILL SHE ALIGHTS FROM THE WAGON, ACHING AND STIFF IN HER muddied clothes. A number of Humphrey's "farmers and mission Indians" are circulating among the buildings, their faces painted with lines and speckles. Some carry bows and arrows; others are armed with double-barreled shotguns sawn in half.

She pulls James to her skirts. "Take Mama's hand, and *don't let go.*"

Thomas, ignoring the Sioux, leads his handpicked staff on a swaggering tour of his new kingdom. Though populated by fewer whites than Redwood, this headquarters appears more solid and secure. Set in a lovely oak grove, its buildings are of recent construction. Their cream-colored brick deepens to salmon-pink in the shade. A two-story brick duplex accommodates the Agency's carpenter and blacksmith shops, along with a manual labor school for the Indians. A similar structure serves as a boardinghouse for government workers. There is also a bakehouse, a livery stable and a jailhouse "for unruly savages."

John smirks at the jail's two undersized cells. "Let's hope the Sioux get unruly in small numbers."

The base of all Upper Agency operations is a two-story brick warehouse, the most imposing building on the Hill. Located inside are the offices for the agent and the physician, as well as storerooms for provisions and agricultural equipment. John hurries off with Thomas to inspect his workplace. Sarah gazes with longing at the window that will be his. In Shakopee his medical practice was in their home. She assisted his surgeries, nursed his patients, prepared his salves and tinctures, kept his ledger, recorded entries in his casebook. Sometimes she even treated patients in his absence, supplementing his drug cabinet with her own command of remedies and bonesetting. Those days, she suspects, are over. That warehouse is a male stronghold.

Situated across the green from the warehouse is another two-story brick duplex. This is where their family will live, with the Galbraith brood rollicking and bickering on the other side of the center wall. She carries Nellie through the front door and exhales, long and loud.

The place is pristine; not overly spacious, but airy. Six-pane windows let in a breeze and ample light. Humming in Nellie's ear, she wanders room to room with James. Yes, she can make this a home. Not *too much* of a home—they won't be here forever—but home enough. As soon as there's money, she will buy an upright piano and a cage of songbirds for the parlor. She will host elegant parties in the dining room. In the kitchen, she will have ice cream in the icebox and fresh-cut herbs drying in bundles. She will cozy up the two bedrooms with quilts and embroidered linens. She will hire a live-in Sioux maid. The help can sleep on a pallet in the capacious pantry.

She shoves up two more window sashes for a cross-breeze, then steps out the back door. Plenty of space for her kitchen garden. She might even hire trellises built.

Feeling almost blessed, she sets Nellie down to toddle. Beyond her future garden are a woodshed, an outhouse with three doors and a fringe of scrubby shrubs. Beyond the shrubs, six hundred feet below, the junction of the Yellow Medicine and Minnesota Rivers. Beyond the junction, a patchwork of weedy reservation fields. Then tallgrass prairie, flattened as if by a level to the skyline, perhaps a hundred miles out. No trees anywhere, except in narrow belts bordering the rivers and streams.

Somewhere out there are said to be two mission stations, both Presbyterian. One is in the charge of an old doctor named Williamson. The other belongs to the Reverend Stephen Riggs, compiler of her Dakota dictionary. Aided by that book and the women of Šakpe's band, her Dakota had once been passable. "Your ear is fat and your tongue is thick," Mother Friend told her in Tiŋta Otoŋwe, "but your heart is good. You come to us in a good way." Now, where the Sioux are concerned, even her heart needs practice.

The endless expanse of prairie below Agency Hill smites her with a sense of her insignificance. She feels like an ancient seafarer on a great ship at the edge of the known world—beyond which, the maps warn, lay sea monsters, dog-headed giants and cannibals.

A thunderhead is forming to the west, unearthly and wicked black. Not pigeons this time.

❧ 2 ❦

JUNE 20, 1861

THE CANNON EXPLODES in the bow of the *Franklin Steele*. Its breech blows back, blasting a deck railing and cabin door to smithereens. Standing in the expectant crowd on shore, Sarah is overcome by laughter. Her poor form raises eyebrows all around, but she can't contain herself. Spectacle, turned debacle. No one is injured—not Governor Ramsey or the other dignitaries on board; not any of the high-society ladies and gentlemen, up from St. Paul; not the bevy of sightseeing settlers, up from the river towns; not a single member of the press; not even the crewman who lit the fuse. After a momentary lull the brass band on the boat plays on.

Cannon-fire was to have announced the arrival at the Lower Agency of the much-ballyhooed "Grand Pleasure Excursion to Witness the Annual Sioux Payment." With the Minnesota River fifteen feet below normal due to drought, the *Franklin Steele*'s captain had done well to navigate upstream. Debarking passengers are telling tales of the sidewheeler scraping bottom and hanging up on cottonwood snags all the way from St. Paul, four days and two hundred meandering miles. At full fare, each person had shelled out a whopping $10 for a round-trip ticket "to visit the last of the continent's vanishing race."

Sarah presses her lace handkerchief to her brow. The heat of early summer is intense, even at nine in the morning. John had spurned the landing, but she'd popped her parasol and insisted on hiking down to meet the boat. She believed the newspapers' boast that Henry David Thoreau would be aboard, traveling with the junior Horace Mann, a companion of tender years. A man like Thoreau, who had sung the praises of John Brown from his raid on Harper's Ferry to his hanging on the gallows, must be met.

The last excursionist steps ashore. The musicians in the band start packing up their gleaming trumpets and trombones. With a frown she turns to scan the backs of the throng toiling up the wooded footpath to Redwood. A man like Thoreau should be conspicuous by his mere presence. How has she missed him? A quick spin of her parasol on her shoulder, and she bustles to catch up.

IN COUNCIL SQUARE A CONTINGENT OF INFANTRY DISPATCHED FROM FORT Ridgley is ranked at attention in mismatched uniforms. Governor Ramsey receives their salute, his double-breasted frock coat ready to pop its buttons. He then greets a party of chiefs and headmen from the two Lower Sioux tribes, the Mdewakantonwans and the Wahpekutes. Philander Humphrey, flapping his hat against the bugs, identifies some of the Indian leaders for Sarah and John: Wakute. Wapaśa. Taoyate Duta, or Little Crow—

"So *that's* Little Crow," Sarah murmurs, recalling how his villagers swarmed their wagon train when it was bound for the Upper Agency. Like the other chiefs, he wears the frock coat and pants of a farmer Indian, having agreed to live as white men do. Yet by old custom he wears his hair shoulder-length and a blanket folded over his arms. She doesn't know what to make of him.

As the Governor draws even with him, Little Crow slips a crooked wrist from beneath his blanket and awkwardly shakes Ramsey's hand.

"He's a cripple?" John says to Humphrey.

"Somebody shot up his arm-bones in a family feud, years ago. But don't be hoodwinked by his deformities. He's shrewd as a hawk, an instrument of Satan."

"Who's that?" Sarah says, nodding to another, much younger chief, clearly no farmer Indian. He's about her height, just over six feet, but he looks even taller for his erect bearing and magnificent headdress of eagle feathers. His face is painted in quarters of red, white, black and yellow. A hoop necklace and mirror pendant adorn his neck. A blood-red blanket robe, draped around his shoulders, falls loosely to his feet.

"That's Standing Buffalo," Humphrey says. "The only Upper Sioux chief I've seen today. The Sissetons and Wahpetons will be paid later, without all this hullabaloo. Their gold went north with your train."

Sarah can readily spot the farmer Indians by their cut hair and white man's clothes. They also appear well-fed compared to the long-haired blanket Indians, who vastly outnumber them. She's about to remark on this when Clark Thompson, the pug-faced Superintendent of Indian Affairs, addresses the assembly at the top of his voice.

"I regret to inform you"—his bawl is loud as an auctioneer's—"for reasons beyond my control, there will be no annuity payment today."

A loud groan from the excursionists. The Sioux stand like slabs of granite. On one edge of the patchy crowd, a short man in a straw hat breaks into a spate of coughing.

Superintendent Thompson swabs his face and jowls with his kerchief. "I've assured our Indian friends that this delay will be brief, a matter of days. The Great Father in Washington won't forget his promises. In lieu of the annuity payment, we'll hold a grand council in a few hours near Reverend Hinman's. The trees will offer some shade—"

"We didn't come all this way for windbag speechifying!" an excursionist yells. He is seconded by a host of others.

Thompson pats the air, trying to calm the crowd. "Down the road you will tell your children about this day, when you witnessed the Sioux speaking in council. Oratory is much prized by the red man—"

"But we want to see the gold!"

"Refund our tickets!"

"Where's the thousands of Indians we paid for? There ain't but a few hundred here!"

Thompson appeals for quiet. "After the council, we'll enjoy a great feast. The Sioux have prepared a dance for your amusement. I daresay, those of you who danced away your nights on the boat, coming up, will revel in the comparison."

The short man in the straw hat is still hacking away, his kerchief splotched with blood. The fresh-faced fellow beside him pounds a fist on his back. In age, they might be father and son.

Thoreau and Mann.

"A SHORT DISTANCE FROM HERE IS THE GREAT FATHER'S FORT. WE'VE stationed the garrison there out of respect for your nation, and to protect you against any who would do you harm. Some of its troops have joined us today. Again, out of respect."

Infantry surrounds the council gathering. Governor Ramsey is squeezed into an altar chair installed like a throne on Reverend Hinman's porch. Chiefs and headmen occupy benches on the grass, sometimes rising to dip a gourd from the barrel of sugar water provided for their refreshment. The blanket Sioux listen to the interpreter's relay of Ramsey's remarks, passing their pipes, saying nothing. Clusters of farmer Indians sit apart.

Thoreau and Mann are late to the proceedings. They stretch out amongst the flock of whites, not far from Sarah. Over the interlude of these past hours, she observed them from the bluff as they waded through prairie grass up to their thighs, roaming into swatches of blooming yarrow and daisy fleabane, bristly sarsaparilla and larkspur, milk vetch and purple clover. Occasionally Thoreau would stoop and knife up a plant; study the specimen; sketch and jot in his notebook. Plagued by his consumptive cough, he would often drink from his canteen, or let Mann shoulder his knapsack and bear him up. George Gleason's pup trailed him like she would a master, no matter how many times he kicked her away. Free at last of the fawning dog, he cushions his head on his pack and crosses his legs at the ankles.

John elbows her in the ribs. "Thomas is up next."

Their friend Galbraith bounces up from his parlor chair at the Governor's right hand. Between his enthusiasm and the heat, his face is nearly as red as his beard. "I've been sent here to look after your interests. I'll care for you as a father should care for his children. Having only recently assumed my post, I'm behind on my duties. The last agent left much undone." A jab at his predecessor, Joseph Brown. "My first priority, after paying out the annuities, is to finish planting the corn. One thousand acres."

Such a waste of good seed, Sarah thinks. No farmer worth his land would plant corn two months late.

Thomas drones on, directing his speech at the farmer Indians. Thoreau pulls his straw hat over his eyes. On the ground beside him lie several buckskin garments decorated with quills and beads, likely obtained in trade with the Sioux; more natural specimens, no doubt, like wildflowers dug up for study.

"My name is Red Owl. I am Mdewakantonwan, from the band of Wapaśa."

Thoreau sits up, rubbing his hound-dog eyes. Red Owl, the spokesman for the Lower Sioux soldiers' lodge, has risen from a bench to address the officials on the porch. At the commencement of the council, this same

Indian offered prayers, lifting a ceremonial pipe to the sky, to the four corners of the winds, to the earth. Though slight of build, he cuts a frightening figure. One half of his body is painted black, the other red. He wears a headdress of owl feathers dyed scarlet and a red sash decorated with quills.

"All these things you white men have promised today you have promised us before," he says, "and every time we have been cheated out of them." The government interpreter flattens his voice, as though to douse the fire in Red Owl's oratory. "In the treaties we gave almost all of our homeland to the Great Father in Washington. In return we were guaranteed money, provisions and land on which to live. But we scarcely possess enough to cover the nakedness of our women and children. While the Great Father and his people have full round faces and fine clothes, my people are ragged. I myself am so hungry, I can hardly stand up to represent them."

The blanket Indians send up an approving chorus. "Haŋ! Haŋ!" *Yes, it is so.*

"The last agent, Crooked Foot, paid wages to his family and friends who did little or nothing to earn them. He and his men violated our women. He built a score of worthless little houses for the farmer Indians, using funds set aside for educating my people. He took provisions paid for by our money to a distant part of the country for storage. Many were never returned to us, or came back spoiled. The tainted food killed women and children. We need a storehouse of our own, right here among us, where our goods can be well-kept and not slip through anybody's fingers."

Red Owl's voice is mounting, bolstered by the cries of the Sioux around him. Up on the porch, Thomas is twisting his wedding band, a nervous tic.

"Now we hear that our new white father, Major Galbraith, wants us to sell even more of our land to white settlers. I say no. I say the Great Father in Washington has plenty of land elsewhere to give to his white children!"

Thomas balls his hands into fists. He glares at the porch floor. Red Owl isn't done talking, but Thomas, Sarah can see, is done listening.

AT THE CLOSE OF THE COUNCIL, GOVERNOR RAMSEY PRESENTS THE INDIANS with two fat oxen. After the Sioux slaughter the beasts, Sarah watches them position the carcasses on their backs, skin the hides and empty the stomachs. The livers they lift to their lips and sink in their teeth. They pass them around with bloody mouths, offering them even to white spectators, all of whom blanch and decline.

The Sioux butcher the balance of the meat into manageable pieces, slivering their blades between joints and along seams of flesh, respecting the contours of the animals. After long labor amidst flies, they stand the four rib sections beside a hot fire. They vanish then with the remaining beef, presumably to return for the evening's feasting and dancing. Only a few of their women remain, to tend the fire and the roasting meat.

WHITE CHILDREN RAMBLE DOWN THE HILL TO SPLASH AND FLOAT IN THE LAZY current of the shallow river. Men whiffle their hats at clouds of gnats and mosquitoes. In the dappled light beneath an elm, Sarah lounges on a quilt, sponging the flushed cheeks and necks of her napping babies with a moist cloth. All around her, women flutter their scalloped fans in the sweltering heat. Henrietta Galbraith and Jannette DeCamp are grousing about their living quarters and bemoaning the dearth of social functions at the Agencies. Susan Humphrey counsels them to concentrate on the proper instruction of their children. "Worry less about what surrounds you," she says. "Tend the souls of your little ones."

Sarah has had enough of their chinwag. Her eyes are on Thoreau, still seated on the ground amidst a standing gaggle of men. He's the sole reason she rode that wretched road back down to Redwood after only ten days at the Upper Agency. The Sioux, in their language, have been calling him *The White Man With The Spider Crawling Inside His Chest,* or something like that. For the moment, he's at peace with his cough.

After one last sponging of her babies' faces, she stands up, tidies a few sweaty strands of hair and snaps open her hand fan. "Ladies, will you please?" She gestures at James and Nellie. "I'll soon be back," she says, already walking away.

The men are talking the War. She maneuvers into place at John's side, coyly waving her fan. He and the others will deem idle her female opinions. She will have to guard her tongue; speak little, and speak well.

J.B. rolls down his wet pant-legs, fresh off a frolic with his hound in the river. He's more free-spirited than John; the birthright, she supposes, of a younger brother. His decision to take leave of his law practice in Blue Earth City to serve as Thomas's right hand at Redwood had heartened her.

"You *do* realize," he says, looking down at Thoreau, "that Minnesota was the very first state in the North to commit troops."

"And yet...." Thoreau lays a dirt-stained finger along his prodigious nose. He appears even more sickly, up close. Wasting cheeks. Premature gray in his thick waves of beard. Baleful eyes, bulging amidst pleats of crow's feet. "You Minnesotans seem cold on the subject of the War, as if your participation were perfunctory, and the War's outcome immaterial. As if the War were merely an *inconvenience*."

J.B. hurls a stick. His hound gives chase. "The War does look different here on the frontier."

An excursionist in a checkered waistcoat spits a chew. "I say leave the Union as it was, the Constitution as it is, and the Negroes where they are."

Humphrey wrinkles his nose. "You sound like a politician. Slogans are no substitute for conscience, or debate."

Thoreau props himself back on his arms. "We must preserve the Union, yes, but we must abolish the abomination that is slavery, and expand the cause of liberty across this entire continent."

"You sound quite certain of yourself, Mr. Thoreau." A clean-shaven clergyman strolls up, peeling an apple. His long hair, swept back from a pronounced widow's peak to hang down his neck, verges on Indian-style. He introduces himself as Henry Whipple, Episcopal bishop of Minnesota. A tall man, he is one of those rare people that she must look up to, a little.

"I'm certain of the truth only," Thoreau says. "We must follow where it leads. The Sioux who spoke so splendidly in council—Red Owl—we must learn to know things as *he* knows them. We must learn to live in that knowledge."

The men are flummoxed. Sarah can read it on their faces. To know as an Indian knows, and live accordingly—to them, the notion is blasphemy, truth stood on its head. No Indian could ever be superior to a white man, and no heathen to a Christian.

"Mr. Thoreau"—Whipple's apple peel curls toward the grass—"I consider myself a friend of the Sioux. There's much to admire in them. They aren't idolaters, they believe in a Great Spirit. They have strong pride of nation, and love of their own, just as we do. They're generally virtuous and civilized, in their way, despite their degradation and poverty—a curse that we ourselves have stamped upon them.... *Much* to admire. But I'll never believe them our betters."

Thoreau buckles his arms around his knees. "Compared to Red Owl, that weasel of a Governor and this man here"—he throws a nod at Thomas —"had eloquence to snore through!"

Thomas splutters in indignation.

"Now, Mr. T...." Horace Mann chides.

"Red Owl is a natural man," Thoreau says, "while we're nothing but drudges. We cut down and grub up the forests, we till up the prairies, but we can't converse with the spirit of the trees we fell, or the spirit of the land we plow and bring to harvest. We're estranged from nature's truth! Yet we believe ourselves superior—"

"Ah, but we are, most surely!" John's nostrils flare. His ears are reddening.

"I think not."

"But these savages are—are—"

"—merely different from ourselves. One revelation was made to them, another to us. Natural truth is what we hold in common. But we Americans have lost all sight of it." That niggling cough again.

Bishop Whipple carves a fat slice of apple. "In the end, Mr. Thoreau, our own revelation is higher, is it not, and therefore necessary for progress? The Bible and legions of Christians have produced Western civilization!"

"Any man wearing a collar would say so." Thoreau is digging in his knapsack.

Whipple bristles. "Don't dismiss me, sir."

"Surely, Mr. T.," Mann says, "you must admit that Indians like Red Owl are exceptional."

Thoreau works to stifle his cough behind a clean kerchief. "Your point's well taken, Horace," he says at last, with a sniff. "I should revise. There was a time, not so long ago, when every Indian might have taught us how to live again in our original relation to Nature. Simpler. Freer. More in sympathy with our surroundings, unburdened by acquisitiveness and depravity. If the Indian, generally, had remained who he was, with his instincts intact, we might one day have become—through his example, and our own intelligence and imagination—more indigenous than he himself. But today ... most Indians *might* be inferior to us—precisely—because we've tamed them—and—clamped upon them—the chains of our institutions—"

A heavy spate of coughing and wheezing. Mann kneels and pulls the cork from Thoreau's dented canteen. Thoreau grips the young fellow's shoulder with a bony hand. "Thank you—my boy...."

He's dying a slow death. Anyone can see it. Sarah waits for him to calm. Then: "Mr. Thoreau"—all the men look at her, except for the man who matters most, who seems averse to looking at anyone—"sir, don't you think the Indian is as entitled to liberty as the slave?"

"Sarah!" John warns her off with a glare. J.B. heaves another stick, with a snort.

She wouldn't risk saying such things, were they driving back to the Upper Agency tonight. But they don't depart until tomorrow. By then, John's wrath will have passed. "Don't you think," she continues, "that a reservation might be as loathsome to an Indian as a plantation to a Negro?"

Thoreau clears his throat. "Perhaps. But the African and the Indian are *not* the same, in either their character or their condition within this country."

She begins to dispute him, but he isn't finished. "The African is a survivor. He's docile, childlike, able to adapt ... by this he has endured the evil that is slavery. If we don't end slavery for him, he'll be enslaved forever. He hasn't the blood to throw off the yoke. He must be *given* his liberty." He folds over his kerchief, concealing the blood on the cloth. "The Indian is too much a man, too much a warrior. He'll die before he allows anyone to enslave him or force him to live against his nature. He'll never shuffle and dance. He'll refuse to submit. Therefore, he will perish."

She thinks of Ćaske, the Indian who in Shakopee once traded a string of fish for a peek at her bookshelves. "But surely if we allow the Indian his liberty, and we permit him to live in his own way, in relation with us...." She breaks off, disarmed. Thoreau is looking her straight in the eye.

"My good woman, a warrior must *win* his liberty, and fight to the death to keep it. But it's too late for that now. The Indian has become too much like us, in our vices. He cannot win. In time, there will be nothing left of him."

ॐ 3 ॐ

HANDMADE INVITATIONS HAVE BEEN DELIVERED, even out to the mission stations. The decorations are ready. The sky is clear.

Back in Shakopee, before the Panic, she always spread a fine board for her guests on the Fourth of July. Today's fare, from necessity, will be more simple and spare—biscuits, pickles, hard cheese, cold baked beans, potato salad, smoked ham. But, by Heaven, she and Henrietta plan to outdo themselves on the sweets: puff pudding; peach and blueberry pies; a procession of sponge cake, coconut cake, gold cake and silver cake; and to crown the day, strawberry ice cream. Their guests will be talking about this lawn party until Christmas, unless the Indians ruin it.

All this past week, the encampment of Upper Sioux was swelling in the valley of the Yellow Medicine. As the noise of the Indians' drumming and singing rose night and day on the smoke-threads of their fires, she fretted about a possible disturbance. "They sound so restless," she remarked to Stewart Garvie only yesterday, browsing the newspapers on the counter of his store. He's her favorite trader; an animated fellow who sports jaunty vests and colorful string ties. She likes his strong Scottish burr.

"More Indians than usual coming in," he said, handing her a piece of peanut brittle from a tin.

"Why the delay? Their gold came up with us last month. Why not pay them, so they can be gone?"

"Nae, the rations are late—flour, sugar, lard…. They always get doled out the same time as the money."

"It seems imprudent to make them wait."

The Scot laughed, baring his yellow teeth. "The Sioux are used to waiting, Mrs. Wakefield. Happens all the time. Either the gold's here and not the goods, or the goods are here but not the gold. Sooner or later, the Indians will get their due." He patted his wallet. "Then we'll all be happy, aye!"

But now, outside her window, a mixed-blood is wheeling his pony on the green, warning of trouble like Paul Revere. His hollering rousts the clerk Noah Sinks from the warehouse. The rider reins in to deliver his intelligence, then gallops on up the lane. Sinks sprints back inside. A minute later, a man she doesn't recognize strides out the warehouse door, clanging a brass hand bell. He's armed with a revolver.

"Everyone to the jail!" he yells in a lusty baritone, as if he runs the place. *"Now!"*

She rushes to corral James and Nellie. A child in each arm, she pushes through the screen door just as Henrietta herds her youngsters off the stoop. With others on the Hill they scurry toward the pint-sized jail, though surely the warehouse would be more defensible.

"Henrietta, where's Thomas? Shouldn't *he* be giving the orders?"

"He isn't back from Redwood. But I'm sure he'll make the party."

"Who was that with the bell?"

"Major Brown."

"The last agent?"

"Thomas asked him and his son up, to review the books. Shall we invite them to the party?"

John's waiting with his Derringer at the busy jailhouse. Together they huddle with the children on the floor along the far wall as traders and government employees stream in with their families. By the time Joseph Brown bars the door, Sarah has counted forty-five souls, about half of tender age. Their names mostly escape her, she has lived among them less than a month, yet today they might die together in this pen. The men have four guns among them to hold off a horde of thousands.

Joseph Brown dispatches his son Samuel for reinforcements from Fort Ridgley, more than forty miles to the southeast. A heavy duty; Samuel's no longer a boy, but not yet a man. As he races for the stable, the trader Garvie sticks his shotgun out a loophole in the jail wall to cover him.

"Sarah," Henrietta whispers, "shall we invite the Browns to our party or not?"

· · ·

"CHRIST!" JOHN SMACKS THE WALL BESIDE THE BARRED WINDOW. TWO HOURS they've been in the stink of the jail. "Where's their goddamned gold? Let's break it out!"

Joseph Brown bares tobacco-stained teeth. "Money may not be their grievance at present."

"So what the hell is?" Garvie says, staring down the barrel of his shotgun.

"I suspect they're not happy I'm back here." A glistening bead of sweat drips from the cleft of Brown's chin. Crooked Foot, the Sioux call him. Considering what she has heard recently from Thomas and Margaret Williamson, Sarah thinks the name well-deserved.

The Williamson mission is three miles from Agency Hill. Twice she has ridden there on her mare for Sabbath service, then taken afternoon tea with the balding old doctor and his wife. The Sioux call Thomas Williamson Peżihuta Wićaśte, *Medicine Man,* out of respect for his healing powers. But only a handful attend his church, despite his conducting worship in their tongue.

Over tea last Sunday, Dr. Williamson railed at length about Joseph Brown's tenure as agent—his embezzling, his collusion with traders, his bestowal of favors on relatives, his rustling of Sioux cattle, his "immorality" with Sioux women. "In summation," he said, fingering his bearded chin, "the man is totally destitute of religious principle. But to be fair, I'd have to doubt the character of any man who signed on as agent, aiming to retire after four years with an ample fortune."

BY EARLY AFTERNOON THE JAIL IS AN OVEN. HAND FANS ARE FETCHED. Clothing is peeled off to the limits of decency. Buckets of water are drawn on the quick from the nearest well, and everyone gulps from the ladle. Kerchiefs are dipped and tied around necks. The whining children's heads are doused and their flaming cheeks mopped with their mothers' dampened aprons.

"How long," Sarah asks Brown, "do you intend to keep us here?"

"Long as necessary."

She stands up and dusts her skirts, no longer convinced of the danger. "I have a party to prepare."

"Sit down, woman!"

"You're not my governor!"

She gathers James and Nellie, but barrel-chested Brown blocks her path to the door. "If the Sioux have a problem with *me*, woman, they have a problem with *you*. In the Indian mind, there's no separating one from the rest."

"If we're to die, Mr. Brown, I might as well die in my own house. And if we're to live, we'll all soon be hankering for food. Either way, I aim to leave and see to my cooking. Kindly step aside."

John snatches James from her grasp. "Don't be a ninny, Sarah!"

"Look at your son, Husband—he's dying of this heat! And for what?"

A pounding on the door interrupts. Garvie peers out the corner of the window. "Aye, let him in, it's Little Paul."

John hurries to unbar the door. A pudgy Sioux sidles in; a farmer Indian, by appearance. After conferring quietly with Brown in Dakota, he slips back out.

Brown wipes the back of his hand across his upper lip. "Standing Buffalo and the other chiefs have met in council. They've decided not to attack, at least not before they present their grievances to Major Galbraith. In the meantime, they've posted guards below. We're free to move about, but there's no way off the hill."

"Then by all means, Major," Henrietta says, "you must come to our party."

Garvie cradles his shotgun. "Those laddies from Ridgley better get here quick."

SARAH IS HANGING THE LAST OF THE HOLIDAY BUNTING WHEN THE MISSIONARY families roll up in two buckboards. Dr. Williamson reins in his team. "Is there trouble? Indians searched the wagons at the bottom of the hill. They're painted for war."

Margaret, beside him on the seat, holds up an empty wicker basket in liver-spotted hands. "Mrs. Wakefield, I'm afraid we can't contribute to your feast. They took our molasses cookies."

Sarah assists Margaret down from the wagon. Then she goes to the second buckboard to greet Stephen and Mary Riggs, whose mission station, Hazelwood, is two miles beyond the Williamsons'. She can't fathom why the two Presbyterian families don't unite their missionary efforts.

She greets Mary Riggs with cool cordiality. The woman's face has a dour cast, as if she would prefer to be anywhere else. She likely inherited her dowdy calico dress from a barrel of mission donations.

As Reverend Riggs swings his youngest children down from the wagon, Sarah smoothes her hands over her own flag dress, sewn special for the occasion. She has been counting toward this moment ever since her arrival at Yellow Medicine. Meeting the man who had compiled the Dakota dictionary is a little like meeting Noah Webster in the flesh.

The missionary turns to face her, with a genial lift of his hat over his wild side-whiskers. "Mrs. Wakefield, I presume?"

"Reverend Riggs." She offers her hand. "Happy Independence Day! Might I award you the honor of reciting the Declaration after the meal?"

"I am humbled, Madam." He bows and touches his lips to her knuckles. His generous nose is peeling from sunburn.

Smudge pots with yarrow are lit against the mosquitoes. The men talk and smoke. The women circle up, fanning, as the children frolic at their games. Sarah and Henrietta lay their cold supper on linen-covered tables set end to end and decorated with wildflowers and bunting.

The meal is subdued. Liquor would have married the mood, but to placate the tee-totaling Presbyterians, Sarah serves only water and milk. After dinner, the company toasts with lemonade to each colony that rebelled against King George. Under the circumstances, the men forgo the customary volleys of gunfire.

Reverend Riggs delivers the Declaration of Independence in his best preacher's voice: "We hold these truths to be self-evident, that all men are created equal, that they are endowed by their Creator with certain unalienable Rights...." He bellows down the litany of grievances against King George:

> For Quartering large bodies of armed troops among us:
>> For protecting them, by a mock Trial, from punishment for any Murders
> which they should commit on the Inhabitants of these States ...

—a rousing declamation, his hand punching at the sky for emphasis—

> For cutting off our Trade with all parts of the world:
>> For imposing Taxes on us without our Consent:
>> For depriving us in many cases, of the benefits of Trial by Jury—

The crack of a gun freezes the scene. Then a lone scream rends the air. Sarah dives with Nellie beneath the cloth-covered table. Her guests press to the ground all around her, shielding one another.

A gangly boy hurtles by, out in the open, as a second shot rings out, even closer. Sarah lunges and brings him down by a leg. Frenzied with terror, he kicks and flails. She slaps his face to daze him, and drags him under the table.

She searches out James's towhead, further down the line of bodies, in the arms of Margaret Williamson. Beside them, curled over his knees, is Joseph Brown.

Flies buzz. The wind shifts. Smoke from the smudge pots sweeps beneath the tablecloth. The gangly boy, nine or ten years old, buries his face in Sarah's chest, whimpering for his mother. From somewhere a baby mewls. When Nellie answers, Sarah feels her milk let down, dampening the stars on her dress.

THERE ARE NO MORE SHOTS. THE MEN RECONNOITER. A HARMLESS SCARE, Joseph Brown decides.

Desperate to save the party, Sarah claps her hands like a schoolmarm. "Sing for us, Mr. Gleason!"

The good-natured Irishman has driven up for the holiday from his clerk's post at the Lower Agency. He scoops up his dog Sadie, tilts back his pheasant-feather hat and leads the company in a few patriotic tunes. Sadie howls as he croons.

John turns out the strawberry ice cream on a serving tray in front of wide-eyed children. The neat four-quart pyramid is met by oohs and ahs and Mama-can-I-have-somes. Sarah strikes off wedges of ice cream with a meat cleaver, for dramatic effect, while Henrietta plates.

"Is that safe to put in your stomach?" Mary Riggs asks, in a mousy voice. "If you're not of rugged constitution, I mean."

"It's like eating a snowball, Mother!" The boy Sarah had slapped. She stops cutting wedges to watch him. He's burbling with pleasure, licking his spoon clean after each bite.

"Is it really so delicious, Robert?" Mary says. "Shall I be brave and try some?"

"Oh, yes, Mother, you *must!*"

In a flash of inspiration, Sarah snatches up the tray of ice cream and whisks it back to the house. Cries of dismay trail behind her. Henrietta catches up to her in the kitchen.

"Sarah, whatever are you doing?"

"Put the ice cream in the ice box! Don't let it melt. You hear me? *Don't let it melt.*"

. . .

SARAH'S DINING ROOM IS PACKED WITH TIGHT-LIPPED CHIEFS AND HEADMEN. She stands in front, flanked by Dr. Williamson and Reverend Riggs, praying nothing goes wrong. The missionaries have closeted Joseph Brown in an upstairs bedroom, where his presence won't provoke.

From behind the dining table she extends a plate of ice cream to Standing Buffalo; a generous portion, the color of buttermilk, pinked by frosted red berries.

She clears her throat, from nerves. The missionaries will have to atone for the errors in her Dakota. "Woyute." *Food.* She pokes the ice cream, licks her finger and smiles. "Waśte!" *Good!*

Standing Buffalo touches the ice cream with a fingertip. "De daku he?" *What is this?*

"Wota," she says. *Eat.*

The chief accepts the plate. He studies the ice cream at arm's length, face pinched by doubt.

She looks at her boy, standing with his father at the front door. "Little man, come to Mama!"

James pulls free of John's hand and beetles a path through the Indians. Reaching the table, he drops to his knees and crawls under. When he pops up on her side, she hefts him up and presents him with a spoon. "Sweetie, show Standing Buffalo how much you like strawberry ice cream."

She dips him toward the blue earthenware bowl on the table. With a giggle he scoops up a man-sized bite and plugs it into his mouth, grinning through his dimples, a smear of ice cream on one cheek.

Standing Buffalo trades glances with the other Sioux leaders, dark eyes twinkling.

"Wota," she repeats, to encourage him, dabbing at James's cheek with the tip of his Stars & Stripes bandanna.

The chief works the edge of his spoon to load a puny bite. The room hangs.

"Strawberry!" James squeals.

"Skuya!" Wonderment in the chief's voice. "Waźuśteća! Waśte!" *Sweet! Strawberry! Good!* He spoons up a second, bigger bite, to a burst of laughter and scattered applause. "De wa naćeća he."

She shakes her head. No, not *snow*. "Pte asaŋpi ćaġa." *Cream frozen.* For confirmation of the Dakota she looks to Riggs. He nods in obvious surprise at her proficiency.

Hoping she has enough ice cream to go around, she beckons all the Sioux leaders toward the table. "Wotapi mitakuye!" *Eat, my relatives.*

A ripple of murmurs runs around the room. "Wiŋyaŋ taŋka waśte do," the Indians are saying. *The big woman is good.*

LATE THE NEXT AFTERNOON, THOMAS DISMOUNTS STIFFLY OUTSIDE THE warehouse, back from the Lower Agency a day later than expected. No sooner has he shambled inside the building than Standing Buffalo and other Sioux leaders come riding up the hill in full regalia. Pouring in behind them are hundreds of warriors, mounted and on foot, and a river of women, children and old people. Sarah watches from her stoop, hands on hips, as the Sioux encircle the warehouse across the lane. John's still there, in his office.

Thomas pushes up a second-story window. Through Antoine Frenier, his mixed-blood interpreter, he greets the Sioux below and asks their business.

"More than a moon ago we received word to gather for the payment. We came like obedient children."

Sarah apprehends the rough meaning of the Dakota before Frenier interprets. The speaker sounds like Standing Buffalo, but she can't see well for the crowd.

"You have done well, coming in as I ordered." Thomas's words are a slushy mumble, as though he might have kept company with a bottle on the ride up from Redwood.

"By treaty, my people must be fed until the payment is made."

"I have nothing to give you."

"The warehouse should be opened."

"I say again, I have no food."

"Another Crooked Foot!" a Sioux yells. Frenier chooses not to interpret the insult.

Standing Buffalo: "You allow the cut-hairs to get food from the warehouse whenever they wish. But you allow us food only once a year, and then only when it suits you."

"If you don't like the arrangement," Thomas snaps, "cut your hair!"

Sarah's hand flies to her mouth. When Frenier interprets, the Indians send up a terrifying whoop, raising the hairs on the back of her neck. Retreating into the house, she bars the front door, then rushes to the open dining room window.

"Cut-hairs who are fed for living like whites are no longer Dakotas!

The government should give them no more money, no more food." This Sioux voice she doesn't recognize. "The annuities are payment for Dakota land. Only Dakota people should be paid!"

Sioux guns fire into the air. Sioux fists pound the warehouse doors.

Thomas: "I'll give you each a cup of flour."

"My people's bellies are empty! Our white father must keep his word!" Another riot of gunshots.

"Listen to me!" Thomas braces his arms on the window sash. "I know the provisions were to have been here by now, but the War against the South has caused many delays—"

"Major, look!" Frenier points down the lane.

"What the hell? Sweet Jesus...."

Sarah hastens to the window at the far end of the parlor and parts the lace curtains. Teamster wagons are inching up the lane through the crush of Indians, advancing toward the warehouse. Three, four, five of them. They look to be laden with barrels under canvas. She crumples a curtain in a hopeful fist. She doesn't think much about God and such, but the arrival of these wagons seems more miracle than luck.

She resumes her post in the dining room. Thomas has withdrawn from his window, perhaps to deliberate with his staff, or perhaps with a bottle. His clerk Sinks greets the first teamster to drive into the warehouse yard. He soon gives a big thumbs-up to the air.

Thomas reappears. The barrels in the wagons, he tells the Sioux, contain flour. He offers them to the chiefs, a sign of good faith, and pledges to distribute the rest of the overdue provisions on July 16, eleven days off.

The Sioux leaders huddle. After several excruciating minutes, they remount. Standing Buffalo's pony prances sideways as he lifts his staff of eagle feathers toward Thomas. "We accept this flour from our white father. But when we come back, we expect him to deliver what has been promised, in full."

MOONLIGHT TOSSES A PALE ORANGE MAZE OF SHADOWS ON THE BEDROOM ceiling and walls. Sarah lies beside John in bed, their bodies not touching.

In early evening, young Samuel Brown rode in from Fort Ridgley ahead of 125 soldiers and a howitzer. His father went posthaste to the stable and saddled his horse, to return with Samuel to the family mansion, nine miles downstream.

Outside the duplex, insects drone. Bullfrogs rrumm. Beneath the night sounds the Sioux drums pulse, refusing to sleep. Sarah doesn't know what the drums mean. By now, more than 4,000 Indians are said to be camped in the valley; a perfect double circle of tipis, a half-mile across.

"John … I'm thinking we should go home."

He searches out her hand in the bedclothes and presses it to his chest.

$\maltese$ 4 $\maltese$

SUPERINTENDENT CLARK THOMPSON steams up from St. Paul with the paymaster to supervise preparations for the annuity distribution. Drunken curses fly day and night from Thomas's office in the warehouse.

"Bloody Democrats! Fine mess they've left me with…."

"Washington can go to hell! Bloody bureaucrats can't shit and piss at the same time. The sons of bitches can't be bothered with savages, with a war on…."

"Bloody Sioux! They want the whole world handed them in a pail. Lazy swine…"

A month ago, stepping off the *Jeanette Roberts* at the Lower Agency, Sarah thought Thomas laughable, ignorant of Indians, unsuited for the office of agent. But she didn't foresee him coming unhinged, so drunk on power or liquor he can't properly weigh benefits and risks. He's apt to get them all killed, even his own wife and children. "Can't you or Thompson *do* something?" she complains to John. "The whole Hill can hear him! At least he could shut his window. *Tell him to shut his window!*"

AT SEVEN O'CLOCK ON THE MORNING OF THE SIXTEENTH, SARAH HEARS A BRISK rapping at the Galbraiths' door. "Morning, ma'am," says a business-like voice. "I'm Clark Thompson's deputy. He sent me for the Major. The Superintendent expected him at the warehouse an hour ago."

"My husband has taken to his bed with illness," Henrietta fibs through her screen, as though nobody could possibly overhear. "Mr. Thompson will have to manage the distribution without him."

SARAH FANS HERSELF AT AN UPSTAIRS WINDOW, OBSERVING WITH PITY AS THE Sioux approach the green to be counted. After officials record their names, they settle with their water bags in scant shade under withering sun. The wind, usually such a beast, has lain down for a rest.

Hot, airless hours peel away as heads of families are summoned to the paymaster's table for their gold. Once they quit the table, they're beset by traders demanding the instant settlement of debts. Garvie, the Scot toward whom she has felt kindly disposed, struts about in a turquoise paisley vest, waving his ledger in their faces. The Sioux aren't bookkeepers. They likely have no idea what, if anything, they owe anyone. The measure of a Sioux's worth among his people, Dr. Williamson has told her, isn't what he saves, spends or borrows, but what he shares and gives away. There's a reason why Standing Buffalo is skin and bone. A chief's people must eat before he does.

Superintendent Thompson addresses the Sioux from the same second-story window where Thomas spoke on July 5. The annuity gold has been disbursed as pledged, he says, but the distribution of provisions must again be deferred due to lack of inventory. "A copious bounty will be yours, come autumn—a gift from your Great Father Lincoln, who proposes to treat you with benevolence."

From where is such bounty to issue, the agitated Indians want to know, especially in the middle of the great white man's War?

"I can't tell you any details at this time," Thompson says, "but I promise the gift will satisfy you. In the meantime, you must go home to your villages and not return till you're sent for." His "must" is reinforced by the howitzer's maw.

"Is your government so weak?" Standing Buffalo declares. "Is your nation so poor? What manner of men are you, shedding the blood of your brothers and breaking your promises to us? Why should our people suffer and die so you can win your war?"

Sarah quits her window. "The warrior," Thoreau said at Redwood, "will fight to the death." A day of reckoning will surely come. She prays not to be around when it does.

THE SIOUX OBEY THOMPSON'S ORDER TO "MOVE OFF." AGENCY HILL SINKS into a routine calm. Though slow to trust it, Sarah applies herself to constructing her reservation life.

She hires a Sioux servant. The girl will need schooling in how to keep a proper house, tend children, all the essential crafts of service, but her mind is supple and her body strong. She can be trained.

Sarah presents the girl to John just after his daily ride. He lifts the girl's chin on the end of his riding crop to study her face. He draws the whip down her neck, over the front of her blouse, and rests its tip on her belly.

Five days in, they waken to discover the girl gone.

"What did you do to her?" Sarah asks John, laying breakfast.

"She was lazy."

"She was *learning.*"

She hires another girl. This one lasts three days.

"Husband, you'll not be the cause of our next girl leaving, or I'll be leaving next." She lobs a napkin over the top of his newspaper.

A week later, sixteen-year-old Dinah arrives at her door with a letter of recommendation from Margaret Williamson. Blanket Indians recently shot the girl's father dead while he was planting corn, in punishment for cutting his hair and renouncing Sioux ways. "Any Indian who forsakes the hunt for the plow can expect to be targeted," Margaret wrote. "It's a story old as time, Cain killing his brother Abel."

In the arts of preparing and serving meals, Dinah will require instruction, but she's quick at washing laundry, making beds, scrubbing floors, tidying up. When she proves a natural nursemaid, Sarah moves the girl's floor pallet from the pantry up to the children's room and plumps it with more straw. On the girl's one-month anniversary, she presents her with a cheap bottle of eau de toilette, selected from the assortment of perfumes atop her vanity. Servants are less apt to steal, *Godey's Lady's Book* says, if sweetened.

She converts the far end of her large pantry into a sewing nook and stocks it with linen, flannel, calico, plaid, gingham, cashmere. In anticipation of the holiday season, she measures Henrietta for a party gown that will subtract years from the woman's wrinkles. One look at that gown and other government wives will surely seek out her needle for frocks of their own. Orders in hand, she will impose on John to buy her a Singer sewing machine, like those advertised in *Godey's.*

In the privacy of her nook, she teaches Dinah about fabrics, patterns, seams, stitches, linings and fittings. To her amazement, Dinah is already adept at the rudiments of sewing. She will speedily surpass in ability most white girls her age.

SARAH TIES THE RIBBONS OF HER BONNET. SHE HAS ALREADY PACKED A LUNCH and, like most Sundays, smuggled into the saddlebags as much extra food as she dare. "James and I are off. Dinah will see to your dinner."

"Williamson's today," John says, "or Riggs?" He has plans to dissect a cur.

"Wherever I end up."

In the government stable she saddles Belle and sets James behind the pommel. "Got my wings on, Mama!" he says, bouncing on the mare. "Let's fly!" She mounts behind him, astride like a man.

On their Sabbath rides they always pass the farm of Pasu Kiyuksa and Opa, their nearest Sioux neighbors. The old couple raises corn, potatoes, turnips and rutabagas on their twenty acres, along with chickens and a few cattle. During Joseph Brown's tenure as agent, the government built them a one-room house, windowless and brick, but they prefer the buffalo-hide tipi erected in their yard. It's a hunter's lodge. Painted riders on ponies launch arrows at painted buffalo and deer. Perhaps it was while hunting that Pasu Kiyuksa had lost most of his nose.

Today Sarah stops by with a length of calico, intent on trading for some of Opa's wildberries. "Greetings, my relatives!" she calls, in her best Dakota. James dashes off in mad pursuit of a year-old pup, one of the couple's thirteen flea-bitten dogs.

Opa sticks her gray head out the tipi door. "Good Big Woman! It is good you are here! Please, can you help?"

Inside the roomy lodge Pasu Kiyuksa lies bare-chested between two dogs on a bed of buffalo robes. His veiny left hand is fanned over his right shoulder. This morning, Opa tells Sarah, a new pony spooked and bucked him off. "Green horses are for young men!"

Sarah nudges a dog away to kneel. "Touch you?" she says to the old man, in halting Dakota.

Pasu Kiyuksa nods, with gritted teeth.

The shoulder is bruised and swollen. Opa hovers as Sarah probes. "It is out of joint?"

"Yes."

"Good Big Woman is strong enough to reset it."

She examines the upper armbone. Presses the collarbone. Both are intact. She shares a knowing look with Opa.

The kuŋśi positions herself at her husband's head, to help restrain him. "Old man," she says. Her crooked fingers comb the untidy gray bangs from his eyes.

Sarah stands up, reviewing in her memory the two times she reset a shoulder, back in Shakopee. "Courage," she says in Dakota, as much to herself as to Pasu Kiyuksa. The old man closes his eyes.

She angles her foot into his right armpit for leverage. Takes up his right elbow. Slides her right hand into his and firms her grip. Steels herself, for his sake, then jerks with a twist.

In the wooded heights above Rush Brook, she reins Belle to a walk. Here, the air has a distinct tang. The oaks are yellowing, the maples tilting toward their autumnal blaze. Far below, Sioux women and children are bathing in the shallows. Men spearfish in the rapids and stalk small game through the brush.

Only on occasional Sundays do she and James actually attend worship. When at the Williamson mission, she's always glad for a spot of tea, after. But on those rare Sabbaths when she rides clear to Hazelwood, she never drinks tea with Mary Riggs. An insufferable woman. Despite her husband's monumental achievement in compiling the Dakota dictionary, she despises the tongue and allows no one but him to speak it in her presence. She has erected a tall picket fence around her house in an attempt to shut out the Sioux and limit their influence on her children. She exhorts Sarah to follow her example lest James and Nellie "become little Indians."

And how can Sarah forget what she witnessed on the doorstep of the Hazelwood church, not long after her lawn party? A Sioux woman had just trooped half the day to present Mary Riggs with fresh berries, a way of honoring her on the Sabbath—the most wakaŋ, or *sacred*, day among whites. Mary Riggs thanked the "degenerate squaw" by dressing her down for breaking the Fourth Commandment. In English, of course.

The Sioux call Mary Riggs Oĥanśića, *The Stingy*. She can drink her own pot of tea.

She shifts her weight back in the saddle and her feet forward in the stirrups, keeping a tight hold on James. Belle minces down the steep grade toward the stream. The hillside falls away so sharply, James begins to fuss. She sings in a low voice, to calm him and the horse both.

The wiŋyaŋ below, accustomed to their visits, wave from their cook-fires. "Doctor Boy! Good Big Woman!"

James scoots off to play with the littlest Sioux boys. Once he exhausts himself, he will curl up somewhere and sleep. Sarah settles in a circle of women under a brush arbor to share a smoke on their long-stemmed pipe. The mixture of tobacco and willow bark yields a smooth, warm taste with a hint of apple, mild on the tongue. As she smokes the kinnikinnik, she listens hard to the women's banter, as in Tiŋta Otoŋwe, years before. She has a good ear, but she's still reticent to talk. Dakota must be spoken with proper courtesy, without hurry. Every word matters. Every syllable carries weight. She pays rapt attention, careful not to fidget during customary stretches of silence.

The wiŋyaŋ portion out the food in her saddlebags. Cutworms are mowing down their corn, beans, squash and pumpkins. The "great bounty" of provisions guaranteed by Superintendent Thompson hasn't yet materialized.

As the women smoke, they make a flatbread from government flour, mixing, kneading, shaping, frying. Sarah eats the soft, greasy round they urge upon her, tearing it with her teeth.

♨ 5 ♨

DAYS ARE SHORTENING. Dun grasses bend flat in the wind. Sarah doesn't want to think about winter, but she must. By all accounts, it will be brutal. The rivers will freeze. Snow will bury the road to the Lower Agency and Fort Ridgley below it, impeding the delivery of supplies and mail. Planning ahead, she acquires through Garvie six buffalo robes and seven bear hides. She stockpiles food in the pantry like a mouse burying beans. She even orders Christmas presents—a sled for James, a dolly for Nellie, and for John, a new chessboard with timer.

As trees empty of their leaves and birds, Sioux straggle from their villages back to the valley below the bluff, even more wretched than before for lack of food. Cutworms have chewed through the crops of farmer Indians and blanket Indians alike. Local game has grown scarce from over-hunting. And now the Sioux must miss their fall buffalo chase to collect the "great bounty" of treaty goods pledged by Superintendent Thompson in July. Without those provisions—flour, sugar, salt, baking powder, coffee beans, rice, salt pork, blankets, gunpowder, shot, lead—they might not survive the winter.

But the Agency warehouse still isn't stocked. Thomas, awaiting inventory, stalls for time, releasing to the Sioux a pittance more flour and pork. Fearing an outbreak of violence, he directs his staff at Yellow Medicine to prepare their families for an evacuation to Redwood.

"Will evacuation really be necessary, Thomas?" Sarah asks. From behind her right shoulder, Dinah refills her wine glass without dribbling a drop. The girl has done her proud, waiting table this evening with such skill as to seem not even there.

The Galbraiths are to dinner, along with Captain Marsh, up from Fort Ridgley with a howitzer and a company of volunteers. Minnesota's best troops are away fighting in the South, but Marsh, with two gold bars on his shoulder straps and a full head of chestnut curls, seems an able commander. He drills his men to exhaustion on the green.

When Marsh had arrived for tonight's affair, she saw him pause in front of the duplex to admire her new window shades. Their hand-painted rose bouquets, illuminated by the warm glow of her new house lamps, outclass Henrietta's lace curtains, next door. Upon entering the house, the Captain regarded her décor with visible appreciation. Her main rooms are now painted a fashionable bronze green, with white woodwork. New Persian carpets in green motifs set off her new black walnut furniture. In the parlor, next to her new piano, hangs a full-sized reproduction of "Shakespeare and His Friends." Side tables are arrayed with vases of flowers, miniatures and popular magazines like *Harper's Weekly* and *The Eclectic Magazine of Foreign Literature, Science and Art*. A new French clock stands on lion-paw feet on the parlor mantel. James delights in winding it each morning, with his papa's help.

"I do expect it will be necessary to evacuate, yes." Thomas quaffs his glass. Beside him, Henrietta pushes around her peas.

John stops buttering a slice of bread. "I thought it was all just talk."

"We'd hoped." Captain Marsh crosses his knife and fork on his plate. "But there's apt to be trouble."

"Once you distribute the rations, shouldn't the crisis be past?"

Thomas toys with his ring, waiting as Dinah tops off his wine. "Might as well tell you. Everyone will hear, soon enough—"

"Thomas…." Henrietta lifts an eyebrow.

"What?"

She nods toward Dinah. "The *squaw*," she says softly.

The girl doesn't flinch.

"Dinah," Sarah says, "please see to the children, till I ring."

"Yes'm." The girl places her decanter and linen towel on the sidetable.

They all watch Dinah through the parlor. "You were saying?" John says to Thomas, once she makes the stairs.

"There will be no 'great bounty.'"

"Christ." John looks from Thomas to Captain Marsh. "No goods *at all?*"

"Less than ten thousand dollars' worth," the Captain says. "Not nearly enough to tide them over till the next distribution."

"And *I'm* the one who must tell them. The bastards." Thomas guzzles his wine to the dregs.

Sarah plunks down her fork. "Trouble isn't the word for what's coming."

"Thus my order to evacuate," Thomas says. "You think me a fool?"

John takes off his pince-nez. "As agent can't you procure more provisions *somewhere?*"

"Can't *you*, O physician, raise the dead?"

ONCE THE DOOR CLOSES ON THEIR GUESTS, SARAH REPAIRS TO THE PIANO stool. She presses a few keys, the start of a lullaby by Tennyson she's been committing to memory. "I'm not going to Redwood. When they evacuate, I mean."

John notches the foot of a cigar. "Don't be daft. Think of the children."

"*Whose* children?"

"The only children that matter." He lights up, puffing smoke.

"What about the children of the Sioux? You're their doctor. Don't they matter to you, even a little?"

"Don't James and Nellie matter to *you?*" He shakes out his match. "No, the three of you will go below with the rest." He pours himself yet another brandy and drops into his armchair by the fire. "It's all for show, you know." He stares into the flames. "A magnificent lie, like the 'great bounty.'"

"What is?" She closes the lid over the piano keys.

"The treaties, this reservation, my work … it's all a farce. A charade. An act."

"I don't understand."

"Ah, my pet, but I think you do. We're not here to help the Sioux survive. We're here to help them toward *extinction*. We'll take their land, their assets, their way of life…. In a twinkling, there'll be nothing left of them. They're in our way. It has to be done." He streams smoke toward the ceiling. "You watch … after forking over this ten thousand dollars' worth of rations, the government will reduce next year's annuity payment by the same amount. It's a shell game. The Sioux will never be the wiser!"

She sinks into a chair opposite him. "I don't believe that."

"Ask Thomas. I'll wager I'm right."

"Then someone must tell Standing Buffalo!"

"And risk every white scalp between here and St. Paul? Are you insane?" He plucks up the brass poker and stokes the logs. Sap sizzles.

"And *you*"—he levels the rod at her chest—"with your charity and your monkey talk, your raiding of my medicine cabinet! Don't think I'm unaware of your pet enthusiasms! But none of it will save your precious Sioux. Their race is passing from this earth, and I, like all the rest, intend to make a merry profit as they go."

She rises, trembling. She crosses to the window, away from his poker.

"Oh Sarah, don't play the innocent! Not even half a year, we've been here, and how many birds do you have locked up in those pretty cages of yours?" His reflection looms in the dark glass, still brandishing the rod. "*How many*, I said?"

"Six."

"And how many fur muffs in your closet?"

"John, stop—"

"Where do you think the money's coming from, to spoil you so? Do you suppose I've *earned* it all? My dear, to the victor go the spoils. If it hurts you to admit it, pretend to be naïve, but don't be looking down your snout at me. And don't you dare be putting James and Nellie at risk for love of *them*."

ACROSS THE GREEN GOVERNMENT FAMILIES ARE MUSTERING INTO WAGONS, THE evacuation to Redwood underway. Only essential personnel will remain. Even through the windowpane Sarah can hear James screeching for her. Nellie is too tender in age to be without her mother, but James will be delivered to the Humphreys. Henrietta, so many others, will think her reckless to stay behind on the Hill and heartless to forsake her boy. But they don't know what John has done. She's too bruised to quit her room. She can scarcely get from her bed to the chamber pot.

Over and over, she revisits the night it happened, less than a week after her dinner party. She remembers that J.B. had ridden up from the Lower Agency, his hound trotting alongside. She remembers him announcing in the parlor that he'd resigned as deputy agent, only four months in, and would depart at once for Blue Earth City.

She remembers him alerting John of looming scandal. The trouble concerned Azariah Pierson, another Masonic Brother on the reservation staff, serving as Superintendent of Schools. Recently he had uncovered "serious irregularities" in the education fund. Brother or no Brother, he was ready to point fingers, and not just at Thomas. J.B. urged John to quit his post as physician and catch a boat before the river froze.

She remembers tottering around John's chair, whiskey in hand. A pox on the Sioux, she called him. A leech. A conniver without shame. Things she would never have risked saying, sober. She harangued him about the children along Rush Brook, who were going blind from sore eyes and dying of trifling colds. She mouthed off about their mothers, reduced to selling their bodies to white men for a moldy loaf of bread, a bit of rancid gristle, a single dose of medicine—

"That's right," she remembers telling J.B. "Don't you know? Your dear brother has his *squaws*. I'm no stranger to the gossip. They're part of the *spoils*."

She remembers inching down through cigar smoke into John's face. "You're afraid of *Pierson*? Husband, you should be afraid of *me*! I'll write the newspapers, that's what I'll do! I'll expose all of you. Why wait for scandal to break when I can ruin you myself—"

That's where her memory of that night ends, though sometimes a random impression flashes. The taste of blood, spilling warm and brackish down the back of her throat. The force of being yanked, then slammed. It must have been J.B. who saved her. The younger, more honorable brother.

"I NEED YOU TO SAVE ME, MRS. BUTTS. MAKE ME A PROPER MAN." THAT'S how John had proposed to her in Shakopee, five years before, buffing his pince-nez on a spotless kerchief. Appearances mattered, he told her. To thrive in his practice, he must wed. "A man approaching forty must settle."

By then she'd lived two years in Minnesota. In all that while, she never thought about taking another turn at marriage and motherhood. Managing the household of a reputable doctor in a burgeoning frontier town left no time for woolgathering. Besides, she had serious designs of her own; designs that involved no man. In only a matter of weeks, her unorthodox contract as John's housekeeper would end. She meant to open a dressmaking shop with her accumulated wages.

"You don't know what you're asking," she told him.

"You've had heartache, losing a husband." She can still hear his voice, surprisingly kind. "But perhaps enough time has passed?"

He believed her to be a widow then. She thought him a man of nettle-some opinions and unpredictable temper who overindulged in drink and cards. But he was also a graduate of Yale. He remained a serious student of his profession, devoted to his medical books and animal dissections. If too cerebral in treating his patients, at least he was prudent enough to let her attend their suffering, to compensate.

"You just don't know," she said again, even as she took inventory of his person. Not as handsome or sturdy as his younger brother, but not without qualities. Dark, intelligent eyes, set off by the gold rims of his spectacles. A contemplative face beneath his well-groomed goatee. Straight white teeth. A trim, erect frame, filled out on her cooking. And he was tall enough. She only had to look down on him a little.

Still, she felt no madcap temptation to meddle with him. She couldn't imagine touching him, or him touching her, in regions concealed by their clothes.

"We're not incompatible, Mrs. Butts. Please consider it."

Perhaps romance, she told herself, was best left to silly girls and senti-mental novels. She was nearing thirty. If she ever wished to have prospects again, she couldn't afford to be fussy. Especially when thought bossy and plain. Especially when bigger than most any man she would ever meet. The fit between herself and this doctor might do, like a second-hand suit. With his medical practice and his land speculations, he would be a good provider. He wielded his knife and fork like a gentleman. And not once had he laid a hand on her in anger. That much she could say in his favor.

"I need time, Dr. Wakefield. Give me time...."

JOHN ENTERS THE BEDROOM. HE CHECKS THE BINDING AROUND HER RIBS, examines her black eyes, applies more salve to the cuts on her purpled face. He tries to dose her with laudanum, as he has every morning since. "Take after I eat," she lies through swollen lips, eyes smarting with tears.

He washes his hands in the basin. Toweling off, he probes her with his eyes.

"Girl," he says to Dinah, "stay with your mistress, keep the cloths fresh." He dons his coat. "Should you have need of me, I'll be in my office."

His descent of the stairs is rapid. Dinah watches out the window until he's safely gone, then bolts the bedroom door. Sarah exhales.

She opens her battered mouth to receive rabbit-tobacco leaves. Sioux medicine. When they soften, she tries to chew. Her gaze follows Dinah about the room as she tips another dose of laudanum into the chamber pot, then sets about preparing an herb poultice. These last days, she has been seeing the girl as though for the first time. The shapely figure beneath the blue calico dress and starched white apron. The glinting trade ring on her left pinky. The heavy black hair, plaited back from a middle part. The smooth bone earrings. The strong neck, decorated with strands of pipebeads. The lips that seldom smile. The enormous eyes, bloodshot from lack of spectacles…. She looks and looks and looks at the girl, to keep from hearing James crying across the green.

Sarah sags in her vanity chair, wrapped in a quilt, straining to hear through the open bedroom window. It has been two days since the evacuation. Thomas and the Upper Sioux are in council on the hoary green, encircled by Army guns. Chief after chief has risen to speak. The "great bounty," they now know, is a trifle.

"We have been waiting a long time." This orator, Dinah tells her, is Maza Śa, *Red Iron*. From here, she can only see his back. A short, spindly chief, he wears the clothes of a farmer Indian, but his hair, decorated by two eagle feathers, hangs in braids. His midsection is wrapped in a blue blanket.

"Snow will soon be on the ground," the old chief says, Frenier interpreting. "We are poor; you have plenty. Your fires are warm; your lodges keep out the cold. Meanwhile, we have nothing to eat. Our hunting season is past. A great many of our people are sick for being hungry. We may die."

Maza Śa falls quiet, opening a space for his words to form. Thomas, elbows propped on the arms of his chair, begins twisting his ring.

"We may die, Major Galbraith," Maza Śa continues, after a long interval, "but if we do, we will leave our bones on the ground, that our Great Father may see where his Dakota children perished. We have sold our hunting grounds and the sacred burial grounds of our ancestors. We have sold our own graves. We have no place for our dead. And still you do not give us what you promised."

Thomas has nothing more to offer. The council ends in stony silence. Maza Śa, Standing Buffalo, all the chiefs and headmen mount their mottled ponies, dig their heels and charge off. A few wagons of provisions grumble after them. The meager rations are an insult, but the Sioux are in no position to reject them.

"Dinah, please help me back to bed."

The next day, Standing Buffalo sends a messenger to Agency Hill. He and his most able men are leaving the reservation. Though they might freeze to death, they will go west after the buffalo on their winter ranges. "The weakest of my people are dying—the women and children, the sick, the elderly. I ask you, with a good heart, to feed them while I am away."

SARAH IS HAVING a late breakfast of milquetoast and tea at the dining table, the first meal she has eaten downstairs since her beating, when John plows through the front door.

"You wanted to ruin me?" She shrinks from his temper and the liquor on his breath. "You've succeeded! Now you must live with it, *wife!*" He throws a newspaper in her face before slamming out of the echoing house.

The Saint Peter Tribune. A weekly Republican rag; full of notices, mostly. Every town in the Minnesota Valley has at least one such paper. Garvie keeps all the latest editions on the counter in his store.

This issue is dated October 9. She lays it on the table and scours the pages until, under LOCAL AFFAIRS, "Wakefield" stops her eye. She eases forward in her chair, hugging her sore ribs. The story runs half a column; its source, three soldiers lately deployed to Agency Hill. She doesn't recognize their names. Hardly a surprise. She has only ever fraternized with Captain Marsh and his lieutenants.

She props her head in her hands, squinting at the type. Almost two weeks after her beating, reading is still a strain.

DOES THE GOVERNMENT PAY HIM FOR IT?

A striking example of connubial felicity came under our immediate observation during our stay at the Upper Sioux Agency.

A man in the employ of the Government as Indian Physician, by the name of Wakefield, gave to the public, and more particularly to the post guard, an exhibition of the manner in which he treats his wife. During the evening the notice of those posted near the residence of the wretch was attracted by an uproar in the second story of the building, when the animal was seen to knock down and abuse his wife most inhumanly. She appeared at the time to be entreating of him to desist, and by her manner was earnestly trying to evade public exposure.

She might be reading a novel: some other "wife," some other "wretch" of a man. *How did we come to be fighting upstairs?*

This brutality continued with little intermission until about midnight, when the cry of *"Murder! Murder!"* was heard coming from the same house in a woman's voice, and a file of the guard went over. In going upstairs, they heard the bolt of the door slide, fastening the couple in and the guard out. A woman in a weak and suffocating tone could be heard to say, "You are killing me!" and "O, my God!" and such other sentences as those, broken by sobs and cries of despair. The guard tried the door and found it locked, and then knocked and demanded entrance, whereupon Wakefield's brother appeared below and suggested the couple should be allowed to settle their own domestic affairs in their own way.

Why, J.B. didn't save you at all....

By the coldness of his manner and tone, we felt this was the customary way in which the doctor arranges his domestic affairs. It may be a very pleasant way for him, but certainly not quite so pleasant for his wife, and those who are compelled to live in his immediate neighbor-hood.

The guard had no authority to arrest him, and therefore he received no punishment for his brutality.

The signatures of half the company can be obtained if necessary.

T.G. SCOTT
B. SYLVESTER
D. DONALDSON

"Half the company." Fifty troops. And how many other people on Agency Hill heard her cries? Thomas and Henrietta, surely. The clerk Sinks and his family. The carpenter Nairn and his wife. The Faddens, Mrs. Murch, the Patoiles....

She pillows her brow on her forearm. She'd been a fool, believing if she cloistered herself until the evidence healed, no one outside the house would learn of her beating. Believing that J.B., a man of honor, would surely keep her secret.

J.B., she sees now, is a Judas. But there was never a secret for him to keep. Everyone on Agency Hill had witnessed her humiliation, if only with their ears. The evacuees packed up the story and carted it down to the Lower Agency, where it would have swiftly spread. And after this published report, everyone in the Minnesota Valley will be privy to the unpleasantness that had transpired behind her rose window shades. Nothing sells newspapers like a scandal. A respected physician had whipped his wife. And his brother—a former judge in Blue Earth City with his eye on the state legislature—dismissed the guard marching to her defense. The sordid story will burn like a prairie fire all the way to St. Paul.

One long tear slides hot. *John and J.B. will never forgive you.*

What had these three foot-soldiers hoped to accomplish, squealing to the press? Did they peddle the story for money? Set out, as Democrats, to humiliate some reputable Republicans? Act out of misguided chivalry? Whatever their motive, she will have to counter their version of events. Defend John. Say and do whatever she must to save him, his reputation, his livelihood. Not for his sake, but for her own, and the children's. She has no choice. Having already run away from one husband, she won't run away again.

IN THE ABSENCE OF STANDING BUFFALO AND HIS MEN, THE CRISIS ON THE reservation cools. Over the next few weeks, as evacuees dribble back to the Upper Agency from Redwood, Thomas conducts an obligatory investigation into Sarah's "whipping."

Seated uncomfortably in the same parlor where she suffered the first blow of John's wrath, Sarah writes a sworn statement absolving him of any wrongdoing. "Let there be no doubt or gossip," she pens in closing, as Thomas hovers. "I alone am to blame for the events of that night, which have stained my Husband's Honor, and besmirched the good Name of his Brother." Her signature at the bottom, painfully inscribed, looks like a stranger's.

Thomas manages to collect several other exculpating affidavits from his senior staff. He extracts one from Henrietta as well, though she must have heard the whole episode through the center wall. Perhaps every woman will lie for the man she lies with.

At John's urging, Thomas then crafts a letter to the editors of *The Tribune*. He assures the newspaper's readers of an impartial and thorough inquiry. He promises to send Superintendent Thompson the affidavits and a detailed report of his findings. He then delivers a rebuke to Privates Scott, Sylvester and Donaldson, if not the entire Minnesota Valley:

> I respectfully suggest that in all cases it is usual, and perhaps proper, before a man is tried, convicted and executed, to hear both sides of the case. This rule exists even under the rigid regime of courts martial.

Very Respectfully,
THOS. J. GALBRAITH
U.S. Agent

The editors of *The Tribune* publish the letter in full. To Sarah's relief, it proves to be the last public mention ever made of the matter.

7

SARAH CAN'T RECALL LIVING through such a winter. Nor can anyone else on Agency Hill, from Old World or New. January is a constant dig, with two feet of snow. On the windward side of buildings, it piles up in banks twice her height. Most days, the mercury fails to hit zero, and sometimes plummets to thirty below. When she steps outside the house, the air scours her eyes, knifes her face and lungs. Stacks of firewood are reduced to their last stick, and men are forced to cut trees in the bone-chilling cold.

Toward the end of January, temperatures tease, ballooning into the twenties. On the second day of warmth, Sarah grants Dinah leave to check on her kin. The girl straps on snowshoes, wraps herself in a buffalo robe and sets off on the seven miles home.

Agency children romp, giddy at being free of walls. They populate the Hill with snow-Indians, crown them with headdresses of scruffy crow feathers, riddle their bodies with sticks, for arrows. Sarah lifts Nellie atop sparkling snowdrifts, to plop and slide on her rump. She pulls James on his new sled, straining at the rope. Were her Sioux friends to see her wearing her sun goggles, a Christmas gift from John, they would call her Wića Ite, *Raccoon Face*. But from here on Agency Hill the Sioux seem far away as the sea. After three months, there's still no word of Standing Buffalo, out hunting on the plains.

IN FEBRUARY ARCTIC AIR SLAMS THE HILL LIKE AN ANGRY FIST. TREES POP AND snap like gunshots. A dismal gray sky clamps itself upon the ice-locked reservation. Many days there's no horizon. By the Agency thermometer the month averages two degrees.

As February rounds toward March, the wind rears up out of the north like a mama bear afraid for her cubs. It slaps snow around for four days straight. White blots out the sun. Two feet of fresh powder top off the snowpack, further burying the government road and any connection to the world beyond. Sarah can't sleep for the storm's howling, a sound known to drive hardy souls mad.

In the midst of the blizzard, John stuffs a satchel with clothes and his last two boxes of cigars. Hand over hand he drags himself to his office on a guy rope strung between their stoop and the warehouse door. There he hibernates, day and night.

Sarah acts the part of dutiful wife, sending Dinah across the rope with hot meals and changes of clothes. She imagines John's hours occupied with the dissection of rats, the reading of old *Harper's* magazines, card games with other restless men. And of course he's drinking. Their house out of liquor, at the warehouse he can tap the barrel of alcohol meant to supply his practice, or even the laudanum in his medicine cabinet.

She envies him having a place of his own to escape to. Once, she had her sewing nook, but since the onset of winter, that room has felt more like a crypt than a refuge.

Dinah lures her to the dining table with seed beads and pieces of tanned hide. "Mother and aunties sell traders," the girl says, in limping English. "Missus try make?"

Stuart Garvie and other traders purchase Sioux handiwork to resell to reservation visitors, officers at Fort Ridgley, even collectors in St. Paul and Chicago. Buckskin suits, belts, knife sheaths and pipe pouches are in demand, but Dinah has her own specialty. "Moccasins, your people like. Sell good."

The moccasins she wears are symmetrical, each fashioned from one piece of leather. The moccasins she crafts for the traders are cut more like Sarah's slippers, with definite left and right feet, and separate rawhide soles. These she beads and quills with ornate floral designs. After lining them with thin muslin, she pierces the hide with her awl and adds silk ribbon lacings. "Fancy, your people like."

Now and then, from out of the concentration of her moccasin-making, she tells a story. Her voice, speaking in quiet Dakota, opens space between her and Sarah like a silver moon emerging between night clouds.

· · ·

MY FATHER HAD MANY NAMES. MY PEOPLE REMEMBER HIM AS TAKES MANY Ponies. Medicine Man — Dr. Williamson — called him Henry.

My father has walked on to the spirit world. He was a great warrior, but he did not die in battle. He died because he laid down his tomahawk. He buried it in the ground. He said our world was passing. He said your people were blowing our world away on their breath.

"The white people's god must be stronger than ours," my father said, "or we would not suffer as we do." And he put away his war-shirt. Medicine Man cut my father's hair in front of the people. While he was cutting it, my father was shaking like a white man with a gun at his head. He was a brave man. That is when he died.

He was plowing his land. Some of my people were taunting him, calling him a woman. They told him he must come away with them like a man to raid the Chippewas. When he refused, they called him a coward. They said he was no longer Dakota. They killed his horse. Two days later they shot him dead in his field.

He meant to plant that field to corn. He meant to live, the only way your people would let him live. And for that, our people killed him.

SARAH SENSES THAT A SINGLE MOCCASIN CAN TELL A STORY, ITS INTRICATE designs a secret language of color, inscrutable as the Indian carvings she remembers from the rocks above Narragansett Bay. Those slabs of sandstone were so crusty with lichens and moss, the carvings could easily be missed, especially if the sun was low, but her fingers had been familiar with every groove: a horizontal zigzag, like mountains; the number eight, tipped on its side; a coiled snake; a crude face, with rays emanating from the crown; crosshatched lines, like the tracks of sandpipers; a creature with wings, though clearly no bird.... Neighbors said the pictures were senseless chicken-scratches, or signs of the Devil, but her father considered them art, or even language — a message, he said, for those who could understand. In early memory she sits in his lap, guessing at their meanings. A perfect left handprint is pecked into the rock, the same size as his. "Stop," she thinks it means. "Come," he thinks. Her hand will outgrow it in her teens.

She strings seed beads and stitches them on scraps of cloth, learning by her mistakes. If she ever proves ready to work with hide, Dinah might explain the symbols in her colorful beadwork and quilling.

· · ·

My mother is big like you. She is as big as a man, bigger even than my father was. And she is strong. She is called Warrior Woman. Your people, they call her Jane. When she was a girl, she would race against the boys, and she would win. She could wrestle them to the ground. She could outshoot them with her bow. People still tell the stories.

My mother's eyes are sore now, but once she was skilled at the hunt. I remember this. When she went out on the chase, she took no more meat than she needed, and she gave thanks in the proper way. So the four-leggeds and the winged ones sacrificed their lives to her arrows. The fish in the river would leap to meet her spear and swim into her nets. She always returned home with plenty. She would share her catch.

Today her eyes are bad, and there are no more animals. There are too many hunters on the land. The deer and the beaver, the otter and the elk and the muskrat, all have gone to live underground. Even the buffalo is going underground. I remember my mother saying to my father, "The buffalo nation has always been with us. They numbered more than all the beads our women have ever stitched. Now we look and look and we cannot find them. Someday they will not be anywhere. Without them, who will our people be?"

My father said, "The world is blown away."

The dining room table is soon mounded high with fabric, hides, bundles of trade beads, ribbon, sewing boxes and baskets, books, slate and chalk. Sarah and the girl bend over their needles in almost companionable silence. They trade stubs of stories and bits of knowledge. With John holed up in his office, Sarah and the children take all their meals with Dinah in the kitchen, like servants.

Sarah stitches "Dinah" in beads.

The girl learns to write all twenty-six letters of the English alphabet. She learns to write her own name.

From the day I was born, I have watched my mother sew and quill and bead. Her hands are a man's, but her fingers are a woman's. She learned these arts from her mother, and her mother from her mother, a long string of mother and daughter beads, back to the beginning. I am next. I must learn from my mother before her eyes are gone. I am her only daughter who has not walked on to the spirit world.

I am Hapstiŋna, Third Daughter. Medicine Man named me Dinah when my father had him put us in the water. That day, Medicine Man said he was marking me in my heart. He said I would carry the mark as long as I lived, so I would never get lost. He said because I was marked, my father would always be able to see me, and I would know where I was. I did not want ever to be lost from my father. So I raised my right hand and said, "Yes, I will honor my father." And I do. My father sees me from the spirit world. I try to do what honors him. But I am not Dinah. I am Hapstiŋna. That mark is deepest on my heart.

"Hapstiŋna," they say, "has her mother's blood. Look at what her fingers make." But my mother's needle has a better eye than mine. I must learn fast.

The grandmothers, the aunties, so many women ask my mother to make special gifts for them. They are things no white person could ever understand. My mother's eyes are sore, but she still makes these things talk. The things she makes for the traders do not talk. The mouths of those things are shut. Those are the things I help her make most.

I am also called Śina Zi. Yellow Shawl, in your tongue. But when you call me Dinah, I answer.

SARAH FREQUENTS THE FROST-COVERED WINDOWS, PEERING OUT FROM BEHIND the shades into blue shadows. At the moment, a lamp in John's office is burning faintly through another squall. Whenever he decides to come back home, he mustn't blow through the door to find her relations with the girl too familiar.

❧ 8 ❧

EARLY APRIL. The wind softens. The land forgives. Tiny wildflowers bloom under the last snow. Frozen ruts thaw. The river ice cracks and breaks open with a roar. Thatches of green sprout in brittle-brown grass. Yellow-breasted meadowlarks whistle. Noisy frogs swell in chorus.

John moves home from the warehouse. Steamboats run again. Amidst the news of the bloody Union victory at Shiloh, reports of Standing Buffalo trickle back to Agency Hill. The chief and his hunters are back from their chase, empty-handed, defeated by Waziya, who draws near in winter and blows terrible storms from his mouth.

On her first ride with James since their long winter confinement, Sarah finds Pasu Kiyuksa and Opa in fair health. But at Rush Brook she shakes hands with elders whose arms are sticks. She holds wasting children who are too weak to shoo the flies from their nostrils. The wiŋyaŋ tell her they're peeling the bark of young cottonwood trees and foraging for mushrooms and nettles to feed their families.

In the hunger of the Sioux, she sees her own, of a different sort, and understands what her life has come to. Its extravagance almost begs to be destroyed.

She declines the women's pipe. As soon as her bags are emptied of the food she has brought, she reties them to her saddle. "Time to go, James!"

"But Mama, we just got here!"

"Do as I say!" She drags him sniveling from his play and hoists him roughly onto Belle. "Dokśa ake waćiŋyaŋ kin kte ye," she calls to the wiŋyaŋ, as she mounts. *I will see you again.* In Dakota there's no word for goodbye.

She flees Rush Brook, riding with James further out into the wild countryside than ever before, galloping into the wind, going nowhere. She pushes down in the stirrups and leans forward in the saddle, pressing her boy low over Belle's neck. Her hair spills loose and flies. The mare's shoulder blades toil between her thighs.

Atop a ridge she slows to a trot to wend through a quiet grove of mature cottonwoods. The crowns of the trees are tossing, but here in the shelter of the lowest branches, it's quiet. The only sounds are the thudding of Belle's hooves and the whisper of new leaves—

"Mama…." James points a timorous finger.

She reins up with a cry and forces Belle hard to the right, to spare James further sight of the burial tree. The bundling around the dead Indian has worked loose. The emaciated torso, having slipped free, is hanging down between the cradling branches. Birds have pecked out the eyes. Strings of hair flutter on the breeze.

She walks the mare off the ridge, an arm tight around her boy.

"Was that a man, Mama?"

"Yes, James, that was a man."

CROPS GO INTO THE GROUND EARLY. RAINS FALL IN GOOD SPELLS. VISIONS OF A bumper harvest ease the memory of last year's cutworms. But many of the Sioux are still eating a diet of wild grapes and berries, marsh grass, lichens and tree bark. Meat is the occasional muskrat or duck. John admits to seeing all kinds of disease due to malnutrition.

Then, in mid-June, the rain stops, and nobody's prayers can make it start again. The air smells parched. Grass crackles underfoot. The earth cracks. In places on the Minnesota, steamboats drag bottom. Everyone worries over the prospect of all river traffic drying up.

Sarah waters her thirsty garden from the well, shooing away hungry Sioux until, from exasperation, she hires a mixed-blood to build a tall picket fence. She doesn't mean to be another Mary Riggs, and the Sioux don't mean to steal. She has finally wised up: Because she has sometimes accepted their mouse beans, their frybread, their chokecherries, the Sioux are entitled to her lettuce, her onions, her peas, her hoe. No need to ask first. Since what's theirs has become hers, what's hers has become theirs. It's the Sioux way. They can't help being who they are, any more than she can. This is what she tells herself, as she instructs Dinah on whitewashing pickets.

After a full year on the reservation, she is feeling the weight of its extremes. She braces herself as the Sioux assemble again for their annuity payment, their camp spreading in circles below Agency Hill. She fears a repeat of last year's troubles, or worse. Rumors are swirling: Because of the War against the Southern rebels, the government is short on gold. It might underpay the Sioux by half, or substitute unsound greenbacks. It might not issue any money at all.

On June 25 the Upper Sioux chiefs and headmen meet Thomas in council on the green. Standing Buffalo is even gaunter than he was in October. His hair, so black before, is grizzled. "It is customary," he tells Thomas through Frenier, "for the treaty payment to be made to my people during The Moon When the Strawberries are Red. The hooves of our horses are stained with berry juice. It is time."

"I can't give you what I don't have," Thomas says. "I doubt the money will be here for another month."

The chiefs plead with Thomas to release the provisions in the meantime. By treaty, they remind him, they have full right to whatever goods are stored in his warehouse.

He won't be moved. "We must adhere to protocol. Provisions must be distributed the same day as the payment. For now, you must disperse, and feed yourselves by the hunt."

"You have to talk to Thomas, Henrietta. Last year taught him nothing."

Henrietta repositions her embroidery hoop on her coverlet. A floral pattern, with lovebirds. "I don't involve myself in Indian matters, Sarah. No lady should."

Tiresome, these thorns in their conversations. Their friendship is fraying at the seams. "Suppose it was us. Suppose there was a warehouse filled with food—*our* food—yet the authorities refused to release any, while our children were dying from lack. My James and Nellie! Your Jacob and—"

"Thomas told the Sioux not to come till sent for. They should have listened."

"They came according to custom. He's obligated to feed them till the distribution."

"Not for weeks at a time!"

"They have nothing to eat."

Henrietta lays aside her needlework. She begins fanning her wrinkles. "I'm not without pity for the Sioux. God help them! But Sarah, you mustn't keep harping on their welfare."

"God help *you,* the first one that dies on our stoop."

"Oh, come, it isn't as bad as that."

"Oh, isn't it?"

"If it is, perhaps you should tear down that pretty white fence around your garden!"

❦ 9 ❦

AUGUST 4-5, 1862

SARAH JERKS AWAKE to her own bed and her own four walls, awash in morning light. She'd been dreaming. Ćaske, an Indian from Shakopee, was hanging down dead from a cottonwood in her yard. In the next tree, another dead Indian. An absolute forest of trees, growing Sioux bodies.

She rolls over, stretching a clammy arm above her head, reluctant to start into the heat of the day. The air is already sultry.

How strange, after all these years and such slim acquaintance, for Ćaske to appear in her dreams….

Commotion threads into her waking—singing, yelling, the whinnying of horses. She dons her robe and slippers and goes to her window.

Hundreds of Indians are stampeding the grounds around the warehouse, dressed in regalia, outfitted as if for show. But this isn't one of their fancy dances, meant to entertain or beg. Guns are firing into the air. Mounts are dashing about in every direction.

She sticks her head out the window to sight the soldiers' camp, a furlong off. Young Lieutenant Sheehan and a hundred soldiers from the Fifth Minnesota have been bivouacked there since July, to maintain order until the payment. A raconteur with a taste for whiskey lemonade, Sheehan has been twice to dinner. Now Indians on horseback have overrun his post.

Her eyes shift back to the warehouse. Though the hour's early, John might well be inside, drinking coffee with some of the men. Sioux guns are leveled at every soldier stationed around the building. The clerk Noah

Sinks is dancing to bullets, dust flying at his feet. The farmhand Parker Pierce is standing stock-still on the green, a tomahawk poised over his head. Milk streams from bullet holes in his pail.

A chief wheels his horse with a battle cry and charges the main warehouse door. When he sinks his hatchet into the wood, she runs for her babies, across the hall. They're still in bed. Dinah's straw pallet is empty on the floor.

She drags James and Nellie into her bedroom, meanwhile shouting for the girl. The house gives a vacant reply. She storms back to her window and searches the desperate scene below.

There, steps away from the chaos on the green. "Dinah!" she yells, from the floor of her belly. *"Hapstiŋna!"*

The girl spins around and looks up, eyes wide and bright.

"Get in the house! Lock everything!"

The girl seems paralyzed, the only unmoving thing. To lure her back from the melee, Sarah picks up James and leans him out over the windowsill. Dinah adores the boy like her own blood.

"Mama," James asks, at the sight of the Indians, "is it a party?"

She's holding onto him for dear life. "James, wave at Dinah! See her there? *Wave!*"

Dinah stares up at them with parted lips.

"An Indian dance, Mama? Can we go?"

"Hapstiŋna! Please!"

Another frightful second longer, then Dinah hurries back toward the house. Sarah whirls from the window, thrusting James away. "Scoot! Under the bed, you and Nellie! Hide! It's a game—"

Out the window, a bullet cuts the halyard on the main flagpole, dropping the Stars & Stripes like a wet rag. Indians swarm her yard. She charges down the hall to a back window. Indians are tumbling over the fence into her garden.

Dinah tops the stairs. Sarah tows her by the arm into the bedroom as fists start pounding the front door. She points to James and Nellie under the bed skirt. "Lock the door! Hide the children!"

She slips out of the bedroom. The door closes behind her. The bolt slides into place.

She pads down the stairs in her slippers and steals into the parlor. She pulls the loaded Derringer from John's desk drawer and taps the muzzle on her forehead, a sort of prayer.

At the banging front door, she reties her robe. Then gingerly she lifts the bar. Raising her pistol, she breathes one last time, and twists the knob.

Warriors spill past her into the house, shouting for axes, every oŋspe Good Big Woman has, to breach the warehouse doors. Weak-headed with relief, she slips the Derringer into the pocket of her robe. All they want is what's theirs. Her finger still on the trigger, she levels her chin and cuts through the roomful of Indians like the prow of a ship parting the waves. Indians accompany her to the pantry, where she offers them a trade axe. They reject it, having already tested their own. They need a heavier head.

She thinks of John's tools, locked in the woodshed. A felling axe, a splitting axe. A maul wedge, a splitting wedge, a sledge.

She thinks of John, likely in his office, surrounded by Sioux.

She takes down the cast-iron key-ring from its hook.

FROM A CORNER OF HER BEDROOM WINDOW, SHE WATCHES THE ACTION AT THE warehouse. With John's tools the Indians soon break through the fortress doors and surge inside with triumphant whoops. Several soldiers lie on the ground, bloodied from blows, but so far this is a bizarre battle. No guns fired by either side seem to have inflicted any harm.

As some warriors reemerge from the building toting sacks of flour, a line of infantry fans out before them, muskets at the ready. In the center of the line is Lieutenant Gere, Sheehan's second-in-command, practically a boy. Next to him is a howitzer, trained on the warehouse doors. One sight of that big gun, and the Indians fall back from the line of aim. Afforded the opening, Lieutenant Sheehan, whose camp she'd thought overrun, rushes a squad of men inside. He and his troops oust the remaining Sioux without bloodshed.

Sheehan barks commands in his Irish brogue. A squad of soldiers runs to the riven warehouse doors and crosses their gun barrels to bar entrance. The rest of the company assumes battle formation in front of the building. The boy Gere repositions the howitzer to defend.

GOVERNMENT FAMILIES SWEAT OUT AN ANXIOUS NIGHT IN THE WAREHOUSE, guarded by Sheehan's troops. Meanwhile, in a show of hostility, all 5,000 Sioux camped below Agency Hill pull up stakes and move several miles off. Word comes from Standing Buffalo that despite his opposition, Sioux leaders are planning to attack. Sheehan dispatches Gere for reinforcements, but any help from Fort Ridgley will arrive too late. Thomas sends a frantic message to Reverend Riggs through Little Paul, the farmer

Indian, imploring him to put to use any wisdom in the Bible that might pertain.

As a ruff of first light illumines the horizon, the women and children are loaded into buckboards for evacuation to the Lower Agency. Sarah and John make their goodbyes wagonside, each with a sleeping child nestled against one shoulder.

"Listen, Sarah, when you get below, go straightway to the Humphreys. Tell Philander everything that's happened. Redwood should prepare. Any violence here is apt to spread—"

"Let's be moving out!" the wagon driver bawls.

She should say something. "Be safe." Trying not to think of the axes she gave the Sioux.

He touches the back of his knuckles to her cheek. She flinches, despite herself. He seems not to notice. "Best you be off. Oh, and here"—he slides her sun goggles into her dress pocket—"you'll be needing these."

She lifts Nellie up to Henrietta in the wagon and climbs aboard. When she swings around for James, John still has him tight in his arms, chin snug against the boy's brow. He's turning in place with his eyes closed, as though stuck on the axis of a dying world.

At least there's one of us he loves.

"Last call, folks!" the driver says.

John gives James up to her, tears skidding down his cheeks.

"We'll see you soon, Husband." Reassurance against all reason.

He takes off his pince-nez and backs away from the wagon.

She's arranging herself on the seat next to Henrietta when Thomas, stinking of gin, plops down beside her, hat slouched over his bloodshot eyes. "Surely you're not leaving!"

"Whether he stays or goes doesn't concern you!" Henrietta says, settling her boys at her feet.

"What other men do you see in these wagons? Is *my* husband running off?"

Thomas wedges his hands between his thighs.

In the end it's the Sioux who prevent Thomas from going. A party of warriors stops the train below the trading post. They allow safe passage to the government families, but Itoŋśni S'a, *The Liar,* will have to stay.

❧ 10 ❧

IN THE KITCHEN of the Humphrey home, hard at the family's wash, Sarah wrings out a dress she sewed for Susan last spring. A brown gingham dress, with faux wood buttons and a drawstring waist. A dress she stitched together as a gift after learning Susan was expecting her fourth child. A dress she should probably throw in the fire to spare the woman more grief.

On Tuesday she had arrived at Redwood to find Susan in labor. Around two in the morning, Philander delivered the baby, stillborn, a knot in the cord tighter than a hangman's. For three days after, the bereft woman lay gray on her embroidered pillowcase, scarcely making a sound, refusing to eat. Only this morning has she taken some broth.

Philander sloshes through the kitchen door with two more buckets of water. It's his bull-neck, not this dress, Sarah would like to be wringing. He disguises his sorrow so well, driveling on about the righteous judgment of God, the wages of sin and the curse of Eve, she's tempted to sneak brandy from her flask into his teetotalling coffee. Poor Susan isn't to blame.

She towels the sweat from her forehead and neck. Her arms are one throbbing ache, from shoulder to wrist. If only she could do the wash in the yard, for the breeze! But outside the kitchen window, the Lower Sioux are demonstrating around the new government warehouse. Red Owl, who had so impressed Thoreau, didn't live to see it built. Alas, neither did Thoreau.

"It's getting ugly out there." Philander crouches to splash his face. "Gleason refuses to open the warehouse without Major Galbraith's say-so."

"Plain foolishness!"

"'Withhold not good from them to whom it is due, when it is in the power of thine hand to do it—'"

The crack of a musket startles them both. It's the first shooting in this week of unrest since the flour raid at the Upper Agency. Sarah spies out the window. The Indians around the warehouse seem no more agitated than before. "Likely just shooting the air."

Philander takes down his gun from above the fireplace and sets about loading shot and ball.

"Can't the traders do something to help?" she says.

"They're refusing to extend any more credit."

She looks out at the warehouse again. "T.J.G. Agt., 1861" is engraved on the stone lintel above a second-floor window. More of Thomas's vainglory.

In four days they have received no report from Yellow Medicine. Had the Upper Sioux attacked Agency Hill, as once seemed foregone, the Lower Sioux would surely have raided the warehouse next door. No locks and chains could have kept them out. So she tells herself, over and over.

On the Sabbath she ventures out to St. John's church. Scattered in the pews when she enters are a few other evacuees from Yellow Medicine, some government whites from Redwood, and a handful of Sioux. She sits down beside Jannette DeCamp, her old friend from Shakopee. Jannette's "darling Joseph" occupies a pew with his sons on the men's side. He operates the Lower Agency sawmill and gristmill.

Little Crow seats himself across the aisle. He's thinner than when she last saw him, swimming in a black velvet-collared coat. At least on this day, red is his favorite color. A crimson cravat is tied around his shirt collar; his fringed deerskin trousers are trimmed with intricate red and green beadwork. Swathed around his waist is a red blanket. Up close, she gauges his age at around fifty.

"Taoyate Duta"—using his Dakota name—"ćante wašte ya nape ćiyuza pi ye!" *I greet you with a good heart and a handshake.*

To her astonishment, he leaps up to greet her. "Madam," he says in

BENEATH THE SAME STARS   63

English, with a slight bow. Despite his crippled wrist, his handclasp is firm.

"I am Mrs. Sarah Wakefield. My husband is the physician at Yellow Medicine."

A disarming smile lights his lips. "You are here at Redwood to visit friends, Mrs. Wakefield?"

His English is excellent, but his lying needs practice. He knows precisely why she's here.

DURING THE SERMON A PIGEON IN THE RAFTERS SWOOPS LOW AND WILD OVER the heads of the faithful. Babies crawl about on the plank floor. Flea-riddled dogs wander in and nose about until, with much yelping and pattering of nails, they're dragged out again.

Reverend Hinman, a protégé of Bishop Whipple, is a passable speaker, but rambling. Sarah keeps nodding off in the August heat. She wags her fan harder against drowsiness and the bugs. From behind its cover, she surveys the church for Mother Friend and other familiar faces from Tiŋta Otoŋwe. As Lower Sioux, this would be their church, if they chose to attend.

Three rows back on the men's side, an Indian appears to be sleeping. Or perhaps he has closed his eyes, the better to listen. There's something about him....

She considers him in stolen glances. His hair, parted to one side, is short as a white man's. Apart from his fingerwoven armbands, he's dressed in the clothing of a settler. His face is ordinary—except for that scar on his forehead, fading back into his hair....

Ćaske!

AT THE SIGHT OF HIM PEERING IN HER PARLOR WINDOW, AT HOME IN Shakopee, she'd set down her teacup. She tracked him window to window as he circled the house, shadowed by his woman. In the kitchen she hurried to open the back door before he walked right in, as Sioux were wont to do.

"Hello," she said through the screen. His bangs were cut low over his almond-gray eyes. Short plaits of hair hung at each side of his head.

"Haŋ, Peźihuta Wićaśa Tawiću." Calling her *Doctor Wife,* as did all Śakpe's people. "Ćante waśte nape ćiyuza pi do." A traditional greeting, something about a *good heart.* She didn't try to repeat it.

He held up a string of walleyes. "Books see?"

His use of English took her aback. She looked at his big, gleaming fish —half a dozen, at least. He seemed to be proposing a trade, his catch in exchange for a peek at her bookshelves; a generous swap, even if John wasn't fond of freshwater fish.

She wagged her finger at his gun. "No mazawakaŋ in tipi."

With obvious reluctance he propped his gun against the house. She opened the door to admit him and showed him a hook above the sink for his fishline.

She escorted him to the large walnut bookcase in the parlor. As he stepped toward his reflection in its glass doors, she studied him from behind. The striped trade blanket folded over his shoulders. The long braid hanging down his back, decorated with ribbons. The blue calico shirt. The typical buckskin leggings and breechcloth. The filthy bare feet.

He flattened his palms against the glass pane, squinting through the door to her little library. "Book house."

She smiled at his unwitting poetry. "No, not book house. Bookcase." She could see him watching her mouth in the glass. "Book *case.*"

"Book ... case."

"Very good! Waśté! You read?" She pointed at him and made the sign of a book.

"Learn. Wasiću wakaŋ Pond."

"Reverend Pond taught you?"

"Haŋ." *It is so.*

He understood English better than he spoke, like she did Dakota. "Books are good," she said. "Books waśté."

"Haŋ, waśté. Books wakaŋ?"

His question stole her breath. Wakaŋ was a word she knew well, embedded as it was in so many others. *Holy,* it meant, or *sacred;* perhaps anything powerful that couldn't be understood. Wakaŋtaŋka—*the Great Mystery,* God of the Sioux. Wakaŋ iźa—*children.* Śuŋka wakaŋ—*horse.* Mazawakaŋ—*gun.* Wakaŋhdi—*lightning.* Wasiću wakaŋ—*a white minister,* like Samuel Pond. Why, wakaŋ was even at the heart of this Indian's band of Dakotas, the Mdewakaŋtuŋwaŋ—*People Of The Sacred Lake.*

"Books wakaŋ?" he repeated.

She unlocked the bookcase doors and retrieved the Wakefield Family Bible from the bottom shelf. "This book is wakaŋ."

"Book. Woyapi."

"Yes, woyapi. This woyapi is wakaŋ." She pointed to the words gilded on the ancient leather cover. "Ho-ly Bi-ble." Tapping each syllable as she read.

"Haŋ," he said without interest, or perhaps he hadn't understood. Suddenly he stretched out his arms, as if to embrace the bookcase. "Books wakaŋ!"

Fire spilled down her spine. *She* was the one who hadn't understood. The Indian wasn't asking. He was declaring. *Books are sacred.*

"Haŋ, koda," she said, calling him *friend.* "Woyapi *are* wakaŋ!"

His name, he told her that day, was Ćaske. "Chahz-KEH," she said after him, easily enough, and met with his approval. For him, "SAIR-uh" proved difficult, his alphabet having no equivalent for *R.* She applauded his best attempt.

After he left, she looked up his name in her Dakota dictionary. "The name of a first-born child," it said, "if a son."

II

𝕤 I 𝕤

JOHN TURNS the wagon up the government road toward home.

"So," Sarah asks, "the Sioux have left Yellow Medicine?"

"For now." He stretches his legs against the buckboard's footrest. "Captain Marsh rode up to reinforce Sheehan. After a series of councils, he and Reverend Riggs prevailed upon Thomas to issue more flour and pork. Then they sent the Sioux home till the gold arrives. *If* it arrives." He reaches back to reposition her parasol over the sleeping children. "It's been quiet for a couple of days. Marsh is withdrawing his troops to Ridgley."

"So soon?"

"We're apt to meet his train."

"Down here, Indians were rioting all week around the warehouse, demanding food."

"Thomas promised Little Crow to distribute some rations down here. That should appease them."

"I just saw Little Crow yesterday at Hinman's church!" Such a long-winded service. By the benediction Ćaske had already spirited himself away.

"Somehow he got wind of the flour raid and the parleys after. He rode up, showed off his ribs in council, said if Thomas was going to open one warehouse, he must open both. Thomas was cornered." He pulls at his goatee, gray with road dust. "Andrew Myrick didn't help him any."

"The trader?"

"Idiot jack-ass told the Sioux for all he cared, they could eat grass or their own dung."

She covers her mouth in dismay.

"Damned lucky Riggs was able to smooth their ruffled war bonnets." He unstoppers his flask, takes a long draft. "Would you believe, in the middle of this mess, Thomas is aiming to go off to War? He's holding a meeting tonight to raise a company of half-breeds for Lincoln."

"And *he's* planning to lead them?"

"Leaving tomorrow, first light. He'll stop at Redwood long enough to muster more volunteers, then they'll be off to Fort Snelling."

"What does Thomas know about fighting a war?"

"Let's hope more than he knows about keeping the peace."

"Henrietta never even hinted! I wonder if she had any warning. Did *you* know he might enlist?"

He fiddles with the slack reins. "Last spring, he figured to go off and fight, play the hero, make everybody forget the Pierson business." An allusion to the scandal that precipitated her whipping. Azariah Pierson, the reservation's Superintendent of Schools, had accused Thomas of charging $5,000 in false claims to the Indian education fund and either splitting the money among his friends or purloining the entire sum for himself. Though he held no proof, Pierson was certain that other accounts were also being embezzled. He'd since resigned his post in disgust.

"So why didn't he enlist back then? Oh, if only he had!"

"Superintendent Thompson told him to hang on till after the annuity payment, to squeeze all the milk he could from the cow. But Thomas must be fed up with waiting. It's been one crisis after another, ever since he got here. Christ...." He drains the last of his brandy. "I should probably join him in the ranks."

"You?"

"Pierson's a righteous son of a bitch. There's no telling how far he might push this. Efforts have been made to quiet him, but so far it hasn't been rigged."

"So J.B. was right. Pierson could destroy you."

"I'd rather take my chances with him than with the graybacks."

They drive some minutes in silence.

"Sarah, I've been doing some thinking.... It might be wise for you and the children to go back East."

"To Shakopee?"

"No, *East.* To your friend Julia, if you'd like, or my family in Connecticut. Just till the mud settles."

She slides her sun goggles up onto her brow. "Don't trifle with me, John. Not about this."

"I'm not trifling. I'm not sure when yet, but be making yourself ready to go."

IN A REVERIE SARAH OPENS HER TRUNK AND CONTEMPLATES ITS EMPTY TRAYS. When she rose this morning, the sun was a mammoth red ball, tinting the clouds a fiery crimson. The grass, stained a dull golden red, bowed in homage. An auspicious sign, that sun must have been, for after all these years, and all her trials, today she's going home to Rhode Island.

Moments ago, John strode into her sewing nook and pressed a thick leather wallet into her thimbled hand. "Traveling money," he said. "George Gleason's driving you and the children down to Fort Ridgley, to catch the stage."

"Gleason?" was all she could manage. Despite John's remarks last week on the government road, she hadn't actually believed he would ever let her go.

"He's itching to get back to Redwood. I told him if he took you on down to Ridgley, he could borrow my team. You'll leave at two."

"I can't possibly be ready in an hour!"

"Dinah will help."

"But it's so late. Why not wait till tomorrow?"

"I told you, Gleason's got to get back. You should make it to Ridgley by nightfall, or thereabouts."

She lifts the trays from the trunk, trying to quell her misgivings. Most people driving to Ridgley stop overnight at the Half-Way House. She would rather not gamble, racing the sun. The road is too treacherous in the dark, even with a high moon. Still, she's going home, and the children are going with her.

She bustles room to room, gathering, sending Dinah on the run to fetch. Piles accumulate on her bed—books, toys, clothing for every hour and season. She stacks, she sorts, she folds, she rolls. Her trunk will never be big enough.

MORE THAN EIGHT YEARS EARLIER, SHE'D STOOD BEFORE JULIA PAULL'S dressing mirror, bandaging her chest as tightly as she could bear. Trying not to think of her baby, just down the stairs, nursing her best friend's breast. Trying not to think of Richard, and how he slept the night before with a hand upon her bosom.

He would never hit her again.

She loosened her hair from its pins, shook it free, parted it to one side. She picked up the shears, drew a sharp breath and cut, not letting herself look at the floor.

Richard, she knew, would search the streets, the stagecoach stops, the railroad depot. But he would be searching for her, not for Thomas Jemison. And Thomas Jemison would be gone.

She whipped her fingers through her hair, amazed at how light she felt without her tresses. She'd left the nape somewhat longer, after the current male fashion. Lucky for her, beards were out of style.

At the foot of the bed, a neat mound of clothes. Julia's George was a big man, and his clothes, compared to a woman's, were effortless to put on. Drawers, with buttons. Trousers, with suspenders. An undershirt and long-tailed top shirt, pulled over the head and tucked in.

She slipped on the plain black vest. She tied the black cravat into a proper bow. She pulled on the brown frock coat and shrugged the shoulders home. In the mirror the clothes hung on her body like a man's—arms big enough, chest flat enough, waist thick enough, though some wadding might help behind the fly.

She planned to end her imposture once she felt safe enough—west enough—from Richard. Her sights were set on the Minnesota frontier, where, by all accounts, all people were welcome, all fortunes were possible, and all prior sins were wiped clean, like Heaven.

She descended the back stairs to the kitchen where Julia, done nursing Florie, was cutting soda biscuits. When Julia saw her in her getup, her mouth dropped open. "Well, I'll be bound! Turn around, will you, let me look at you...." A melancholy laugh. "My, but you're a fine-looking man!"

"Would you ever suspect?"

"Not till you dropped your pants. You even sound like a man, looking like you do."

Sarah tipped her hat. "Name's Thomas Jemison." A man in one of her father's old books.

"This is truly what you want?"

Little Georgie toddled into the kitchen with a sugar tit in his mouth. Florie waddled in behind him, dragging a pull-toy tipped on its side. She headed straight for Sarah's knees. "Mama!"

She caught her baby up, buried her face in the side of her neck.

· · ·

FIVE MONTHS IT TOOK, WORKING HER WAY ACROSS THE COUNTRY, DISGUISED AS Jemison lest anyone be after her. When she started out, she was terrified of betraying herself, doing one of the million woman-things she was apt to do without thinking: primping, eating too daintily, showing some sign of her monthly Curse. She never knew when someone might catch her adjusting the binding on her breasts, or chance into a privy while her pants were down. She steered clear of taverns, barbershops, billiard halls, anywhere men were loitering. Young men, especially. They always had something to prove and were quick to pick a fight.

The further west she went, the more comfortable her pretense became. As a man she was remarkably free to go where she wanted, when she wanted, according to her own good judgment. She could indulge in drink and tobacco as she pleased. To a degree, if someone told her what to do, and how to do it, she could choose not to. She could issue orders of her own and, owing to her size, reasonably expect obedience from most. She was no longer any man's servant or possession.

She traveled by stagecoach from Providence to Albany; by packet boat through the Erie Canal; in steerage on a palace steamer across the Great Lakes to Chicago; by train over to Galena; by steamboat up the Mississippi. Debarking from the *War Eagle* at the landing in St. Paul, she almost knelt and kissed the ground.

Her return East, by comparison, will be an excursion; mostly by train in first-class comfort, as a reputable woman instead of a runaway wife. With any luck she should reach Providence by midweek next. Julia will answer the door and faint dead away.

Apart from Florie, Julia Paull is the closest thing to kin she has left in Rhode Island. For that, she has only herself to blame. She'd fled Providence without any word to her family in North Kingstown. For three years after, she sent them no news of her whereabouts. By late '56, when she posted them a notice of her wedding to John, they might well have thought her dead. She intended the clipping from the *Shakopee Independent* as a gesture of reconciliation, hoping all might be forgiven by reason of her joy. But when an envelope arrived at last from North Kingstown, addressed not to her but to "Dr. J.L. Wakefield," she smelled trouble.

"Your new wife is a harlot," her blessed mother had written, in a letter only six lines long. "Your children will be bastards. Set Sarah's hand upon the Good Book. Ask her if she didn't desert the bed of J. Richard Butts, her rightful Husband. Ask her if she didn't abandon her own Daughter to strangers. Then tell her she is dead."

Six cold-blooded lines, but they didn't contain the whole truth. Yes, she'd run away from Richard Butts. How else could she get free of him? The man was sucking the marrow from her bones. And yes, she'd abandoned her baby. Were she to have stolen Florie away, Richard would have chased them to kingdom-come, out of sheer spite. What kind of life would they have had, always on the run, Florie not two years old?

No, loving the child had meant giving her up. Not to strangers—that was a lie, born of her mother's hurt—but to Julia Paull, her best friend. Julia promised to love Florie like one of her own, if Richard consented, and they both knew he would, for Richard's greatest fear in life, after his dread of being alone, was being alone with his own child.

"Tell her she is dead." Plainly she'd injured her mother beyond repair by not running home to her; by not letting her raise up Florie in a circle of kin. But she couldn't allow her daughter to live in the same house as her stepfather. She couldn't allow her daughter to go out into the dark of that barn whose door would creak on its hinge, warning that you were no longer alone with the warm cow and the rhythm of your milking.... No, Pitt Vaughn wasn't the sort of man any girl should grow up around. And her mother wasn't the sort of woman who could admit the sort of man her second husband was.

"Your new wife is a harlot." Though she explained everything to John, justifying herself, only his fear of scandal saved her from a thrashing. Shakopee was too small, his practice too fledgling, to risk talk around town of a beating. "But don't mistake me, *wife*," he said, his cigar dripping ash on the bloodstained wood of his office floor. "If you *ever* post another letter to *anyone* in Rhode Island, I'll make you wish you'd never left your darling Mr. Butts."

IN THE BOTTOM OF THE TRUNK SHE PLACES HER SEWING BOX, HER FAVORITE books and sheet music, her jewelry box, a shoe bag. She fits them together like puzzle pieces, leveling the top, then covers the layer with a towel. Next, she lays in flannels, linens, everyday dresses and petticoats, undergarments, shawls and cloaks, her finer apparel....

In the years after her mother's fateful revelation, she gave John a son. She entertained the flower of Shakopee society to curry his favor. She nursed his patients and kept his accounts. She helped him survive the Panic of '57. She fulfilled all her wifely duties without complaint until right after Nellie was born, when, to her surprise, he grudgingly allowed her to correspond with Julia Paull. "But I forbid you to write the girl," he said, "or any of your blood."

How her pen trembled, composing that first letter:

Shakopee, Minn., January 1860

My dear Julia

I cannot say my feelings as I write this. How are you faring? By your great Help I am here in Minnesota with two Babies and a Husband who cannot forgive me for Richard Butts. My Prayers for your Family and my Florie have been unceasing these many years but I fear they are of no account. If you receive this and it is in your Heart to give me a kind reply I will cry tears of joy as I am ever

Your humble Friend
Sarah

In due course an envelope from Providence appeared with the florid arcs and loops of Julia's handwriting. When she slivered it open to a glad reply, she understood how a sinner feels, redeemed.

She fills the trays of the trunk: gloves, handkerchiefs, lace collars and cuffs, parasol, slippers, dressing gown, perfume, a jar of cold cream....

In Julia's recent letters there has been a turn. Her second son, Walter, is in the thick of the War, and Albert, her oldest, is planning to enlist. "I do not know how to bear Albert's going too, but he has caught the Union Fever like his brother and wishes to place his name upon the Rolls."

Sarah smiles to herself at the prospect of according Julia some cheer in her boys' absence. At the prospect, too, of reuniting with Florie. About her firstborn, now ten years old and a mite sickly, she can't hear enough.

Florie is her Father's in face and frame, her Mother's in mind, and her own Self in spirit. She is a good girl but holds her thoughts closer than a penny. I cannot pry many words from her though she keeps near me as a shadow. The Child is not without affection for her Father but she wishes always to remain with us. Richard has provided well as he could but ours is the only Home of which she has memory. I will tell you my Dear that Richard lately took a Wife, a pretty young thing named Addie. I feared he would soon remove Florie to his own house to raise her up but he is going to the War. He wishes I keep her till his return and of course I am willing if God is, she is my greatest comfort with my Boys in the Fight.

Once Richard's regiment dispatched to the South, Julia entreated her to come for a visit:

Your journey across the Country will be the easier part of your coming here. Richard has always told Florie her Mother is dead and he long ago swore me to it, a condition of raising her up. So my Dear if you are to visit you must be Sarah Wakefield, not Sarah Butts. You cannot let on who you are. Much as I love you do not come if you cannot do this.

She dons a two-piece day dress, her golden toffee moiré with crinoline skirt. As she clads James in his bolero suit, she senses a strange clairvoyance between Julia's months-old invitation to come East and John's sudden impulse to remove her and the children from the frontier.

"Be Mama's little man, now." She works at taming James's cowlick with her comb. "We're going on a big trip."

"Where to?"

"To the sea, where I grew up! Far, far away! We're going to ride the train!" She tucks the comb into her carpetbag, weighty with necessaries for the journey. "Dinah, please close the trunk."

She ties her green velvet hat over her coiffed hair.

"Sarah?" John calls, from the bottom of the stairs.

"Ready!" She pulls Dinah into an embrace. "Go home," she whispers in the girl's ear, as John enters with Gleason to collect her luggage.

James rides the trunk down the stairs and out the front door. She hangs back in the house, heavy with sentiment, Nellie babbling away on her arm. Has it been only a year she has lived here? In the parlor she closes the key lid on the piano and feeds a handful of berries to her canaries. She centers the white queen in her square on the chessboard. She touches the doorjamb where her pencil marked the children's heights on their birthdays. She stares at the fireplace poker.

John appears in the doorway. She gestures at the miniature family portraits on the mantel. "I want to take those."

"Christ, is there still room in that trunk? One would think you were never coming back."

Gleason is waiting in the buckboard, Belle and Mick in the harness. He's snapping his whip at the weeds. His dog Sadie thumps her tail as John helps Sarah and the children into the rear bench seat.

"Drive fast, George!"

"Will do, Doc. Thanks again."

Sarah notes the sun's position. "You *do* have a gun, Mr. Gleason?"

The Irishman pats the side of his coat. "Got her right here."

"A pocket pistol? After all the Indian troubles we've had?"

Gleason releases the foot brake and flicks the reins. "Be seeing you, Doc."

The last sight she has of John, he's twirling his pocketwatch on its chain, feet planted wide as he watches them go. His shirtsleeves are rolled up, his hair mussing in the breeze. Behind him, squatting on the white-washed stoop, is Dinah, head down, arms hugging her knees.

❧ 2 ❧

AUGUST 18, 1862

STEWART GARVIE IS SITTING atop a dry goods box outside his store, sharpening his Bowie knife. He hails Gleason down.

"Bound for Redwood, George?"

"After I take Doc's wife down to Ridgley."

"Nae, laddie, best you be staying here! Sioux killed some settlers over in the Big Woods."

Gleason spits a stream of tobacco. "Ain't the first time."

"*Mine!*" Nellie says, fumbling for Sarah's goggles.

"Joe LaFramboise was by," Garvie says. "He told me the Sioux's all riled up. They been meeting up and down the river."

"Another scare's all." Gleason scratches Sadie's ears, the dog panting.

"Nae, there'll be hell to pay, and the Sioux know it."

"Mama, *mine!*"

Sarah parries with Nellie's arms. "Mr. Gleason, perhaps it would be best if we—"

"Mama," James says, "let's go on our big trip!"

She touches a finger to his lips.

Garvie bends the rim of his hat. "Joe says there's a lot of Sioux itching to fight. Says I ought to shutter the store—"

"Mr. Gleason," Sarah says, "please, I think—"

"Close up shop on the word of a half-breed?" Gleason spits again.

"Joe's a righteous enough fellow—"

"Mr. Gleason, take us back up the Hill!"

"Don't get yourself in a lather, Missus—"

"*This instant!*"

"You think I'd drive below if it might cost me my neck?"

"Forgive me, Mr. Gleason, but at the moment it isn't *your* neck I'm most worried about."

"Doc ain't in a sweat."

"You mean … my husband's aware of this?"

"Joe was telling us all about it over coffee. Doc called him a fool to worry." He clucks to Belle and Mick, with a light pat of the reins on their rumps. "Be seeing you, Garvie. Next time you're below, let's catch us some fish."

"THERE SHOULD BE MORE TRAFFIC."

Gleason leaves off his whistling. "What you say, Missus?"

"A cart or wagon, an Indian … this road always has *some* traffic. In two hours, we haven't seen a soul. Where *is* everybody?"

"Wherever they ain't, I expect."

"Mr. Gleason, for the last time, turn this wagon around."

"Say, you like to sing, don't you, Missus?"

James jumps up from the seat. "*I* like to sing, Mr. Gleason!"

"How about Aura Lea?" He begins to sing. "'When the blackbird in the spring, on the willow tree' … C'mon, Jimmy, let me hear you—"

"Mr. Gleason, *please!* This isn't a pleasure trip!"

"You better behave, Missus, or I ain't going to take you nowhere again." He laughs from his belly. "Sounded like an old married couple right then, didn't we?"

"Mr. Gleason, have you been drinking?"

"'Aura Lea, Aura Lea, maid with golden hair' … sing, Jimmy! Sadie loves a good song, don't you, girl?"

Sadie yaps.

"Know what I think, Missus? You'll live to see the day when you'll be thanking me."

"*Thanking* you? Whatever for?"

"For going on down this road instead of going back!"

THEY CREST THE BURIAL MOUND, ALMOST HALFWAY BETWEEN THE UPPER AND Lower Agencies. Ahead, smoke hangs low to the horizon in the vicinity of Redwood.

"Fire!" Sarah cries, startling the children. "The Agency!"

Gleason regards the pall, shakes his head.

"Mr. Gleason, stop!"

"Prairie fire is all."

"Here, James, take your sister!" She makes ready to jump from the wagon. Gleason grabs with one hand at her skirts. She kicks his arm away. "Either turn this wagon around or let me and my children off! *At once!*"

Gleason brakes the wagon hard. He swings around in his seat, glaring up at her. "Now you listen! I'm tired of your fussing. We ain't going back to Yellow Medicine, might as well get that through your head. And you ain't getting off, out here in nowhere. So sit down and shut the hell up!"

Sadie whimpers. Sarah tosses her head, glowering behind her goggles. He's right, of course. On wide-open prairie there's no place to run to, and nowhere to hide. But that doesn't mean they should drive willy-nilly into trouble. She has half a notion to tear the feather from his hatband and stuff it down his throat.

"See there"—the first Gleason has spoken, these last few miles —"we're coming up to the Half-Way House, sitting there pretty as you please." He checks his pocketwatch. "Quarter past six. How about stopping for a quick bite of supper?"

She cleans the dust from her goggles. With smoke still thickening the sky over the Lower Agency, ten miles on, reaching the Reynolds' inn will be a relief. Gleason can do as he pleases, but she and the children will go no further. Joseph and Valencia will surely accommodate them until any danger is past.

Sadie rises up on all fours with a growl, baring her teeth.

Sarah nudges Gleason's shoulder from behind. "Up ahead—"

Two Indians with guns show themselves out of the tall grass. Both are wearing traditional dress, but one is a cut-hair. He sports a red bandanna around his neck.

"Out hunting," Gleason decides.

She wraps an arm around James. "Your pistol, Mr. Gleason!"

"Quiet!"

"Hurry the horses!"

"*Quiet*, I said! I know these fellows." He reins the wagon to a stop. Sadie whines, ears flat against her head.

"Haŋ," Gleason says, greeting the Indians, "where you boys headed?"

. . .

THE CHARGE OF SHOT BLOWS GLEASON BACK OVER HIS SEAT ONTO HER LAP, trapping Nellie. She stares into his face, suddenly such a boy's, eyes wide and amazed, lips working without sound. She scarcely registers the blood oozing from his right shoulder before a second charge strikes him in the gut. With a groan he rolls over the side of the wagon and lands hard on the ground. Sadie bounds after him with a bark. Belle and Mick bolt in a panic, pitching her to the wagon floor.

The runaway wagon is like a skiff on a heaving sea. She latches onto the sideboard and pushes to her feet. If only she can regain control of the team, she might charge the wagon on up the road to the Half-Way House. But there the reins are, trailing on the ground.

Cumbered by the wagon, the horses are slow to gather speed. The Sioux with the red bandanna has jettisoned his gun to give chase. Feet flying, he outpaces the wagon. When he draws even with the team, he makes a grab for Belle's bridle. The mare bites, kicks. The Sioux hangs on and wrenches her head to the side, once, twice. Again. She bucks, can't keep stride. Beside her, Mick falters.

The Indian wrangles her in. As the wagon careens toward a halt, he lets go and tumbles free.

When the wagon stops, the whole world stops, a bubble of quiet bothered by restless hooves, an occasional snort, the odd jingle of harness. Sarah casts about, searching the wagon bed on the off-chance Gleason's pistol spilled from his coat. Meanwhile, the Sioux scrabbles to his feet, dusts off his leggings and goes to retrieve the lines.

Sarah hides James and Nellie behind her as the Indian approaches. He's undersized for a man so strong. Smaller than herself. She steals a glance at the wagon whip, still in its socket.

"Haŋ." He sets the brake. Blood streams from a cut above his eye. He stands there, studying her. "Peźihuta Wićaśa Tawiću." *Doctor Wife.* Her name among Śakpe's people.

She nods. She hasn't heard that name in years.

He motions toward her bloody dress. "Doctor Wife no good?" he says in English.

"Waśte. Wopida." *I am well, thank you.*

The wiry Sioux lifts the reins up to her. "Doctor Wife, horses."

Not quite believing, she accepts the lines.

He saunters around to the front of the team. "Doctor Wife no talk. Hepaŋ"—his gaze shifts back to the Indian who shot Gleason—"drink big." He natters to Belle and Mick, rubbing their necks and withers. "Śuŋka wakaŋ waśte." *Good horse.*

He mounts the buckboard from the off-side. She backs away with the children. When he steps forward, offering his hand, she relinquishes the reins. He takes them, then reaches out again, inviting her to shake. As though in a dream, she lets him have the ends of her fingers.

He rests his palm briefly on Nellie's head before leaning down to James. "Doctor boy?"

James looks up at Sarah, a fringe of tears on his lashes. Somehow he knows not to ask aloud the questions in his eyes.

The Sioux smiles and taps James's chest. "Doctor boy wakaŋ."

His words part the veil of her fear. Yes, there on the bridge of his nose, right below the line of his disheveled bangs, is the tail end of his wicked scar.

Ćaske.

AS THEY DRIVE UP TO GLEASON, SADIE IS LAPPING THE IRISHMAN'S DIRT-streaked face. Hepaŋ is pouring powder down the muzzle of his gun. Horrified, Sarah springs from her seat. "No hurt babies!" she shrieks in Dakota.

Ćaske twists around in the front seat. His pained expression warns her to be quiet.

"Oh my God, Missus," Gleason moans. Her green velvet hat lies beside him on the ground.

Ćaske jumps down from the wagon to recover his gun. Hepaŋ rams his ball home.

"No hurt Doctor Wife!" she begs in Dakota. "Doctor Wife fry bread! Sew! Cut wood!"

Hepaŋ shoulders his musket.

"Children sacred!"

Gleason stirs a limp, bloody hand. "God … help me, Missus…."

Hepaŋ aims at the Irishman's head. Pulls the trigger.

"Mama—" James presses against her legs. "I want to go home."

She nuzzles him. "Soon. We'll all be going home, very soon."

Suddenly she gets a close whiff of rum and sour sweat. She feels a pocket of heat at her temple. Instinct braces her for the shot—

The gun clatters to the ground. Hepaŋ lunges after it, nearly toppling over from drink. He snaps at Ćaske for knocking it away. Once he steadies himself, he shoulders it again and prepares to fire.

God—

Ćaske lays hold of Hepaŋ's arm and forces the gun down. He leads him a short distance from the wagon. Snatches of Dakota carry on the breeze. Back in Tiŋta Otoŋwe, he's saying, Doctor Wife shared her food and medicine with their band. She traded for his fish. After a Chippewa ambush she and her husband treated the wounds of many warriors.

"All whites must die!" Hepaŋ says.

"No." Ćaske's voice is calm but firm. "Doctor Wife has a good heart. She saved my life."

In Sarah's memory it was John who saved Ćaske's life. May 27, 1858. A party of Šakpe's Sioux had wandered off their new reservation to hunt and fish near their former village. Chippewa warriors ambushed them across the river, below Shakopee. Though vastly outmanned, the Sioux fended off the initial attack and eventually routed their old enemy. The Chippewas carried off their injured in the direction of Lake Minnetonka. As the Sioux retreated toward the deserted ruins of Tiŋta Otoŋwe, the missionary Samuel Pond prevailed upon them to entrust their most seriously wounded to John and Dr. Weiser, the only physicians in town.

She was helping to convert one bay of Mrs. Apgar's barn into a field hospital when the first Sioux casualties arrived by wagon. At the sight of them, she reeled into the weeds and retched.

John shored her up. "Take the carriage and go home, for the baby if not for yourself."

She hung onto him, needing to cry, wanting not to. After mastering herself, she refused to leave, despite the child in her belly.

They bedded down on hay a total of fourteen Sioux wounded. She assisted John and Weiser in treating them, holding them down as their wounds were probed, stitching and dressing their minor injuries, setting bones, administering ether during surgeries. John muttered at the waste of the ether. "Why not rum?" He drew his needle, a lit cigar between his teeth. "Surely they don't feel pain as we do."

Weiser called John over to examine a Sioux in a grave fettle. A flap of the Indian's scalp was torn back, exposing skull-bone. Even through the profuse bleeding, she could see the dent in the skull, big as a silver dollar. From a war club, perhaps.

She let her eyes gravitate to the Indian's face. The baby rolled inside her. Feeling faint, she headed for the light of the open barn door.

This Sioux she had recognized.

. . .

"THAT WOMAN," HEPAŋ says, "IS THE LIAR'S WIFE! I WILL KILL HER!"

"No, I know this woman. She is tall. She is strong. I visited her lodge, long ago. She saved my life after battle."

The argument loops around and around. Soothing Nellie at her breast, Sarah sneaks the flask of brandy from her carpetbag and unstops the cork. A nip for James and another for her nerves, then she stuffs the flask down her corset.

"She is the wife of Humphrey?"

"No. She is the wife of the doctor at Yellow Medicine."

Hepaŋ drinks long from his bottle. "The Liar is a bad man. I will cut his woman and his children to pieces!"

"This is not The Liar's family. It is the doctor's family."

"They will be trouble!"

"I will care for them. I took them prisoner. They are mine. If you want to kill them on this road, you will have to kill me first."

IN MRS. APGAR'S BARN SHE WASHED THE BLOOD FROM ĆASKE'S BODY. Changed the saturated compresses on his scalp. Sponged his clammy skin. By sundown, he hadn't improved.

Not a single Sioux patient had yet succumbed. Even John seemed pleased behind his pince-nez. But she dreaded the closing in of night. Souls were more tempted to slip the bonds of the body in the absence of light. To ward off extremity and death in the dark hours, she hung her brightest lantern on the post near Ćaske.

She should have made him the gift of a book, that day he brought his fish; instead, she let him walk off with his woman, empty-handed. Next time, she told herself. But no next time ever came.

Mrs. Apgar wrapped her in a moth-eaten quilt. "A woman in your condition must have her rest. Why do you care so about this Indian?"

"I don't know. It's just … he came by the house, to trade."

She settled near him in a rocking chair, turning the lantern wick higher, ignoring the churning smoke.

IT'S NEAR DUSK WHEN THE TWO INDIANS END THEIR QUARREL. HEPAŋ BUMBLES up into the wagon and drops with a grunt on the bench next to James. He sits cockeyed with his bottle, the muzzle of his gun leveled at her ribs. Up in front, Ćaske assumes the reins, musket across his thighs.

A sound escapes Gleason. Less than a moan, more than a breath. She'd thought him long dead in the creeping pool of blood. He still has his scalp, his thin ribbon of red hair apparently not worth the effort of a blade.

Ćaske rubs his eyebrow. "Get out and shoot him again. Do not leave the white man any life to suffer."

"My brother and I will both shoot."

Ćaske's fists go slack on the lines. Grim-faced, he hands the reins back to her. "Horses run, Doctor Wife dies."

Sadie, guarding Gleason, up and growls as the Indians close in.

Hepaŋ fires. Sadie yelps, darts away.

Ćaske raises his musket, pulls the trigger. The gun snaps fire, but there's no charge, as if the barrel hadn't been loaded. He lowers his gun with a shrug, slings it over his shoulder.

Sadie slinks back toward Gleason, whining and sniffing. Ćaske picks her up and hoists her into the driver's box.

"IF YOU WANT to kill them on this road, you will have to kill me first." Tough words. Did Ćaske truly mean them? In Shakopee he seemed kind enough, even civilized, able to tell right from wrong. She doesn't much care whether he learned his scruples from the missionaries or from walking abroad in the world, tussling with life. As the buckboard trundles toward God knows where, steered by his able reins, she clings to her slender faith in him like a lifeline.

Masked by her goggles, she steals furtive glances at Hepaŋ when he slugs back his bottle. Though evening has cooled the air, he wipes his face again and again on his shirtsleeves. If not for drink, he might be a handsome Indian. Taller and stockier than Ćaske, he has the bloated middle of a man gone to idleness and booze. Razor-thin brows curve over sunken red eyes. His complexion is ruddy and pimpled. She breathes through her mouth to avoid his smell.

At the foot of a gentle hill, they drive past a half-naked Indian armed with a gun and tomahawk. His torso is smeared with blood, his hair tangled and wild. He goads along a white woman cumbered with two youngsters in her arms, two on her back and two more trailing behind.

Ćaske reins in. He gestures the family toward the wagon.

"My brothers should drive on." The Indian prods the woman with his gun. He's missing a notch of his nose above the right nostril. "These prisoners are mine, to do with as I please."

. . .

They enter a sizable Sioux village. Ćaske restrains a snarling Sadie as noisy wiŋyaŋ swarm the buckboard, shouting, "Peżihuta Wićaśa Tawić   u! Peżihuta Wićaśa Tawić
u!" *Doctor Wife!*

Sarah tugs off her goggles. These are Śakpe's people, from Tiŋta Otoŋwe.

The women help her down from the wagon. They guide her toward a cookfire, worrying over the blood on her dress, exclaiming over her babies. After spreading a rug upon the ground, they supply her with a feather pillow and woven wool coverlet, and entreat her to rest on the plundered bedding. They pour her a basin of water. They set before her some frybread and a wooden bowl brimming with greasy meat.

At the sight of the food, bile rises in her throat. She has just seen a man slain and her children menaced. She was nearly murdered herself. She might yet be killed or dragged off and molested in unspeakable ways. She might even be made some warrior's wife, never again to live white....

She puts her goggles back on. Her reception here is no happy reunion. The hospitality of these wiŋyaŋ is no ritual of friendship. To her, this is war.

"I'm sorry to find you here, Mrs. Wakefield," a mixed-blood man says, in clipped but fluent English.

She tears up. "It's a sorry day."

He drops to a knee beside her, clutching a bottle of rum. "You're safe for now," he says. "You should get some rest."

"What do you mean, 'for now?'"

"Our soldiers have sworn to kill everyone with white blood in their veins."

She tightens the coverlet around her shoulders. "So I suppose they'll be killing you, too."

He twiddles with his bottle. "Whose blood is that on your dress?"

More tears behind her goggles. She tells him about Gleason, in brief.

"George Gleason? The clerk at Redwood? That's a damn shame, sorry to hear it."

He tips the neck of his bottle toward her lips. She waves it off.

"Ćaske's a good man. Trust him, do what he says." He eyes her bowl of food. "You should eat."

"I'm not hungry."

"Don't refuse what's offered. You can't be sure when you'll eat again."

She hadn't considered this. Not far away, women are feeding James and Nellie. Old men are rumpling James's blond hair and ribbing him about his freckles. Despite everything, the children look content. She sets the bowl of meat in her lap, breaks off a piece of frybread and forces it down.

"Mrs. Wakefield, I can tell you one thing about my people. Best not to complain. Always oblige them. Act like you trust them … like they're your own kind." The mixed-blood stands up to go. "It's your only chance to stay alive."

SHE DIPS UP MORE MEAT WITH HER BREAD, THE GREASE SOURING HER STOMACH. As she eats, she takes stock of what she knows about Indians. How very long their memories are. How seriously they regard the act of speaking, and what's been spoken. How they're quick to make friends, if you treat them well. How they don't let you lie to them twice. How they're apt to punish you when you wrong them—like white folks, but different. How they can't hold their liquor. How they blur the line between mine and yours, yours and ours. How they give away what little they have as though they had plenty, and expect you to do the same. How they love their pipes, and swallowing the smoke. How they each can have multiple names. How they joke and play, even in extremity. How they don't let you see what they're thinking. How they love their children above all else. How they believe the whole world is wakaŋ, and every wakaŋ thing is a relative, and must be treated accordingly. How they make long greetings and short goodbyes. How they terrify with their war whoops….

Her tiny bank of knowledge about the Sioux likely trades in more error than fact. Until today, her life hasn't depended on her ability to understand them; to the contrary, their lives have depended on understanding her. No Indian could ever have injured her, or any American, without the government exacting more than its full measure of revenge. Meanwhile, she herself has always done pretty much as she pleased, when she pleased, among the Sioux. However much she might have enjoyed their company, as a people they have always been, at bottom, subordinate to her: a curiosity, a diversion, a source of labor, a cause for charity, a source of shame.

"Don't be complaining," the mixed-blood said. "Oblige them. Treat them like they're your own."

She slings off her goggles. *You shall not defy them. Whatever they give you to eat, eat. Whatever they tell you to do, do. If they scold you, grovel. If they're hungry, cook. If they suffer wounds or sickness, nurse them. Laugh when they laugh, mourn when they mourn, pray when they pray. Abide by their courtesies, conform to their manners. Make yourself useful. Show no fear, don't even let them smell it, lest it excite their blood….*

It is, as the mixed-blood advised, the only way. In this perilous time, the Sioux have no reason to trust her; no reason, in fact, to bother with her at all. Already she and the children are eating their food, drinking their water, using their bedding. If she isn't careful, even the Sioux who feel for them a degree of goodwill might soon resent them as an encumbrance.

"COME! I WILL TAKE DOCTOR WIFE TO A LODGE TO SLEEP. YOU WILL BE WARM there."

In a fog of exhaustion, she gets to her feet, uncertain whether she has understood Ćaske's Dakota. She sets Nellie in the crook of her arm and takes a sleepy James by the hand. "Can we take my things?" she asks Ćaske in English, nodding at the wagon.

He fetches her carpetbag. The trunk they will have to leave.

She notices a difference in his bearing as he parades her among his own kind. She can't say what it is, precisely. An air of triumph, perhaps. The glory of being a warrior. Pride in possessing a white woman. Whatever accounts for the alteration, it troubles her, like the red bandanna now tied around his head instead of his neck. It causes her to doubt him. But he's all she has.

About a mile on, he consigns her to the care of a wiŋyaŋ outside a tipi. "Doctor Wife will rest here until I come back," he says in Dakota.

The wiŋyaŋ orders her out of her hoopskirt, if only to fit through the tipi door. Sarah's glad to shed it. Her full dress has been catching every gust of wind, snagging on every briar, posing a peril near every fire.

Inside the tipi a white woman cowers, suckling a tiny baby. Through her sobs the woman tells Sarah how she saw four members of her "Familie" horribly butchered—"meine Vater, meine Bruder, meine Schwester, meine Ehemann." After birthing her child two weeks ago, the frau is suddenly a widow among "wilden Indianern." Her grief pours out non-stop. "Ach, meine liebe Federbettens! Fünf Federbettens! *Fünf!*"

Sarah tries to calm the wretched woman lest her crying provoke the *wild Indians* who slashed open her *family* and *five featherbeds*. Suddenly Ćaske ducks through the tipi door, followed by several warriors. She chokes back a cry. Atop one Indian's head is Gleason's pheasant-feather hat. Another warrior, wearing Gleason's sack coat, lifts the Irishman's trousers by the suspenders and turns out the empty pockets, to raucous laughter.

Ćaske presses Gleason's watch to his ear, its crystal broken, its hands intact. The time is nine o'clock—the very hour at which Gleason promised to have her and the children to Fort Ridgley.

Amidst Gleason's plunder, no pistol.

ĆASKE MOVES HER AGAIN, THIS TIME TO A BARK HOUSE. WHEN THEY ENTER, A settler woman, young and delicate, shrinks into the shadows against the far wall.

Ćaske sets down Sarah's carpetbag. "Doctor Wife will sleep here tonight. In the morning, someone will take you to My Mother."

"Ćaske no go!"

"Doctor Wife will be cared for. When you meet My Mother, she will give you a proper dress." Ignoring her protests, he steals out the door.

Abandoned, she takes stock of the lodge. A fire burns low at its center. A raised platform overlaid with hides and dried grass runs along all four walls, a couple feet off the floor.

Where they say sleep, you must sleep.

She lays Nellie and James on the soft bed, then sinks down between them and the captive woman.

"Wie geht es dir?" the woman says. *How are you?*

"Gut." She isn't *good* at all, but she doesn't know the German word for *alive.*

The frau's face brightens. "Sprechen Sie Deutsch?" *You speak German?*

She pinches her forefinger toward her thumb. "Ein bisschen." *Only a little*; a few common phrases picked up from settlers around Shakopee. "Sprechen Sie Englisch?"

The young frau slumps.

SARAH LIES ALERT AND TENSE IN THE DARK, HER ARMS AROUND JAMES AND Nellie, trying to expel from her mind every specter of torture, death, ravishment, loss of her babies. Outside the lodge is bedlam. Jubilant Sioux are reveling in a sudden abundance of food looted from settler cupboards and cellars, barns and fields. They're shooting holes in the sky like settlers on the Fourth of July. Ponies are whinnying. The darkness shivers with pounding drums, the tread of dancing feet and spine-chilling ululations. Panicked voices of white women and children float in; accents from New England and Old World countries. *What's become of their menfolk? What's become of John?*

Andrew Myrick told the Sioux they could eat grass or shit. This uprising is their reply.

The young frau shivers against Sarah's backside, hanging onto her ribs, whispering the same prayer, over and over. "Mein Gott, mein Gott, mich nicht im Stich…." *My God, my God*—beyond that, Sarah can't say what it means.

$$\text{ॐ} \quad 4 \quad \text{ॐ}$$

ĆASKE'S MOTHER is making her morning prayers, wreathing her body in a light cloud of smoke. Sage and tobacco smolder in an abalone shell on a bare patch of earth near the fire pit.

Sarah averts her eyes and glances around the lodge. Firewood, beside the door. A water keg. A carpet of buffalo hides. Bedding, rolled up. Two willow backrests. Multiple parfleches for storage. Everything in order, and vibrant with color, even in dim light.

She hoped to recognize Ćaske's mother from Tiŋta Otoŋwe. But the fine-boned kuŋśi who rises from her prayers to greet her is a stranger. Short and slender like her son, she has the start of a dowager's hump. Patches of pure white hair at her temples pull back into gray-black braids. Age has whittled a stack of furrows into her forehead and puckered the skin around her thin lips. Her eyes give the impression of seeing everything and revealing nothing.

"We must make Doctor Wife one of us," the kuŋśi says, shaking hands. "Do you understand?"

She nods. "Bad talk Dakota." Apologizing in the kuŋśi's tongue.

The old woman points at her mouth and wrinkles up her beak of a nose. "No 'merican," she says in English, with the hint of a chuckle.

She sits Sarah down and loosens her hair from its combs and pins. She oils it with tallow from a tin trade box, then plaits it into two braids drawn tight as piano wires. The ends she bands with fragrant ties. After dipping her gnarled finger into a second tin, she runs it down the center part.

Sarah surrenders her shoes and stockings, her dress, her petticoats and chemise. Her corset she insists on keeping. It braces her weak spine, she explains in gestures, but in truth, it contains her flask of brandy. Over her corset she's supposed to wear a brown calico dress, cinched with a beaded belt. The dress isn't big enough. She rips it at the neckline to open the back.

The kuŋśi folds a grubby white blanket shawl around Sarah's shoulders, then steps back to inspect her. "Come."

They emerge together into dawn. The camp is quiet, barren of men. A short distance away is the wagon, right where Ćaske parked it last night. Belle and Mick have vanished, but somehow her trunk is still in the wagon bed, unmolested.

The kuŋśi scoops up some dirt and begins to rub it into Sarah's face, her neck, her arms, darkening her skin. Then she shoos a cluster of women away from a looking-glass propped against a split-rail fence. The large wall mirror has cherubs carved into its gilded frame. Sarah could swear it once graced the parlor at the Reynolds' Half-Way House.

The old woman draws her toward the glass. "Doctor Wife looks Dakota now."

"But … this can't be…." Sarah fondles one of her braids. Her golden brown hair, always her greatest vanity, has overnight turned white as bone. It's shot down the middle with blood-red paint.

JAMES, DELIGHTED TO PLAY INDIAN IN NEW FRINGED LEGGINGS, STRIPS OFF HIS stockings to run barefoot. Sarah tracks him down and rubs dirt on his bare torso and face until he begs her to stop. For his long curls she has no remedy. He's a tow-head, her golden prince. No matter how much dirt she massages into his stubborn mop, his hair remains flaxen, almost as light as hers. With her white hair, she could be mistaken for his grandmother.

Nellie is easier, having the black hair and swarthier skin of the grandmother she will never know. Once Sarah strips her of all but her skirt, wiŋyaŋ from neighboring tipis lower beads over her head and pronounce her a doll. Sarah's watching them pass Nellie around when a solidly built woman, short but broad in shoulders and hips, struts up to her in the tipi yard. Masses of colorful beads burden the wiŋyaŋ's strong neck.

The wiŋyaŋ reaches up to flick one of Sarah's dangle earrings. "Pretty."

Sarah relaxes a bit at the flattery. These sterling acorn earrings are her sentimental favorite; the very first pair she acquired, free of Richard Butts. She manages a smile, just as the wiŋyaŋ's hands flash up and rip the earrings out.

She caterwauls in pain, pressing her ears flat against her head. The winyaŋ substitutes the sterling acorns for her own tin teardrops. Then she springs with a rock into the wagon bed. She hammers at the lock of Sarah's trunk until it breaks. With a shrill tremolo of triumph, she throws back the lid and starts chucking the truck's contents over the side of the buckboard.

Sarah's ears are bleeding like tiny fountains, and now her precious possessions are in the dust. The winyaŋ leaps from the wagon. She grinds the children's toys beneath her heel. She heaps the miniatures in a pile and pounds them to pieces. She breaks the binding of the books and shreds their pages with the knife from her belt. She holds up the silk dresses, one by one, laughing at their large size; then she tears them into strips and rolls them up like bandages to save. Slipping into one of Sarah's finest undergarments and best bonnets, she promenades among nearby tipis, showing off her vulgar costume.

The winyaŋ, Sarah learns with dismay, is Ćaske's half-sister, Winuna. She owns this tipi, where Sarah and her babies are meant to live. And her husband—*dear God*—is Hepaŋ.

MID-MORNING, ALL THE WOMEN OF THE BAND PACK THEIR HOUSEHOLDS AND strike their tipis. The ensuing hours are riddled with false alarms—white soldiers, said to be on the march; Sisseton and Wahpeton warriors, said to be riding down from Yellow Medicine. To Sarah, the winyaŋ of Śakpe's band seem almost as afraid of the Upper Indians as of the Americans. Perhaps the various Sioux tribes aren't the natural allies she always believed.

With every new rumor, a detail of warriors relocates the people out of harm's way. At the moment, they're biding time alongside the government road. The sun is directly overhead, Sarah wishes for a bonnet. Her exposed skin is pinkening beneath its film of dirt. Her calico dress is sopping with sweat.

News trickles in of an assault on a village of iasića, *bad speakers,* at *The Place Where There Is A Cottonwood Grove On The River*. That can only be New Ulm, a prosperous German town on the southern margin of the reservation, at the junction of the Minnesota and Cottonwood Rivers. Between the Sioux and the Germans there's notorious bad feeling.

A kuŋśi Sarah remembers from Tiŋta Otoŋwe settles on the ground beside her with a pipe. The shriveled hunchback, near dark as a Negro, is called Lightfoot. She's keen on games. Sarah once saw her gamble away her tipi, playing dice. Whenever Lightfoot smiles, the tip of her tongue pokes out between toothless gums.

Despite the heat Sarah accepts Lightfoot's offer of a smoke. Chuffing on the pipe pacifies her nerves. Thanks to Ćaske's mother, her torn earlobes have stopped bleeding. The kuŋśi had cleaned the slits, stitched them shut and treated them with herbs.

"It is sad," Lightfoot says in Dakota, gumming her words.

Too weary to work at the Sioux tongue, Sarah answers in English. "All this fighting, yes, it's very sad." She tips back her head and puffs out the smoke of the kinnikinnik.

"Doctor Wife will die soon."

The statement, so impassive, impales Sarah like a spear. "What Lightfoot say?" she asks in Dakota.

The kuŋśi's eyes are buried in thick folds of skin. "Doctor Wife will die soon. Our people will keep your babies. When they grow big, we will ask the Great Father for much money. He will buy them back."

Sarah vaults to her feet. Before she can know her own mind, she charges a nearby winyaŋ, whips the work knife from her belt and sprints to catch up Nellie. Pinning her against the flesh of her ribs, she puts the blade to her baby's throat.

Shouting erupts from all sides. Sarah's blood throbs as a loud circle of winyaŋ shrinks around her. If what Lightfoot said is true, killing her babies would be an act of mercy. The government will never buy back white children who have grown up Indian.

"Me die, baby die!" she yells, in Dakota.

"Mama, *down!* Nellie *down!*"

Ćaske's mother inches toward her with arms opened wide. "Doctor Wife is safe. Your baby is safe."

"Baby mine!" She pivots left and right, nowhere to go.

"Doctor Wife will keep her baby." The kuŋśi taps her palm. "Give me the knife. I will not let anyone hurt you or your children."

Sarah looks at the kuŋśi's eyes, so steady, so calm. She looks at the tight ring of winyaŋ. She looks at the knife in her hand. At the mark its blade has made on Nellie's tender neck, not quite drawing blood.

She lets the knife fall. Staggering, she knots a whining Nellie in her arms, kissing forehead and cheeks and chin.

CURLED UP WITH NELLIE IN THE DRY PRAIRIE GRASS, SARAH RELIVES THE KNIFE episode over and over, no longer trusting herself. Her emotions are distorting her perceptions like a magic mirror. *What if Lightfoot merely meant to warn you?*

"Wake up! Wake up!"

A foot prods her in the back ribs. She rolls over, shielding her bleary eyes from the late afternoon sun.

"We must go!" Ćaske's mother is folding Nellie in her blanket shawl. "Hurry! Bad men are searching for Doctor Wife!" The kuŋśi hoists Nellie onto her back and is off at a run toward a dense stand of cottonwood trees.

"Little man, come to Mama! Now!"

James scampers over from a stick game with some boys. Sarah scoops him up and hightails it after the old woman.

In the cottonwoods they crash through the undergrowth to the edge of a gorge, sides steep as a roof. The kuŋśi plunges straight down like a woman a third her age.

"Up on Mama's shoulders! Quick! Arms around my neck! Hold on tight!"

Sarah slips and slides down the grade, hooking onto tender saplings to stay upright. At the bottom, she pauses with Ćaske's mother beside a small stream, her breath in jags, a stitch in her side, until a crack of gunfire sends them scuttering through deadfall along the ravine floor.

Once they're into tall horsetail, the kuŋśi deposits Nellie on the ground beside the brook. Stops. Listens. "Sit down here, all of you." She hands Sarah a pouch from her belt. Inside are a cup and some hard crackers. "I must go. Be very quiet. I will be back when it is safe. Understand?" She drags brush to cover them over, then is gone.

SARAH CAN SMELL the storm coming through the trees. Around sundown, she detects the first rumble. Rain starts to patter and dribble through their cover of brush. When it bursts down in sheets, she tilts her head back and lets it pelt her sunburned face, lets it spill over her lips into her parched mouth, lets it wash over her dirt-caked body, lets it coax her into crying. If any Indians are still pursuing her in this downpour, they won't be able to hear. She cries like she has needed to cry, ever since Gleason.

Thunder crashes. Lightning flashes and pops. Somewhere above them, a tree splits and bursts into flame. The air smolders. The children, terrified, lock themselves to her body. She bends low, sheltering them from the rain with her drenched blanket shawl. Their skin is gooseflesh. She rubs and rubs their arms and legs, trying to stop their shivering. She mixes them a dose of brandy with rainwater in the old woman's cup, then hugs them against her in a ball.

Rocks tumble down the hill in the darkness. Mud begins to slide.

Suddenly she laughs. Of all the Sioux who might have attacked their wagon, it was *him*.

ALONE IN MRS. APGAR'S BARN, ĆASKE YET IN HIS COMA, SHE SAT IN THE rocker, telling him stories from her past. How as a child she traced petro-glyphs in the rocks by the sea. How she sailed with her father in his skiff. How she grew up in the lanes of North Kingstown being taunted for her size. How even her mother said she should have been born a boy. How her one-armed stepfather sent her to work in Davis Mill. How for four years she earned credit there on his account without ever seeing a penny. How she ran away up the coast to Providence, where she sewed shrouds for an undertaker. How she meddled with Richard Butts, and bore his child, and abandoned them both to live free, only she wasn't free at all—

"Mni."

She stopped rocking. One word, *water*, faint as a ghost's. His mouth was opening and closing like a hungry bird's.

She dipped her cloth into the basin. Dabbed at his cracked lips.

"Mni." A croak.

He sighed. Before she could dip him some water from the bucket, he was spent, and all her coaxing couldn't bid him back.

AFTER THE STORM, THE DRIPPING. EVERY LEAF THAT DROPS ITS WEIGHT OF water is a footfall. Every bough that cracks overhead is the report of a gun. Once, she mistakes the pounding of blood in her ears for the trotting of feet on the ridge. A wolf … no, a muskrat … noses around them in the dark, its beady eyes gleaming.

The brook swells over her ankles. Up to her calves. Up to her knees. She labors to keep her babies from sliding in. The cold water numbs her legs, yet she's loath to leave their hiding place unless it rises higher. Up above, the night air is alive again with gunfire, the noise of ponies, singing and hooting, blood-curdling cries. Sioux are likely all around them in the ravine. She's certain of it.

O God … dear Father … how to pray?

"Mama, let's go home." James, waking from a twitchy dream. "I want my own bed."

"Hush, sweet." *Can You see us, down here in these woods?*

"Please, Mama, I'm so cold! Papa wouldn't approve."

"Mustn't talk, not even a whisper." *I know what the preachers say, but in my heart, forgive me, I don't know if You decide who lives and who dies or if You're up there loving everybody or if You're out there not paying much attention. It's all a babble, and I can't pretend to believe what I don't know, but if You have any say-so, please, I'm begging You, I'd kneel if I could, spare me and my children—*

"I want Dinah!"

"Shhh." She tells James again in his precious ear what the trouble is.

*And my husband—I know he hasn't much use for You, or for me either, mostly …
but still, if he's alive somewhere—*

"Oh, I forgot about them Indians…." He's almost back to sleep.

*If we don't make it through till morning, or if the old woman doesn't come
back, please God, be gentle putting us to sleep. And then … if You can stir yourself, bring my people someday soon to find us. Don't turn us to bones here all
alone and lost forever—*

God please ….

That's all I have to say till

If I think of more

Amen

WHEN MORNING SUN CREEPS OVER THE SIDE OF THE RAVINE, SHE'S SORRY FOR
the light. She feels more vulnerable to discovery, even under the brush. But
all she hears is birdsong and the brook. Not a sound out of place.

The sun climbs higher, spraying amber light through the trees. Still no
sign of Ćaske's mother. *Perhaps the kuŋśi wants you to perish. Perhaps she will
leave you to starve.*

She feeds her last soggy cracker to James and nurses Nellie again. She
dips water from the creek to rinse away the mud from their skin. She fans
the merciless mosquitoes, so thick she breathes them in, every breath. The
children's faces are swollen with bites, scratched to bleeding.

She pours them more brandy. She re-paints them with mud, to coat
them against the bugs.

Still no sign.

O God

SADIE NUZZLES IN, ROUSING HER FROM A FEVERISH DOZE. ĆASKE'S MOTHER
emerges like an apparition. When she drags away the brush from over
their heads, Sarah tries to get up to greet her, but her legs won't obey,
numb from the brook. She arches her neck to kiss the kuŋśi's wrinkled
cheek. "Thank you, thank you, thank you!" Her voice hoarse.

James throws his arms around the kuŋśi's neck. She lifts him and Nellie
further away from the water before helping Sarah scoot up the muddy
bank. She kneels to massage the feeling back into Sarah's feet. "Our band
has moved to Taoyate Duta's village, below The River Where They Mark
The Trees Red. Doctor Wife will be safe with us there. Fighting and plun-

dering have distracted the men who would do you harm. But the village is far. Understand? It is far."

Even with Nellie on her back, the kuŋśi sets a relentless pace. Sarah, carrying James, strives to keep up. They avoid the government road and every footpath, breaking a rough trail through scrub and prairie grass, in some places five feet high. Only when Sarah falls does the old woman stop.

Anchoring her vision to her trudging feet, Sarah sinks into their leaden rhythm. Looking ahead is too hard. Any distance to go is too great. The prairie grass cuts, drawing blood. Jackrabbits bound away.

As they wade through a slough, the old woman tells her that the Indians have attacked the soldiers' lodge of the Isaŋ Taŋka, the *Big Knives*. Ćaske is in the fray.

Sarah suspects that Fort Ridgley will fall without much of a fight. Captain Marsh, Lieutenant Sheehan and the boy Gere are gallant officers, but the troops in their command are few and unseasoned. The fort itself lacks palisades and earthworks. Deep wooded ravines border three of its four sides, offering substantial cover to advancing Indians.

She barrels through berry bushes toward the river, trips over grapevines and ivy, steps on a snake. Were the Sioux to overrun Ridgley, they would have a clear path down the Minnesota Valley. They will lop off the river towns, one by one, all the way to St. Paul.

She hikes James higher on her back. She wants the attack on Ridgley thwarted and the uprising put down. She wants Marsh and his lieutenants alive and well. She wants herself and her babies safe. But Ćaske....

She raises her eyes to the kuŋśi toiling ahead of her, Sadie at her heels. That woman's son once bartered fish for a gander at her books. He wrestled Death in Mrs. Apgar's barn, and survived. He saved her and the children from the murderous Hepaŋ. And the old woman herself came back for them rather than leaving them to die in that miserable ravine. If God is keeping score, such acts must count for something.

At last, Little Crow's village. Hundreds of lodges. A horsetail flies like a giant scalp above Little Crow's tipi, adjacent to his frame house.

"Slide off Mama's back," Sarah says to James. Her arms and legs are convulsing with cramps. She's chilling with fever.

Winuna appears ahead, bent over a cookfire. At the sight of her, Sarah collapses. The old woman squats beside her. Sadie nudges.

"Water...." she begs, her mouth dry and gritty, as though full of sand. Before she can drink, she passes out.

SHE COMES TO IN THE DOWNY COMFORT OF A FEATHERTICK, COOL IN THE SHADE of a wagon. She has no memory of how she got there. Flies are thick on her torn legs and feet. All around her, women are jabbering. Some of Little Crow's soldiers, they say—"men with bad hearts"—are threatening to visit sića upon her. *Evil.*

Ćaske's mother crouches beside her. "Doctor Wife must go."

"No." The sun hasn't crawled an inch since she blacked out.

"I cannot protect you from this."

"No strength ... help babies...."

The old woman pats her arm. She rises and calls for James. He races over straightaway, his hands full of frybread. Having mingled so often with the Sioux along Rush Brook, he comprehends much of what the kuŋśi says. He also understands she must be obeyed, because she's a grand-mother. It's the Sioux way, to honor elders. Sarah's throat tightens. If he has to, her boy will be able to survive amongst these people without her.

The kuŋśi rests a palm on his head. "We will play a game now."

"Oh, yes!"

"Lie down here, next to your mother."

He drops and snuggles up against Sarah with his bread.

"No talking. You hide." The old woman arranges some buffalo robes over them, then a large sheet of canvas. The day goes black as night.

"Mama, is this hide-and-seek?" James says, in the suffocating dark.

"Yes. We must be very quiet."

"Who is hunting?"

"*Shhh,* we must whisper, be very still." She kisses his crown. His little heart is racing against her, but his breathing is easy. He has bought the old woman's ruse.

It's a miracle that he is here. Struggling to ford the Redwood with him on her back, she slipped and went under. She lost him to the current. Had he not somehow caught hold of a rock, he would have been swept away.

"James, Mama wants you always to be a good brother to your sister."

He wriggles against her.

"Try not to move."

"It's hot."

She works her hand through the pile of robes and raises the canvas for a whiff of fresh air. The kuŋśi is marching back and forth in front of their pile with Nellie in her arms.

If only Ćaske were here.

She lowers the cloth. "James, what's your sister's name?"

"Nellie, silly Mama!"

"We do call her Nellie, don't we? But I have a secret. Her real name is Lucy Elizabeth."

"Lucy?"

"Yes."

"Do *I* have a real name?"

"You're my little man!" She fumbles for his nose, pretends to pluck it from his face.

He giggles.

"Shhh." She puts his nose back on.

"I'm not afraid of the dark."

"I know, you're very brave…. Mama wants to tell you something very important. Are you listening with both ears?" She feels him nod. "You must always remember your name. And you must teach Nellie her real name. Don't let her forget who she is."

"Nellie is Lucy!"

"Practice each day, in secret, when you're all alone. Say, 'I'm James Beach Wakefield, and my sister is Lucy Elizabeth.' Tell yourself, in your heart, each night before you go to sleep. Promise me."

"I promise."

"Good boy."

"Can we come out now?"

"You must always stay with Nellie and help her, no matter what. Will you do that for Mama?"

A spirited nod. "But Mama, please, I don't want to play anymore."

❦ 6 ❦

THE SUN IS TRYING to push up through dense black clouds in the east. Stray beams of light filter through the cloud cover; under their influence the colors of the landscape are eerily vivid.

An ill breeze begins to gust out of the northwest. Sheet lightning flashes. Thunder rolls. The Sioux scramble to close the smoke ears of their tipis and tighten the anchor ropes. They hammer the tipi pegs deeper into the earth. Old people do ceremony, seeking to fend off the tempest, but their rites don't appease. Rain cascades down, blowing sideways.

For this day, at least, there will be no war. The wind howls, a sustained gale, shoving at Little Crow's village one turbulent wave of storms after another.

Sarah rests, uneasy but snug, in the shelter of Winuna's lodge. After her ordeal in the ravine, her spirit is desolate; her body, a bag of hurt. She listens across the hours to the pelting rain, the rattling poles, the creaking of the tipi cover. Bells jingle and deer hoofs clatter from one of the tipi ropes.

She studies Ćaske as he burns sweetgrass, smokes his pipe, cleans his gun, draws in an old ledger book. Upon arriving home from yesterday's battle, he'd exhumed her and James from their pile of buffalo robes. "Come out!" he said, lifting her up by the hands. "Do not be afraid! I will shoot anyone who tries to harm Doctor Wife."

Hepaŋ wasn't with him. His whereabouts since her capture have been a mystery.

Ćaske's mother is making a doll for Nellie from cloth and rawhide. James plays with Winuna's two little boys, charging his toy buffalo against their toy horses. Winuna runs melted lead through her bullet mold.

The constant barrage of rain and wind against the tipi punishes the nerves. It's so dark, she can't gauge the time. She decides it must be night when all the children, by some habit of the body, crawl into their beds and drop off to sleep.

Ćaske burns more herbs in his abalone shell. His mother brews more coffee. Winuna stirs the fire. No one speaks.

Sarah is nodding off when Ćaske leaps to his feet. The tipi is starting to rock. He yanks her up and propels her toward the door.

"My babies!" she screams, as he shoves her out into driving rain. "My babies!" she screams into the wind, as he drags her toward the buckboard.

He hauls her down in the grass beneath the wagon. She stretches panicked hands between the spokes of a wheel, desperate for her babies. By flickers of lightning she sees Winuna squeeze James and her boys out of the crippled tipi. Just as the tempest pries the last tipi stakes from the soggy ground, the old woman escapes with Nellie. The lodge billows up. It sweeps against the wall of another tipi, forty or fifty feet away, and collapses in a heap.

SHE SHIVERS AWAKE IN A MASS OF SLUMBERING BODIES BENEATH THE buckboard, the family molded against one another for warmth. Half asleep, she lifts her head and peers out. The morning star is dazzling in the southeast. Two fingers of geese cross the moon.

A while yet until dawn. Tipis are down. Fires are burning out of place. Household possessions are strewn hither and yon. Animals are roaming free.

She spoons tighter against the body beside her and founders down into sleep.

A FLUSH BRIGHTENS THE EASTERN HORIZON. DESPITE LAST NIGHT'S STORM, A second attack on the stubborn fort of the Big Knives is imminent. Wiŋyaŋ run bullets, give out battle rations, and ornament war ponies with ribbons, jangling bells and feathers. Warriors make their prayers, put on paint, wrap fire-arrows to set Ridgley's roofs ablaze.

Naked to the waist, Ćaske smears his face and body with grease, then applies pigments with a buffalo sponge. "This earth that I use as paint," he sings, "makes the enemy afraid."

For a second time his mother reddens the part in Sarah's hair. Then she streaks red paint across Sarah's forehead and down her cheeks. She ties colorful silk ribbons to her braids. Allowing Sarah to retain her corset, she dresses her in Sioux clothes that actually fit: a loose calico blouse, a blue broadcloth skirt trimmed with ribbonwork, beaded leggings, a green blanket shawl, even beaded moccasins—her first shoes of any sort in three days. Bewildered by the sudden fuss over her appearance, Sarah is glad not to have to stand before another mirror.

"Doctor Wife no stay here," Ćaske tells her, in broken English, his habit when sharing confidences. "Hepaŋ no safe. Tuŋkaŋsidaŋ house go. Ḣuya-pa." He intends to deliver her and the children to his grandfather, Eagle Head, for safekeeping.

The painted warriors progress toward Ridgley in a slow muddy train behind the white steed of Little Crow. Ćaske drives the buckboard through their midst. The clean, earthy air is replete with war songs and the jingling and tinkling of bedecked ponies. If not for knowledge of the Indians' purpose, Sarah would thrill at the spectacle.

The sun is gaining when they turn into the yard of a half-painted brick house encircled by a village of tipis. Such a house could belong only to a chief. Wiŋyaŋ at morning chores pause to watch their wagon roll to a stop.

"Who is that dear child in your arms?" a familiar voice says, in fluent English, as Sarah alights with Nellie.

"Oh, Mother Friend! I'm so happy to see you!" Sarah rushes to embrace the kuŋśi. In former days Mother Friend had traded her fingerweaving and beadwork in the streets of Shakopee. Whenever they chanced to meet, the old woman would coax her into speaking Dakota. Eventually she coaxed her all the way out to Tiŋta Otoŋwe; a world apart, though only a couple miles from town.

Life on the reservation has carved the extra flesh from Mother Friend's frame, but her eyes haven't lost their bright warmth, and her braids are still wrapped with brilliant woven ribbons. She reaches to enfold Nellie. "Pretty, pretty girl! And the little doctor"—she rumples James's hair—"has grown so tall!"

Ćaske releases the wagon brake. "I must go. My grandfather is in the brick house. Doctor Wife will be fed and taken care of. I will return by nightfall."

"I will feed her myself." Mother Friend passes Nellie to one of her grown daughters to cosset. "Doctor Wife gave me food many times in the white man's town. Today she will eat with me."

The kuŋśi provides Sarah with water and soap to bathe. She cooks a porridge of wild rice and venison broth. She spoils James with nuts and chunks of maple sugar. But her kindnesses can't distract from the battle once it erupts, somewhere above Eagle Head's house. Ridgley cannons boom and rip. In the woods across the ravine, warriors can be seen falling back from the fort, reloading their guns and rushing uphill again.

All day long, Sarah tries not to listen or watch. All day long, she prays to the sun to budge, plumes of smoke high in the sky.

THE EVENING TURNS MUGGY. SARAH JOINS THE WOMEN AND OLD PEOPLE WHO are gathering in Eagle Head's yard to wait for news. Nellie climbs in and out of Mother Friend's lap, flicking the kuŋśi's braids.

Around sunset a messenger lopes in, causing a stir. Upon hearing his report, Eagle Head rises on slow knees and asks for his gun and shot pouch. "The white soldiers' lodge has not been taken. I must take Doctor Wife to the woods. Taoyate Duta has made threats against her."

"Ćaske say stay!" she says, afraid of fleeing with the old man. He's too frail, in his eighties at least.

"My grandson is not coming back. Doctor Wife will be killed if she does not leave."

Mother Friend lays a firm hand on Sarah's arm, letting her know she mustn't argue. "Take your girl. Leave the boy with me. I will be a good grandmother."

A BRAMBLE SNAGS HER ANKLE. SHE GOES DOWN HARD. THE BLOW TO HER midriff takes her wind. Nellie, in a sling on her back, lands on top of her. By some mercy, the child doesn't scream.

"My grandson is not coming back."

The Ridgley cannon have gone quiet, but the near woods aren't far enough away to be safe. Too many close gunshots, too many galloping hoofbeats. She crashes on and on through the trees, the old man directing the way from behind. He can't keep up. Again and again, she must retrace her steps. This time, she finds him bent over in the moonlight, wheezing, clutching at his chest. "I must rest," he gasps, "or I will die...."

What did he mean, "Ćaske isn't coming back?"

. . .

IN THE TRANQUILLITY OF DAWN, THEY VENTURE OUT OF THE WOODS INTO THE lush bottomlands of the Minnesota. She could outrun the old man, hunt for a low place to ford the river. Cross over, hide in the brush until dark. Set out for a white settlement downstream, should any be yet standing.

But like a fool she left James behind. "I will be a good grandmother," Mother Friend had told her, almost as if not expecting her to return.

Eagle Head hurries her through golden stubble. The meadow is cut clean, studded with haycocks and heady with the smell of grass. In the middle of the field he stops to burrow out a hole in a haystack. He urges her inside.

"I will come back." He rearranges the stalks over her and Nellie. After a few feathery footfalls, she can hear nothing except Nellie's breathing.

THE HAY RUSTLES WHENEVER THEY MOVE, THREATENING TO BETRAY THEM. SHE nurses Nellie to keep her quiet until she's empty of milk. She could scream from the close air, the heat and thirst, the confinement of her corset, the dry itch. She shakes off the image of a probing spear running them through. A torch being put to the stack. A fire-arrow whizzing in.

She probes deep into the haycock for moist hay and lifts a few stalks to her lips to suck. James will be crying himself sick. Only once have they been apart for more than an hour or two. "Mama's indisposed," John told him, right after her whipping, barring him from her room. The boy begged and begged at her door, whining about his belly burning and his heart beating out of his chest, until his evacuation to Redwood. When he came home from the Humphreys with a hacking cough and signs of hectic fever, John had no remedy. "You've spoiled the boy so," he told her, "he could droop and die. Homesickness can kill even a soldier." Until her face was passable, she could only love James through the door, sweetening him up as best she could.

Nellie rubs at her eyes. Yawns. Clicks her tongue.

How long will this dreadful outbreak go on? Everyone expected the War against the rebel states to last a month, but after a year, there's no end in sight. Might it be the same against the Sioux? Mr. Lincoln's called up so many volunteers, we might not have enough men in the state to quash the uprising. Even if the authorities do marshal a force, how will it ever liberate us captives without mowing us down? Cannon shot and musket fire don't discriminate—

The ground's trembling. She clamps her hand over Nellie's mouth and strains to hear beyond the hay.

Ponies.

She sticks a frantic fingertip between Nellie's lips, inviting her to suck.

"*No!*" Nellie pushes it away.

She doubles her palms over the little mouth. The ponies halt nearby. Hooves paw. Battle adornments jingle. Nellie strains against Sarah's hands, her little eyes, so wide, so afraid—

A faint gurgle issues from the child's throat, loud as a crashing wave in Sarah's ears.

Please, Nellie—

She folds herself over her baby's body.

The riders, all quiet.

A muffled whimper leaks out from beneath her.

She searches out the pulses on either side of the little throat. She listens for some sign that the thing must be done, or not.

The resting ponies huff. Tails swish. Bells jangle, light and pretty.

A war whoop will be too late. She hardens herself to stone. Presses the throat with her fingers. Smothers the flailing little arms and feet with her body until they slacken, and go still.

SHE FLOUNDERS awake with a sharp sob, surfacing from sleep so swiftly, she can't place where she is. Her eyes strain for light, for recognizable forms. There, Winuna and her boys. There, Ćaske's mother. There, Ćaske himself, back safe from Ridgley. She begins to breathe again.

James is attached to her like a barnacle. He hasn't let go since she got back. When he first spotted her at a distance, being escorted into Little Crow's camp by Eagle Head, he broke into a sprint and came leaping at her without breaking stride, nearly knocking her down. "Oh Mama, you're here! I thought you were gone to Heaven!"

They all might have gone to Heaven if not for Ćaske removing them to Eagle Head's before the battle. During the fighting, three shells from Ridgley exploded in Little Crow's new camp. A number of Sioux and even a few captives were torn by shell fragments or mowed down by canister. No one had believed the cannons could strike from such a distance.

Ridgley still hasn't fallen.

The wiŋyaŋ who had lost kin cut off their hair. They sliced the calves of their legs and fleshy parts of their arms with the tips of their knives, just enough that the cuts would weep. With their heads shorn and blood trickling down, they sat on the ground, moaning, rocking and wailing. Hour after hour, they wailed. They're wailing even now, in the grip of night. Sarah has never witnessed such expression of grief.

By accident of Fate or the Hand of God, she has avoided heartbreak of her own. She still has her James, and Nellie's breathing against her is even and deep. She brushes the girl's forehead with her lips, praying that whatever fugitive memory survives in the child of being choked cold in the haycock will soon pass. She herself will have to live with it, long after the marks of her fingers have faded from Nellie's neck.

She's drowsing off again when a drunken growling rouses everyone in the tipi.

"Where is the white woman?" Hepaŋ roars, keeling over onto his boys. "I want the white woman! Let us talk!"

Ćaske scrambles out from beneath his sleeping robe. His mother, drawing James to her bed, whispers to Sarah not to move. In terror beneath her blanket, Sarah feigns sleep, fighting to keep her breaths regular, her eyelids still.

Through the barest squint she sees Hepaŋ regain his feet. He unsheathes his dagger. Once he distinguishes her in the dim firelight, he lets loose a garbled string of English curses. She stifles the impulse to flee.

Ćaske circles the fire pit, blocking Hepaŋ's path to where she lies. "My brother is drunk."

"I will have the white woman for my wife, or I will kill her!"

Ćaske dips his head at Winuna. "*There* is my brother's wife! Why do you act this way?"

"I must have *her*"—pointing his blade at Sarah—"or she must die!"

"Go lie with your own woman."

Hepaŋ glares, playing with the weight of his dagger.

Ćaske inches closer to him. "Lie with your woman!"

Hepaŋ swings a sorry swipe with his knife.

Ćaske yields no ground. "I do not want to fight. My brother is drunk. Go to your bed. I will take the white woman for my wife."

Sarah catches hold of the old woman's hand.

"I have no wife," Ćaske says. "It is proper."

Hepaŋ sways on his feet, studying his blade. "Yes, it is right. My brother should take her."

"I will take her when I know for certain her husband is dead."

"My brother must take her now!" Wagging his dagger.

"He drink big," Ćaske says to Sarah in English, not taking his eyes off Hepaŋ. "Ćaske sleep Doctor Wife, he no kill."

One more look at Hepaŋ's gleaming knife, and she lifts her blanket. Ćaske slips in next to Nellie, stretching out on his back. "Do not worry," he says to Sarah, in Dakota.

She turns on her side, away from him. Across the tipi, Hepaŋ spills into bed. She'd been hoping he might have slunk off to die after stopping a bullet. But there he is, passed out and snoring a few feet away, sprawled like a boar in mud. She almost feels sorry for Winuna.

"My wife is in the spirit world," Ćaske whispers. "She knows my thoughts. I will not harm Doctor Wife."

In her memory his wife has no face, no age.

"Whenever I am not here," Ćaske says, "Doctor Wife must stay inside. I have claimed you as my woman. You will be safe in the lodge where I sleep. Even Taoyate Duta will be unable to harm you."

Skeptical, she curls herself into a ball. "Hepaŋ knife!"

She hears him raise up on an elbow. "Hepaŋ will not try to touch you again, or he will be punished." His breath is warm on the nape of her neck. "But if you leave the lodge, I cannot protect you. Taoyate Duta and his soldiers want Doctor Wife dead."

"Why?" The English bursts from her lips. "What have I done?"

He doesn't speak. He doesn't move.

He doesn't understand you.

She hugs her knees. "I am all alone!"

"I am responsible for Doctor Wife and her children. But we need an ally." He lies back. She can still feel his heat. "We will appeal to Śakpe Daŋ. We will help him remember you from Tiŋta Otoŋwe. We will ask him to take you under his wing."

Śakpe Daŋ is seated cross-legged in the tipi's place of honor, hair curling out from his black calico headband. Apart from his steadfast scowl, he bears an uncanny resemblance to his father, Śakpe, who died shortly after his people's removal to the reservation. By reputation he has none of his father's best qualities and exaggerations of his worst. Fortunately for Sarah, he comprehends English as well as she does Dakota. They can both speak freely in their own tongue.

"I knew Śakpe Daŋ's father to be a great man," she says. "You have the chance to be even greater." Wearing her fancy clothes as a gesture of respect, she sits with her long legs folded to one side, like a wiŋyaŋ.

"I have heard many stories. Doctor Wife was once a friend of our people."

"I am still your friend. I wish your people no harm." She glances at

Ćaske, packing tobacco into the polished red bowl of the family pipe. He'd advised her to wait until the pipe was passed before getting to the heart of it, but she lets her question fly. "I must ask if I am to die."

Śakpe Daŋ relaxes against his willow backrest. His face is slate, his eyes empty as barrels. Somewhere in the silence of the tipi, a cricket begins to chirp.

"Is my life in danger?" she asks. "I know there are many captives in this camp, perhaps hundreds. Taoyate Duta safeguards some of them in his own lodge. Others, like myself, he threatens day and night. I have heard he hates me most of all."

Śakpe Daŋ grunts. Ćaske offers him the pipe.

"Am I the only white from Yellow Medicine among his captives?" she asks.

Śakpe Daŋ puffs on the pipe. Smoke issues from his nose. "It is so."

"I have heard that Taoyate Duta is angry because Thomas—Major Galbraith—escaped. He wants to kill me in his place."

"The agent has not acted honorably. He is a liar."

"That doesn't answer my question!"

She sees Ćaske grimace. She's being too direct, too white. Yet this is no time to be mealy-mouthed. Fort Ridgley, despite the odds, is still standing. The German settlers at New Ulm have staved off multiple assaults. And an American army under the command of former governor Henry Sibley—Long Trader, the Sioux call him—is said to be advancing up the Minnesota Valley from St. Paul, to suppress the uprising. Tate Mi Ma, the camp crier, has told the people to make ready: They will withdraw north toward Yellow Medicine, to join forces with the Upper Sioux.

At first, she'd welcomed the news of retreat. In the territory of the Upper tribes, Standing Buffalo's influence might shield her from Little Crow. But then Tate Mi Ma wended through the lodges with a direr pronouncement. "The white captives are weak as chickens, slow as turtles. They eat too much of our food. They will burden us when we go north. Better they die now!" Her emotions have since been spooling away.

"Please, Śakpe Daŋ, out of respect for your departed father, let us hold the pipe together—you by the bowl, and I by the stem!"

Śakpe Daŋ props an elbow on his thigh and rests his head on his palm. His eyelids are heavy, like he might fall asleep, but in an instant he could pull the dagger from his chest sheath and make orphans of her babies. She opens her mouth to make one last plea, not yet formed in her mind.

If John gets through this war with his life, and the children with theirs, he won't care what wicked bargains you had to strike....

"If Śakpe Daŋ spares me and my babies ... if you give us our lives—" she squeezes out the words like fishhooks through flesh— "I will be a good Dakota wife to Ćaske! My children will belong to your people. We will live with your band the rest of our days!"

꿢 8 ꚛ

HER WORLD IS ONE VAST, snarly Indian train. Hundreds of women are on foot, bent beneath heavy bundles and cradleboards, some leading pack-horses. Hundreds of men are on mounts and in every kind of conveyance, from two-wheeled ox-carts to fine coaches, light chaises and teamsters' wagons. Most of the settler vehicles have been loaded without regard for size or capacity; some founder beneath the weight. A number are hitched to steers, milk cows and Indian ponies. Unused to a harness, the animals rebel, spilling their loads, sometimes maiming and killing.

Everywhere infants are crying, mules are braying, cows are lowing and cattle bellowing, wolf-eared dogs are barking and yelping, plundered musical instruments are being plucked and blown—a deafening Babel of confusion. Warriors race back and forth on horseback, whooping and singing their war songs. They're absurdly outfitted in plunder, with pock-etwatches tied to their ankles, ladies' furs girdling their waists, clock wheels dangling from their ears, silk shawls wound like turbans around their heads. They wield the lash without mercy, trying to marshal the chaos and prevent anyone, white or Indian, from escaping or lagging behind. One of the cruelest warriors is a curly-haired mulatto in Indian dress, a most peculiar sight.

The wind flattens her clothes against her body. Her dress is plain and her feet bare, her moccasins having been put away with the rest of her fancy things. She can't figure out why she's still alive. Śakpe Daŋ promised nothing over the pipe. Little Crow and the soldiers' lodge must have decided to keep her and the other captives a while longer, to hold them for ransom or to use them as bait, as leverage, as shield.

Somehow in the crowd she has lost Ćaske's mother. Uŋćiśi, she's been told to call the old woman; the first *mother-in-law* she has ever had. She hastens with James to catch up to Winuna and her boys, getting clear, for the moment, of Hepaŋ. He has been stalking her most of the day.

Winuna scuds along with her pack, bound by a hide strap to her forehead. "My Brother's Wife is too slow. Keep up, or our soldiers will kill you."

Sarah licks the dust from her lips and spits. Winuna seems to have softened since the storm almost killed them all. Or since Ćaske forbade Hepaŋ to ravish her. Even now the wiŋyaŋ is slackening her pace a bit, to help her keep up. The peace between them might not last, but it's a truce in which to breathe easier.

WITH NELLIE ON HER BACK, SHE FLOUNDERS WITH WINUNA AND HER BOYS across the river, up to her waist in yellow water, muck sucking at her ankles. James paddles along behind, one pudgy hand tight in hers. This time she won't let him be swept away.

A pot-bellied mule splashes up beside her. "Good Big Woman!" the rider says, in Dakota. "My heart is glad to see a friend from Yellow Medicine."

She lowers her head. She doesn't want to be associated with the Upper Agency. Thomas has too many enemies. "I am Dakota!" she hears herself say, and Winuna laughs.

The Indian on the mule laughs, too. "Good Big Woman must not tell lies."

Uŋćiśi is suddenly beside her. "Be careful, my daughter," she murmurs. "That man is Wahpeton."

What does that matter? Sarah almost blurts, grabbing onto the roots of a toppled tree to steady herself. *Why are you and the other grandmothers so afraid of the Upper Sioux?* She drags herself along the tree trunk and sloshes up the riverbank onto dry land. There she lets her babies go and doubles over, out of wind.

The Wahpeton crowds her with the muzzle of his mule. "Good Big Woman does not recognize me?"

"Little Paul!" James cries. He raises his sopping arms, to be picked up. With a grin the Wahpeton swings him up on the mule.

Sarah peers at the pudgy Sioux through a haze of sunlight. Little Paul has abandoned his farmer clothes. From his porcupine roach to his fringed leggings and breechcloth, he appears every inch a blanket Indian.

He stretches a stubby arm down to her. "Come! I will take Good Big Woman to my lodge."

She retreats a few steps. She might be tired and footsore, but she isn't about to climb up on that mule.

"Take me! Take me!" James squeals, bouncing on the mule's back, as Ćaske bumps the overloaded wagon up onto the riverbank. "Little Paul can take me to Papa!"

"James, sweetheart, you can't go without Mama. You'll cry no end when it gets dark."

"Oh no, I'll be your little man! *Please!*"

Little Paul has followed their English. "Let the boy come. Good Big Woman will have one less child to worry over."

"That man is Wahpeton." Uŋćiśi eases her pack to the ground. "Understand?"

Uncertain what to do, Sarah beckons to Ćaske. She would like to spare James's little legs the long march to Yellow Medicine. She can't have him riding the buckboard; it's so laden with plunder, she's afraid it might tip. But were she to send James off with Little Paul, she might never see him again.

She seats herself on a log. As she nurses Nellie, she keeps one eye on Ćaske, who has drawn the Wahpeton aside to smoke and talk, and the other on Hepaŋ, wading with his boys in the shallows. Sadie is growling at him from the bank.

Perhaps she should trust Little Paul. A leader at the Hazelwood mission, before the war he was a clear favorite of Stephen Riggs. On at least two of her Sabbath visits, he led the tiny congregation in Dakota hymns. His singing was intolerable, but after meeting he played with James like a favorite uncle.

Her milk isn't letting down. Nellie's fussing will soon be a squall.

"What My Husband say I do?" she asks, when Ćaske rejoins her.

"My Wife may go with the Wahpeton, but he wants you for his woman."

Her jaw falls open. "He has wife! He go church!"

He shrugs. "He is Dakota." Multiple wives, he means; not much practiced among the Sioux, but permitted, to the consternation of the missionaries.

He examines her sorry feet. "My Wife must not walk any further. You must either go with the Wahpeton or drive the wagon."

"Go, or drive." How can he so casually let you choose between himself and this stranger? Would it be so easy to give you up?

He calls her "wife"; she calls him "husband." She shares his bed—chastely, but enough to convince. Everyone seems to believe they're a couple. Even so, does he secretly wish to be free of her and her babies? Is he weary of having to provide for them, and protect them? In this crush of people on the riverbank, she dare not ask, even in English. Ears are everywhere.

"I stay," she says.

The slightest nod. "And the boy?"

The decision about James is too fraught to make. "What My Husband say I do?"

Ćaske stands up.

"What My Husband say?" she says again.

He pulls off his red headband. "I am not a wise man. But the journey we are making is long." He strides to the river, crouches, splashes his face, drinks from his hands. He dips the headband in the water, wrings it out and reties it.

Her mind clears. She passes Nellie off to Uŋćiśi, then limps over to Little Paul. "Guard my son with your life," she says to him in English, "or may God strike you dead!"

Little Paul remounts in front of James. Sarah reaches to hug her boy close. Then she squares him on the mule's back and wraps his elfin arms around the Wahpeton's thick ribs. "Hold on tight, little man. I love you."

Little Paul kicks his heels into the mule's sides. James breaks out in a yowl. "You ride too, Mama!" Tears coursing down his cheeks. "Mama, *please!* You ride, too! Come find Papa!"

"Soon, James!" She waves after him. "Mama will come after you!"

"Mama! *Mama....*"

She waves and waves, until she can no longer hear his cries on the wind or search out his golden head in the throng of Sioux.

Uŋćiśi lays Nellie back in her arms. "My Daughter must sit." She helps Sarah hobble back to the log. "I will bind your feet with herbs. I will nick the stitches from your ears."

Ćaske sits down beside her to share some pemmican. "Wahpeton know doctor?" he asks, in English.

"Yes." Sucking sweetness from the dried meat.

The muscles are working in his jaw. "Wahpeton say Dakota come, doctor run. Doctor no dead. You wife."

FOR A SECOND DAY THE SIOUX TRAIN SNAKES UP THE GOVERNMENT ROAD toward Yellow Medicine. Sarah drives the buckboard behind Belle and Mick, sweating beneath the unmerciful sun. Plundered goods are piled high around her. Her bound feet rest atop a full pantry: a crock of molasses, hot metal canisters of flour and sugar, a jar of lard melted like oil....

"Doctor no dead."

Among the scores of white captives, she has counted only two men. If the gruesome stories told by the settler women are true, Indians butchered most all the white men in the vicinity of the Lower Agency during the first hours of the outbreak. The men's kin often died with them. She harbors little hope for the Humphrey family, Jannette and Joseph DeCamp and their boys, Reverend Hinman, or her other acquaintances at Redwood. She can only pray that, against all odds, they might have slipped away to safety.

Lately she has gotten wind of atrocities on the Upper reservation as well. Of her friends there, only Thomas seems to have cheated death, having ridden off to St. Paul with his half-breed recruits. Henrietta and her children, Stuart Garvie, the Riggses, the Williamsons—everyone she knew, including John, was said to have been shot, clubbed, tomahawked, gutted, scalped, dismembered, burned alive.... Doubting their sources, she has refused to invest the grisly stories with full belief. But in the innermost chamber of her heart, a voice has been whispering that John was likely among the slain.

Now, for John at least, Little Paul might have supplied proof of life. As an Upper Indian, he could well have witnessed, or even been involved in, whatever unfolded on Agency Hill after her departure. *But on whose side was he?*

Here's the Half-Way House. No trace of trouble. By appearance, Valencia might be inside changing bed linens and Joseph out mucking the barn. *What's become of them?*

Gleason's body will be on the road, not far ahead. She lifts her eyes to the sky.

· · ·

THE SIOUX SOLDIERS HALT THE TRAIN TO CAMP FOR THE NIGHT. SARAH HELPS Winuna haul water. On her last trip, she lags behind at the spring. After rinsing her dusty face and neck, she fills a large pail, seats herself on a rock under some burr oaks and timidly unbinds her feet.

She inches her right foot into the pail. The cool water pinks with blood against the white of her skin.

What if John's alive, after all?

She shudders. Lowers her left foot in.

What if he meant you to die, that day he sent you away? He'd heard about the troubles, Gleason said. Yet he hurried you out the door. Stood there watching you go, with a driver who had no gun. Stood there twizzling his watch, Dinah behind him on the stoop—

A black hole yawns in her chest.

But surely he wouldn't have hurt the children, his own flesh and blood....

Winuna races up, yelling, wagging her finger. Uŋċiśi and Ċaske come running. Upon seeing Sarah, they burst into scolding. She drowns in their angry torrent of words. Her Dakota has been improving, immersed as she is in the tongue, but she can't grasp the nature of her trespass. It concerns the pail somehow. Ċaske enlists a mixed-blood to explain in English.

"All vessels belonging to a tipi are wakaŋ," the mixed-blood tells her. "You know the word?"

"Yes. Sacred. Holy."

"Something like that. Pots, kettles, pails—no woman may put her feet in them, or even step over them. To do so is strictly forbidden."

"Oh no!" She pulls her feet dripping from the pail. "I sorry," she says to Ċaske, dumping the water. "I clean!"

"No."

She sets the pail in front of him. He turns it upon its rim and stalks away. Helpless, she holds out her hands to the mixed-blood. "I fouled this pail because I'm a woman?"

"You didn't *foul* it. A woman, too, is wakaŋ.... How do I tell you? If you were Dakota, you would understand."

"I CANNOT FIND THE BAG OF LEAD SHOT," WINUNA SAYS TO HER MOTHER AS they're breaking camp, the third day of the march. She thrusts the tipi cloth into the back of the buckboard. "Where did you put it?"

Uŋċiśi picks up a willow backrest in each hand.

"Old woman, did you hear me? *Where is the shot?"*

Uŋčiši stows the backrests in the wagon.

"You cannot remember, can you? Foolish old woman! You are always losing things!"

Sarah cowers by the cookfire, feeding Nellie bites of roasted potato. Spats between Winona and Uŋčiši are as common as the wind, but this one is especially ugly. She has never seen an elder treated with such contempt.

With full hands Uŋčiši marches back and forth to the wagon, while Winuna screeches blame. Finally, with the authority of age, the kuŋši sets loose her own tongue, lamenting her daughter's insolence and poor management of the household.

Winuna grabs up the coffeepot and hurls it at her mother. It misses the old woman's head by an inch. "I will not live with you any longer!" she squawks over her shoulder, strutting out of sight.

Sarah glances at Časke. He's watching his mother without expression. Uŋčiši climbs into the wagon and begins to sort through the family's possessions and plundered goods. After bundling her share, she piles them on a travois and lashes them down. Just as the Sioux train starts to move out, she and Časke hitch the travois to Belle. The mare prances and kicks, bothered by the unaccustomed load.

Hepaŋ drives off in the buckboard behind Mick and an Indian pony. Winuna and her boys slouch amidst the cargo.

"Grandmother! Ride with us!" the boys call out.

Uŋčiši raises both hands in the air, as if in blessing. Her daughter fixes her stare straight ahead.

Little by little, Belle quiets. Uŋčiši walks the mare in easy circles on a lead rope, acquainting her with the sound and feel of the drag.

"My Wife will ride," Časke says, once Belle is ready enough to join the caravan. He boosts Sarah up over the travois poles into a worn Indian saddle. She strokes Belle's neck, humming and singing to soothe them both.

HER SPIRIT LIGHTENS AS SHE NODS ALONG, MILE AFTER MILE. THE SUDDEN falling-out in the family has freed her of Hepaŋ. It has also put an end to the squabbling and silent clashes of will between Winuna and Uŋčiši. Life's misfortunes seem to have poisoned the blood between them, much like herself and her own mother.

On this leg of the journey north, Uŋčiši and Časke accompany Eagle

Head. The war has forced Ćaske's grandfather from his brick house. The tough decisions faced by members of this family since the start of the uprising are gaining shape in her mind. She has been piecing their story together like a crazy quilt ever since her capture. After hostilities broke out, Little Crow and the soldiers' lodge ordered all cut-hairs among the Lower Sioux to throw off their white dress, leave their white housing and join the campaign against the wasiću. Ćaske and Uŋćiśi complied, out of loyalty to their people and concern for their own survival. Displaced from their tiny farm, they took refuge with Winuna and Hepaŋ, who were blanket Indians, hot for war. Though close kin, they dwelled together in the same tipi about as peaceably as Unionists and Rebels in the same house.

Eagle Head, meanwhile, resisted the war. Much as he resented the wasiću, he thought it foolhardy to attack white settlers and challenge the might of the Isaŋ Taŋka, the *Big Knives*. Early on, Little Crow and the soldiers' lodge tolerated his dissent. He was, after all, an elder and a chief. But once they resolved to retreat north, their indulgence ended. Only by going along would Eagle Head and his band prove themselves to be true Mdewakantonwans. Else they would be destroyed.

She rests her shins atop the sturdy poles. Up ahead, Eagle Head is dozing in his saddle, head drooped on his chest. A kuŋśi who must be his woman straggles behind him, bent beneath the load strapped to her back. She leads a packhorse. Judging by the size of the tipi cloth bundled to her travois, her lodge will be too small to shelter the entire family. Some relatives will be sleeping under the stars tonight.

She smiles. Sleeping under the stars is a price she will happily pay to be clear of Hepaŋ.

FROM A DISTANCE, THE BRICK BUILDINGS ON AGENCY HILL LOOK JUST AS THEY did the afternoon she left home with Gleason—about two weeks ago, near as she can figure. Days have become hard to reckon.

At least her house isn't rubble like Joseph Brown's. Less than nine miles back, she'd spied the charred ruins of his three-story mansion. Brown himself was away when the Indians attacked, but his Sioux wife Susan, his son Samuel, and several more of his children are among the captives being safeguarded by Little Crow. The chief will probably try either to broker a fair price from the American authorities for their safe return or use them to win concessions.

She cants into Belle's silky mane, out of the moaning wind. *Why should Susan Brown be so untouchable, while you yourself must live in constant fear for your life? Are you not also the wife of an influential white man? Didn't the Upper Sioux spare your house on Agency Hill, out of respect?*

The mare's distorted shadow moves over the road.

❧ 9 ❧

BRACED BY UŋĆIŚI, Sarah hobbles against the wind through the new Sioux encampment. Pitched a couple miles beyond Agency Hill, the camp has mushroomed to a city of a thousand lodges.

"Who is this 'Little Paul?'" the Sioux say, when she inquires after him and James. "By what name do our people know him?"

She bites back her frustration. If she knew his Dakota name, she would use it. "Ta Makoće is friend," she tells them, using their name for Stephen Riggs.

They shake their heads.

"The man is Wahpeton," Uŋćiśi tells them, and describes his appearance.

They shake their heads again.

After searching for several hours, Sarah limps with Uŋćiśi back to Eagle Head's. By the fire in the tipi yard, she again lets the old woman wash and bind her feet.

"I go Ta Makoće mission," she tells Ćaske in Dakota, as he pours her a cup of coffee. "Ta Makoće help find James."

Ćaske sets down the coffeepot. He's kind enough not to say what she already knows: Either the missionaries at Hazelwood are dead or they fled long ago.

"Hapstiŋna know Little Paul," she says, on inspiration. "Hapstiŋna know James. Mother is Warrior Woman. House is near Ta Makoće mission —" She tries to rise but Uŋćiśi stops her.

"My Daughter must not walk anymore."

Ćaske fetches his gun, his shot pouch, his powder horn. "If My Wife tells me where to go, I will go. I will find this Hapstiŋna."

"SARAH?"

For so long, she hasn't been Sarah but Doctor Wife, Good Big Woman, My Daughter, My Wife. When her English name leaches in, she lifts her chin.

"Sarah, is that really you? Your *hair!*"

Standing over her in tatters is a filthy white woman, far along with child. Her head is turbaned with red gingham. A sleeping toddler fills her sunburned arms.

Sarah pulls herself upright. "Jannette? Jannette DeCamp?"

The woman tumbles into her arms with her Benjy. "Oh Sarah, it's been so—so—*awful!* Not a decent place to sleep! Nothing fit for even a pig to eat! I roam around begging, like one of *them* … can you believe it? I swear, Sarah, I shall die!"

Sarah embraces her friend from Shakopee, whom she last saw at Hinman's church. Little more than a year ago, their families had steamed up to the reservation together aboard the *Jeanette Roberts*. Jannette's "darling" Joseph managed the sawmill and gristmill at the Lower Agency. Considering the bloodshed there, Sarah is amazed to see her alive.

She wraps up Benjy like a rag doll and nudges toward Jannette a bowl of food she hasn't touched for worrying about James. The woman tears into the boiled potatoes and dried beef.

"Which Indian has been keeping you?"

"We wander like rats … eat what we can … sleep where we can." Jannette washes down a mouthful with Sarah's cold coffee.

"Your other boys are with you?"

"Somewhere…." she says, attacking the frybread.

"No Indian has claimed you as his?"

Jannette talks as she chews. "There was … a friend of Joseph's … can't look after us properly … he was shot at New Ulm.… I swear to Heaven, never in my life … have I been treated so! I'll never … trust an Indian again … absolute devils!"

"Not all of them, Jannette, as your own experience attests, and mine."

"But look at you, Sarah! You're less the woman you were by half! And your hair—it's as white as my grandfather's wig!"

"It turned color the very first night, from fright, I suppose. George Gleason was killed right in front of me!"

"Not *George!*"

"He was driving me and the children to Ridgley to catch the stage. We were ambushed near the Half-Way House. We'd have all been killed, if not for our Indian friends. Just like you…. More coffee?"

"That horse piss scarcely passes."

"It's all we have."

"You have plenty enough." Jannette's eyes roam away to a towel, soap and washbasin. "The Sioux must think well of you."

"Of course they think well of me. I've always shared with them what food and medicine I could, I talk with them in their language…. If you cast your bread upon the water, in time it returns."

"I cast whole loaves, coming to this reservation!"

"That might be true, but whining and fretting will make them cross. I'm warning you as a friend, guard your tongue."

Uŋčiši walks wearily into the yard. She whisks up the coffeepot and empty bowl. "Do not let this woman stay long," she whispers in Sarah's ear, "or those who dislike her will learn to dislike you."

Sarah nods, with a smile at Jannette.

Uŋčiši seats herself nearby to sew on a new tipi cloth. Sadie's nose rests on her thigh as she plies her needle.

"What did that squaw say?" Jannette asks, under her breath. "Was it about me?"

"She'd welcome my help, is all."

"Isn't that George's dog with her?"

"Tell me, what's become of Joseph?"

"How I wish I knew! The day before the outbreak, my darling started for St. Paul, to buy a new blade for the sawmill. He didn't want to leave— Benjy was sick—but Lord help me, I told him to go. I'll never forget the last thing he said to me: 'Don't be lonely, my love, and don't let the Indians carry you off.' For true, that's what my darling said, in jest. I don't think I've had a good hour's sleep since."

"I'll pray for him. And for you and your boys." She passes Jannette a wriggling Benjy.

"And I'll pray for you, Sarah, all alone in this godforsaken world…. You *do* know John's dead, don't you?"

"Why, no, I don't."

"Oh, but he is! A mixed-blood saw his body in your yard, his head was … cut off."

That one again; so many ghastly stories. And against them all, Little Paul's assurance of life. "If John's dead, as you say he is"—Jannette's callousness has put her in a mood to vex—"I might as well pass the remainder of my days among the Sioux. Here's as good as anywhere."

"You can't mean it! This is the Devil's Hell! God forgive me, but if not for my boys, I might end my ordeal this instant."

Sarah adjusts the binding on one of her feet. "I've lived through worse, among my own kind."

Jannette frowns. "Your whipping, you mean? But you brought that humiliation on yourself. You admitted as much."

"No, that's not it." She has said too much. She struggles to get up. "I'm sorry, Jannette, but you'll have to excuse me, I've a tipi cloth to sew."

✾ 10 ✾

EAGLE HEAD PASSES his lit pipe to Dowaŋ S'a. "Tell us what you saw."

Ćaske's cousin, *The Singer,* is regal in appearance. His chiseled features are prepossessing, his skin smooth and exceptionally deep in tone. A turban of red, turquoise and yellow cloth crowns his head. His neck is heavy with beads; his upper arms, graced by red quilled bands with feather tassels.

"A hundred Sissetons, Wahpetons and mixed-bloods came riding in. They were painted and armed for battle, yelling, firing into the air." Dowaŋ S'a speaks like a troubadour sings, his voice liquid and full, easy to hear without being loud. "They galloped straight at the headquarters of our soldiers' lodge. They fanned out to surround it, singing a warrior's song. They were not afraid to die. After they dismounted, they stood alert, holding their horses by their bridle bits, facing our soldiers down."

Sarah has heard some talk of Upper Sioux tribesmen organizing in defiance of Little Crow. The camp of this "peace party" is said to be located near Riggs's mission, across the creek, a mile or so to the west.

"The representative of their soldiers' lodge stepped forward and declared their intention to keep apart from us. He was a Wahpeton, called Maza Kute Mani. He spoke straight." Dowaŋ S'a closes his eyes as he smokes, as though drafting his thoughts through the stem of the pipe. "The Wahpeton said, 'You think you are brave because you have killed a lot of defenseless women and children. But you are cowards. You think to get me and my people to help you in this work? I tell you no. Never.'"

Dowaŋ S'a's memory is like ink on paper. "'These prisoners you have taken,' the Wahpeton said, 'they will have to be given back to their people. The sooner you do it, the better it will be for you.'"

"It is so," Eagle Head says, with approval.

Dowaŋ S'a himself is inscrutable. His face is painted with the black stripe of the soldiers' lodge, but like Ćaske, his heart might not be in the fighting. "The Wahpeton said, 'In attacking the whites you are doing battle against thunder and lightning. You will all be killed off. You might as well try to bail out the River of the Falls as to whip them.'"

"It is so!"

"'You have threatened to kill me. So be it. I am not a woman. I am not afraid, nor am I alone—'"

Mother Friend barges into the tipi. "One of our men," she tells Uŋćiśi, "has killed a white boy."

"Who has done this?"

"Short Bull. He had too much drink. He told the white boy to swallow a live crayfish. When the boy refused, Short Bull pulled his tomahawk."

"It is wicked to kill without cause." Eagle Head slumps against his backrest. "This morning, a rival soldiers' lodge rode straight into our camp. Now a captive has been murdered. Our soldiers are not keeping good order. There is too much chaos, too much rage, too much fire water. I fear a rampage." He nods in Sarah's direction. "I think my grandson's wife should leave us until there is calm."

Visions of the ravine and the haystack cloud Sarah's mind. "No, *please*. I stay inside lodge."

"I agree with My Grandfather," Dowaŋ S'a says. "It is not safe for you here."

"I wait for Ćaske! I wait for my son!"

"My cousin has been gone for a day and a night. No one can say where he is, or when he will return."

Uŋćiśi helps Sarah to her feet and binds Nellie to her back. "We have a relative. You must go to him. He is a farmer, here in the valley. He is called Pasu Kiyuksa."

"And Opa! I know them!"

"Do not go to their farm," Dowaŋ S'a says. "They are in the camp across the creek."

Sarah looks at him in surprise. "The camp of the Wahpeton?"

"I saw them there last night. Our soldiers went over to compel the peace party to join us. We did not succeed."

"My Daughter must not talk more." Uŋćiśi guides her toward the tipi door. "Dowaŋ S'a will escort you to the edge of this camp. On the way he will tell you how to find Pasu Kiyuksa."

She kisses the kuŋśi's cheek. "Tell Ćaske come."

SHE CHARGES THROUGH THE COVER OF A CORNFIELD WITH NELLIE ON HER back, keeping low among the stalks. She expects every moment to be overtaken by one of Little Crow's men. Dusk can't fall fast enough.

This might be Hell, after all. Nowhere to feel safe. Nowhere to belong, truly, for more than a little space....

The rhythm of her running has lulled Nellie to sleep. She deadens herself to the pain in her feet. At least her trek will end among friends. She repeats Dowaŋ S'a's directions to herself, over and over, afraid of getting lost.

An evening mist is changing over to drizzle when she shambles into the peace party camp. She wanders like a trespasser among the few dozen tipis, all glowing from fires within. Each step is agony.

A lodge just ahead is painted with buffalo hunters. Outside the door is Pasu Kiyuksa, curled up in a blanket with his gun.

"Good Big Woman!"

Hearing her name, she falls on her knees. Pasu Kiyuksa runs to her, grasps her by the arms and hefts her up. And here is Opa, picking up Nellie....

INSIDE THE TIPI SARAH SINKS ONTO A PILE OF BUFFALO ROBES. PASU KIYUKSA shoos away a dog wanting to nose and sniff. He prepares an ointment for the sores on her feet, singing a low song as he works. Opa, meanwhile, sets about cooking some jerked beef with dried vegetables. Both of them are in full Indian dress. On their farm, Sarah only saw them dressed white.

She washes in a basin of water and swallows down some coffee. In Dakota she tells about her flight from Little Crow's camp.

"It is good that Good Big Woman has come," Opa says, in her quavery voice. "The old man and I will do what we can to protect you."

Pasu Kiyuksa crouches with his salve by her feet. "This will hurt, but the pain will leave you."

"Why you camp here?" Sarah asks.

"Our house was burned. Our fields were laid waste."

"Taoyate Duta?" Through clenched teeth.

"No, but men in league with him. Some were from our own band. Our young men have angry hearts. Our change of dress was not enough to appease them."

"Resist Taoyate Duta is dangerous."

"He could smack us like a flea," Opa says, with an elderly swat on her arm.

Pasu Kiyuksa finishes with his salve. "We cannot win this war. The Lower tribes should not have started it. They are wrong to drag us into it."

"Eagle Head say fight no good."

"And Ćaske?" he asks, massaging her tight calves with oil.

"He fight. No happy."

"These are hard days for our people." He smiles faintly. "Good Big Woman's tongue is not so fat as it once was."

Knowing the couple must be wondering how she'd wound up with Ćaske, she tells them enough of the story to satisfy.

"But Ćaske did not bring Good Big Woman here," Opa says, her question implied.

"He search for James. Wahpeton ride James on mule from Redwood."

"What is this Wahpeton's name?"

"English name is Little Paul."

Opa looks at Pasu Kiyuksa. She chuckles. "Wakaŋtaŋka has led Good Big Woman to our tipi. Tonight, Good Big Woman will rest. Tomorrow, we will retrieve your boy. The Wahpeton you seek is one of us. You call him Little Paul. We call him Maza Kute Mani." *He Who Shoots As He Walks.*

THE NEXT MORNING A BUGGY WITH A WHITE CLOTH OF TRUCE TIED TO THE dash wheels up outside Opa's tipi. Ćaske is driving, with Dowaŋ S'a alongside. Squeezed between them is James.

"Oh, thank Heaven!" Sarah cries, limping toward them. "Oh, my boy! My boy!"

James folds his little arms across his chest. "I want to go back to Little Paul's!" Head to toe, he's decked out in the fancy dress of an Indian: beaded headband and armbands, a hide vest, buckskin leggings with fringe, a breechcloth, beaded moccasins; all, she supposes, the handiwork of Little Paul's wife.

"Aren't you glad to see me?" she asks. "Mama's been so worried!" She reaches to help him down from the rig. He tries to push her back.

"I'm no baby!"

"Of course you're not. I'll bet you can jump down from the rig all by your big-boy self."

"Watch me!" He leaps with a whoop.

"That's my little man!" She snatches his hand and runs him headlong into waist-high prairie grass. She grabs up fistfuls of wildflowers to shower over his head. She swings him round in a circle until they swoon in a happy heap.

"Again, Mama!" James squeals, trying to tug her back up.

For a happy space, she forgets the war.

Ćaske tells her that he got to Eagle Head's last night as the drizzle became a soaking rain. His search in the vicinity of Riggs's mission had turned up no evidence of Hapstiŋna or Little Paul. But upon hearing Dowaŋ S'a's account of the peace party demonstration outside the soldiers' lodge, he pressed for more details about the Wahpeton—what he looked like, what he sounded like, how he carried himself. This Maza Kute Mani, he began to suspect, was the very man he'd been hunting for.

This morning, shortly after sunrise, he and Dowaŋ S'a borrowed a buggy and drove across the creek to locate Maza Kute Mani—Little Paul— in the peace party camp. "He refused to relinquish the boy unless we agreed to let him meet with you."

"Why?"

"He will tell us when he comes."

Across the fire in the place of honor, Little Paul wraps his arms around his knees. Sarah has endured the Wahpeton's overtures for at least an hour, attended by Ćaske, Dowaŋ S'a, Pasu Kiyuksa and Opa.

"I no want you for husband!" she says again, in Dakota.

"But if Good Big Woman comes with me," Little Paul coaxes, "I will protect her, just as I protected her son. Is he not finely dressed?"

"You have wife."

"My first wife will do all the work. Good Big Woman will have her own tipi. I will paint it and make you proud. You will sit in the honored place. While my first wife collects wood, you will make moccasins. Your life will be easy."

"You go church. You know 'One man, one wife.'" Even as she says the words, she feels the flush in her cheeks. She hasn't exactly lived her life according to "one woman, one husband."

Little Paul rubs his chin. "Will Good Big Woman stay with Ćaske?"

"Yes. He has good heart."

"You will stay *as his wife?*"

She chews on her lip. "He takes me to my people. One day."

Between them, the bed of the fire is dancing, red-hot.

"I am the better man to deliver you," Little Paul says. "It is so."

She raises her eyes to look at the stout Wahpeton, straight on. "Listen to me carefully, Little Paul." She has reverted to English, for eloquence. Their chaperones won't understand every word, but he will. "Here in the presence of these witnesses whom I am glad to call my kin, I tell you this: I am obliged to you for opposing the war and trying to shield captives like myself. I am grateful to you and your wife for taking good care of James. But if you believed such actions would entitle you to possess me, you were mistaken. *I will never be yours.*"

She repeats her final sentence in Dakota. Little Paul doesn't move. Opa taps out the ashes from the pipe on the altar of the tipi and replaces the pipe in its beaded bag. When Little Paul still doesn't leave, she is forced to dismiss him.

"The heart of Maza Kute Mani is sick with love," she says, once he is gone.

"Why?" Sarah says, "I no want him. He no listen."

"A man's heart has reasons. If you would be free of him, you must return to Taoyate Duta's camp with Ćaske."

"It is so," Pasu Kiyuksa says. "And there is another reason Good Big Woman should leave. The day is coming when Taoyate Duta and his soldiers' lodge will lose patience with those of us who oppose this war. On that day, Good Big Woman will be safer with Ćaske than here with us."

Dowaŋ S'a, wearing the black soldier's stripe on his face, doesn't dispute this. Ćaske keeps his own counsel. Baffling, these silences of his, concerning her.

ॐ I I ॐ

THE FRONT of the council lodge has been unlaced and the two ends of the tipi cloth unfurled like wings. A second tipi cloth has been hoisted alongside on a skeleton of poles. The two cloths overlap to form an enormous crescent. Loose edges of hide ripple on gusts of breeze.

In the shadow of this backdrop, a thousand or more people have mustered to hear the deliberations between the leaders of the peace party and the Lower Sioux. Sarah stands shoulder to shoulder with Jannette in a thicket of white captives toward the back of the crowd. From here, faces of the speakers are blurs of paint and feathers. She isn't always certain who is talking, but the orators are so vigorous and the onlookers so hushed, she can hear quite well.

"We feel as though the world is coming to an end," says an Indian from the peace party. "Deliver your white prisoners to us. We will give them up to the Big Knives and negotiate for peace."

"Not while one of us still lives to shoot a gun!" a Mdewakantonwan cries.

"If you do not give up the captives, our soldiers' lodge will seize them from you!" A bold boast, Sarah thinks, considering the few lodges in the peace party camp.

One of Little Crow's soldiers rises to speak. "I am in favor of continuing the war and keeping the captives in our custody. The Americans will break any agreement we make to give them up. Ever since we first negotiated with the whites, their agents and traders have robbed and cheated us.

Some of our people have been shot, some hanged. Others have been placed upon floating ice and drowned. Many have starved in their prisons." This warrior has a powerful delivery. His eloquence could shore up the will of any Lower Sioux who might be wavering. "It wasn't the intention of the Lower bands to kill whites. But when four of our hunters shot those settlers in the Big Woods, our young men became excited and pushed for war. Our elders could not stop them; the treaties have destroyed their influence. We may regret what has happened, but the matter has gone too far to be remedied. Now we will have to die like Dakotas. Let us kill as many whites as possible, and let the prisoners die with us!"

Śakpe Daŋ agrees. "My arm is lame from killing white people, but I will not quit. I am not afraid to die. When I go into the spirit world, I will look Wakaŋtaŋka in the face, and I will tell him what the whites did to my people before we went to war. He will do right by us. I am not afraid!"

Jannette gropes for Sarah's hand. "What are they saying?"

She presses her finger to her lips.

Little Paul, wrapped in a plaid trade blanket, asks leave to speak. "In times past I have served as the spokesman of my band. Those times are gone, but I want to tell you today what is in my heart. I want to ask, why did you Lower Dakotas not council with us before you decided to make war?" He waits in an expansive silence. "I will tell you why. You knew if you did, we would not allow you to involve our young men! By dragging them into your fight without first consulting us, you have done us a great injustice.

"I am going to tell you something you will not like. Because you have involved our people in this trouble without calling a council and obtaining our consent, I shall use every means to get them out of it, without any regard for you who are our leaders. I am opposed to you continuing this war and committing further outrages. I warn you not to do it. I myself will not participate."

Sarah can't believe this lionheart is the lovesick dog who was after her for his wife.

"I have heard a great many of you say that you are brave men," Little Paul goes on. "This is a lie. Persons who cut the throats of women and children are cowards. You have also said you will easily whip the Big Knives, because they are weak and no match for you. But you will see. The Big Knives will not kill women and children, as you have done, but they will battle hard against you who have guns in your hands. They have much lead, powder, guns and provisions. No one who fights them ever becomes richer for it or remains two days in one place. They are always hungry and on the run."

Jannette squeezes her hand until it hurts. "Tell me what he's saying! I can't make it out!"

"Shhh!"

"It makes my heart hot," Little Paul says, "walking among the lodges of your camp, seeing the suffering of the captives. It is not our way as Dakotas to starve prisoners, and threaten them, and slay them in our villages. We should treat them as kin. I am ashamed.... And since when do we hold captive our own mixed-blood relatives? Our own people's children! There must be three times as many mixed-blood captives as whites in your camp. Let them go! Give them back their horses and wagons!"

"The mixed-bloods are not Dakotas! They are white! We should have killed them at the start!" This is Tate Mi Ma, the old camp crier. She would recognize his bull-frog voice anywhere. "The half-breeds, too, are against us! When we attacked the soldiers' lodge of the Big Knives, many half-breeds were inside, shooting at us!"

An Indian raises his gun above his head. "If we Upper tribes do not agree to join the fight, will you take us captive, too? How many of your Dakota relatives will you take hostage before you end this? How many of us will you try to kill? Mixed-blood, half-breed, Sisseton, Wahpeton, Mdewakantonwan, Wahpekute—we are all Dakotas!"

Bickering erupts, unlike anything Sarah has ever observed in an Indian council. The councils she witnessed on Agency Hill might have been tense, but they were dignified affairs, governed by strict etiquette.

An elder commands quiet. The feuding dies down. "Look at us, ready to rain blows on each other! My relatives, the Americans have done us grievous wrongs. But these choices we are making now, to go against the ways of true Dakotas, we are making ourselves. We are harming our own people. The whites believe their way is the only way. Let us be better than them!"

Little Paul clambers atop a barrel. "I say to you again: Give me the captives, and I will convey them down to the American fort. Perhaps the Big Knives will shoot me—I will risk it. I am not afraid of death. Look at me as fiercely as you please, but I shall ask you once, twice, ten times to deliver these women and children to their friends. Then, if you want to go on fighting the Big Knives, fight! Or, better yet, *stop* fighting! It is folly. You cannot win!" A dramatic pause. The cloths of the council tipi flap and beat in the breeze. "You have promised to kill whoever talks like I am talking now. I tell you, if anyone speaks what is wise and good, listen to him! That is all I have to say." He steps down and seats himself on the ground, to faint murmurs of approval.

Another Indian stands to speak. "I did not sanction attacks on white women and children. I gave orders to kill only traders and agents of the American government."

Sarah bows her head. This is the voice of Little Crow. She has no wish to look upon him. That Sunday in Hinman's church, right before the war, he was almost a gentleman. "Madam," he called her, shaking her hand. What did she ever do to offend him? Why does he suspend her on a string of threats above the bottomless pit?

"But now," he is saying, "we must settle the question of whether we will continue to fight or deliver up the prisoners and run. I say it is impossible to make peace, even if we desire it. Did we ever do the most trifling thing and the Americans not hang us? We have been killing white people by the hundreds! If the Big Knives get us in their power, they will hang us all like dogs. As for me, I will kill as many of them as I can and fight them until I die!"

She pictures Little Crow in her mind's eye—so broad-shouldered and tall, so spare of flesh, leering at her like a hawk, a circle of red painted around his left eye. And yet … wouldn't a chief do anything to save his people, just as she would, to save her children?

"Every band of Indians from Redwood to Big Stone Lake has had some of its members embroiled in the war," Little Crow says. "The Big Knives will punish us all. A man is a fool and a coward who thinks otherwise. Who will desert his nation at such a time? Do not disgrace yourselves by surrendering! Die, if die you must, with weapons in your hands, like brave Dakotas!"

AFTER THE COUNCIL SARAH AND UŊĆIŚI WORK WITH EAGLE HEAD'S WOMAN to fill kettles with beef and potatoes. They pound coffee beans. They begin to fry bread. When darkness falls, a party of men assembles outside Eagle Head's small tipi, each bringing his wooden bowl. They lounge with Ćaske in the yard, eating, smoking, telling stories, gambling at cards. Eventually they start singing, thrumming rhythms on their chests. Soon they are up and dancing to Dowaŋ S'a's hand drum.

After the last man wears himself out and goes home, Sarah and Ćaske lie down together on a bed of buffalo robes.

"The Big Knives will march up soon," Ćaske whispers, in the light of a shrouded half-moon. "My Wife will be released with the rest of the captives."

"My Husband heard Taoyate Duta speak in the council. He has no intention of giving us up!"

"If you are not released before the rivers begin to freeze, I will find a canoe along the river and take you downstream to your people. But it is better to wait. If I try to take you myself and we are discovered, Taoyate Duta will kill our entire family."

Her ears are throbbing with her own heartbeat. Perhaps she should have tried to escape, long ago, without Ćaske's help. But how could a woman with two babies have made her way through the wilderness?

"I am not a wise man," he says, "but I think My Wife should go back to Pasu Kiyuksa and Opa until the Big Knives come. The peace party camp is growing. Since today's council, even Wakiŋya Tawa has moved his lodge. You will be safer there."

Wakiŋya Tawa had once been Little Crow's head soldier. But while fighting at Redwood, the first day of the outbreak, he prevented some warriors from finishing off his friend George Spencer. He gave the trader sanctuary in his lodge, devoted himself to nursing his wounds and ultimately chose to abandon the war effort. His actions have imperiled him and his family.

She heard the entire tale from Spencer himself, visiting him in Wakiŋya Tawa's tipi early in captivity. "The same light of Providence shined on me as on you," Spencer told her in a thready voice, his mouth a pale slit in his heavy beard. "We were both saved by a man named Ćaske." That day, with bullets in his arm, chest and belly, he seemed ready for the angels. Bending low to hear his words, she thought she smelled death on his breath. Yet despite the severity of his injuries and persistent threats on his life, he's still alive. The defection of his protector to the peace party doesn't surprise her.

She twists on her side to face Ćaske. "Does My Husband ever think of joining the peace party?"

His knuckles trace the air above her cheekbone, without touching. He has never touched her as a man touches a woman. He has never asked her for her body.

"That," he says, as the moon slides behind the clouds, "is not a question My White Wife should ask."

C̣ASKE READIES HIMSELF TO LEAVE WITH A RAIDING PARTY FOR THE BIG WOODS. "We need more cattle for the camp," he tells her. "We need more flour." As he paints Belle with medicine symbols, Sarah knows not to ask when he will return. He rides away on the words of a warrior song.

With so many war parties moving out, the camp empties of all but a modest guard. The old people smoke, the children play, and the wiŋyaŋ, like women everywhere who are worried about their menfolk, busy their hands. Sarah sits with Uŋċiśi in the yard of Eagle Head's lodge, hour after hour, working her needle hard through the white canvas of a new tipi cover, double-stitching the flat seams for strength.

Whose cattle, whose flour?

Her fingers ache at the sewing. Her knuckles stiffen. She tries not to think. Not thinking is a dark art, but thinking can be darker.

THE DAYS MELD TOGETHER, nothing much to distinguish one from the next. Sarah absorbs the comfort of routine until that routine becomes another life, another sort of belonging.

Once they finish the tipi cloth, Uŋćiśi blesses the ground where their lodge will stand, adjacent to Eagle Head's. "Come," she says to Sarah. "It is time for My Daughter to raise her home."

After a half-hour's labor, their tipi stands fresh and white, lightly patterned by the stripes of its seams. The new cloth hasn't a single wrinkle. As Uŋćiśi shows her how to rig the smoke ears and door covering, Sarah admires the tipi's simple yet sophisticated architecture of cloth, poles, ropes, pins and flaps.

Inside the lodge they dig a shallow pit for the fire and prepare a patch of earth for the family altar. Outside, they lay large stones along the tipi's skirt to secure it to the ground, then cut in a trench to channel rainwater away.

Uŋćiśi spreads an offering of tobacco around the new tipi. She purifies the lodge with cedar smoke, blessing every part. "She is our grandmother. She shelters us in the face of the wind." Blackbirds perch on the tips of the poles.

"We will need to sew a lining," Uŋćiśi tells Sarah, as they arrange the family's belongings inside. "It will help keep the lodge warm and dry. And at night it will prevent our enemies from seeing our shadows on the wall."

With the new tipi up, Sarah helps the women in neighboring lodges melt bar lead and ladle it into bullet molds. She cuts hide for new moccasins to supply the warriors, who can't wear old ones into battle. She pounds jerky into a fine powder and mixes it with fat and berries to make pemmican, food for fighting. She pounds, pounds, pounds some more.

The women her age call her Ićepaŋśi—*Cousin,* or something like it. So many Dakota words can't be reduced to dictionary definitions. She's living her way into their meanings, one day at a time.

SHE'S NURSING NELLIE IN THE NEW TIPI WHEN SHE HEARS A VOLLEY OF gunfire, signaling a war party's return. Warriors' horses race full-tilt around the edge of camp. The earth beneath her trembles with hoofbeats.

Minutes after the ground goes still, she sees on the wall of the lodge the distorted shadow-play of an Indian dismounting in the yard and Uŋćiśi giving him welcome. *Ćaske.* A tingling of pleasure blooms low in her belly, spreads soft and warm between her thighs; a sensation she hasn't felt in years.

Ćaske dips through the tipi door. She blushes. From modesty she shifts away in her willow backrest. Nellie pulls off her breast with a whimper.

"My heart is glad to see My Wife."

"My heart is glad to see My Husband."

"The new lodge is well made. It will be a good home."

Home. A place you're faithful to. "I am happy it pleases you."

"Mother say Nellie sick," he says, switching to English. His use of her language is improving, like her Dakota. They're growing in toward each other like the roots of two thirsty trees.

"She has a fever. She needs a nap."

He squats beside her. "Wife sing, Nellie eat, Nellie go sleep."

"I should sing her a lullaby, you mean? A cradle song?"

"Lull-a-by," he tries, seating himself on the carpet of buffalo hides.

She hums, to start, then floats into a lullaby by Tennyson she learned from *Godey's.*

Sweet and low, sweet and low
    Wind of the western sea;
Low, low, breathe and blow,
    Wind of the western sea!
Over the rolling waters go,
Come from the dying moon, and blow,

Blow him again to me,
While my little one, while my pretty one sleeps....

By the end, Nellie has latched onto her breast again and locked a cluster of fingers on her chin.

Ćaske draws up his knees. "My Wife will tell me what the song means?" In Dakota, now.

"That is too difficult," she continues in English. "There are too many things your language has no words for."

"If a thing exists, it has a name," he says. "It can be spoken." His smile, she notices for the first time, is a tad crooked, to the right.

She sighs. *Where to begin?* "The sea is a great body of water that stretches around the world."

"It is so. We call it the Big Water."

Mniwaŋća. Her turn to try a word. "But how do your people know about the sea? You live so far from its shores!"

"We travel, we trade, we visit other tribes. I have not journeyed to the end of the land, but I have been there in stories. It is said that many different peoples live there who do not understand one another." He winds a finger in one of Nellie's curls. "How does My Wife know the Big Water?"

"I was born beside it."

"My Wife was born far, far away." He lets the curl slip free. "It is said that the Big Water is alive. It is said that it comes and goes like the sun. It is said that it tastes like blood."

The salt, he must mean. "Yes, something like blood."

"The home place of My Wife, beside the Big Water, is where the sun rises, or where the sun sleeps?"

"Where it rises. We call that place Rhode Island."

He rises to collect a comb and the tin of tallow, then reseats himself at her right. "I sometimes wonder why My Wife left her homeland and came to mine." He loosens one of her plaits, a thing that women do for each other. She thrills at the touch of his hands in her hair. "It is a long way to come," he says, applying the tallow.

She removes Nellie's fingers from her chin and folds her little arm down. The child's eyelids are drooping; her rosebud lips, still puckered but no longer sucking. "The Big Water ... hurt me. Long ago. I was seven winters." She covers her breast, scarcely breathing.

His combing is tender. "My Wife was hurt by a sea monster?"

So they have their monsters, too. "The sea stole something precious from me. I couldn't get it back. After that, nothing was ever right again."

"Your heart was very sad."

"Yes."

"So ... you left the Big Water to punish it."

She stares at him, hard.

He begins to rebraid. "But the Big Water does not die. It cannot be slain."

"No."

"So the one who seeks revenge is the one who is punished." He unsheathes his dagger. "I am not a wise man. But I think My Wife will go on being punished until she puts away the knife." He lays his dagger beside her.

He ties off the end of her new braid. Attaches to her right earlobe a loop of tiny shells. Moves around to her left, to attend to her other plait.

She picks up his dagger. Its handle is still warm from the sheath against his body; its triangular blade, sharp as guilt.

And you, My Husband, when will you put down the knife?

Ćaske and Dowaŋ S'a sneak her out of Little Crow's camp to hike to the Williamson mission station. The men carry James on their shoulders by turns. Bringing him along is a risk, but she can't bear to be separated.

She creeps all alone through the Williamson house. Room after room is heaped with debris. Books and clothes, ripped apart. Tables and bedsteads, upended and smashed. Upholstered chairs, knifed through. Feathers from pillows and ticks, strewn about. China, in shards. Flour and sugar, spilled on the floor. The good Doctor's medicine bottles, all broken or emptied....

Her heart sinks. It's medicine for Nellie that she walked all this way for, to nurse the nagging fever Uŋćiśi's remedies can't break.

The mission bell is clanging. She picks her way through the mess to peer out the front doorway, the plank door shot off its hinges. Sioux boys with torches are ransacking the white frame church.

She sags down on the doorstep and lays her forehead on her bent knees. She came here not only for medicine, she realizes now, but for consolation. Instead, she has found loss, and more loss. Nothing can be salvaged.

At least there are no bodies. No evidence at all of bloodshed. Perhaps the Indians allowed Thomas and Margaret to escape, out of respect for the kindness in their wasiću hearts.

"Mama, look what *I* found!"

She dries her tears on the back of her hands and puts on some cheer. "What have you got, little man?"

James holds up a leather-bound Old Testament, torn and dirty. Then, from behind his back, a ripe tomato, bigger than a fist. "There's more in Auntie Margaret's garden," he says, trying to haul her up. "Come see!"

He drags her by the arm toward Ćaske, bent over in the vegetable patch, scavenging. When she glances back over her shoulder, the Williamson church is an orange silhouette of fire.

❧ 13 ❧

AT DAWN THE NEXT DAY, the lodge of Little Crow is flapping in the wind, a sign of its dismantling. Within minutes Uŋćiśi and Sarah have their own tipi flat on the ground. They fold the cloth, bundle the poles, pack the household and load the travois behind Belle.

The family falls into a caravan that must be miles long. Draped over Sarah's shoulders are two bags of shot, each weighing twenty-five pounds. She trudges along near Nellie, jouncing on the travois, her face shaded from the sun. Still listless with fever, the child is sucking her thumb toward sleep.

As they desert the valley of the Yellow Medicine, moving north, Sarah stops to look back at the blue-gray smoke hovering over the Agency. That smoke is the last of her house, her beautiful things, her old life. Little Crow's soldiers have torched the remaining structures on the Hill lest the Isaŋ Taŋka, in giving chase, try to occupy them as a fort. Every brick building will be reduced to a shell.

She turns again into the wind. The pace is fast. Little Crow's soldiers are on edge, despite their recent victory at a place called Wakpadaŋ Taŋpa, *Birch Creek*. They claim to have inflicted great losses there on a party of Isaŋ Taŋka sent to bury dead wasiću in the countryside. Long Trader and his army, no doubt stinging from that loss, are reportedly in pursuit, advancing from Redwood toward the Upper Agency. Rather than wait around to greet them, the Sioux are retreating toward the Red River, gateway to Uŋći Makoće, *Grandmother's Land*.

She must brace herself. There's no prospect anymore of deliverance. Before long, she will be too far north for Ćaske to canoe her and her babies downriver to Fort Ridgley; too far north for Sibley's army to catch up before they cross into Canada.

"Might as well pass the remainder of my days among the Sioux," she'd told Jannette. "Here's as good as anywhere." Crazy words, as though a demon had possessed her mouth.

Yet her feet have toughened to leather. Her skin is tanned dark. A couple nights ago, she dreamed a fragment of a dream in Dakota. Truth is, she is turning into a white wiŋyaŋ, and she'd best make her peace with it. Her future, and James and Nellie's, lies with Ćaske and Uŋćiśi on the exposed plains of Canada. In another month they will all be dragging across a wasteland of swirling snow.

Her eyes rest again on Nellie, so sickly. On James, riding Belle, his blonde hair bleached white by the sun. *How will you ever survive?*

AHEAD IN THE CROWD, JANNETTE DECAMP IS LAGGING BEHIND THE PACE WITH her boys. She trips again and again in the prairie grass. Sarah quickens her stride to catch up.

"Here, let me." She frees Benjy from Jannette's arms and sets him on her hip. Light as he is, she won't be able to carry him long, laden with her bags of shot.

"Oh Sarah, have you heard? Little Crow's planning to spare any captives with Indian blood—even one savage drop—but the rest of us, we're traipsing to our graves! My Welly, he says to me, 'Mama, will they kill us with knives?'—he has a horror of knives, Welly does. Sometimes I think I should put my boys to sleep myself—"

"Hush now! The boys can hear you."

"Don't tell me you've never thought about it."

"I'm grateful we're alive. Besides, if what you're saying about Indian blood is true, my babies and I are perfectly safe."

Jannette stops mid-stride. Sarah hikes Benjy higher on her hip and walks right on, astonished at the machinations of her own mind. She'd interrupted Jannette merely to stanch the woman's gush of talk, but some-how, with her last words, she started to spin a lie. That demon again, possessing her mouth.

Jannette scurries back up, sputtering. "Sarah ... whatever did you mean ... 'perfectly safe?'"

If she delivers her next words with care, she can turn her fib to advantage. "My grandfather, back in Rhode Island … he married a Narragansett full-blood."

"I don't believe you! You've never said a word—"

"—about my Indian blood? Of course I haven't! What white woman would?" She embellishes her fable. "My mother took after her mother's people. She was often assumed to be Spanish, or Italian. Nellie favors her strongly…. Why, you yourself have remarked on how very dark she is!"

Jannette's face sharpens. "I never suspected…."

"Please, Jannette, don't tell a soul. I don't want anyone else to know unless it becomes necessary."

"Not a whisper. I swear to Heaven!"

Jannette will no doubt squeal to the first fellow captive with ears. Her lie of "Indian blood" will soon be common knowledge, and perhaps a shield to her and her babies.

"Sarah, I have to ask … did you ever tell John?"

"Had you been in my place, would you have told your *darling* Joseph, and spoiled your chance for happiness?"

"But John had a right to the truth!"

"I'm white in every way that matters."

Jannette steps in front of her. She wrests Benjy away. "They were right about you, back in Shakopee! And they're right, what they say about you here! I'm done defending you. Let's go, boys!" She storms ahead with Welly and little Joe. "Heaven help you, Sarah Wakefield! You and your Indian *lover!*"

THE SIOUX TRAIN HAS ADVANCED AROUND SIXTEEN MILES WHEN THE Wahpeton chief Maza Ša and a large party of warriors speed out from their village on horseback, whooping and yelling, firing their guns. They demand that the caravan halt.

Sarah recognizes the spindly chief. Not long after her beating, she'd sagged in a chair at her bedroom window, straining to hear his words during a council on the green. "We may die from hunger," he told Thomas that day, "but if we do, we will leave our bones on the ground, that our Great Father may see where his Dakota children perished."

Now Maza Ša tells Little Crow to go home. "You commenced this outbreak, and you must do the fighting in your territory. We do not want you here, exciting our young men and getting us into trouble. We will not allow you to pass."

A serious row ensues, with warriors from both sides shooting into the air. Before they come to blows, a temporary agreement is reached: The train will go no further, but neither will it turn around.

Little Crow's soldiers order the people to pitch camp, right on the spot. The site is level enough but farther than usual from sources of water and wood. Without benefit of hills, it's fully exposed to the wind. Most of the grass has already been grazed. The place is hardly ideal. Yet in no time tipis extend to the horizon in all directions. As Sarah lugs pails of water from the distant river, she can distinguish no clear boundaries between Maza Śa's village, Little Crow's camp and the lodges of the peace party, whose members have been compelled north. She learns to navigate the maze of tipis by sighting flags planted for that purpose.

TONIGHT'S DANCING IS THE FIERCEST SINCE THE FIRST WEEK OF HER CAPTIVITY. For several hours, painted warriors have been spinning and leaping and spearing the air, proving the strength and agility the drums seem meant to test.

A new song, now, with women in the lead. Sarah sinks into the gloom, away from the torches. A tiny kuŋśi with silver hair, stepping in time, carries before the people a tall red staff ornamented with eagle feathers, strings of beads, ribbons, trinkets. From the top of the staff dangles the scalp of a wasiću, painted vermillion, stretched upon a hoop. Sarah shuts away every thought of the white man who lost his hair.

Women in black face-paint and blanket shawls trail behind the kuŋśi in single file, their feet talking the beat of the drum. Slowly they form concentric circles around the grandmother, facing her staff, shoulder to shoulder, erect and dignified. They lift their heels and slide to the right in rhythm with the drum strokes. The circles turn by inches. Despite the hideousness of the scalp, the dance isn't fiendish or violent. The women exude a sense of power that lures Sarah back toward the front of the crowd. Among the dancers she locates Mother Friend and the women who call her Cousin. Uŋćiśi is stepping with new energy. The hump on her back seems less pronounced.

Perhaps a scalp dance isn't a hellish glorification of slaughter, as she previously believed. These women are the life-givers, the mothers and grandmothers of the people; so wakaŋ they can't wash their feet in a pail. Honor is owed them. Honor is owed their men, who have been fighting to protect them, their children, the entire nation. And honor is owed their enemies, around whose scalps they dance.

Near the kuŋśi in the center of the circle, a bonfire seethes. Torches flare. Gunshots crack. The drum pounds. Rattles shake.

So many times during the war she has watched the women dance this dance, her blood running ice cold. But tonight some of their blood is in her. She arranges her shawl over her head and plunges into line beside Uŋćiśi. After one steady pass around the circle, she has learned their basic step. She relaxes into it. She doesn't look at the kuŋśi with the swaying red staff. She doesn't look up at the scalp. She doesn't look for Ćaske amidst the men who are joining the dance, all feathers and horns and bustles, their bare feet tattooing the earth. Like a good wiŋyaŋ she keeps her eyes on the ground, her spine straight as a tipi pole.

The hypnotic cadence intensifies. The land breathes through her feet. The drummers' song is defiant. Their words repeat like a chant: "This I have killed, and I lift up my voice...." At intervals the women ululate in response to the singers, some raising weapons supplied them by the men. She joins their tremolo, throwing her voice high and shrill, pouring out her heart to the sky.

AT LAST, EXHAUSTED AND FULL OF ACHE, SHE SLIPS OUT OF LINE. SHE EASES into the darkness beyond the circle of the dance. Darkness deeper than shadows. Darkness deep as a womb.

That's where she and Ćaske find each other, out in the prairie grass beyond the light. He wraps her in his blanket and steers her away, toward a near stretch of the river. No wind against them. No moon, no stars overhead. She doesn't ask herself what's happening; she understands and is unafraid. They stride in rhythm, buttressing each other as they stumble over the black land.

Trees loom. River sounds rise.

In a soft place where deer might have lain, they stop. He draws her down within the tipi of his blanket. They sit trembling, knee to knee. Water sings over rock. In the close air she breathes him in: the smoke of prayers and fires, sweat of the dance, the scent of desire.

Here are his fingertips on her temple, her cheek, her chin. Her neck. Her breast....

His hand falls away in invitation. She reaches for him. They fold in upon each other, molding themselves to flesh and earth. They taste the sea upon each other's skin until they're washed out to a place where self and other vanish.

ꙮ 14 ꙮ

STANDING Buffalo rides in to meet with Little Crow. Most of his warriors are said to be days away, out on the buffalo ranges, but he and his modest retinue are still a fearsome sight in their regalia. The council lodge has again been opened wide to the people. The Sissetons approach to the beat of two hand drums, singing a song that curdles the blood.

Women hustle their children into the tipis. The men stand armed and wary. Ćaske shields Sarah with his gun. "Stay behind me."

From almost the first day of her captivity, the Lower Indians' distrust of the Upper tribes has puzzled her. Perhaps they expected the Upper Sioux to retaliate for their fatal breach of protocol, which Little Paul had decried in council. Little Crow and his soldiers' lodge violated custom by initiating a full-scale war without first consulting all the tribes. They spurned the wisdom of the elders and circumvented the authority of the chiefs. Their rush to war has put all the eastern Sioux in the crosshairs of the Isaŋ Taŋka.

The Lower Indians moved north hoping to form an alliance with the Sissetons and Wahpetons. But Maza Śa has halted their advance with a show of force. The peace party, represented by Little Paul, is refusing to join the fight and demanding the surrender of all prisoners. And here is Standing Buffalo, summoned from the hunt, looking grim and formidable.

He is the help she has been waiting for. Once he dismounts, she slips past Ćaske to greet him. Had the chief not stayed his men, she might well have taken a bullet.

"Good Big Woman! It is you?"

"I greet Standing Buffalo with a good heart!"

Their handshake is firm.

"Good Big Woman is among the captives?"

"Yes, from the first day."

"And the doctor? The boy who likes ice cream?"

"Both my children are with me. I do not know my husband's fate."

"You are well treated?"

"We live with a man who has a good heart. But Taoyate Duta would have me dead."

Standing Buffalo gazes past her to the council tipi, where Little Crow is waiting. "My heart is sad to see your suffering. When I heard of this trouble, I did not believe it. I have come here to find out for myself who disturbed the peace with the Americans, and for what reason. I want nothing to do with the fighting."

"Can Standing Buffalo return me and my children to our people?"

"These are things I cannot do. You are not my captives."

"Then we will die."

"Good Big Woman must trust me. There are things I can do, and will do, to protect you. But at present you must stay under Taoyate Duta's control."

Her body is quaking. She wills her knees not to buckle.

"Good Big Woman must not show her fear. Trust what I tell you: *You will not be harmed.* I will see to this. My heart is saddened by the suffering of all the captives—so many are children of my own people! But I am not strong enough to gain your release here." He clasps her hand. "If Taoyate Duta presses further north, into my lands, I will come and take Good Big Woman under my wing. I promise you this, with a good heart."

He starts toward the council lodge, then pivots on his heel. "Who is the man who has cared for this white woman?" he says, in a full-throated voice.

Ćaske holds his gun aloft.

"My brother is a good man!" The overt statement of praise is perhaps freighted with warning for Little Crow.

Standing Buffalo is soon joined for the open-air council by Maza Śa and other chiefs and headmen of the Upper tribes. To a man, they refuse to lead their bands against the wasiću or to assist the war effort in any way. They threaten the confiscation of Lower Sioux horses and cattle if Little Crow marches any further into their territory. They advise him to free his captives and treat for peace with the Isaŋ Taŋka.

Little Crow and his soldiers are isolated now, pinched between the stubborn Upper Sioux to the north and Sibley's army, marching up from the south.

SARAH SLIDES UP HIGHER ON ĆASKE'S CHEST. A RARITY, THE TWO OF THEM having time alone, here in the tipi. His hair lies in limp strands streaked with gray. She twines some around one finger. It has grown almost long enough to braid.

"I needed to feed My Wife," he tells her. "I needed to feed My Mother.

"The agents favored cut-hairs. They gave them double payments, extra clothes, better food. So I cut my hair and tried to make them happy. I plowed a couple acres. I planted like a woman. I built fences. I even lived in a little log house. I could not breathe in that house. My Wife died in that house."

She traces the old scar over his forehead and back through his scalp, as though it might lead her to some recollection of his woman's face.

"My Wife died in The Moon of the Sore Eyes. All winter I had hunted to feed her, but there were no tracks. All winter I fished through the ice, but we were still hungry. And she was sick with a child that would not be born. It did not want to be in this world, so it stayed where it was. No charm, no medicine, could make it jump through the circle of fire. It went back to the spirit world, and my wife walked on.

"I did not tell the missionary Hinman. I did not want My Wife buried in his churchyard. It is not our way. I painted my face black. I sat with her until her soul was gone from her body. Then I bundled her up and laid her in a tree in a high place where she would not be found.

"When Hinman heard, he told me her death was an omen from the white God. He told me I must be baptized. He told me I must worship like a white man or die."

She touches the two pronounced nubs where his collarbones meet his breastbone. The architecture of his body is too plain for want of flesh. She knows every inch. Her hands have traveled around his ribs to the sharp, crusty ridge of his spine; her mouth, along the distinct cords in his neck....

"Your God is good to your people. He has much magic. My people see this. But the white God is no good for us. He has made white men to be farmers. Wakaŋtaŋka has made Dakota men to be hunters and warriors. The agents and missionaries were wrong to make us choose. Wakaŋtaŋka will be angry if we give up our ways, and we will die. And when we die, we will not be allowed to journey to the spirit world, where our ancestors live.

"I am not a wise man. I am willing to learn from any man who walks in balance. But the missionary Hinman had a troubled spirit. He said my people were living in great darkness. He said he was bringing the true light to save us. He said when we saw that light, we would love it and learn to walk in it. I did not know what Hinman meant. The same light came to us each day as came to him. We walked in it together. The light is the good road."

She wants to say, "I am not like Hinman."

She wants to say, "I do not think you are living in darkness."

Instead she says, "I saw My Husband at Hinman's church."

His eyebrow arches quizzically, by his scar.

"It was only a week or so before you ... before the uprising began."

"Sometimes the spirits told me to go, to keep the white man happy. The next week, too, I was there." It was on that last Sabbath, he tells her, when an argument with wasiću settlers over near the Big Woods precipitated the war.

"I will tell My Wife how this happened. This is the story we were told by the four young men who did the killing. They were from our band. I know them well. They said they did not go out to kill white people. They went to hunt. They had been away two or three nights when they came to the farm of a white man. It was near the town your people call Acton. A hen flew up from her nest by a fence. One of the hunters took the eggs from it, but another said, 'Leave them, we might get into trouble.' The first man was angry, for he was very hungry. He dashed the eggs to the ground and said, 'My brother is a coward! You are half-starved, yet you will not take even an egg from a white man.' His companion said, 'I am not afraid. To show you, I will go up to the settler's house and shoot him. Let any who are brave enough go with me.'

"That is when the settlers died. Our men killed four or five of them. When it happened, My Mother was in the cornfield, chasing away crows. I was sitting in Hinman's church, a few pews behind Taoyate Duta. The meeting was like a steamboat's paddles churning in the river, drowning out the voices of the spirits."

He kisses the corners of her mouth. "My Wife's people believe they can only find what is sacred inside the pages of a book or the walls of a church. I do not understand this. Mysteries are everywhere. If your people believed that, they might have walked with good hearts upon this land, and there would have been no war."

"Does Taoyate Duta walk with a good heart?" she asks gently.

"He did not want to do battle with your people. But at a council meeting after the killings, our young men threatened him. Hotheads called him a coward. He agreed to lead them, out of shame.

"When our force started down to attack Redwood, I went along. I had to go with my band. I had to be a good relative. But like Taoyate Duta I did not want to fight. I took no part in the killing.

"For years I had done everything I could to live in peace with your people. Nothing I did was enough. Yet it was too much. A Dakota man cannot live like a white man and remain Dakota. A Dakota must hail the sun each morning, and pray with the pipe. Dance to the drum. Purify and strengthen himself with his brothers in the sweat. Share his possessions with his village. Walk with a good heart among the lakes and trees and rivers, among the four-leggeds and the winged ones. Sacrifice himself for something truer than himself.

"This is the Dakota way. And I will walk in it until my breath is gone and I walk on, up the star path."

⁂ 15 ⁂

SARAH PUSSYFOOTS around stinging nettles to get at the raspberry patch, astonished to find berries so late in the season. She gobbles them down fast as she can pick. The best fruit hangs on prickly canes in the middle of the thicket, plump and tangy-sweet. Barbs scratch and rip.

After eating her fill, she harvests the remaining crop in her water pails. James and Nellie will eat the berries by the fistfuls. If she can rustle up some flour and sugar, she might even bake them a cobbler.

Kneeling by a pool along the Minnesota's edge, she scrubs at the red stains on her stinging skin. A turtle flops from a rock with a plunk. A squirrel sits up and scolds. She will be wearing these stains for days. In the glass of the water, her lips look painted on.

She shakes off her hands and seats herself against a maple whose leaves are firing with autumn. She has earned a rest before fetching the berries home. She must have made a dozen trips with her water pails.

This morning, in the blue light before daybreak, she'd wakened happy. For an odd instant she was a little girl again, back home in North Kingstown, up in the mow of the barn. She could smell the sweet hay, the damp coats of the sheep, the smoke of her father's pipe....

Then she felt Ćaske breathing against her body.

SHE CARRIES A LOCK OF HIS GRAY-BLACK HAIR IN THE FRINGED WORK POUCH AT her waist. A lock of her white hair is plaited into one of his braids. At dawn each day, they rise together and give thanks. He greets Grandfather Sun, burning sage, from which evil spirits flee. They talk no more about her canoeing downriver or absconding to the peace party camp. Neither do they talk of always being together. The circle of life opens and closes. A path wide enough for two can become no path at all.

Since the council with Standing Buffalo and Maza Śa, the Sioux have fought no major battles, but another full-bore attack on the Isaŋ Taŋka can't be far off. Meanwhile, Little Crow has held more contentious negotiations with the peace party. His soldiers have several times attempted to bully the dissenters into line, swarming their camp, knocking down tipis, scattering households, even killing ponies—one final, terrible warning. Slay an Indian's horse, Ćaske says, you all but slay him.

Yet in recent days, according to Dowaŋ S'a, the peace party has succeeded in moving off to a well-fortified hollow near the mouth of the Chippewa River. Emboldened by the maneuver, more Indians are shifting allegiances. The Lower chiefs Wapaśa and Wakute have gone over, as has the Wahpeton chief Mazomani. The peace party camp, once so thin, has swelled to a hundred lodges.

Ćaske paints their tipi, plays cards, hunts ducks. He's carving a spinning top for James. Ćaske, he calls her boy; *First Son*, like him. "I have Papa," James tells her, "and I have A-te." *Father.*

She sews on the tipi lining, butchers and jerks meat, makes frybread almost like she was born to it. She dries corn and potatoes foraged from Upper Sioux fields. She sews sacque dresses for the aunties and pullover shirts for the men. She boils juniper needles and oak root to treat Nellie's chronic diarrhea. And yes, she humps water from the river.

White captives sometimes sit within earshot of her, picking the nits from each other's hair. "She's one of *them* now," they say loudly. "But then, she was never one of *us* to begin with, was she?" The lie of her Narragansett blood.

At night, she and Ćaske school each other in their native tongues, tenting with a candle beneath a blanket so as to cast no shadows on the tipi cloth. In muffled conversations they swap vocabularies and practice pronunciations. He teaches her about writing with pictures. She tutors him in alphabets. They read together from an *Old Farmer's Almanac* presented by Dowaŋ S'a in trade for a new shirt. From the Williamsons' Old Testament, with its stories about the Chosen People's conquest of the Promised Land and their slaughter of the Canaanites, she refuses to read him.

. . .

He offers his ledger book and a stub of pencil. "Teach me wakaŋ words." After pondering, she writes wowićada, *faith*. Woape, *hope*. Caŋtekiyapi, *love*. She prints these words in big, bold strokes, like when she taught her little brothers to spell. He copies them dutifully in a child-like hand, but for him, she can see, they possess no power.

"Does My Husband know these words?"

"They are missionary words. They are not Dakota."

"If you will tell me a wakaŋ word, I will try to write it for you."

He brightens. "Waćiŋ taŋka."

A phrase she has heard often. "Waćiŋ taŋka ye," the grandmothers say to the warriors. "Waćiŋ taŋka ye," they say to the children. It seems to be an admonishment to have great patience, to act with deep purpose. But as he copies her spelling with care, she realizes it must signify considerably more.

"What is the meaning of these words?" she asks.

To answer, he tells her a story about a strange woman who comes on a journey from another world, bearing gifts. At first the people can't tell whether she's an enemy or a friend. But she speaks their language. She prays their prayers. She dwells among them, sharing everything she has, until she walks on.

A woodpecker hammers a rapid tattoo. Sarah skims the trees on the riverbank for its red head. The loud drumming doesn't repeat.

The wind soughs through the thin branches. Stitches of birds, too high to hear, migrate south across the sky. Fallen leaves skitter along the ground. The musky smell of decay permeates the air.

Further down the bank, on an outcropping of granite, a young woman drops her empty pails to greet her sweetheart. His blanket wraps her in a standing embrace, a moment stolen for unchaperoned love.

Down by St. Paul, just below the citadel of Fort Snelling, this river flows into the Mississippi, which the Sioux call Ȟaȟa Wakpa, *River Of The Falls*. And where those two rivers meet, Ćaske has told her, is Mdote, a wakaŋ place. Long ago, before time began, it was there that Wakaŋtaŋka formed the first Dakota man and woman, creating them from the very land upon which they were meant to live.

Here, on the upper reaches of the Minnesota, that land has no echoes, few shadows and wind that doesn't stop. It's a land that turns your soul inward upon itself and drives it like a tipi peg deep into the earth, a hard teacher of what matters most. But it's a land, too, with room enough to loosen everything inside you that is stretched too tight and battened down too fast. Something like grace abides here. Something necessary, like mercy, gotten by giving in.

She contemplates the warped reflection of the courting couple in the slow, glassy water. They giggle and coo beneath the loafing ducks.

❧ III ❦

❧ I ❧

SCOUTS RIDE IN, mid-morning, ponies in a lather. The Isaŋ Taŋka are advancing from Yellow Medicine. Their force is much larger than expected. They have many mazakaŋ taŋka. *Big guns.* Cannon.

Old Tate Mi Ma makes his rounds with orders from the soldiers' lodge. "All men, prepare to leave to strike the Americans! We will destroy them, once and for all! Any warrior who takes the scalp of an officer or captures an American flag will be awarded the honors of the tribe!" This battle, Sarah senses, will be the people's last stand. Triumph, or perish. "We will move camp tomorrow at dawn! Any captive who cannot walk will be killed! If any captive runs away, all others will die!"

In the yard of the tipi, Uŋćiśi dresses Belle for battle, masking her head and bobbing her tail with red cloth. Ćaske ties a medicine bundle around the mare's neck. Sarah, in a sulk, brings him cakes of pemmican for his sash and an extra pair of moccasins.

"I ask My Husband not to go! Something terrible will happen!"

"If I do not go, Taoyate Duta will believe My Wife is the cause, and kill us both."

She wraps herself around him, though outside the tipi the act is unseemly for a woman and humiliating for her man. He eases her away.

She wraps her arms around herself. "Why must the soldiers' lodge move us again?"

"This position is too exposed."

"But Maza Śa has forbidden Taoyate Duta to move further north!"

"The camp will move west. Not far."

"Perhaps I should take the children to the peace party until after the battle."

"I forbid it! Do not try to go there, under *any* circumstances. You will be put to death if you are caught. Your death will be slow."

"No one will catch us. The camp guard will be thin."

"You will die even if you succeed in escaping. Taoyate Duta has vowed to destroy the peace party after the battle unless its men take part."

"But Opa and Pasu Kiyuksa … Little Paul …."

"Everyone in that camp will be killed."

"And My Husband will help kill them? Your own relatives?" She throws herself into his chest, knocking him off balance. This time he lets her hang on.

"Do not talk to any half-breeds or white women while I am gone. Stay inside with My Mother. When darkness falls, lie down by the fire, so your shadow does not show on the tipi cloth."

"I beg My Husband again, do not go."

"I must take my gun and dagger, but I will leave you my club and my jackknife—"

"No!"

"My Wife must let me go. I have nothing more to give you, except my prayers."

THE DISTANT BOOMING OF SIBLEY'S CANNON SIGNALS THAT THE BATTLE HAS been joined. The women driving relief wagons say that the fighting is near Ćaŋ Waŋźidaŋ Mde, *Lone Tree Lake,* a dozen or so miles below the camp.

Confined to the tipi, Sarah keeps vigil across the hours. Sunlight creeps across the floor. Wind howls down the smoke flaps and disturbs the fire. She offers to the air her dread of Ćaske not coming back. Uŋćiśi sings prayers.

If only, instead of hiding out, she could have charge of a wagon team, to be closer to him. To help preserve him. Death has too many ways in war to sniff out a man who, in his marrow, has no passion for the fight; even a man wearing a wakaŋ-bag for protection, and a lock of his wife's hair as an amulet.

AT LONG LAST, IN THE DARK OF A NEW MOON, INDIANS BEGIN TO STRAGGLE back from the battle. The camp flares into sudden chaos. The cold air bristles with the wailing of women, tales of defeat, curses on traitors, threats against the captives. In the tipi yard Sarah drops kindling on the dim fire and fans it up with a hawk wing. With Uŋćiśi she puts on coffee, fries bread, reheats a kettle of stew … all acts of hope, prayers in the flesh.

As if sought in a vision, Ćaske finally materializes in their faint circle of light. He kneels by the fire, sets aside his gun, slips off his shot pouch. She brings him water. As he gulps it down, she inspects his body with her eyes. No blood, no scrapes. If not for his sullied war paint and his powderhorn, shot through, he could be a hunter returned empty and dog-tired from the chase.

She stoops to remove his moccasins. She washes his leathery feet, dries them on a linen cloth and soothes them with velvety sage leaves. It's the only display of affection she can properly offer him outside their tipi, painted with stars.

THE SOLDIERS' LODGE CONVENES THE PEOPLE IN ONE LAST COUNCIL, BONFIRES burning all around. Little Crow cradles his gun in his arms. "I am ashamed to call myself a Dakota. Seven hundred warriors, whipped by the cowardly Big Knives! We should run away and scatter out over the plains like buffalo and wolves. Our enemy had bigger guns, better arms and more soldiers, but we should have crushed them! We are brave men! I cannot account for this disgrace. It must be the work of traitors in our midst.

"The Big Knives will soon be upon us. In their anger they will want to cut me to pieces and boil me in a kettle. I will fight them to the last—but for now, we must all flee, to save our women and children. No time should be lost! The Big Knives will punish anyone who stays behind, even those who wanted no part of the fighting! Let us retreat north toward Spirit Lake. After one moon, I will lead a delegation to our relatives beyond The River That Runs Fast And Muddy. We will persuade them to unite with us and renew the war in the spring!"

Sarah has heard of Mni Śośe Wakpala. That river, the women say, is far out on the plains, where the prairie grass is short, buffalo herds are still thick and blizzards kill even the strong.

"The captives will slow us down," Little Crow says. "No bargain can be struck for their safe return. We have no reason to keep them any longer. They will only be a burden."

The warriors nearest to Little Crow whoop in agreement, firing their guns into the air. This is what Sarah has feared for weeks—her fate, and James and Nellie's, passing from Ćaske's control. She presses into Ćaske's side. He presses back.

Little Crow silences his men. "The Big Knives will chase us to the ends of the earth if we kill their women and children. They will give us no peace until every last one of us is dead. I say let the white captives go back to their friends. Let Maza Kute Mani deliver them."

Her heart beats triple time. Can Little Crow be believed? Will he really let Little Paul deliver the captives to safety? That decision might not even be his to make. After such a devastating defeat, his soldiers might choose to defy him. They might exact their revenge on every white in sight.

MANY TIOŚPAYE IN THE CAMP ARE RIPPED ASUNDER. LODGE SPLITS FROM lodge, kin from kin. Some Indians want to flee west with Little Crow or continue north toward Grandmother's Land. Others believe it better to throw themselves on the mercy of Long Trader. Sarah, suddenly on freedom's brink, stands alone amidst the keening and cleaving, the swirls of words, the despairing silences, the hurried packing and decamping. One thing is clear, even to a wasićuu-win like her: The things being said and done this night will alter the Sioux people forever.

Dozens of relatives muster near Eagle Head's tipi to deliberate. They can't agree on what to do. Eagle Head argues for staying. The youngest men are set on going with Little Crow. Ćaske and Dowaŋ S'a wish only to get away and start a new life, far from the Americans.

The circle of relatives dwindles through the night. In the pre-dawn dark, Ćaske directs Uŋćiśi to dismantle her tipi. "We cannot delay any longer," he tells Eagle Head. "Let us retreat to Big Stone Lake. We can regroup there and deliberate upon the wisest path forward."

He kindles a torch in a campfire and walks toward the tipi. Sarah rushes after him, feeling desperate, events beginning to tumble. "What will happen to us?" she cries.

He locates the travois, propped against the back of the lodge. After positioning it on the ground, he begins fumbling with its rawhide thongs. "Half-breeds are being sent down to Long Trader with a letter of good heart. You can ride down with them to the camp of the Big Knives."

"But Taoyate Duta's soldiers might ambush us on the way!"

"Then you can wait with the other captives for Long Trader to march up here. He should arrive before the sun is overhead."

"But I want to stay with My Husband!"

"Then bundle the children. We must go!"

"No, that is not what I mean—*please*—my babies will die if we flee to the plains!"

Ćaske rubs his eyebrow. "You do not want to go down with the half-breeds to Long Trader's camp. You do not want to wait here. You do not want to go out on the plains. What *do* you want?"

She slumps at his feet. She doesn't want to go back to a life with John, if in fact he's alive. But what kind of life is possible with Ćaske? A life of privation she might tolerate, but a life on the run from her own people, always looking over her shoulder, always being afraid, always trying to be someone she wasn't born to be? She'd tasted that life as Thomas Jemison, when she ran away from Richard. It isn't a future she wants, either for herself or her babies.

"Stay with us, My Husband—you and your mother! Wait with us here!"

"I do not trust Long Trader. Once he has custody of the captives, he will kill my people. Is that what you want, to see us dead?"

She rests her brow on one of his moccasins, covering her tears. If only she knew where to go, and how, like a flock of geese migrating from one season to the next.

Ćaske jams the shaft of his torch into the ground. "My Wife...." He folds down beside her, pries her hands from her face, clasps them in a knot against his chest.

THE SKY IS PINKING AND A DAWN BREEZE KICKING UP AS THE FAMILY ENTERS the peace party camp. Outside Opa's tipi Sarah shakes hands with Dowaŋ S'a and Eagle Head, bidding them farewell. "I will see you again," she says, in the traditional way.

She turns to Uŋćiśi. The old woman has set Nellie down and sloughed off her pack. Kneeling, she slips onto Sarah's feet the fancy moccasins she wore the day she met Eagle Head; soft deerskin, beaded with purple and teal flowers, green leaves and vines. When she rises again, she rips her red blanket shawl in two and drapes one half around Sarah's shoulders.

"My Daughter is going back to where she will have a good, warm house and plenty to eat. My heart is glad for you. But what will happen to us? I fear we will starve on the plains this winter, without even potatoes to roast." For the first time, she looks bent and frail.

Sarah leans down to kiss her wrinkled cheek. "Uŋćiśi has been a mother to me, stronger and kinder than any woman I have ever known.

Wherever you go, Grandfather Sun will shine on you, and Grandmother Earth will bear you up." Blinking back tears, she takes the old woman tightly in her arms. "And your son"—she lets Uŋčiśi go but for her hands —"you have raised him to have a good heart. He fights for his people. He respects their ways. He saved me and my babies from certain death and brought us to live with a brave, honorable woman. I will remember you both, and will pray for you always."

James hangs on the old woman's leg. "Come home with us, Grandmother."

"Oh, My Grandchild, I would keep you if I could!" Uŋčiśi makes a great fuss over him as Sadie whines, licking jealously at her fingers.

"Mama, can't we bring her home?"

Sarah digs her fingernails into her palms.

"Let me stay with Grandmother, just a while longer! Can't I?"

"James, we must go find your father."

"But why can't Papa live with us here?"

Nellie lifts feeble arms to Ćaske. "A-te."

He swings Nellie up. "Little Girl Who Sleeps To Cradle Songs. Your mother must keep singing."

Sarah looks away, from emotion. "Come to me, child," she hears Opa say to Nellie.

"Sarah Wakefield." His pronunciation is perfect.

She attempts a smile. "My Husband has been practicing in secret."

His hand enfolds hers. The show of intimacy takes her breath.

"It is a difficult name," he says. The *R*, the *F*—sounds unknown in his tongue.

"It is not my true name." She caresses his long fingers, so calloused and scarred.

"Tell me the name I should call you."

She raises her eyes to the scar on his forehead. Then her gaze slides down to meet his. "The name you call me in your heart is my true name."

A trace of his crooked smile. "My Wife and I will see each other again."

"Whenever we close our eyes."

❦ 2 ❦

A GIRL AGAIN, she's picking wild berries in buttery sunshine. "Careful," her mother says, "they might be poison," but she ignores the warning. She mashes berries into her mouth, handful upon handful, swallowing them with scarcely a chew, choking them down like words she isn't allowed to say, a life she isn't allowed to live....

She wakens to laughter and the scent of apples. Spent and confused, she rolls over onto her back, still tasting the juice of dream berries.

"Mama, come see!"

She sits up in the bed of buffalo robes. Still trying to get her bearings, she adjusts Uŋćiśi's red shawl around her shoulders. Beside her, Nellie is sound asleep beneath a quilt. James is seated at an overturned washtub, his blue eyes big and eager. Atop the tub rests a golden-brown pie in a cast-iron frying pan. The aroma of hot apples is stunning.

"Can you believe it?" James says, in English. "Pie like *you* used to make!"

"Good Big Woman!" Opa waves her over with a horn spoon. She portions out the pie into wooden bowls. "Wash! Eat! There is plenty!"

"Where did you ever find apples?" Her nose whiffs for cinnamon.

"The old man scavenged them from Hazelwood before the move north."

Mary Riggs's apples, they must be, from the fruit trees behind her picket fence. "We must save some pie for him," she says.

"He has no stomach for such sweets. I made it for the children."

James is soon scraping his bowl clean with his finger. "Mama, may I have some more?"

"Not unless you want a bellyache."

Opa pours her some coffee. "Good Big Woman slept well?"

"I was dreaming." The pie crust is perfection, better than her own.

"I hope you were visited by good dreams."

"I cannot say." She licks sugar from her fingertips. "My heart is sad. My body is tired." She reclines against a beaded backrest, warming her hands on her cup. "Shall I replenish your water and wood after my coffee?"

"It is best we stay inside until Long Trader comes. Many Indians who fled after yesterday's battle are returning. They are setting up their lodges among us."

"They will cause trouble!"

"Our men are keeping watch."

James is rubbing at his eyes, ready for a nap. Crawling in beside Nellie, he wriggles beneath the quilt and nestles against her, burying his head in the curve of his arm.

Opa folds down stiffly beside Sarah. "When Long Trader gets here, he will want to punish those who have done bad things."

"Yes."

"He will not know which of our men to trust." She pulls out a blanket coat she's been sewing. "Maza Kute Mani, whom you call Little Paul, corresponded with Long Trader during the war, seeking a way to peace. A number of letters passed between them."

"How is Opa aware of this?"

"Our party chose Maza Kute Mani to be our spokesman. He acted with our consent." Her knotty fingers are stitching the coat's hood toward the neck. *She Who Is Part Of Everything,* her name means. "He believes Long Trader counts him as a friend. But his position would be more secure if he could deliver up one of Taoyate Duta's captives."

Sarah catches the kuŋśi's meaning. "He wants to surrender *me?*"

Outside the tipi, a man clears his throat, wishing to pay a call. Opa ignores him, intent on her needle. "If Good Big Woman were to allow Maza Kute Mani this honor, he would win favor in Long Trader's eyes."

"But you and Pasu Kiyuksa should give me up!"

The visitor rattles the tipi door on its willow frame.

Opa shakes her head. "The old man and I have lived enough winters. Long Trader can do with us as he likes." She looks at last toward the door. "Enter!"

• • •

SARAH STARES UP IN DISBELIEF. SHE LIFTS THE REMNANT OF UŊĆIŚI'S SHAWL TO frame her face. "My Husband has come back."

"Yes."

His red headband. His one slender braid, still plaited with her white lock of hair. His wakaŋ-bag, hanging around his neck. "And your mother?"

"We are all here. I have come to ask you back to our lodge."

"Would that please My Husband?"

"The family would feel safer if you are with us when Long Trader comes."

She rises. "Opa, may I let the children sleep?"

The kuŋśi winks. "That pie must be eaten before I let them leave."

"About Maza Kute Mani...."

Opa dismisses her with a wave. "We will say no more about him."

UŊĆIŚI'S TIPI IS ALREADY UP, A FEW RODS AWAY, ITS TOP QUARTER SPLASHED with blue and yellow stars. When Sarah appears in the yard, the old woman smiles but, like Ćaske, offers no explanation for the family's abrupt change of heart. Sarah puts on her own mask. She picks up a hatchet and starts to split kindling, flattening her tongue against the questions gnawing at her teeth. Not all questions need to be answered. Not all questions can be.

The sun scrapes across the sky. Ćaske occupies himself carving the spinning top he began making for James before the battle at Lone Tree Lake. Sarah broods. "I do not believe that Taoyate Duta and his soldiers will let us captives live. They will come back in vengeance and kill us."

"My Wife must not worry." Ćaske blows off some shavings.

"But Taoyate Duta has been a torment! He has made so many threats!"

"Yet after all this time, My Wife is still alive." He smiles a little. "I am not a wise man, but I believe Taoyate Duta has two hearts. One heart is Dakota, the other is white. Two moons ago he was worshiping in a white man's church, wearing a white man's clothes, living in a white man's house. When our young men clamored for war, he blackened his face and covered his head as a sign of mourning. He did not want to fight. Then someone called him a coward to his face." He falls quiet, his blade peeling wood, perhaps seeing something of himself in the grain. "A two-hearted man cannot be fully trusted. But I think Taoyate Duta will not come back. He is too Dakota to butcher his own people, and he is white enough to let the white captives go."

She sighs. "Long Trader cannot get here fast enough!"

He tests the sharpness of his jackknife against his thumb. "Much as I do not trust Taoyate Duta, I trust Long Trader even less. He has always claimed to be a friend of our people. He has hunted and trapped and traded with us. He has negotiated treaties with us. He married the daughter of one of our chiefs and sired a child. These things I know, but I do not know if his white heart is good. I do not know if a friend, once he becomes an enemy, can still be a friend."

MID-AFTERNOON, SIBLEY AND HIS ARMY STILL HAVEN'T APPEARED.

In the bed of an empty wagon, Ćaske tries to teach James how to whip his new spinning top. The floorboards are too rough. "It will spin best on ice this winter. First Son will see."

"Will My Father come to my house and show me how? On the river ice?"

Sarah turns away.

ĆASKE SHOOTS A CANADA GOOSE. SARAH PREPARES THE FAMILY A FEAST, WITH wild turnip cakes. As she cooks, he crouches with his gun, staring holes into the ground. Pops up and paces. Crouches again, rubbing his eyebrow. "When I came into this world, I knew who I was. Now I do not know how to live as a Dakota. If I go to the plains, I will wander alone, cut off from my people, a fugitive of war. If I stay and submit to the Big Knives, they will be my death."

She lights his wasićun pipe to calm him. "I will protect My Husband from Long Trader!"

A dejected laugh. "My Wife is a big woman, but Long Trader's guns are bigger." He blows a long stream of smoke through his nose.

She watches the smoke hang and clear. "Long Trader has promised to shake hands with every Indian who abandons Taoyate Duta and gives up his captives. Pasu Kiyuksa and Opa believe Long Trader will keep his word."

"I do not trust Long Trader as they do." He passes back the red clay pipe. "If not for My Mother, I would leave. But she would not survive winter on the plains, and I will not abandon her to the Big Knives."

"Your mother ... my children ... they are the reasons we must stay."

"What of the doctor?"

She puffs on his pipe. "My white husband does not have a good heart."

"Yet you wish to go find him. You refuse to put him away."

"Among my people it is not so easy to leave a man." She puts the polished reed pipe stem to his lips. He draws on it, swallowing the smoke.

"My Wife is two-hearted like Taoyate Duta. One heart is white, the other is Dakota."

"I ask My Husband to trust me, as I trust him."

He dips a rag in grease and begins to oil the stock of his musket. "I will speak the truth," he says, polishing hard. "I have never trusted any white person with my whole heart. I am trying to trust My Wife. But if I am killed, I will haunt you forever."

DOWAŊ S'A DUCKS THROUGH THE DOOR. HE TELLS THEM THAT SCOUTS FROM the peace party have searched out Long Trader. He and The Big Knives have advanced only eight miles since the battle at Lone Tree Lake.

Sarah brushes the tip of a braid across her sickly girl's cheek, eliciting a feeble smile. "Were one of the captives in this camp named Sibley," she mutters in English, "that army would be marching up on the quick."

A second kinsman joins them in the tipi. A third. When Eagle Head, too, presents himself, Uŋćiśi greets him solemnly, then smothers what's left of the fire. "My Daughter," she says, "we must go." She bustles Sarah and her babies out of the lodge into dusk, dropping the door behind them. She crosses it with two sticks, forbidding entry.

An eerie hush pervades Camp Lookout, as the peace party camp is now being called. Firelight flickers in neighboring lodges. Uŋćiśi tosses a lacrosse ball toward James. It slips through his hands. Full of giggles, he scoots after its indistinct form in the twilight, Sadie bounding alongside.

With Uŋćiśi distracted, Sarah sidles around back of the lodge, Nellie on her hip.

"Pretty!" Nellie says, with a weak jingle of the beads around Sarah's neck.

"Shhh, baby," she whispers, clenching the beads to kill them.

Inside the tipi two gourd rattles begin to talk. Sarah detects the faint scent of sweetgrass. And now she hears the music of Dowaŋ S'a's voice. She can't quite apprehend the words of his prayer song, as though they belong to a different dialect. The other men unite with him, in low unison.

"Get away, get away!" Uŋćiśi skirts around the tipi, shooing her off, hissing and flapping her arms like a furious goose.

Embarrassed, Sarah seats herself with Nellie near the smoldering remains of a fire. She uproots some dry grass, chucks it onto the embers and watches it flare. Dowaŋ S'a must be a wićaśa wakaŋ. If Ćaske is consulting a holy man, he might yet break and run. He's like a mariner in fog. No stars or landmarks by which to navigate; no beacon by which to judge whether to hold course or change heading. She prays a bit of light will glimmer through Dowaŋ S'a's divinations.

❄ 3 ❄

MORNING SUN IS MELTING the delicate hoar frost from the prairie grass when Ćaske escorts two older Indians into the tipi yard. He introduces the men to Sarah as Wapaśa and Wakute. Before now she has only seen these Mdewakantonwan chiefs from a distance, in council. According to Jannette DeCamp, each played a role in saving her and her boys during the first hours of the uprising.

Inside the tipi the chiefs seat themselves against the willow backrests reserved for honored guests. Wakute perches his dusty stovepipe hat on a knee. Except for his moccasins, he's dressed like a scruffy settler; shirt misbuttoned, tie lapping one point of his collar. "We are told Doctor Wife is a writer," he says.

"Yes, I can write," she says, noting the cloud of disease in his right eye.

"We are dispatching a messenger to Long Trader with words of our good heart. We want to send along a letter from Doctor Wife. We ask you to tell Long Trader how you have been helped by Eagle Head, Ćaske, Dowaŋ S'a, all who have been your friends. Make him understand that every Dakota in this camp wants peace."

"There is no reason for such a letter. I will be certain to tell Long Trader in person when he arrives."

"We cannot wait." Wapaśa cups his hands over his blanketed knees. Unlike Wakute, he wears traditional garb. On his head is a fingerwoven turban adorned with buffalo horns. Wings of feathers ornament his shoulders like epaulettes. A necklace of grizzly bear claws covers his chest. Tied to his waist is a belt of wampum and a double holster with pistols. "Long Trader seems not to trust us. His advance is too slow. We must impress upon him again how we have cared for the captives, and how much we desire peace."

"We do not wish to burden Doctor Wife with this entreaty," Wakute says, toying with the brim of his hat. "But the trader Spencer is wounded in the arm. He cannot write for us." George Spencer, he must mean; shot three times, yet alive, thanks to his friend Wakiŋya Tawa.

"We know that Doctor Wife will write well," Wapaśa says. "We know that Doctor Wife has no fear."

She weighs the chiefs' request. If a letter of commendation is warranted, they're shrewd to seek one from her, a white captive of some importance, kept safe for weeks by their own tribesmen. She nods to Ćaske. He retrieves his ledger book and pencil stub. She will gladly speak her mind in defense of her Dakota kin.

FUGITIVE SIOUX CONTINUE TO RETURN AT NIGHT UNDER COVER OF DARKNESS. By dawn on the third day, Lookout has grown to a few hundred lodges. Indians throughout the camp are digging in, suspicious of Long Trader's lead-footed advance.

Sarah helps Ćaske excavate a large, deep hole in their tipi floor. Over the top they construct a false floor of tree branches and buffalo hides, substantial enough to sit upon. In case of attack, this hole will be a last refuge where she, the children and Uŋćiśi can huddle below the line of fire. Ćaske will defend them from behind a low breastwork, built with the earth displaced by their digging, just outside the door.

Toward noon, news spreads that the Isaŋ Taŋka have been spotted a few miles to the south. While some Sioux seclude themselves straightaway in their tipis, others scramble to festoon the camp with strings of beads and eagle feathers. They raise a huge Stars & Stripes above the peace party's council lodge. They replenish the camp's supply of water to slake the thirst of Long Trader's men. Where there are clothes enough, Indians exchange leggings and breechcloths for trousers, and wasićx captives are dressed like wasićx again. Many Sioux paint their faces, though not as they do before battle, or in mourning. Perhaps they're marking a change of worlds.

"Paint me, Grandmother!"

Uŋćiśi glances at Sarah for permission. James is still clad in his fringed

Indian jacket and leggings. Like Ćaske, he has balked at putting on trousers. The old woman gives him a ghastly yellow face, with a bold red stripe across his forehead and down each cheek.

Now Uŋćiśi washes Sarah's face and loosens her white hair from its braids. She is combing out the crimps when Mother Friend appears.

"I have found an American dress for Doctor Wife!" she says, holding up a brown gingham dress with faux wood buttons and drawstring waist.

Sarah gasps. It's the maternity dress she sewed last spring for a pregnant Susan Humphrey.

"Look at the stars! Look at the stars!" A little white girl is bouncing with excitement in a wagon box, clapping, pointing south.

Not stars. Soldiers. Over the wide plateau floats the faint pulse and lilt of martial music: fifes and drums at the head of the troops. Even from afar, the Army is a grand sight, with colors flying and bayonets glinting in the sun. Sarah, squeezed into Susan Humphrey's dress after crude alterations, can't believe her ordeal is about to end. For so long, she has tried to guard herself against much thought of the future. Now the future is marching in. All around her, captives are jumping up and down, screaming, praising God and Colonel Sibley. But she is rooted where she stands. Her head feels like a fist.

Camp Lookout is one huge declaration of submission. Strips of white cloth flutter from wagon wheels, the tails of Indian ponies, lances stuck in the ground. White flags made from bed linens flutter from the tops of tipis. Little Paul, astride his mule, is waving the biggest flag of all on a tipi pole. As the troops mosey over the prairie, he trots his mule out to greet them, the flag of truce sailing above him in the wind.

Sibley advances like a snail. He's a former governor, no military man, and his pace is a politician's. His troops could be on dress parade rather than claiming victory. Impatient soldiers begin to break ranks. They barrel toward Camp Lookout, frantic, Sarah supposes, to learn if their kin, unaccounted for in the madness of war, are by some miracle among the captives. At the onslaught of men, Ćaske and other Indians shoulder twitchy guns. Voices yell from every direction to keep muzzles pointed at the ground. James cowers behind Uŋćiśi. Nellie shrieks. The world teeters.

"Papa! *Papa!*" Two girls no older than James run screaming toward a soldier who is sprinting toward them. The private throws down his musket. "Elizabeth! Minnie!" Catching them up, he swings them round and round.

Sarah pulls her portion of Uŋćiśi's shawl tighter around her. She searches the faces of the oncoming men, blood hammering with contradiction. She wants John to have survived. She wants him to have stepped up to fight for her and the children. She wants him to be among these troops, desperate for some glimpse of her. Yet she wants never again to be his.

She expects the column of troops to halt at the camp's perimeter. But at the head of the cavalcade, Sibley rides right on by, to the music of the fifes and drums. His officers round up their undisciplined men and impose order on the ranks. Hundreds of troops pass by, marching and mounted. A modest train of artillery and tarpaulin-covered mule-wagons brings up the rear and is swallowed by dust.

The white captives send up bewildered cries. Many weep. James, recovered from his fright, chases after the soldiers with a band of Sioux boys, shouting, "Sibilee, Sibilee!" They soon traipse back, coughing on dust, trailing their rags of truce behind them.

Dowaŋ S'a rassles James onto his shoulders. "Most of the Big Knives are old men with stubs of teeth. They move like turtles."

"Their young warriors," Eagle Head says, "have gone to fight their brothers in the great white war."

The troops dig in on the ridge to the northeast, between Camp Lookout and the Minnesota River. They hoist rows of white tents. Then, in plain view, they train howitzers on the Sioux.

Lookout erupts in panic. Half-breeds from the peace party mount their ponies and race off under a flag of truce, to ascertain Long Trader's intentions.

Ćaske squats by Uŋćiśi's fire and lights his wasić021 pipe, gun across his thighs.

Two hours after the Army's march-by, a squad of Sibley's men gallops down from the sun-washed plateau. So still and tense is Camp Lookout, Sarah hears the thudding of the approaching hoofbeats from far off. As the soldiers reach the outermost tipis, white captives run out to meet them, bawling, begging, screeching. Two of the soldiers' mounts spook and rear up. An officer, reining in his sorrel, stands high in his stirrups and demands quiet. The cavalrymen space their prancing horses in a line, either side of him, arms at the ready.

The officer, dashing in his gold bars and buttons, raises a gloved hand. "I am Captain Hiram Grant." Beside him, a half-breed in Union blue interprets for the Sioux. "I greet you on behalf of Colonel Henry H. Sibley, who will shortly advance with a contingent of troops to this camp. At that time, he will accept the unconditional release of all captives into his custody." The captives raise a rousing cheer.

"All captives," Grant continues, his mouth obscured by a full, bushy beard, "should separate themselves from the Sioux and remain inside till Colonel Sibley comes."

"The easier to kill the nits," a soldier jokes under his breath to the rider beside him.

Overhearing, James tugs on the fringe of Sarah's shaw. "Mama," he says, "what are nits?"

ĆASKE LEADS SARAH INTO THE TIPI. WHERE ONCE A FIRE WOULD HAVE BURNED, the hole they dug lies concealed.

"Long Trader will part us now," he says, fingering the brown gingham over her bosom. "My Wife must talk to her people, or they will kill me."

Her throat is too full to speak.

"My Wife is a good woman. You have a good heart."

"I wrote Long Trader a letter. I promise My Husband will not be harmed."

His hand slides down to the pouch at her waist. "My Wife must tell her people I am a good man. If I were a bad man, I would have fled with Little Crow, like Hepaŋ and the others."

"Yes, I told them."

"You must tell them again." He removes the locket of his hair from her pouch.

She tears up. "I will tell them as many times as it takes. But please, My Husband must not be afraid."

"I am not afraid. But I do not trust."

✼ 4 ✿

SARAH DEFIES Captain Grant's order to remain sheltered. In mid-afternoon she observes the first movements of troops in the soldiers' camp and hears the faint fifes and drums. She begins to cry. Anything, suddenly, can make her cry.

Sibley parades two companies of infantry and a convoy of empty wagons down the ridge at a leisurely pace. At the edge of Camp Lookout, he orders a halt and sends a camp crier to announce a council. Then, escorted by his officers and trailed by wary Sioux, he walks his black stallion into the maze of tipis. He sits like a lord in the saddle, muscular and trim even in his fifties, but his blue uniform is shabby, his boots thick with dust. His chevron mustache needs snipping. The dark bags under his eyes lack weeks of sleep.

He dismounts at the council lodge. Above him, the American flag beats the wind. His officers remain on horseback as Indians assemble. Sarah hovers at the outskirts of the crowd, one of the few wasićú who hasn't retired to a lodge.

Sibley shakes hands with Little Paul, Wapaśa, Wakute, Maza Śa and other Sioux leaders she can't name. From what Ćaske has told her, Sibley has a history with many of these Indians, but any trust that might formerly have existed has collapsed. Too much has happened. War has many means of killing; many casualties beyond the wounded and the dead.

Sibley climbs into the bed of a buckboard. Close behind is Captain

Grant, and a third man ... the Reverend Riggs, alive and well in the uniform of an Army chaplain. Sarah's heart leaps at the sight of him. If he has survived, many others on the Upper reservation might have as well.

"I am here on the authority of the Great Father in Washington and the Governor of Minnesota." Sibley's Dakota is fluent. "During the past six weeks, many of my people have been made to suffer by your people. Most were defenseless civilians. They were made to lose their property and their lives after dwelling for years as your neighbors in Christian friendship."

Sibley digs his thumbs into his sword belt. "My force is large. All guilty parties will pay the price for their transgressions. Even now, detachments of my cavalry have been dispatched after Little Crow. I intend to pursue all hostiles with fire and sword until I overtake them. But I assure you it is not my purpose to punish the innocent. If you have not been involved in the massacre of civilians and related outrages, then place yourselves this day under my protection. I am the friend of all who are friends of the great American Father."

A murmur passes through the crowd. Wapaśa steps forward to speak. The chief has changed out of his shoulder feathers and breechcloth into farmer clothes. "This war was wrong. The hearts of those who started it were sick. But they thought our Great Father, who is so busy fighting his own people, might have forgotten his Dakota children. The agents he sent to us paid no heed to his words. Everything they did, they did in confusion. They made promises, sealed with the pipe, never fulfilled. They were thieves. The annuity money was always late. This year it was not paid at all. Meanwhile, our people were starving, and the traders were like rats. Our hearts were very heavy.

"We in this camp wanted nothing to do with the raids. When the war broke out, we found ourselves amidst those who had started the killings. We were compelled at the muzzle of a gun to either go with them or die. All we have done has been with the intention of saving our white friends, protecting the white prisoners and ending the war. We have neither blood on our hands nor hatred in our hearts."

A Mdewakantonwan named Taopi echoes Wapaśa. "We would not have dared to come and shake your hand if our own hands were stained with the blood of your people. There is no bravery in killing helpless men, women and children who have no means of defense. That is cowardice, and it is only cowards who would boast of it. Taoyate Duta has got himself into trouble he cannot get out of. He tried to involve those of us who are still your friends in the murder of white settlers. We were told we would be killed if we did anything to help the whites. But we have gathered all the prisoners we could, and with our families, we have waited here for you, as you told us to do."

Sarah's eyes roam the crowd. What the Indian orators have said is true, to a point; without the peace party, she and the other captives might long ago have met their demise. Yet some of these Sioux are known to be staunch Little Crow loyalists. Unlike Ćaske, they hadn't fought under duress but with a thirst for blood. They're only masquerading as peace party Indians, whether to save themselves and their kin or to do mischief. They might yet opt for treachery. Every Sioux gun is still loaded with ball. She wishes Ćaske weren't standing so close to Sibley's wagon.

"The Mdewakantonwans started this war upon your people, then they fled up here among us." Little Paul is speaking now. "I asked them many times why they did this, but I do not yet understand it. 'I feel as though the world is coming to an end,' I told them. 'Why have you made war on the Americans? They have given us money, food, clothing, plows, tobacco, guns and powder, knives—all things by which we might live well. Why then have you made war upon them?' This is what I asked them."

He extends an arm toward Sibley. "Long Trader, I take your hand as a child takes the hand of his father. My hand is clean. I have regarded all white people as my friends, and from this friendship has issued a great blessing. This is a good work we do today. I am glad. Yes, before the great God I am glad."

"FORM SQUARE!"

The infantry maneuvers into a hollow square, a double line of men facing out on all four sides with bayonets fixed. The Army's colors are marched into the center of the formation. Sibley stations himself there with Captain Grant. Reverend Riggs seats himself at a field desk and prepares to act as scribe.

White captives surge out of the lodges. Most of the women are in rags. The children, like James and Nellie, are all dressed like little Indians. The most frenzied captives push along the rest, mobbing Sibley and his men, grasping and clawing to the point of seeming mad. Sarah, hemmed in among them, locks onto her babies with such ferocity they writhe to get free.

The captive Hattie Adams is planting kisses on the soldiers. The frau who lost her five featherbeds swoons. The girl Mattie Williams drifts like a wraith, a husk of a self. George Spencer shuffles along, weak with his wounds, buttressed by Wakiŋya Tawa. Jannette DeCamp and her boys are nowhere to be seen.

Sibley dabs at his welling eyes. Once his officers establish a semblance of order, he clears his throat and issues instructions in English: "White captives will proceed to the colors, one at a time, and present yourself to Reverend Riggs. Point out the Indian who has had charge of you, if he's here. Mr. Riggs will record your name, and that of your protector. Thereafter you should wait within the square until the full census has been taken. Once the white captives have been secured, mixed-blood captives will be recorded. Thereafter my men and I will escort you in wagons up the hill to Camp Release."

The Sioux observe the proceedings in silence, guns pointed obediently at the ground. Sarah catches sight of Uŋćiśi and Eagle Head. Sitting between them, in the place where Ćaske last stood, is Sadie.

"Mrs. Wakefield?" Riggs's face pinches with concern. "I'm relieved to see you and your children. For a long while I thought…. Well, never mind that, how are you faring?"

Sarah blots her tears with the heel of her hand. "My baby is low, Reverend, but we're otherwise well. And you? Your family?"

"We're all alive for another day, thanks be to God."

"And what day *is* this, may I ask?"

"Friday. September twenty-sixth."

Not even six weeks. Yet a lifetime.

"Are you quite sure you're well, Madam? You look underfed. And your hair…."

"Have you any news of my husband?"

"Why yes, I believe he made it to safety with John Other Day."

"Other Day!" A Wahpeton chief; a mission Indian who farmed on the Upper reservation.

"We must thank the good Lord that in these awful days He raised up among His red children such faithful servants as Other Day and Little Paul. Colonel"—Riggs turns to Sibley—"this is Mrs. Dr. John Wakefield, wife of the physician at Yellow Medicine. You'll remember her letter, written on behalf of some friendlies?"

"Of course." Sibley tips his hat. "Madam."

She tamps down her scorn. "Thank you for coming so *speedily* to our rescue, Colonel."

"We've done our best. Please alert me should you need anything. Anything at all."

Captain Grant brushes James's curious fingers from the hilt of his sword. He looks askance at James's yellow face.

"Your children's names, please?" Riggs dips his pen. "My memory fails me."

"This is Nellie. My little man is James."

Nellie lets her doll fall to the ground. Grant stoops to retrieve it. He leers at its costume. "A *Sioux* doll, Madam?"

"What else would you expect, Captain, our living so long among them?"

"Dear woman," Riggs says, "where's your protector?"

She turns to scan the crowd of Sioux. "Ćaske tokiya idade?" she shouts to Uŋćiśi, just as Ćaske steps up behind her, clenching his gun.

"Haŋ," he says, announcing himself.

"You are the Indian who secured this woman?" Riggs asks him, in Dakota.

"It is so."

"You are called Ćaske?"

"It is so."

"Are you called by any other names?"

"He Who Is Liked By The Stars." *Wićaŋĥpi Waśtedaŋpi.*

Sarah thinks of the blue and yellow stars painted on their tipi. *What else do you not know about him?*

Riggs writes out a phonetic spelling of the name, presumably for the benefit of any white man who might have reason to pronounce it. He neglects a syllable, but Sarah decides not to correct him in front of Sibley and Grant.

Riggs sits back and considers Ćaske's face. "I believe we have met before."

"It is so. We have met several times."

"I'm sorry, I cannot place you.... Tell me, what did you do on behalf of this woman?"

Sarah draws Ćaske closer to the field desk. "As I mentioned in my letter, this man saved my life repeatedly. I cannot thank him enough."

"You speak his tongue remarkably well, Madam," Sibley says.

"I have had good teachers," she says, smiling at Ćaske.

Riggs reaches for Ćaske's hand. "God bless you, my good man, for saving this poor woman and her young ones. Your name will long be remembered for your kindness."

She must leave no doubt. "I tell you again, sirs, if not for this man and his family, my children and I would *most certainly* be dead."

Sibley offers Ćaske a mock salute. "If there are heroes among the Sioux people, you, my red friend, are *most certainly* one of them."

₰ 5 ₷

REVEILLE SPLITS THE STILLNESS. Sarah, wedged between her babies, is already awake, wondering how Ćaske had slept, down in Camp Lookout. Outside the tent, soldiers are assembling, saluting the morning with gunfire, answering the roll call. She smells strong coffee, and sighs. Today, September 27, is her sixth wedding anniversary.

Late yesterday afternoon, when she and more than a hundred other white captives entered Camp Release, the troops had raised three cheers. The soldiers fed them applesauce and hardtack around their campfires. They supplied kerosene for hair-washing against the lice. Then they herded them into cramped tents—in this one, twenty-three women and children, with only straw to sleep on and thin blankets for bedding. After spotting the hole in the canvas roof for a stovepipe, she requested a stove, but none was available. She demanded firewood and was told, "No open fires in the tents."

By the bugler's tattoo, the high spirits of the former captives had descended into whining and whimpering, fears of the dark, questions without answers. The night was too cold and their nerves too frayed to be without the comfort of a fire. Despite the late hour, Sarah cleared the straw from the center of the tent, collected some kindling, and set it aflame. Some rules are worth the breaking.

Axes are thudding along the river. Shouts of warning ring out as cut trees groan and fall. The soldiers, it seems, plan to stay a while. She, most certainly, does not. If Sibley won't provide more adequately, she will return with the children to Camp Lookout until the Army conveys them wherever they're meant to go next. In Uŋċiśi's tipi they were never without a warm fire, adequate bedding, soap and water, and something substantial to eat. She intends to tell Sibley so. But first, she will have a breakfast of Army rations.

"ARE YOU CERTAIN THE SAVAGE DIDN'T ... *INSULT* YOU?"

"Subject you to ... *poor treatment?*"

"The woman's not telling everything!"

"Gentlemen, please—Mrs. Wakefield might not wish to speak of such abuses in our company."

Sibley has appointed three of his senior officers to a panel of inquiry. She is the first former captive summoned for questioning; in deference, she presumes, to her standing as the wife of a government physician. Over the past hour she has tried to offer a compelling account of her weeks in captivity.

Colonel Marshall, the presiding officer, laces his fingers. His balding head is flushed deep red. "Let me suggest to Mrs. Wakefield that if she has anything of a delicate nature to relate, she might communicate it privately to Mr. Riggs."

"I've nothing more to say, Colonel, I assure you. My testimony is complete."

"But sometimes an enemy, a savage especially, will, shall we say, *take advantage* of captive females. Do you not understand?"

"For God's sake, William"—Colonel Crooks, drumming the table "she's a woman! Speak plainly."

Marshall swills a glass of water. "Madam, we're asking in what manner you were *violated.* In what manner the savage *ravished* you."

"I'm well aware of what you're asking. But Ċaske treated me with every dignity. He protected me against every threat to my person."

The three officers exchange glances.

"You have no complaints at all to make?" says Captain Grant. A crooked line of stitches cuts through his heavy beard, over his chin.

"None, thank you."

Marshall writes something on a piece of paper. "You might still choose to speak to the Reverend. I plead with you, Madam, tell him what you have suffered."

·   ·   ·

Upon stepping out of the inquiry, she hikes her dress and sets out at a rush for Camp Lookout. She has been a fool. She should never have urged Ćaske to surrender. She should never have trusted Sibley's promise to let the innocent go free. In the judgment of the Army, there will be no such thing as an innocent Indian.

"God Almighty, who sits on the throne, will make good of this bloodshed yet. But you must submit to Him. Cry in your distress upon the Lord!"

Even from here, on the fresh beeline path through the prairie grass to Lookout, she can faintly hear Riggs shouting in Dakota. A morning prayer service, evidently.

"Those of you who have not yet laid hold on Christ, burn your medicine bundles and forswear your false gods!" Seizing his opportunity to evangelize, Riggs has converted the council lodge into a house of Christian worship. "Jesus Christ is your only salvation! The hand of the Lord is upon you in this time of distress. He will deliver you from your trials and tribulations, if you walk in the way He puts before you!"

She finds the door of Uŋćiśi's tipi closed and crossed with two sticks. She calls in anyway, shaking the door frame. No one answers. *Perhaps the spirits told her and Ćaske to go to church.*

She hurries to the council lodge. No sooner is she inside the door than Ćaske hurries her back out. She winces in pain at his grip on her arm.

"Two men have been arrested," he says. "If the soldiers arrest me, I will know My Wife lied. Then I will lie, too."

"I would never lie about My Husband! I have no reason to lie—you saved my life! But you were right all along—you must run—*now!*"

He relaxes his hold on her. "I am not a coward. I am not afraid to die. I will die without uttering a cry."

"Don't be such a goddamned warrior!" The English is out before she thinks. She reverts to Dakota. "Were My Husband to die here, he would not die a warrior. Please—"

"I will not run."

"But you were ready to run before! What has changed?"

"All is in the hands of the Giver."

"If you are worried about Uŋćiśi, leave her with me. I will care for her, somehow. I promise."

"You promise like a white man."

"Do not say that!"

"Go back to your soldiers."

"I will do everything I can for her—"

"Go!"

AT A GENTLEMANLY HOUR THAT EVENING, CAPTAIN GRANT AND A FEW officers call at the tent. They portion out to Sarah and the other women whiskey and dainties sent by wives and sweethearts to cheer them in the field. Their chivalrous companionship is a welcome relief from the unwanted advances of the rank-and-file. The enlisted men have been so dogged in their amorous pursuits, Sibley has issued an order forbidding them to consort with the captives.

Drink loosens them all. They're soon laughing and singing, flirting like guests at a soirée while children sleep around them in the straw.

"Captain Grant," Captain Kennedy booms over the babble, "how many savages have we locked up? Seven by now, isn't it?"

Everyone falls quiet, looking to Grant. He polishes off his drink. "Yes, indeed! And before tomorrow night, those devils will hang high as Haman."

"But tomorrow's the Sabbath!" one of the women protests.

"The Lord's justice on the Lord's day," Lieutenant Ebell says. "What could be more fitting?"

Emboldened by her liquor, Sarah advances on Captain Grant. "Is Ćaske among the Indians you've arrested? Wićaŋȟpi Waśtedaŋpi?"

"Manacled and in the pen, Madam. He'll swing with the rest."

"Why? Pray tell me what he's done!"

"I should think you'd know, better than anyone."

"To the gallows!" Kennedy toasts from across the tent, and everyone but her chimes in.

She pours out her whiskey on Grant's boots. "I swear to you, sir"— fighting to restrain her voice—"if you hang that man, I'll shoot you dead, if it takes me twenty years."

BY THE NEXT AFTERNOON CAMP RELEASE IS BUZZING WITH NEWS. WITH parties of Sioux still surrendering and renegades being rounded up, Lookout has burgeoned to a thousand people or more. The Army has now cordoned it off and set about confiscating the Indians' guns and ammunition. No Sioux may leave Lookout for any reason, and no one from Camp Release may enter without Sibley's permission.

What's more, Sibley's panel of inquiry has metamorphosed overnight into a Military Commission. Sarah is ignorant of what that might mean, precisely, but on its behalf Reverend Riggs is continuing to question former captives as well as "trustworthy Sioux." Based on his findings, the Army has made more arrests. Last night's count of seven prisoners has become ten, twelve, sixteen. At this rate, the jail will quickly overflow unless the Army somehow reduces its population. As yet, Sibley hasn't constructed a gallows, but the possibility he might string up the Sioux in trees along the river torments her.

She patty-cakes and plays dolly with a listless Nellie. She romps with James at follow-the-leader, then plays catch, tossing a baseball loaned by a soldier. All the while, she stays within clear sight of the crude jail at the center of camp. If Ćaske peers out a chink, he might see she hasn't abandoned him. White women and soldiers venture up to the jail's walls and leer through the timbers. Some spew such vitriol at the imprisoned Sioux that she covers her babies' ears.

The basis for Ćaske's arrest eludes her. Has the Army detained him because he took up arms against the United States, or rather, because he stands accused of crimes against civilians? She understands precious little about the law but senses the significance of this distinction. Everyone knows that rebel soldiers captured by Union troops are confined in prisoner-of-war camps. They're not "hanged high as Haman" like common murderers. Surely Ćaske, in defending his people, is no more deserving of the noose than a grayback.

Two privates stroll by as she and James play catch. "Why bother with arrests and inquiries?" the first is saying. "Ninety-nine hundredths of those devils are guilty. Witnesses in their favor would be useless as teats on a boar."

"I'm with Fogarty!" says the second. "Let's shell all the redskins to kingdom come!"

LIEUTENANT EBELL HAS HIS STEREO CAMERA MOUNTED ON A TRIPOD, POINTED at the jail. Even in his baggy uniform, Sarah can't imagine him a soldier. Such a frail, insipid fellow. Much has happened since she first met him, in passing, the day before the outbreak. A photographer by trade, he and his assistant were roaming the Upper reservation with cameras and a portable darkroom, capturing tourist shots of the Sioux. "Shadow-catching," the Sioux called it. Now he's a commissary officer on Sibley's staff, doubling as a war correspondent.

"Lieutenant," she says, "you might not remember me...."

Ebell straightens from his camera with an air of impatience. Once he sees her, the hook is set. "Oh, yes, Mrs. Wakefield! We met last night."

So regrettable, her drunken outburst to Captain Grant. "Actually, Lieutenant, you and I first met at the Upper Agency, the Sunday before the—"

"Quite right, yes! How fortunate to see you again! Your name's much bandied about." He taps the top of his camera. "Care to pose?"

She reddens. The man has the tact of a squirrel. "Lieutenant, may I ask how you avoided capture at Yellow Medicine? I'm seeking news of my husband, you see. I'm told he escaped with John Other Day."

"Other Day? He's being made quite the hero, that redskin. Saved quite a large party. But no, I fell in with Reverend Riggs and his company. Missionaries, mostly. We made it out by a whisker. Here, I'll show you, it's my best seller—"

He pulls a carte de visite from his breast pocket. The photograph is of a weary, hollow-eyed company languishing in prairie grass, with a two-horse wagon and light buggy in the background. Most of the people in the picture are, indeed, missionary families from Hazelwood—the Riggses, the Pettijohns, the Cunninghams, the Hunters. The caption along the bottom reads, "People Escaping from the Indian Massacre of 1862, At Dinner on a Prairie."

"Indian massacre?" she says. "Is that what they're calling the war?"

"My good fortune to have been there to shoot this! I took it with my very last plate. We'd stopped to rest, too tired to go on. We killed a cow and roasted it, and baked us some bread. It was a risk—the savages were all about, they might have had our scalps, but we were dying of hunger. Joel Whitney was pleased as punch to have this shot for his gallery, once I made it to St. Paul…. The card sells for twenty-five cents."

"Your 'good fortune,' as you put it."

"Care for a souvenir? Send one to your friends back East? No, wait, here's what I'll do: I'll let you have it for free, if you'll sit for me. 'Mrs. Sarah Wakefield, Lusty Captive of the Sioux, Hair Scared White by the Savage Ćaske.' What do you say—will you pose?"

⚜ 6 ⚜

COLONEL SIBLEY CLOSES the drawer in his field desk. "I must ask you to excuse me now, Mrs. Wakefield. I have pressing duties to attend to."

He refuses her return of his kerchief. "Stay as long as you need to calm yourself. I'll tell the guard to allow you some privacy." He settles his hat low on his brow. "This is the second time you and I have spoken regarding the savage. Let it be the last. Understood?"

She turns her head away.

"Good evening, Madam."

Sibley's tent, lit by lanterns, is warm with the heat from a stove. Though primitive and smelling of men, there is solace here. She feels entitled to tarry a while. Sibley owes her. How could he have rejected her petition to release Ćaske, a gesture to honor her birthday? She caresses a chessboard, a match in the endgame, black winning. She lifts the lid on a well-stocked liquor chest. Her mouth waters.

"She's in love with a fiend," the women say of her. "She lay with the devil and prefers him to her own husband...."

One of the thick woolen blankets would be such a comfort to James and Nellie, both ailing with colds. But on such a chilly night, either Sibley or his tent-mate Riggs would miss it.

She leans into a shaving mirror and gazes into the black caves of her eyes. Slides her fingertips down a weathered cheek. Picks up Sibley's comb and starts to untangle the dirty snarls in her white granny's mane. If she has time, she might even use his boar-bristle brush, a hundred swift strokes.

A glance over her shoulder at the tent's door, then she lowers herself into Sibley's chair. His field desk, cobbled together from poor quality wood, is scarcely more than a box with a drop-down lid to write on. Its shelves and pigeonholes contain a few furled maps, a Bible, volumes of infantry and cavalry tactics, poke sacks of tobacco and coffee, muster rolls, a *Manual for Courts-Martial* … nothing of much interest.

She lays the comb aside. Writing supplies, in his left-hand drawer. The opposite drawer, which he'd closed in haste before he left, has a lock. To her surprise, it isn't secured.

She pulls it open. With an ear pricked for footfall, she lifts out the topmost document. She presses it open on the desk's writing surface: an unfinished letter. Multiple pages, in a handsome pen. She must have interrupted his writing when she entered.

I went into the encampment with a few of my officers, leaving a guard of a couple of hundred soldiers on the outside, and after a brief speech, demanded the immediate surrender to me of all the white prisoners. A pitiable sight they presented. The poor creatures cried for joy at their deliverance from the loathsome bondage in which they had been kept for weeks, suffering meantime outrages at the hands of their brutal captors. Most of them were young, and there were a score or more of fine, ladylike appearance, notwithstanding the ragged clothes they wore.

When all were collected, they were placed in charge of the guard, and conducted to my own camp nearby, where tents and other accommodations had been provided for their reception.

She leafs back to the salutation. "My dear Sarah." His wife, no doubt. He began writing her last night, at midnight.

There is one young lady, very respectable and of fine personal appearance, a Miss Williams, who has been very much abused; indeed, I think all of the younger ones have been.

Again with the rape. The worry is understandable; in the beginning, it was one of her own greatest fears. But while Sibley and his officers seem convinced that most female captives had been violated, she herself is aware of only two: the girl Mattie Williams, mentioned here, and Mrs. Cardinal.

She's coming to the end of what Sibley has written, so far.

One rather handsome woman among them has become so infatuated with the redskin who took her for a wife that, although her white husband is still living at some point below and has been in search of her, she declares that were it not for her children, she would not leave her dusky paramour. The woman threatens that if her Indian, who is among those who have been seized, should be hung, she will shoot those of us who have been instrumental in bringing him to the scaffold, and then go back to the Indians. A pretty specimen of a white woman she is, truly!

❧ 7 ❧

SEPTEMBER 30, 1862

"Ma'am." The armed sentry bars Sarah's entry into the tent.

"I'm to testify, soldier." She tries to shoulder past.

He shoves her back with his gunstock. "You'll remain here till you're called, Mrs. Wakefield. Rules are rules."

So, he knows who you are.

She steps aside, biting her tongue. "Rules are rules"—meant as a barb, or not? After so much innuendo and outright slander, she can't tell anymore. "Pretty specimen of a white woman," Sibley had called her, with derision. How she'd been tempted to toss his dreadful letter into the stove!

Sibley's new Military Commission has summoned her to appear. She has made herself as respectable as any woman could in a military camp in wartime. But she's tired. As soon as she wins justice for Ćaske, she will make her way back to Shakopee. She has no house there to go home to— John sold it before their move to the reservation—but in her mind she has already settled into new lodgings. It has a bedchamber with a door, where a hundred randy soldiers can't peer in; a warm bed instead of straw to sleep in; a bathtub and hot water to bathe in; a closet full of clean dresses— her own, instead of a dead woman's; beef and bread to eat, instead of beans and hardtack; quiet and calm, instead of vicious backbiting....

"Sarah Wakefield and her Indian were lovers," the gossips say. "She told me herself she was his woman. She shared his bed from the first. She cooked his food and greased his hair. She ran his bullets and filled his powder. She sang as she sewed for him. She always talked Indian, and wore paint on her face, and danced like a squaw. She's in love with that Indian, it's to be expected, since savage blood courses through her veins—"

From the direction of the jail, a mounting gale of shouts. Sibley has ordered his troops not to pelt prisoners with stones and waste along the gauntlet to the Court. But they still line the way, heckling and jeering, chanting in cadence, "Left!... Left!... Left, right, left!"

Ćaske scuffles into view, hands bound in front of him, legs in irons. His escort is William Forbes, in a major's uniform, acting as Provost Marshal. Owner of stores at both Agencies, Forbes had left most of his trading to his clerks. But with the other traders he attended the last council with the Sioux before the war. "You are not men," he told the Indians. "Eat grass or your own shit," Andrew Myrick said. By the day of the outbreak, everyone on the reservation must have heard some version of the traders' insults.

No wonder that Sioux warriors attacked the traders first. Forbes wasn't at his store, but the Indians murdered all his clerks and brought his business partner George Spencer to Heaven's door. As for Myrick, whom the Sioux called Waćinko, *The Greedy One,* the story of his demise will certainly outlive them all: Shot dead in the back as he ran, and his mouth stuffed full of grass.

As Ćaske limps by in his shackles, Sarah feels their spirits meet in the unacknowledged space between them. His left eye is swollen shut. His face, mottled purple and black. His hair, matted with dried blood. She shudders to think of the injuries his clothing might conceal; to think of the angry boots that might have kicked his ribs and groin as he lay on the floor of the jail, his ankle chained to another Indian.

The fuzzy-faced sentry salutes Forbes. When he draws aside the flap to admit the Major and Ćaske, she slinks around the corner of the tent. She hunkers down between some barrels and a rank of firewood, close enough to the tent to hear a military voice shooting thin and sharp through the canvas: "—convened to try, summarily, any prisoners who may be brought before them by direction of the colonel commanding, and pass judgment upon them, if found guilty of murder or other outrages upon the whites, during the present state of hostilities."

God help us, this is no hearing. This is a full-fledged trial.

"The Military Commission," the voice reads on, "meeting pursuant to Order Fifty-Five, will now be seated according to rank: Colonel William Crooks, Sixth Regiment, Minnesota Infantry, President of the Commission ... Lieutenant Colonel William Marshall, Seventh Regiment ... Captain Hiram Grant, Sixth Regiment ... Captain Hiram Bailey, Sixth Regiment ...

and I am Lieutenant Rolin Olin, Third Regiment, Judge Advocate. Also present are Lieutenant Isaac Heard, Adjutant, Cullen Guards, acting as Recorder, and Antoine Frenier, Interpreter. I would ask the Court to please stand."

Wooden chairs creak, boots chafe, swords and buckles rattle and clink. "Sirs, please remove your gloves and raise your right hands.... Do you swear that you will well and truly try and determine, according to the evidence, the matter now before you, between the United States of America and the prisoner to be tried, and that you will duly administer justice without partiality, favor, or affection, so help you God?" A low grumble of I-dos. "You may be seated."

The Judge Advocate himself is then sworn, and the Recorder and Interpreter, in turn. No officer is tasked with representing Ćaske.

"This Court is hereby called to order." Olin clears his throat. "Case Number Three, We-chump-wash-tee-dun-pay," butchering Ćaske's name.

"THE ACCUSED IS ARRAIGNED UPON THE FOLLOWING CHARGES AND specifications: that on or about the eighteenth day of August, 1862, he did kill George H. Gleason, a white citizen of the United States, and has likewise committed sundry hostile acts against the whites between the said eighteenth day of August and the twenty-eighth day of September, 1862. This, near the Redwood River, and at other places on the Minnesota frontier. What does the prisoner say in answer to these charges—guilty or not guilty?"

Sarah strains to hear a reply, whether from Ćaske or from the interpreter Frenier, who had served Thomas on the Upper Agency staff. The half-breed is fluent in both English and Dakota, but the language of the Court is a tongue unto itself. With little or no experience of the white man's laws and legal customs, how will he ever comprehend the proceedings and explain them sufficiently to Ćaske?

Frenier's muffled voice: "He says the charges aren't true."

"The plea of not guilty will be recorded. Does the prisoner wish to make a statement?"

Frenier: "Yes."

"The prisoner will be heard."

The chink of chains. A cough. Fraught silence.

"Wakaŋtaŋka has brought me alive to this day. I will tell the truth of what happened." Ćaske's voice pours through the wall of the tent, atop the monotone of Frenier's interpreting. "I was with another Indian. The other

Indian shot the white man. I aimed my gun at the white man as he fell, but I did not fire. I have had a white woman in my charge. She is called Doctor Wife."

"Mrs. Dr. John Wakefield?"

"I could not care for her like a white man, but I protected her and her children until I could return them."

"And concerning the other hostile acts with which you are charged?"

"I would have run off with Taoyate Duta if I had done bad things. I was present when the white man was killed. That is all."

"Did you know Mr. Gleason before the outbreak began?"

"I saw him sometimes in the warehouse at Redwood. One time we went hunting."

After a pause, Olin says, "Please explain again how you came to kill Mr. Gleason."

"I did not kill him."

"Then please tell the Court again who killed Mr. Gleason, and how."

"Two of us were in the war party. A wagon came toward us, and the other Indian said, 'Brother, let us shoot the American.' And he did. He shot the white man twice. I aimed at him, because I was told I must kill Americans, or be killed."

"Who said you must kill the whites?"

"Taoyate Duta and the soldiers' lodge."

"When were you told this?"

"That was the order given from the start. Kill the whites, or pay with your life."

"This Indian you say shot Mr. Gleason ... is he now in the Indian camp?"

"No. He went away with Taoyate Duta."

"Does this Indian have a name?"

Silence.

"The prisoner will please tell the Court his name."

A mumble.

"The prisoner will please speak up."

Frenier: "Hepaŋ, he says—Second Son. Like there aren't a hundred of them."

"Were you present at any battles?" Olin picks up, after a lull.

"Yes."

"Where did you fight?"

Ćaske confers a long time with Frenier. At last Frenier says, "Fort Ridgley, New Ulm, Lone Tree Lake. He fought only soldiers. He never killed anyone in cold blood. He *says*."

"Let's return to Mr. Gleason.... Why didn't you stop the other Indian from shooting him?"

"He was wild with fire water. He shot before I knew. I could only stop him killing Doctor Wife and her children."

"Did you fire at Mr. Gleason?"

"I pulled the trigger. It snapped but failed to go off."

"Why didn't it go off?"

"Sometimes a gun does not fire."

"Why did you try to shoot him?"

"The other Indian said I was afraid to shoot."

"So ... it *wasn't* because you'd been ordered to kill whites." Frosty triumph in Olin's voice.

"Yes. I had to shoot."

"Because you didn't like being called a coward."

"I am not a coward."

"How many times did you shoot?"

"I shot over the white man when he fell."

No, only Hepaŋ fired! Tell him about the runaway wagon—

"What do you mean, you 'shot over him?'"

After discussion with Ćaske, Frenier says, "The prisoner claims he missed Gleason *on purpose."*

"So your gun *did* fire," Olin says.

"Yes."

No! Only Hepaŋ fired—two shots—

"Your gun *did* go off."

"Yes."

But there wasn't a third shot—

"A moment ago you said your gun misfired."

"It fired the first time, when the white man was in the wagon. It misfired when he was on the ground."

"You attempted to shoot Mr. Gleason again, when he lay wounded?"

Tell them why. Out of mercy—

"Yes. When he was on the ground, my gun did not fire."

"Is this everything the prisoner wishes to say in his defense?"

Frenier interprets.

"No," Ćaske says to the Court, in English. "I want speak."

. . .

AMONG MY PEOPLE I AM CALLED HE WHO IS LIKED BY THE STARS. I AM Mdewakantonwan, from the village of Śakpe Daŋ. I am the first son of my parents. My father was from the band of Śakpe. My mother is the daughter of Eagle Head, a respected chief. Our spirits come from the Creator down the spirit road.

There is a prophecy among us, passed down from the grandfathers. I will tell it short. Long ago, one of our holy men had a vision. In this vision the buffalo and all the four-leggeds were going back into the earth, and a great spider's web was being woven over the people. When the day came when all this would happen, the holy man said, we would live in little square houses in little pens of barren land. And we would starve and die, because it is not our way to live like that.

It is said that this vision filled the holy man with such sorrow, after sharing it with the people he went back into the earth. Now his vision has come to pass. The dark web has been spun. We have been confined behind fences and made to live in houses that do not move. The animals are gone. The trees are leaving.

Your people have come to our lands to take revenge on where you came from. You think you can defeat whatever has hurt you by turning your backs on your ancestors. You abandon the hunting grounds and graves of your grandparents. You run away and become strangers to your own birthplace. You intrude with giant feet upon our lands, bringing your bad spirits with you. We did not ask you to come. But in the beginning, we welcomed you. We shook your hands. We shared our food. We hunted and traded with you. We smoked the pipe with you. We let you have our women as wives and raised up your children among us.

But now you want to recast us in your image. We are the lead you melt and pour into your bullet molds. You do not respect us. You make us live like you. You make us give up Wakaŋtaŋka for the white God. You make us give up the hunt, our old villages, our medicine bundles, our dances and ceremonies.

You bring us sickness. You bring us fire water. You bring guns and cannon and force us to put our marks on papers we cannot read. Then you break all your promises. Your tongue is forked. One of your words can mean seven things.

We have lost our world, because you did not come to us in a good way. Some day my people will be as the buffalo and the trees.

Our prophecies said you would come from the east, from far across the sea. They said you would arrive by boat on the shores of Turtle Island and march in all directions, devouring everything in your path, like grasshoppers. They said you would have pale skin, and wear odd clothes, and be covered with hair. They said when you spoke, no one would understand. It is all true.

When I was a boy, I would lie awake at night and watch the stars through the smoke-hole of our lodge. "The big, bright stars," the elders would say, "are the wise old warriors, the mightiest hunters. The many small stars are young boys, learning to be men. They are learning to have courage, to be generous, to show respect and compassion. They are learning to be Dakota." I am still learning to be Dakota. Who is left to teach me?

I hear the elders weeping. The earth is weeping, the rivers are weeping. The stars are falling from the sky. Who can put them back?

I am not a wise man. In my dreams I take myself again to a lonely spot and cry for a vision. I paint my face black with soot and stand shoulder-deep in the river, begging the spirits to instruct me. I pray there will be another world. I pray your people and mine will all live again, with good hearts. I pray we will walk together, in good ways. When the winter wind howls at the smoke-hole and ducks down the flaps to make the fire jump, we will keep each other warm and dry. We will tell stories as our lodge rocks, and it will not blow down. The ropes and poles will be too strong, the pegs too many and too deep in the ground. All winter long, while the earth sleeps, we will have plenty to eat. And in spring, when the river ice cracks with a boom, our children will want to be born. The flowers will bloom beneath the melting snow, and our children will run and play together. They will watch the prairie grass change colors as it bows before the breeze. They will watch the ghost-lights leap and dance in the northern sky. They will listen to the cries of the eagle, and honor their ancestors, and grow up to be good relatives of all that lives.

I am not an old man like my grandfather, but the world I grew up in has vanished. I have walked in a great circle and come back to my first steps. I am nothing but a child again. I pray to the spirits to help me walk in a good way. If I cannot walk true, then like the holy man after his vision I should go back into the earth.

8

"THE COURT CALLS Mrs. Dr. John Wakefield."

Sarah enters the makeshift courtroom, still unnerved by Ćaske's oration. He'd sounded like a man touched by Wakaŋtaŋka; a man ordained to utter holy words laid upon his heart. "Gird up thy loins," God told the prophet Jeremiah, "and speak unto them all that I command thee: They shall fight against thee; but they shall not prevail, for I am with thee...."

Up at the front, congregated around a large table, are the five Commission members, in military regalia. Among them is Captain Grant, whom she threatened to shoot dead. At a field desk to the Commission's left sits a militiaman with ink, pen and paper. He must be the Recorder, Lieutenant what's-his-name. And standing ramrod straight before the Commission, watching her approach, is a slim, clean-shaven officer—Olin, the Judge Advocate. His broad forehead is chalky white above his hat line.

Ćaske is shackled in a chair between Olin and a tiny gallery of onlookers. She stops beside him and clasps his bound hands. He raises his chin but doesn't meet her eyes. "Tiwahiŋ da," she wants to say, in the manner of a wife, *I care for you.* But she doesn't dare, with Frenier so near. "Waćiŋ taŋka ye," she whispers, and lets him go.

"Mrs. Wakefield, please step forward and place your right hand upon the Bible.... Do you swear that the evidence you shall give, in the case now in hearing, shall be the truth, the whole truth, and nothing but the truth, so help you God?"

"I do."

Olin returns the Bible to the table. "Mrs. Wakefield, I'll ask you to please state what you know concerning the conduct of the accused regarding the said charges."

"Which are?"

"The murder of George Gleason. Committing hostile acts against whites."

Among the few official guests of the Court she notices both Stephen Riggs and John Williamson, the missionary son of Thomas and Margaret. Young Williamson informed her only yesterday that his parents are alive. They had narrowly escaped their mission station with the help of friendly Indians. Loath to believe the Sioux would ever harm them, they waited almost too long to flee.

"Mrs. Wakefield, I'll ask you again. Please state what you know."

"I assume my testimony will be interpreted for Ćaske?"

Frenier raises an eyebrow at Olin, who nods.

She lengthens her spine. "I was with Mr. Gleason when he was killed. My children and I were riding with him to Fort Ridgley, where I wished to take the stage. I was distressed all the way down from Yellow Medicine— we'd heard rumors of an outbreak—but Mr. Gleason refused to turn back. I pleaded and pleaded. Had he listened to me, he might still be alive."

"Where were you attacked?"

"Near the Half-Way House, above the Lower Agency. It's an inn run by Joseph and Valencia Reynolds."

"Please tell the Court what happened."

"We met two Indians on the road. This man, Ćaske, and another, Hepaŋ, who'd been drinking."

"Is the Hepaŋ in question among the Indians now in the Sioux camp?"

"I don't know. I haven't been down to Lookout since it was declared off limits."

"Was he there the day you were liberated by Colonel Sibley?"

"I doubt it. He and his wife were said to have fled with Little Crow after the last battle."

"This Hepaŋ was a hostile Indian?"

"Yes."

"And the defendant"—Olin points at Ćaske—"was he not also a hostile?"

"Ćaske saved my life, and my children."

"But he was, in fact, a hostile."

"Not to us."

Olin pinches the bridge of his nose. "Please continue with the events of August eighteenth."

"We were approaching the Half-Way House, and we met these two Indians coming up the road from the direction of Redwood. Hepaŋ shot Mr. Gleason outright—twice, in the shoulder and in his middle. Mr. Gleason fell out of the wagon. The horses bolted at the gunfire. They were totally out of control, reins dragging the ground, and Ćaske— you're calling him Wićaŋĥpi Waśtedaŋpi, but I know him as Ćaske—he ran after the wagon and managed to stop it. Had he not, we might have rolled—"

"Please confine your statement to the facts."

"I'm stating the facts as I see them, Lieutenant."

"Continue."

"Hepaŋ had shot both barrels into Mr. Gleason. He reloaded while Ćaske ran after us."

"At this point, was Mr. Gleason still alive?"

"When we drove up, he was writhing on the ground in his death agony."

"What happened next?"

"Hepaŋ shot him again, in the head. Then he aimed at me. He was about to pull the trigger when Ćaske knocked away his gun."

"When exactly did Ćaske shoot at Mr. Gleason?"

"He didn't. I mean, he *did,* but only later. You see, we were about to leave that awful place when a sound came from Mr. Gleason."

"After three bullets, he wasn't yet dead?"

"Ćaske told Hepaŋ to shoot Mr. Gleason again, in pity. But Hepaŋ insisted they both shoot. They got down from the wagon, to put Mr. Gleason out of his misery. Ćaske told me later he'd have wanted the same done to him, were there yet a flicker of life."

"So Ćaske put the last bullet into Mr. Gleason."

"No, Hepaŋ did. Ćaske snapped his gun at him, but it didn't fire."

"Then?"

"We left. In the wagon."

"Mrs. Wakefield, please, if you could shed some light…. The prisoner maintains he shot *over* Gleason, earlier in the attack."

"I saw him shoot just one time, in mercy. That shot failed to fire."

"You're certain?"

"Absolutely."

Olin closes his eyes a moment, as if considering how to proceed. Then: "The Court believes the defendant to be a blanket Indian."

"To the contrary, he lived in a house before the war and farmed his fields. He has had a little schooling, both in English and Dakota."

"Please describe what the defendant was wearing on August eighteenth."

"Shirt, leggings and breechcloth."

"Is that not the dress of a blanket Indian?"

"With all due respect, every man in Little Crow's camp was dressed like a blanket Indian. Everyone had been ordered to wear traditional clothing—to show loyalty, I suppose, or submission. I myself had to wear Sioux dress. So you see, Lieutenant, Ćaske had no choice but to put on the breechcloth. I suggest you forget his clothing and pay more attention to his hair."

"His hair?"

"Not as short as yours, but not nearly as long as the prisoner's you marched in here yesterday. Ćaske is a cut-hair."

"Is he not wearing a braid?"

"A small one. His hair began to grow out during the war. He had to wear it the traditional way."

"Hm, yes, to *show loyalty*.... Mrs. Wakefield, is the defendant a Christian?"

"I've seen him in church. He knows right from wrong. He tries to treat others as he would like to be treated."

"That isn't the question."

"He isn't a savage. He didn't want to kill. He didn't go into this war willingly—he told me so. And he didn't want to attack our wagon."

"I'll remind you again to confine yourself to the facts."

"The *fact*, Lieutenant, is that twice on the government road, Hepaŋ raised his gun to kill me, and twice Ćaske stopped him. The *fact* is that throughout the war, Hepaŋ, Little Crow and others never ceased to threaten me and my children, and Ćaske always protected us. The *fact* is, were it not for Ćaske, my bones would be bleaching on the prairie, moldering into dust, and my babies either dead or headed for the plains. The *fact* is, even if Ćaske had killed Mr. Gleason, I'd have forgiven him, because of the great mercies he showed me—"

"I'm sorry, perhaps I misheard ... did you state you would have *forgiven* him? For *murder?*"

"Yes."

Olin looks at the Commission, then back at her.

"Is it possible, Mrs. Wakefield, that this Indian might have saved you for selfish purposes?"

"Such as?"

"To trade you for clemency, for example ... or to use you, shall we say, in *other* ways."

Captain Grant brushes a trace of lint from his uniform's lapel. Colonel Crooks, presiding from the center seat at the table, crosses his arms upon his chest, his face wrinkled in plain disgust.

"Lieutenant Olin, the defendant did not *use* me, in *any* way, and I resent your implication."

"Mrs. Wakefield, to your knowledge, was the defendant in possession of any plunder?"

She considers how to answer. "Among the Sioux, it's common for goods to be shared, especially with those in need, and there was great privation among the people."

"So your answer is yes?"

"His possession of plunder isn't proof that he plundered."

"Among his spoils, did the defendant have a smoking pipe? A *white man's* pipe?"

She glances at Riggs in the gallery.

"Mrs. Wakefield, I believe the Reverend Riggs conferred with you yesterday."

"We've spoken a few times since my release. Presumably in confidence."

"Tell us, please, about your discussion yesterday as regards a certain smoking pipe."

Her mouth aches for liquor. "May I have a drink of water?"

An orderly dips a cup into a bucket.

"Ćaske had a pipe," she says, after a swallow of river water.

"'Had?'"

"He asked me to destroy it."

"When?"

Ćaske tips his head closer to Frenier, intent on the interpreter's words.

"Last night, at the jail. When I told him whose pipe it was, he gave it to me and told me to burn it."

"To destroy evidence."

"Don't put words in my mouth."

"What other reason could there be?"

Her head is suddenly a drum. "It was a dead man's pipe."

"Louder, please."

"The pipe had belonged to a settler, a man killed the first day of the war. Ćaske wasn't aware of that till I told him last night. He was sickened to hear it. He told me to burn the pipe, out of respect for the dead."

"Those were *his* words—'respect for the dead?'"

"Of course not, he spoke in Dakota, but that was his meaning."

"And how did *you* learn the provenance of the pipe?"

"Reverend Riggs told me yesterday. Some woman had noticed Ćaske smoking the pipe in the jail, and she recognized it as her dead husband's."

"She went mad with grief, seeing it."

"So Mr. Riggs gave me to understand."

"The pipe must have been quite distinctive. Would you please describe it for the Court?"

"I hardly see how it matters."

"I should think it matters a great deal to the dead man's widow." Olin turns toward the gallery. "Mrs. Martha McConnell Clausen, would you please stand?"

A woman rises from the bench beside Riggs. She's so frail, she might blow down in a slight wind. As Frenier's interpreting catches up with the Court, Ćaske turns to look back at her.

"God have mercy," the woman breathes.

"Mrs. Wakefield, this is the widow of the late Frederick Clausen. She saw him shot dead by Indians in their yard. He'd been out haying in his field. At the sound of shooting, he came running."

Sarah tightens Uŋćiśi's shawl around her shoulders. "I'm not uncaring, Lieutenant. My own husband was long rumored to be among the dead. I felt his loss keenly. I only meant … I don't see how a description of the pipe—Mr. Clausen's pipe—pertains to these proceedings."

"The Court will decide what's pertinent and what isn't…. Mrs. Clausen, the Court extends our sympathies. You may be seated." After the woman settles herself, Olin proceeds. "Mrs. Wakefield, I'll ask you again: please describe the pipe."

Sarah can't rid herself of the vision of Mrs. Clausen's stricken face.

"Madam, *please.*"

She gulps down the rest of her water. "The bowl was bright red clay, with diagonal ribbing."

"And the stem?"

"A long reed stem, with a fine polish."

"Would you say it was a handsome pipe?"

"I suppose. Much used, but handsome, and light in the hand. It gave a good smoke."

"You sound like a woman who enjoys a pipe.... Did you ever smoke the pipe in question?"

"Yes."

"You borrowed the pipe from the defendant?"

She rubs the scruff of her neck, and hooks on. "We shared it."

"You and the defendant smoked the pipe *together.*"

"Yes." She fastens her gaze on a horsefly crawling up the wall of the tent.

"Once?"

"More than once."

"Let me be clear. This defendant—your captor—would draw on the pipe, then pass it to you, and you would place your lips—"

"Where *his* lips had been, yes!" She glowers at the Commissioners. "Which of *you* hasn't smoked a pipe with a Sioux?" She wheels around to face the gallery. "Which of *you?*"

"But *you*, Mrs. Wakefield—"

"I've smoked with Sioux women for years!"

"But this was no squaw you were smoking with! And the buck was a *murderer*, to boot!"

She locks eyes with Riggs.

"Madam, I must ask you to turn around and face the Court."

She complies, slowly, trying to steady herself.

"Now, you say the defendant asked you to destroy the pipe."

"Out of respect, yes. When I told him where the pipe had come from, he was distressed. He said he was tired of the killing and didn't care anymore whether he lived or died."

"You never asked him how the pipe came to be in his possession?"

"No."

"That seems curious."

"A pipe's a pipe."

"It didn't look white to you?"

"Many Indians smoke white pipes, Lieutenant."

"When the defendant asked you to destroy the pipe, what did you do?"

"I disposed of it."

"Where?"

"In a tent stove."

"Where you sleep?"

"We don't have a stove. I don't know whose tent it was."

"You didn't consider giving the pipe to Reverend Riggs, to return to Mrs. Clausen?"

The Recorder's mouth is contorting as he writes. His pen scratches loudly, letting in some words, leaving out others, inventing history. Lieutenant *Heard*, she remembers all at once.

"Mrs. Wakefield?"

"No, I didn't consider it. I wish I had."

"It seems you had more concern for the feelings of a savage than those of Mrs. Clausen, a former captive, and a white woman, like yourself."

"Lieutenant, for six weeks I was a prisoner of the Sioux. I saw terrible things. I lived day and night with the fear of being killed, or worse. I had to do things I would *never* have done but to preserve the lives of my children. My hair turned white from the strain. I lost considerable flesh from my bones. Now my husband is said by some to be dead, by others to be alive. I've no home to go home to. I can't sleep, can't eat, can't think straight. What life do I have left? Tell me!" Olin is trying to break in, but she rushes on. "If my actions seem curious to you, Lieutenant—if the dictates of my conscience offend you—you'd do well to remember that in wartime, any woman in my position—a *man*, even—would do whatever is necessary to remain alive."

"Are you suggesting that you destroyed Mr. Clausen's pipe out of fear for your life? I'll remind you, the defendant was confined. He couldn't have harmed you."

She cradles her head in her hands. "You're not hearing me!" She pulls up her chin to address the Commissioners. "I didn't—I *don't*—fear Ćaske. He's a good man. We first met years ago, in Shakopee. My husband even saved his life after a battle, with a pittance of help from me. Now Ćaske has returned that kindness, many times over. He and his mother, others in his family, put themselves at risk repeatedly to protect me and my babies. They made certain we were warm and fed, even if they had to go around begging, or do without, themselves—"

"Has the defendant a wife?" Olin asks, talking over top of her.

The question slams her up against a wall. "A wife?"

"Yes. Does the defendant have a wife?"

"You mean ... oh ... no, his wife is dead. Since midwinter, I believe. They didn't have enough food—"

"So, let me understand. The defendant has no wife, his bed is empty, and suddenly you're living in his tipi, enjoying his care and protection, and sharing his pipe.... What *else* did you share, Madam? Just how did you thank the killer of George Gleason for his many *kindnesses?*"

If only, like a man, you had a pocketwatch to glare at and snap shut, to display your displeasure. But then, were you a man, this nonsense would have ended long ago. Indeed, were you a man, Ćaske wouldn't have been charged at all. Like the Ćaske who saved George Spencer, he would have remained the hero Sibley first pronounced him, for having preserved a white man's life. But you, Mrs. Dr. John Wakefield, are merely a white man's wife.

Olin picks up his *Manual for Courts-Martial*. He must be near done, she thinks, as he's leafing through. She is weary of standing, of being put to the test, of feeling like she's the one on trial. At the initial inquiry Sibley's officers wanted to prove her a victim. Now the Commissioners want to prove her a whore. Some men will twist a woman to suit any purpose.

"Let's address the second charge." Olin lays his handbook on the table beside him. "To your knowledge, did the defendant fight in any battles?"

"He was forced to, like a conscript."

"Why do you believe he fought under duress?"

"Many times he expressed his regret about the war. He told me he'd always considered himself a friend of the whites. But the camp crier would go around before battle, saying every Indian who could carry a gun must fight or be shot—"

"Yes, 'kill or be killed'—we've heard that line before." Olin is strutting back and forth. "A convenient argument, but it justifies nothing. Killing is killing, whether by a savage or a saint."

"You can't say for certain that Ćaske ever killed anyone. I, for one, never saw him with a scalp in his belt, or wearing a new feather. I never saw him in black paint."

"Black paint?"

"Any Indian who has killed during battle must put on black paint before reentering camp."

"For what purpose?"

"I don't know. It's their way."

"Yet you would offer this *lack of paint* as proof of the savage's innocence?"

"Lieutenant, you seem to have little regard for my testimony concerning Ćaske's character. So, I suggest you ask Joseph Reynolds. He's soldiering in this camp."

"What has he to do with this case?"

"As I said before, he and his wife ran the Half-Way House, near where Mr. Gleason was killed. He's an uncle of one of the captives. He's lately spoken with me, and—"

"Mrs. Wakefield—"

"—he confessed to me that he's well acquainted with Ćaske, and considers him a fine man—"

"Hearsay is not permitted!"

"Those were his words—'a fine man.' Ask him yourself!"

"Mrs. Wakefield, I beg you to obey the Court!"

"And I would beg you to listen!"

Her demand hangs in the tent like breath in winter air. Olin shows her his back.

"This Court," she says, under her breath, "has ears of stone."

❧ 9 ❧

THE COMMISSION DELIBERATES in secret all of five minutes before reconvening. Outside the tent, Sarah strains to hear the verdict through the canvas. But without pronouncing its decision the tribunal proceeds to Case #4, Tażu, accused of ravishing young Mattie Williams.

"*Ravishing.*" That one dreadful word from Olin's lips makes everything plain to her, like a brush stroke of varnish bringing out a hidden grain of wood. Though the Court's proceedings over these past few days have been closed to all but official guests, everyone in camp has observed the prisoners being conducted from the jail to the tribunal tent. Rumors abound regarding the cases against them. Case #1 was peculiar. Its subject was a mulatto named Otakte, *Many Kills.* Before the uprising, he lived as a Mdewakantonwan on the Lower reservation. She remembers how, during the march to Yellow Medicine, he lashed without mercy any white captive who didn't keep pace. Charged with heinous offenses against white settlers, he reportedly "sang like a canary" before the Commission for two whole days, trying to save his skin.

The cases since Otakte's have all been of a stripe. Case #2: Tipi Hdonića, charged with "ravishing" Mrs. Cardinal. Case #3: Ćaske, charged not only with Gleason's murder but also "sundry hostile acts"—acts that apparently included ravishing *her,* or even luring her into fornication. Now, here's Case #4: Tażu, charged with "ravishing" the Williams girl. Clearly, the Commissioners have prioritized the cases in which they suspect an Indian of having defiled a white female.

In Ćaske's case, her consistent avowals of his decency must have hamstrung the Commission's prosecution. Without a rape victim, where was the crime? Unable to indict him on that specific charge, the Commissioners, in effect, indicted *her*. They pinned her as a fallen woman; a shameless hussy who had dallied with a red man. Olin's interrogation was her flogging. She can only hope her passionate defense of Ćaske hasn't reinforced the Court's suspicions and further sealed his doom.

SHE DOGS RIGGS INTO THE TENT HE SHARES WITH SIBLEY, HER BREATH IN frosty plumes. "I want Ćaske released! They have no evidence he killed Gleason. To the contrary, they have *me*, a witness in his defense!"

"Kindly lower your voice." Riggs casts his hat onto his cot. "His own words were enough to condemn him."

"They found him guilty?"

"Madam, I'm not at liberty—"

"Oh, stop with your 'liberties!'" She straddles a stool, prepared to do battle. "Tell me, did you recommend Ćaske be tried?"

"Yes."

"Despite everything I told you?"

"You've a distorted view of the man."

"He's a prisoner of war. Lock him up, if you must, but *death?*"

"Whatever sentence the Court imposes in the case will be their doing, not mine."

"It was supposed to be a hearing, not a trial. 'To winnow the chaff from the wheat,' you said."

"Things changed. The winds were too strong against us. Great wrongs demand swift justice."

"What happened in that tent today was not justice. A man can't defend himself if he doesn't know he's in a fight. Ćaske didn't even have a lawyer!"

Riggs frees the top buttons on his frock coat. "I grant you, the lack of defense counsel in these trials is a concern. I've said as much to Colonel Sibley."

"Sibley!" She scoffs. "He means to hang them all!"

"The Sioux will receive but small mercy, I'm afraid."

An orderly interrupts, delivering mail. After dismissing him with a weak salute, Riggs digs through the pouch. He withdraws two letters and tucks them with a smile into his Bible. "I'm sorry, where were we?"

"'Small mercy.'"

"Indeed…. I was saying, justice will require us to execute the great majority of those accused."

"None of this offends you as a man of the cloth? Or are you now just a man in uniform?"

Outside the tent a bugle blares noon mess. Riggs waits it out. "I realize these trials aren't in full accord with military regulations. Nor are they in the spirit of Christianity. They won't get to the facts, they won't resurrect the dead. But Mrs. Wakefield, you *must* understand—"

"Ćaske's an innocent man, a *good* man—"

"He's an *Indian.*"

Her eyes widen. This, from a man who has devoted his life to the Sioux.

"After what the gentlemen on this Commission have suffered," Riggs says, "we can't ask them to try Indians as they would white men." He seats himself opposite her, on a trunk bearing Sibley's initials. "All five of these officers commanded troops at Lone Tree Lake. Three of them were at Birch Coulee. Do you know what happened there? Very grim—let me speak, woman, you need to hear this!"

He closes his eyes and steeples his fingers. "End of August, Colonel Sibley dispatched a detail into the countryside to bury the bodies of dead settlers. Hundreds of bodies, strewn across the prairie. They were rotting in the sun for weeks…. An awful duty.

"Three days out, Sioux attacked the burial party. The camp was surrounded on all sides, totally exposed." His voice is raw with emotion. "I was with Sibley's force, two days later, when he saved what was left of those boys…. I'll never forget it, long as I live. Blood and bodies everywhere. Flies. Moaning. Stench. Tents riddled with bullet holes. The boys had dug in with their bayonets and cups, curled up behind their dead horses, hugged the ground behind their dead fellows, whatever would answer for a barricade. And they held on. No water. A few bites of hard crackers and cabbage for food. When we came in, the living arose from the ground as from their graves. Sibley broke down and wept."

He opens his eyes to regard her. "You knew Joseph DeCamp, I believe? Ran the sawmill at the Lower Agency?"

"Jannette's Joseph?"

"He was among the dead, I'm sorry to say. He'd volunteered to fight, wanting to look for his wife and children. Not long after Birch Coulee, his family showed up at Fort Ridgley with one of my Indians, but by then—"

"They're still alive? Jannette and her boys?"

"Yes, praise Heaven, but imagine their heartbreak…. What I'm trying to say is, these men on the Commission have been to Hell, and they've not entirely come back yet. Now, without any certainty that the war has reached its end, Colonel Sibley has charged them with deciding the fates of the very savages who bushwhacked their boys at Birch Coulee and scalped Marsh and his men at Redwood Ferry—"

"Not Captain Marsh!"

"—who butchered white farmers out mowing hay"—Riggs is preaching, his arms cutting the air—"who brained white babies against the trunks of trees, who committed outrages on white women—but for the grace of God, their own wives and daughters!"

"But the Commissioners swore to be impartial! Upon the Bible!"

"The oath is only as sound as the man. These officers aren't in a condition to give any Indian a fair trial. I've told them several times that I should be sorry to have *my* life placed in their hands. But I daresay, in all of Minnesota, at this hour, there are no men better, or of any wiser judgment. No, the Indians must bear their punishment. The white blood spilled on the ground cries out not only for justice, but vengeance, and these Commissioners, acting as the swift and righteous arm of the government, will visit the wrath of God upon the wretches—even upon those we might still call friends. The Indians are trespassers on our land, and they've done the Devil's work. We're right to seek reprisal, even if our methods are flawed. Lesser men than these might have lined up the Indians in a field by the hundreds and shot them dead without any thought of a trial."

She slumps on her stool. "There's no hope for Ćaske, then."

"With the help of the Holy Spirit, we may yet prepare his soul before he hangs. We may yet rescue him from the thralldom of the Devil."

"There's no chance of appeal?"

He massages his chin, considering. "Not to the Court. But perhaps to Colonel Sibley, and conceivably to his superior, General Pope. They must review the Court's judgment in each case before sentence is imposed."

"Then I'll speak to Sibley again."

"That will do you no good."

"Why not, pray tell? Why won't he listen to me, when he listened to George Spencer?"

"The trader?"

"He's recovering in the hospital tent, but he has already interceded with Sibley from his cot. *His* Ćaske is walking around scot-free."

"You're referring to Little Crow's lieutenant, Wakiŋya Tawa."

"Everyone knows he killed some whites before burying his tomahawk."

"I'm familiar with the particulars. These two instances are not the same."

"I see no difference. My life, my children's lives, are as valuable as George Spencer's. And if my Ćaske, who did *not* kill George Gleason, and who *did* save us, must wait to be hanged, while Wakiŋya Tawa, a murderer, is lauded to the skies for having saved Mr. Spencer, may God strike Sibley down!"

"Tame your tongue, woman!"

"What weapon do I have but my tongue? Sibley and his Commission haven't acted according to justice, but according to favor!"

"Madam, you have done all you could for your Indian—more than you should have. No other white woman plans to testify in defense of a Sioux. That you did so, and with such ardor, has caused people to kindle their whispers, and imagine the worst."

She feels the blood rise in her cheeks. "And you, Reverend, do *you* kindle the whispers? Do *you* imagine the worst?"

❧ 10 ☙

"My son, my son!" Uŋćiśi flails and slaps. "Why does Doctor Wife not save him? Everything he did for you, yet you do nothing to help him! You have forgotten us! Go back to your white friends!"

Sarah yields like a mule under the whip, letting Uŋćiśi's palms cuff her face, her shoulders, her arms. The pain seeps down like blood into the earth, until at last the old woman buckles into her arms, weeping. Sarah lowers her to the ground. She rearranges the shawl on the kuŋśi's shoulders, and waits.

"I tried to take him some bread. The soldiers would not let me."

"No, Uŋćiśi must stay here in camp."

"Yet My Daughter comes and goes."

"I must have permission, and an escort." She nods toward the officer, a Major Cullen, waiting at a discreet distance.

"Can my daughter deliver the bread? Will they let you see my son?"

"I will try. I am doing everything I can to help him, but some people are lying, saying he did bad things."

She won't tell Uŋćiśi that Ćaske has already been tried and sentenced in secret to hang. That her appeals to Riggs and Sibley have been futile. That she hasn't visited Ćaske in the jail since Court, four days ago. That she's afraid to see him again, shackled like a beast to the pockmarked Tażu. That she can't bear to face his reproach. That she worries her affection for him has gotten him killed. That she doesn't know anymore, if ever she did, what she means to him, or him to her. That since her so-called liberation she feels like a woman locked out of her self, without place or people, without a life that fits, without a world that isn't double.

"Your son is called He Who Is Liked By The Stars. I have not heard the story of his name."

Uŋćiśi smiles wistfully. "It happened in The Winter When The Stars Fell. We were camped on the edge of the Big Woods, hunting deer. The first snow was on the ground. One night we wakened to a strange light in the lodge. Ćaske was missing from his bed. He was a boy of seven winters. We hurried outside to find him. Wakaŋtaŋka was emptying the sky. Stars were raining down everywhere, thick and fast, like snowflakes in a storm."

Sarah grasps Uŋćiśi's arm. November, 1833, it had been; she can't recall the precise dates. She was only four years old. Half a continent away from Ćaske and Uŋćiśi, on her family's little farm near Exeter, her father pulled her from sleep to witness the same sky. For three nights in a row, everyone in North Kingstown watched the meteors showering down, thousands each minute, long streaks of bluish-white light coursing after them. While growing up, she heard so many stories about that heavenly spectacle, she can't be certain whether her memories of it are real or imagined.

"At last we caught sight of Ćaske. He was standing alone on a hilltop, clear of the trees. He was small and black against the fiery sky. All the stars were rushing down to greet him. Everyone saw. He was a child of seven winters, and Wakaŋtaŋka sent the stars down." Uŋćiśi caresses the side of Sarah's face, like a mother. "My Daughter must go to him. Take him my bread. Tell him I tried to see him. Tell him I pray without ceasing for him. Tell him the spirits will not desert him."

THE JAIL CENSUS HAS RISEN TO TWENTY-ONE: TEN SHACKLED PAIRS OF SIOUX, and off in a corner by himself, the mulatto informer, Otakte, safeguarded by a soldier. Ćaske and Tażu are slumped along the far wall, playing cards.

"Might you wait here, Major?" Sarah says to Major Cullen. "I won't be long."

The crowded jail is hazy from Sioux pipes and a smoky fire. She covers her nose and mouth against the smoke and the vinegar reek of unwashed bodies. When she is halfway across the straw-strewn floor, Dowaŋ S'a intrudes on her path with an ominous glare. She sidesteps him and his manacles.

Ćaske sees her approaching. He crabs to his feet and hobbles away, to the limit of his chains. He refuses to shake her hand.

"Please!" she says. "I come with a good heart."

He rubs at his eyebrow. The slender side-braid hanging at his ear is no longer twined with a lock of her white hair.

"Why does My Husband treat me so?"

"Why you come?"

"Do not speak in English," she begs, mindful of the guards.

His jaw muscles wrinkle. "Doctor Wife told lies," he says under his breath, in his own tongue. "Your spirit is bad."

"No."

"If Doctor Wife had told the truth, I would not be locked away in this place, away from My Mother, away from my people. Away from the sun." His morning rite: to face the east and greet the rising sun with his tobacco prayers.

"What they have done to My Husband is wrong. You do not deserve it. But I am not the cause." Tearful, she holds out the bundle of frybread. "I bring this from Uŋćiśi."

"You have seen her?"

"This afternoon. She is well but full of sadness and worry. The soldiers have kept her away."

He thrusts the bread down to Tażu. "My Mother and I trusted you, like no one else among your people."

"I have never betrayed your trust."

"I saved your life, many times."

"Yes." She stiffens against her desire to touch him.

"When you wanted milk for your cooking, I traded my coat to get some."

"Yes."

"When your children were shivering, I gave them my blanket."

"Yes."

"When you were crying in the night, I comforted you."

"Yes."

"Then why did you betray me?"

Her fingertips hammer at her temples. "How can I make My Husband understand?" She glances at Tażu, seated with his back against the log wall, chewing on Uŋćiśi's frybread. "I have lost my friends, trying to save you. *All* of them." She inches closer, brushing against the skin of his arm. "It is wrong for you to blame me. I am only a woman, but I have done everything I could for you, like a man. I have sacrificed my good name and my honor, trying to make the Big Knives listen. But when I move my lips, they hear only the twisted words they want to hear."

"You told them I killed the white man Gleason."

"No. I told them you no more wished to kill Gleason than I did. I told them if not for you, Hepaŋ would have killed me and my babies."

"Doctor Wife said these things?"

"Did My Husband not hear me speak in Court?" *Frenier.* "What did the interpreter say? Do not trust what he told you! I did not betray you!"

"But they will put the noose around my neck. Taoyate Duta spoke the truth."

"They might as well hang me as you." She draws her half of Uŋćiśi's shawl over her head. "I am sorry. I believed if I told the Big Knives the truth, they would repay My Husband with kindness. I was wrong. Sometimes words are not enough."

He's looking past her, toward the door. "White words are never enough."

"I have not given up. There is a general named Pope—"

Major Cullen clenches her upper arm from behind. "It's time we leave, Madam."

She wrestles away. "Not yet!"

Guns click to the ready around the room.

"As you were, men!" Cullen says, in command. "Mrs. Wakefield, be finishing up with this buck. *Now.*"

She watches Cullen back to the doorway. *You can appeal to General Pope, you can petition Governor Ramsey, you can beg every son of a bitch who's out there to beg, nothing will help.* "Great wrongs," Riggs said, "demand swift justice." *Wrongs against whites, at least.*

She lowers her head in despair. "I cannot say it...."

"What is this thing you cannot say?"

"I cannot save you."

"We are all in the hands of the Giver."

"I hate myself for it.... Please, I cannot leave you like this. Tell me you believe I tried. Tell me we are parting in peace!"

His eyes search hers. "You are leaving the camp of the Big Knives?"

"Tomorrow."

"Your husband—he is alive? This is certain?"

She nods. *It's all so impossible.*

"Then you will not be alone. It is good. I put My Wife away. It is so."

SARAH LEAVES THE CHILDREN WREATHED IN THEIR DREAMS. SHE WANDERS OUT the tent into bracing cold with a bottle of whiskey pinched from the surgeon's tent. In the morning they will be on a wagon, bound for Fort Ridgley. She has no trunk to pack, no clothes or necessaries to make ready, no goodbyes to make, no last-minute instructions for a servant. She has only herself and her babies.

Uŋćiśi is beyond her help. Ćaske is locked up in a horrid jail she can't free him from, waiting to die.

Stars come down close. Wakaŋ close.

One night he lay beside her, teaching her the sky. The constellation she knew as Orion The Hunter he called Na-pe, *The Hand.* "A chief grew tired of making sacrifices on behalf of his people. He hunted only for himself. Because he was no longer generous, they suffered. At last the Thunderbeings punished him. They took his hand and hid it in the sky."

The North Star, there; Wićaŋȟpi Owaŋźila, he called it. *The Star That Stands In One Place.* "That star was so sad from losing his wife, he froze, and never again strayed from that spot."

Perhaps Ćaske froze in place when he lost his wife. Whoever that winyaŋ had been, he loved her. Not once has she heard him speak that woman's name.

The liquor burns down her throat into her belly. She wants to believe that he has loved her, too, but how can she know? She doesn't even know her own heart. Can love be distinguished from the intimacy of refuge? Lonely desire? Inexpressible gratitude? Affection born of sympathy and longing? All these and more she has felt for him, but love? The two of them exist in contrasts. What unites them, in the end?

Wićaŋȟpi Waśtedaŋpi. *He Who Is Liked By The Stars.* She blots out the moon with her thumb. Perhaps he *did* shoot at Gleason in the wagon.

You know so little about him. Perhaps you don't know him at all. Perhaps no one can ever truly know anybody.

She snugs the Army blanket around her shoulders. She thinks about how these two encampments, soldier and Sioux, must appear to the hooded eyes of God. How from Heaven the sharp boundaries between them must disappear; all the luminous tents and tipis, the flickering campfires, merging together, spangling the black prairie like stars....

From the vantage point of Heaven, this might be the truth of it: All her feelings for Ćaske, and his for her, disappearing into each other. And whatever happens in the place they meet, by some sweet and mysterious alchemy, is what passes for love, and can be known by no other name.

"Ten o'clock, and all's well!" Sentries at their posts around Lookout's periphery call out the hour, tossing the words one to the next.

Her bottle is half-empty. She begins to sing, maudlin and tipsy. "'Sweet and low, sweet and low....'" She drifts down toward Camp Lookout, the cones of its tipis glimmering in the night. "'Wind of the western sea ... breathe and blow ... come from the dying moon ... blow him again to me—'"

"I wouldn't be wandering down here alone, if I were you."

The man's voice, so near, startles the whiskey from her grip. The bottle clinks on the ground.

"I didn't mean to give you a fright, Madam." Tobacco glows red in the bowl of Captain Grant's pipe, illuminating a patch of his face. "But truly, it isn't safe."

By a glint of moon on glass she regains her bottle. She works it into the pocket of her dress. "What threat can they pose now?"

"Not the Indians. Our men. I regret to say, they lack discipline. The squaws in Lookout are a temptation." He offers her his arm. "Shall I escort you back up the hill? Or are you apt to shoot me?"

She starts up the ridge on her own, tottery in her moccasins. "Were you following me, Captain?"

"We just happened to cross paths." Grant puffs loudly on his pipe. "You and your children will be leaving in the morning, I hear."

"Seems so."

"Where will you go?"

"Wherever I'm taken."

"To your husband, most surely."

"Perhaps you can tell me where he is, my hero of a husband?"

"I didn't mean to—"

"Oh, nobody means anything anymore." She wobbles to a stop, sets her hands on her hips. She doesn't want to return to camp, and she can't go back down the hill. "A draft on your pipe, Captain?" Not waiting for an answer, she pulls the pipe from his teeth. A common clay pipe. "The war's made a mess of the world, hasn't it, Captain?" His tobacco is stale. No spice at all. She wants kinnikinnik. "Or perhaps the world was already a mess, and we didn't see it. Here...." She holds out the pipe to him, feeling queasy.

He bites its lip. "All depends where you're standing, I suppose. To us, these Indian troubles feel like Armageddon. But if you were to ask those boys at Antietam—"

"What are your stitches from?"

"Beg pardon?"

"On your chin. I noticed, before."

"Got nicked by a bullet at Birch Coulee." He resettles his hat. "Mrs.

Wakefield, I need to ask if you intend to carry forward your crusade for the savage."

"I've a mind to appeal to General Pope. Governor Ramsey, if I have to."

"Let me urge you off that course. They've decided not to hang him."

Her breath snags.

"Nothing to say for once, Madam?"

"But you crowed he'd swing high as Haman!"

"So I did, and so he should. But your Indian will get prison. Five years. By the time he's out, he'll be as civilized as a devil can be."

She captures Grant drunkenly by both arms. "You're not fooling with me, Captain? This is the God's-honest truth?"

"On my word as a gentleman."

"But I just saw Ćaske yesterday. His spirits were so low!"

"We'll tell him when the time's right, just as I've told you."

"But we met by chance!"

"I was under orders to convey the message before you left."

"Orders from whom?"

"That's of no account. But I've one more thing to say: You mustn't speak of this matter to anyone, even your husband. It's delicate. Can we count on your discretion, as a *lady?*"

THE WORLD FLOATS in a hundred shades of gray and white. The uncanny October fog chills her to the bone. There's no peering down the ridge. There's no seeing to the river. There's simply what's in front of her, to be muddled through, somehow. She stands in the soup, wanting sun.

"Look, Mama, a dead frog!" James lifts it by the toe, a black silhouette.

Yesterday Sibley dispatched to Fort Ridgley an ox train of forty wagons, escorted by eighty soldiers; a considerable number of former captives, most from the Old Country, were among the passengers. Today, the Colonel's sending down a single wagon, drawn by mules, with no escort at all. She and the children will be aboard, along with three other white women and Marian Hunter, the mixed-blood wife of a dead settler. He means them to travel more than seventy miles through war-torn countryside with only their teamster's gun for protection. All the way down, a journey of two days, renegade Indians could be lying in wait behind any bush or tree. In this fog, they could even be waiting in the middle of the goddamned road.

Somewhere a dog yelps. Somewhere, a screech, like a big lost bird.

She hoists James and Nellie into the wagon bed.

"Mama," James asks with a sniffle, "may I try to spin my top?"

"Not now."

Her teeth are chattering, her body quivering. The soldiers won't give her a blanket for her babies. All she has is Uŋčiśi's scrap of shawl. A headache is setting in, pressing behind her eyes.

"I'm so frightened, Mrs. Wakefield," Marian Hunter whispers, as they board the wagon. "Aren't you frightened?"

"It's our only way home."

"My home is gone."

Sarah squeezes Marian's shoulder in sympathy. The woman's white husband was slain in the vicinity of the Lower Agency. The wagon will pass right through.

The teamster whistles to his mules. "Gid-on!" The wagon jerks forward, jarring her onto a seat. Ghostly soldiers laugh and jeer.

"George Gleason laughed at me too," she shrieks into the foggy murk, "and it got him dead!"

James coughs a wet cough. "Mama, are we going to see Papa now?"

She musses his hair. "Will you be happy to see him?"

"I wish he could have come here. I'd so like to live with Uŋćiśi. I miss her and A-te, don't you?"

As the wagon leans down toward Lookout, she smells the Sioux cook-fires. Their smoke is thick, trapped by the fog. She begins to hum a defiant, made-up tune.

Just as they roll past the Sioux camp, a patch clears in the haze. And there, in sudden view, is Uŋćiśi, all alone upon a gentle rise, perhaps waiting for the sun to show itself and receive her prayers: "Taku waśte hena unkupo. Taku waśte śi hena yuȟab." *Put in place all things that are good. Push away all things that are not good.*

Sarah shrinks down, but too late. Uŋćiśi has already caught sight of her. And oh, the woebegone wail that rises from the kuŋśi's tired old throat, as though someone dear has died.

Siege has greatly altered Ft. Ridgley. All the frame buildings previously flanking its north side have burned to ash. Its most impressive building, a two-story stone barracks, looks largely intact, but battle has ravaged the other structures. Walls, blackened and pitted. Windows, shattered or shot through. Shingled roofs, eaten by flames.

An uneven row of graves, two of them long trenches, is fresh in the fort's cemetery. Captain Marsh might well be interred there.

Their wagon grumbles to a stop beneath the faded post flags snapping in frayed ribbons from the pole. Sarah steps down with James and Nellie into a hive of activity—soldiers hauling water and hay, tending animals, unloading and stacking firewood, cleaning equipment, repairing damage to the buildings.

A thickset woman wearing a turquoise headscarf sweeps out of the barracks to greet them. "You poor dears! How terrible, what you have been through!" She introduces herself as Eliza Müller, wife of the post surgeon. Her accent is German, or close to it, but she has complete command of English. Her consonants are so distinct they nick the air.

She shows them into the sooty barracks, already crowded with earlier evacuees from Camp Release. "Tell me, mis schätzli"—she twines her arms over her hefty middle—"who would like a nice hot bath?"

The rosy-cheeked Mrs. Müller distributes what clean clothes she can scrounge up. Her husband, meanwhile, examines the captives in the humble cabin that serves as post hospital. Its one room is heavy with the smell of gun smoke and camphor.

"I do not think there is reason for worry," Dr. Müller tells Sarah, after inspecting her babies. "Good food and a warm bed will soon cure what ails them." But to be safe, he prescribes paregoric for Nellie, twenty drops after each bout of diarrhea.

THE EVACUEES MUST LEARN TO SLEEP AGAIN IN SOMETHING RESEMBLING A bedstead. After much tossing, most make their weary peace with the uncomfortable Army cots. Around them, at Mrs. Müller's bidding, lanterns burn low for those frightened of the dark.

Sarah bends to tuck the blankets around James and Nellie, snuggled in a single cot. Her hand swims through James's hair and lingers on his forehead before traveling down to Nellie's cheek, checking her fever again. The girl's head rests against her brother's chest, rising and falling with his breath. *May they both forget all that's happened.*

She crawls back under the blanket on her cot and pillows her head on Uŋćiśi's shawl. She's sleeping in a muslin work shirt, baggy trousers and a soldier's sack coat in sore need of mending. Though according to Dr. Müller's scale captivity had carved more than forty pounds from her frame, no dress from his wife's pile of hand-me-downs fit.

The smell of gunsmoke is strong. She wriggles onto her side. The wool of the blanket itches. The narrow cot sags. She squirms onto her other side and draws her knees toward her chest.

"I cannot say it...."
"What is this thing you cannot say?"

"I cannot save you."

She kicks her feet free and flips onto her back. High above her, cobwebs sway in the dim lantern light.

After seven long weeks, she is out of harm's way. Yet, here in this barn of a barracks, what she feels most is trapped. A canary in a cage.

Once, while exploring the shore of a cove near their farm, she and her father chanced upon a gannet tangled in old fishing line. Its white wings were outstretched, bound fast by the ravel to a low branch. In the bird's thrashings to free itself, the fishing line had sliced through its flesh, mangled its webbed feet and winched open its pale blue beak to the limits of its jaw. No telling how long the creature had been pinioned there, cruci-fied and helpless. The black dots of its eyes were fixed. They thought it was dead.

Then they heard a sound from it. Something like a sigh, or a breath. Something like Gleason, at the end. She looked up at her father, and he looked down at her.

He went to the bird. Knelt with his knife.

One way or another, she, too, will get herself free.

"PAPA!" JAMES BREAKS FREE, OFF AT A RUN.

Sarah's step falters. The man walking toward them across the parade grounds with a musket—is it him? His pince-nez is gone. His gait is slower than she remembers; his stride shorter, more from the knees. His spine is softer. His shoulders sag, like when he has been drinking, yet he's solid on his feet. His ill-fitting clothes must be another man's charity.

John kneels with his gun to catch up his boy. Watching beside Sarah, Marian Hunter squeezes out a smile. "I hope you'll find happiness again, Mrs. Wakefield."

Sarah tucks some curls behind Nellie's ear. "Happiness might be a far country for us both, Marian."

She carries Nellie across the frostbitten green. James, riding John's shoulders, is scratching his father's whiskers—not his usual clean goatee, but a salt-and-pepper beard, grown up into his cheeks. It isn't like John to be so unkempt. Even when he drinks, his grooming is fastidious.

"My Sarah." John's voice is husky as he greets her.

"Mama, look! Papa's all whiskery!"

John enfolds her, musket in hand. She accepts his embrace, yielding

Nellie to the shelter of his body. The four of them, together again, and apart.

"Your hair…." he says.

"An old woman's."

"Or a swan's." He strokes it like a new lover.

"How is it you're here?"

"I got away with John Other Day—"

"No—I mean *here,* at Ridgley." She isn't ready for his survival tale.

"The newspaper published a list of captives freed at Camp Release. When I saw your names…." Tears stop him. A rarity, in their years together.

"You saw our names, and?"

He swings James to the ground. "I set off. Ridgley was the most sensible evacuation route. The Langenfelds—I've been staying with them —they loaned me fare for the stage to St. Peter. From there I hopped an Army wagon." His hand is resting at the nape of her neck. She wants it off. "I was afraid I'd be too late. I had nightmares of not being able to find you, of hunting you town to town, chasing rumors."

He nods at James, who is begging a soldier to mount him on a mule. "The boy sounds congested."

"Just a cough. Nellie's been low for weeks."

"I swear he's a year taller. And still that sprig of a cowlick!"

She chews her lip. "When must we go?"

"There's a wagon back to St. Peter. We want to be on it." His hand encloses hers. "Don't fret, my dearest, I have my pistol, and Julius loaned me his musket."

The soldier squares James on the mule's bare back. She shudders, remembering how he'd screamed, riding off behind Little Paul.

The mule snorts. James lays his blonde head against its sorrel neck, his fingers full of mane.

❧ IV ❧

I

THE LANGENFELDS ARE LOVELY PEOPLE. They're among the more prominent of John's former patients in Shakopee. When Sarah was still John's house-keeper, Esther had obligingly ordered a new gown from her. Julius owns a boot and shoe store, one of the best in the Minnesota Valley. Yes, such lovely people, these German Jews, and so kind to take in refugees.

Though John chafes at being charity's guest in another man's house, his goatee is neat and trim again. He collects clothing for the children from the Refugee Relief Committee. He rallies Nellie to health. He romps with James, enduring without comment the boy's homesickness for Uŋ́ćiśi and his whipping of Ćaske's top across the Langenfelds' varnished floors.

For her, he draws baths. He brushes her "bewitching" white hair. He lowers the window shades to ease her headaches. He brews her tea, adding milk and sugar just to her liking, unaware she now prefers black coffee. He tolerates her swampy bouts of melancholy. He turns down the bedclothes each night. He kisses and spoons her in bed but doesn't force her affections. In the morning, when she's in blankets on the floor, he asks no questions. His amity, she knows, won't last. She sleeps and sleeps and sleeps.

"JOHN ... THE DAY WE LEFT WITH GLEASON, WERE YOU AWARE THERE HAD BEEN some bloodshed down below?"

"I'd heard rumors."

"Even before we drove off?"

"I thought it best not to tell you. You know how you can be."

"And you thought it best to let Gleason go without a gun?"

"He had a pistol."

"It was a lie."

"Sarah, no man ever went down that road without a gun."

"No man who had any sense."

"So John Other Day helped you escape?"

"Around sixty of us, in all. We didn't have time to collect everyone, but we got Henrietta and her children, the Sinks, Mary Daly, Nelson Givens and his family, the Faddens, the Patoiles…. Other Day led us off the Hill on Tuesday, right before daybreak. I reached Shakopee on Friday. By then I could barely walk, my feet were so bruised—I was in my slippers, see, when the trouble started, and I lost them along the way. Anyway, when I got here, I picked up a newspaper blowing in the street, and there on the front page was a report by that half-breed Frenier—you know, the interpreter. He said he'd been scouting around the Upper reservation and seen every last one of us dead … you and me, Thomas and Henrietta, the Riggses, the Williamsons, everybody."

"Frenier's a liar."

"Christ, of course he's a liar. But that's when it struck me. I'm telling you, Sarah, I stood there in the middle of the street and cried. All I could think of was how I'd sent you and the children down that road with Gleason. I was certain I'd killed you."

"You never once thought about joining up, to come looking for us? Like Joseph, for Jannette?"

"Dearest, *I had no hope.* For six awful weeks I was low as a man can be. Then I saw your names in that list from Camp Release…."

"What ever happened to Dinah?"

"I've no idea."

"You never gave her a thought?

"Why would I? She was one of *them.*"

He reads to her from the Langenfelds' newspapers, squinting without his spectacles, unable to afford new ones. She can see their reading together means something to him; a shred of old ritual. But her soul is raw, and the words in the papers are brine. Each edition carries heartrending pleas for information about the war's missing, that they might be reunited with loved ones; about the thought-to-be dead, that they might be recovered and buried in hallowed ground; about some poor wretch found alive —too young or wounded or demented to name their own name—that they might be identified.

Then there are the hot-blooded editorials.

"Here's your hero up in St. Cloud," John says.

"Jane Swisshelm?" Before the war, the editor of *The St. Cloud Visiter* was one of her favorite writers, full of "uppity" opinions, a flea on the rump of the Minnesota establishment.

"'Every Sioux found on our soil should get a permanent homestead, six feet by two! Shoot the hyenas! Exterminate the wild beasts, and make peace with the devil and all his hosts sooner than these red-jawed tigers, whose fangs are dripping with the blood of the innocents—'"

"Please stop."

"'Shoot them and be sure they are shot dead, dead, *dead, Dead!* If they have any souls—'"

"John, please!" Covering her ears.

"'—the Lord can have mercy on them if He pleases! But that is His business. Ours is to kill the lazy vermin.'" He reads on in silence. "Didn't Swisshelm use to be a friend of the Indians? I do believe she has undergone a genuine conversion."

Other voices in the press are more moderate. Dr. Williamson, for one, considers the ongoing Indian trials a mockery of justice. And Bishop Whipple pens a letter to the editor that even John must approve, indebted as he is to Other Day. "'There is a broad distinction,'" he reads her of the Bishop, "'between the guilt of men who went through the country committing fiendish violence, massacring women and babes with the spirit of demons, and the guilt of timid men who received a share of the plunder or who under threat of death engaged in a battle where hundreds were engaged.'"

He sags the paper to consider her. "This Indian Ćaske...."

"Yes?" She must be steady. What she has told him about her captivity and her testimony at Camp Release isn't even a ripple in the millpond.

"From what you say, he must have been an Indian of the second stripe —a 'timid man' fighting 'under threat of death.'"

"I wouldn't say 'timid,' but otherwise yes."

"And did he plunder?"

"Everyone had plunder. Whatever was plundered was shared."

"But did he *himself* plunder?"

"John, *please,* why all these questions?"

"You'll understand if I'm curious. The savage did, after all, *plunder* my wife."

"You can be glad he did, instead of some other Indian."

"So tell me"—he whips the newspaper closed, folds it on its creases and tosses it on the table—"who was threatening the savage with death when he killed Gleason?"

"How many times must I tell you? *Hepaŋ* killed Gleason! Must we keep going over this?"

He pours them both another cup of tea. "I wish I could remember this Indian of yours from Mrs. Apgar's barn. I can see the wound but not the face."

"Had you not saved Ćaske's life back then—"

"—he wouldn't have saved yours. Yes, yes, yes. What a neat and tidy circle."

Carpet
Dining tables
Chairs
Feathertick
Bed stand
Chamber pots
China

"HOW MUCH MONEY WAS IN YOUR POUCH WHEN YOU LEFT HOME?"

Sarah stops writing Silverware, mid-word. "A hundred and thirty dollars."

"Ah." John pulls on his coat. "Make it one-fifty, will you? And don't forget to put a generous price on the items in your trunk. The Sioux owe us."

"But we have to swear to the truth of our claim."

"Mere formality. Who will contradict us?"

He slides his own inventory across the table. "I know this is difficult, my dearest, accounting for what we've lost. But we have, in fact, lost *everything.* I haven't so much as a scalpel by which to feed us. This is no time for timidity. We must ask for compensation in the measure we deserve."

"What I'm feeling isn't timidity."

"Whatever it is, you must set it aside. The quicker we submit our claim, the quicker we can hang my shingle, set up house again, and put this nastiness behind us." He drops a kiss on her white crown. She flinches inwardly. "I must be off. I may be poorly equipped, but the Relief Committee has need of another doctor, and I, at present, have need of their goodwill. Put your clever mind to work."

Thousands of Minnesotans will be filing depredation claims, seeking restitution for losses incurred in the war. To settle the claims, the government aims to use the annuity money owed the Indians before the outbreak. She and John are entitled to reparation—they *need* reparation, to have any chance of rebuilding a life—but she doesn't want to be paid at the expense of the Sioux people. The losses of the Sioux stretch back years, and they're still multiplying, without hope of redress.

She skims John's inventory, the items listed on separate pages under Tools & Animals, Medical Books, and Instruments. Included under Instruments are his "Relics of Sioux country":

> *One fancy Indian pipe*
> *Bow with arrows*
> *Two Sioux knives and sheath*
> *Buckskin coat and leggings*

He has appraised these "relics" at a hefty $17, a dollar more than his thirteen-piece "Pocket surgical kit." Peculiar as well is his itemization of "Two gold pocketwatches and chains," assessed at $300. The only watch he has ever owned, a gift from his father upon his graduation from Yale, is still in his pocket, right where it was when he fled with Other Day. Clearly he has put to work his own clever mind.

With reluctance she dips her pen and crosses out her meager start. She doesn't want to be part of John's chicanery, but he has been asking too many questions, expressing too many suspicions. Yesterday he burned James's wooden top in the Langenfelds' stove, along with her fancy moccasins and belt pouch. He would have pitched Uŋćiśi's shawl in the fire, too, had she not happened just then into the room.

"What are you doing?" she cried, ripping the shawl away.

"What *needs* doing."

She has no choice but to mollify him. He's her Committee of Relief.

In her mind she travels back to Agency Hill. She drifts into the house she'd made a home.

30 yds. Ingrain carpeting	*30.00*
1 Black walnut center table	*15.00*
8 Black walnut cane seat chairs	*20.00*
1 Black walnut cane seat rocker	*6.00*
1 Black walnut "what-not"	*7.00*
1 Mahogany side table	*9.00*

Logging the furniture is tedious but straightforward. The real art is properly esteeming the little things, the ordinary things, the insignificant and out-of-the-way things. She opens closet doors, dresser drawers and cabinets. She touches nightstands and dishes, fabrics and buttons. She turns the crank on the ice cream freezer. She depresses a key on her piano…. *What are you worth?*

In the pantry she counts jars and bottles and cans of food. By the end of her reservation life, her store of groceries was impressive: 30 lbs. of coffee, 45 of cheese, 50 each of crackers and codfish, 75 each of dried beef and rice, 150 of ham…. And sugar! 100 lbs. of crushed, 50 of brown, 10 of powdered….

What value to assign the cradle in which she'd rocked her babies? Her dear boy's sled? Her canaries? Her miniatures? The old Family Bible, in whose pages she'd inscribed James and Nellie's names among generations of Wakefields? The moccasin slippers made by Dinah…?

Her heart fills suddenly with intimate remembrances of Ćaske. His body, angular and scarred. His ear piercings. The birthmark behind his shoulder blade. The blue-black tattoo on the flat bone between his breasts. The broad rim of his cheekbones. His crooked smile. His eyes, the color of a thunderhead just starting to form. His gravelly voice. *"I am not a wise man…."*

If he was seven winters old when the stars fell from the sky, he must be younger than he looked. She'd always thought him older than John.

She pours a tumbler of the Langenfelds' schnapps. Last night, in the heat of a dream, she embraced John in bed, rousing him from desire. It was their first time, since before the war. After she began to feed him, to taste him, she fathomed her mistake, and groaned. Pleasure, he mistook it for. "Now," he moaned, but even as their bodies locked, she uncoupled from him in her mind. She stole just enough of him to make-believe, her nipples chafing to flame beneath his rocking.

"Such a big woman," he said, after.

She resettles herself at the table with her schnapps and bends over her pages of figures. Tallies her columns with ink-stained fingers. Carries the balance forward, one sheet to the next. Adds her estimated loss to John's.

She slumps back in her chair. $4,316.05. A fortune they can start over with. Every cent of it stolen.

She hurls her pen. The wall bleeds.

❧ 2 ❧

"'CLEMENCY AND MERCY?' What do Easterners know about the frontier? Yet they meddle in our affairs and presume to tell us what to do with our savages!" J.B. is up from Blue Earth City, where for a span of the war he commanded the City Cavalry. Upon his arrival at the Langenfelds', Sarah had greeted him coolly. The last time they were together, on Agency Hill, he allowed his brother to beat her within a shade of her life.

In the parlor Julius has poured everyone a delicious apple and pear schnapps. Across the chessboard from J.B., John is pondering his next move. "Easterners suffer the same affliction as the missionaries. Do-gooder blindness! Contagious as the plague."

J.B tosses a scrap of biscuit to his hound. Elizabeth, Sarah can see, would banish the dog to the porch, had she a say in the matter.

"How humiliating for those missionaries," J.B. says, "being forced to flee from the very souls they'd baptized! To witness the savagery of their disciples, then be made to answer for it in the press!"

"They sold the government and the mission boards a bill of goods." John captures a pawn. "'Send us your money, we'll turn these wild animals into saints.' What a wise investment *that* was! One sniff of blood, and their converts slit the throats of their good white brethren on the blade of their Christian knives—"

"But John," Sarah cuts in, "think of Other Day! He proved his faith, saving your life!"

"For every Other Day, dearest, there was a legion of pretenders! No telling the good from the bad."

J.B. attacks the center of the board. "You ask me, we'd best be rid of them all."

Esther's embroidery needle stops mid-air. "Be *rid* of them? And how would you propose to do that, Judge Wakefield?"

Julius bangs down his schnapps. "Esther, I think it's time we retire. Sarah … gentlemen … if you'll excuse us, we'll wish you good night."

John pushes back from the game in surprise. "How can you not want revenge, Julius? They murdered your kin at New Ulm."

"The guilty should be punished. No more."

"Ah. And how do you propose we sort the goats from the sheep?"

The hound whines for another scrap. J.B. makes him roll over. "The goats and the sheep are all wolves, beneath."

Julius begins to pace. "All races have their wolves, I'll grant you. But no race is *all* wolves."

"And *our* race," Sarah says, relieved to have an ally, "has more than its share of wolves, though they're sometimes well-disguised. As traders, for instance. Politicians. *Lawyers.*"

J.B. ignores her dig. "This Indian who spared your life, Sarah, how do you judge him? Innocent or guilty?"

"I refuse to judge him at all."

"Curious." The tip of his tongue plays at the corner of his mouth. "George Gleason is dead because of him. Even if we assume Gleason was his only victim, which is doubtful, who forgives a wolf that killed one lamb because he didn't kill more?"

John inspects his fingernails. "Someone, perhaps, who's grown *overly fond.*"

THE DEBATE OVER THE FATE OF THE SIOUX RAGES EVEN UNTO THE HALLS OF Congress. Most Minnesotans seem to agree that, however long it might take, the Army must pursue Little Crow and his fugitive Sioux across the plains and crush them. But with winter imminent, the more confounding issue is what to do with the thousands of Sioux already detained and the hundreds convicted of wrongdoing. In little more than a month, the Military Commission has heard 392 cases. More than three-quarters of the trials have resulted in a death sentence.

Now, in the first week of November, the newspapers announce that

Sibley, on the order of General Pope, will convey the guilty Indians to Mankato, the principal town in the Valley, to await their punishment. Though Ćaske's death sentence has been commuted to a prison term, Sarah assumes he will be in the transport.

Meanwhile, Lieutenant Colonel Marshall will transfer the rest of the Sioux to St. Paul. They will be detained at Fort Snelling until state and federal authorities can decide their future. Marshall will have only 300 troops to escort his train of thousands on the six-day march. He appeals to the public not to molest the Sioux:

> I would risk my life for the protection of these helpless beings, and would feel everlastingly disgraced if any evil befell them while in my charge. I want the settlers in the valley, on the route we pass, to know these are not the *guilty Indians* (some 300 of whom are to be executed at Mankato) but *friendly Indians, women and children.*

Sarah reads and rereads Marshall's plea. His train will travel the St. Anthony-Fort Ridgley Road, the same route she and John traveled back to Shakopee, a month ago. Shakopee is twenty miles overland from St. Paul. The Sioux will pass right by town.

UNLIKE SETTLEMENTS FURTHER UP THE VALLEY, SHAKOPEE WASN'T SERIOUSLY threatened during the war or inundated with more casualties and refugees than it could handle. Still, by the time lookouts spot Marshall's train on the afternoon of November 11, the town has been frothing for days with vengeful talk. There has been general praise for the settlers upstream who have visited "a hot time" upon the Sioux. Despite Marshall's cavalry escort, the Sioux have been assailed in town after town with rocks and bricks, rotten vegetables and eggs, the contents of chamber pots. Children and elders have been dragged out of wagons and beaten. Clothing has been ripped from the bodies of women. Babies have been torn from the breast and dashed on the ground. In Henderson, settlers tossed kettlefuls of scalding hot water out second-story windows, burning some Sioux so severely, their skin peeled off.

Sarah prays faces. Uŋćiśi. Eagle Head. Opa. Pasu Kiyuksa. Mother Friend. Little Paul. Her saviors and friends in the terrible procession likely don't know where they're headed, or why, or what's to happen next. They likely don't know what's in store for their male relatives who, like Ćaske, were shackled in pairs, loaded into wagons and made to vanish over the horizon.

John proposes they wrap up some wedges of Esther's kuchen, bundle the children and go down to the landing at Murphy's ferry, to watch "the parade" go by. "The whole town will be out. It's our last time seeing such a herd of Sioux."

"You sound so pleased."

"It's been a long time coming. The end of an era." He assures her there will be no bloodshed. "Most people around here don't want the Sioux dead so much as gone."

"Go, if you want, and eat your blesséd kuchen. But the children and I are staying here."

Once he's out the front door, she dons her hand-me-down coat and repairs to the Langenfelds' backyard. If she listens closely, she can already hear the dogs and the awful shrieking of wooden wheels. There might be as many as 2,000 Sioux in the miles-long train. Women bent beneath their packs. Babies peeking out from cradleboards. Youngsters tramping over the frosty ground. Gray-hairs stumbling along, or sagging in the saddle, or bouncing along in a Red River cart. A mere handful of younger men, leading packhorses; the only "good Indians" left, say the papers. Hundreds of bluecoats will be driving the Sioux like cattle, harassing laggards and strays.

She walks to the woodpile. Picks up Julius's axe.

Somewhere on this long march a baby will be born trailside, its mother's womb not waiting. Somewhere a child will perish from the ordeal, be wrapped in a blanket and abandoned to the crows. Somewhere a grandmother will be shot for not pissing fast enough. Somewhere an auntie will be dragged out of sight by a soldier and defiled…. She can see it all, and she can see nothing.

She sets a piece of wood on end, and swings.

$$\underset{\sim}{\mathscr{F}} \quad 3 \quad \underset{\sim}{\mathscr{F}}$$

JOHN OBLIGES her to dress in borrowed black.

"Be sensible, Sarah. You owe him."

"I owe him nothing! I begged him to turn around!"

"He was on that road because of you."

"No, because of *you!*"

"Quiet down. You want Julius and Esther to hear?" In a fury he ties off his white Masonic apron, borrowed like her mourning dress. "Gleason was a Brother. I have to perform the rites." His third time explaining. "Here, help me with this—"

A sprig of evergreen, for immortality. She pricks herself, pinning it to his lapel. "I'm not stopping you from going." Sucking the blood.

"You *have* to go. You're my wife, the woman he died for—"

"Don't make him out to be a saint. I'm sorry he died, he was a decent enough sort, but he was a buffoon."

"The whole town will talk if you don't go."

She ignores the telltale crimson of his ears. "They're already talking."

"You want to add fuel to the fire? You didn't go to Joseph's funeral either."

"I was unwell."

"You were drunk."

"Well, isn't that the pot meeting the kettle?"

"Christ. Finish getting dressed!"

She doesn't budge. He won't dare strike her with the Langenfelds in the house.

He waggles an envelope in her face, addressed to her, in Julia Paull's writing. She swipes at it, and misses.

"This letter, my pet, you must earn."

"'LET US SUPPLICATE THE DIVINE GRACE, TO ENSURE THE FAVOR OF THAT Eternal Being whose goodness and power know no bounds; that, when the awful moment arrives, be it soon or late, we may be enabled to prosecute our journey, without dread or apprehension, to that far distant country whence no traveler returns....'"

Even blind without his spectacles, John can read with emotion. But she can't forgive him for compelling her to attend the funeral; for putting her on display before the mourners. The cemetery is a gallery of whispers and stares.

The aproned Brothers, Gleason's only family in Minnesota, ring the plot with their wives. Assembled behind them are the gawkers, attracted to the last rites for a local hero: "George H. Gleason, slain by the savage Chaska while defending the wife and children of Shakopee's Dr. J. L. Wakefield."

The Galbraiths are up from St. Paul for the service. Henrietta, shielded by Thomas from the buffeting wind, looks remarkably unchanged by the war. Still the gray hair and wrinkles, still the stoop. Thomas, who fought in the uprising with his half-breed recruits, is hobbled by a battle wound suffered at Birch Coulee. Rather than enlist in the Union cause, he has resumed his duties as Indian agent, helping to oversee the Sioux confined below Fort Snelling. The public has laid much of the blame for the uprising at his feet. He twists and twists his ring.

Mr. Lincoln, as Commander-in-Chief, has initiated a review of all 303 cases in which Sibley's Commission condemned a Sioux to death. He apparently means to distinguish between Indians who perpetrated violence against unarmed civilians and those who participated in battle. The implication is clear. If the President has his way, those Sioux deemed guilty of heinous crimes will die. The rest will likely be held as prisoners of war.

To Sarah this is a fair and reasonable distinction, conforming to the views of Bishop Whipple. But John has lost all patience. "The truth is," he told Thomas before the funeral, "Lincoln doesn't have the stomach for hanging Indians. But if he doesn't hang them all, he won't have the stomach for what happens next."

Now he's fighting to keep his page. "'May we be true and faithful, and may we live and die in love.'"

"So mote it be," the Brothers say, in muted chorus.

"'May we profess what is good, and always act agreeably in our profession.'"

"So mote it be." The language cultish, archaic.

"'May the Lord bless us, and prosper us, and may all our good intentions be crowned with success.'"

"So mote it be."

Sarah wonders who exhumed Gleason's body from its hole along the government road. So many funerals, these days. So many of the slain, being recovered.

"'In respect to our deceased Brother, George Gleason, whose memory we revere, and whose loss we now deplore, we have assembled in the character of Masons to resign his body to the earth....'"

She nods a greeting at Jannette DeCamp, off to the right in widow's garb. The woman is a shell of herself. She glares back until Sarah, discomfited, looks away.

"SARAH!"

Eager for Julia Paull's letter, she pretends not to hear Jannette's voice, coming from well behind her. She continues across the cemetery, her hand in the crook of John's arm.

"*Sarah Wakefield!*"

Disbanding mourners stop to stare. She dismisses John with a pat. "I'll be along."

She turns around and retreats toward Jannette. They face each other, bracing themselves, the wind bitter out of the northwest.

"I thought you'd already left," she says. "You're looking well." A white lie, in kindness. "How are the boys?"

Jannette sticks out her chin. "As one might expect."

"John said Joseph's service was well attended. I'm so sorry I couldn't be there."

"Are you?"

She lays a gloved hand on Jannette's shoulder. "Show me where he's laid."

Joseph's lot isn't far from Gleason's. The disturbed earth of the grave is crusted with light snow.

"Someday," Jannette says, "I shall give my darling a stone."

"What will you do now?"

"My father's fetching us down to Missouri, where my people are." She raises the collar of her ragtag coat higher against the wind. "At least for a time."

Sarah steps around to the head of the grave. "You were with child, last I saw you."

"A boy. Resembles his father, around the eyes." The woman, always so chatty, is tight-lipped as a bottle.

"For a long time," Sarah says, "I feared the worst. The four of you were gone from camp without a trace."

"An Indian canoed us down to Ridgley. All the way down, I thought we'd die."

A canoe. Ćaske promised that, once. "Where's the Indian now?"

Jannette shrugs. "In the stockade at Fort Snelling, I suppose."

"Did they ever put him on trial?"

"Why on earth would they try him? He *saved* us."

"Ćaske saved *me,* yet he's locked up in Mankato."

"You just had to defend him, didn't you?"

Sarah bristles. The proceedings of the tribunal, closed to reporters and casual observers, had supposedly been secret. Yet a great many people who never stepped foot in Camp Release, including her own husband, are bloated with opinions about her testimony.

"I want to tell you," Jannette's saying, "out of respect for our past friendship, I've not told a single soul what you did."

"Is that so?" Sarah lets her voice bite. "And what did I do, exactly?"

"You know very well what you did. With *him.*"

August 24, 1862
Providence

My dear Sarah,

Are you yet alive? How dreadful not knowing! This day I opened the Times to the terrible news that you and your Husband and precious Children are lost with 500 other Souls, massacred by Indians! Is it possible? How I weep to think of it!

I am sending you the clipping from the Times as a charm. May it travel posthaste across these many miles to discover its own Intelligence false and you and

*your Family far from the grave. If the report of this man Frenier is to be believed
there is no Hope. But oft the best witnesses are numbskulls or snakes and our
greatest Certainties not worth the paper they be written upon.*

*It is said horses and weapons are being gathered with all speed and Volunteers
raised against the marauders. If indeed you are in harm's way may Heaven guard
you till Help searches you out.*

*In these times when War is North to South and East to West it feels like God
has turned His Eyes from our drear country. Is this a Day of Reckoning? The walls
are tumbling down but Who is blowing the Horn?*

*If you set eyes on this Letter please send word with haste. Till then I will keep
Vigil in the papers for I am*

Brokenhearted,
Julia

A MIRACLE, THIS LETTER FROM PROVIDENCE. POSTED THE VERY FIRST WEEK OF
the war, it was intercepted with other reservation mail by the authorities in
St. Paul. Even by then, Frenier's lies had sped across telegraph lines to
break in *The New York Times.*

She picks up her pen.

November 23 1862
Shakopee Minn

Oh Julia

What can I say
            We are all alive
      but I am Oh so lost

❧ 4 ❧

A MEASLES EPIDEMIC sweeps the Minnesota Valley. Shakopee's gravediggers, still busy with war dead, lay many victims of the disease to rest. Children, mostly. Out of caution John sequesters James and Nellie in the Langenfelds' house. Sarah constantly checks their brows for fever and examines behind their ears for hints of a rash. She isn't about to lose her lambs to sickness after shepherding them through an Indian war.

"I'm sending you and the children to Lu," John decides in early December, when the epidemic doesn't weaken. His elder sister and her husband Eli live in Red Wing, down on the Mississippi.

"You're not going with us?"

"At Gleason's funeral Thomas said he could use me as Indian physician at Fort Snelling. The income will tide us over, till the claim's paid."

"We could come with you."

"Snelling has the measles, too. No, it's all agreed, Eli's sending your fare. By the time our claim's settled, the epidemic will have run its course, and we can all come home."

"Home...." She weighs the word on her lips. *A place you're faithful to, like a lover. The place you belong.* "Where *is* home, John?"

He falls back into the curve of his chair. "We were happy once, weren't we, rather?" His hair is thinning, gone to gray. The tip of his goatee is white. "I'm so tired of charity. Tired of living off Julius. Tired of begging the Relief Committee, and Eli, and ... everyone." He rubs at his bloodshot eyes.

She leans toward him in her chair. "It isn't only charity you're tired of, is it? You're tired of all the talk." She strokes his knee, in consolation. "Perhaps you're even tired of me."

His eyes thicken with tears. "What if, after all that's happened...." He presses his lips together, struggling, she can see, not to cry. His face sinks into his hands. He sits sobbing, without sound.

AFTER DECADES OF CHILDLESS MARRIAGE, LU AND ELI HAVE COME TO RESEMBLE each other like sister and brother. They have the same fleshy body and round face, the same laugh lines, the same intonations of voice, the same refinement in dress and manners, the same smell of money. They finish each other's sentences, anticipate each other's jokes and mock each other's opinions, in good fun.

"I suppose you've heard how Henry spent the war." Eli is speaking of his close friend Bishop Whipple. "He set up a hospital at St. Peter—"

"—with help from Cornelia, don't forget—" Lu says.

"—in the courthouse, for the refugees."

Lu hums softly as she works her silver tatting shuttle, making lace. "The way Cornelia tells it, Henry became fairly deft with a needle, stitching up wounds."

"So deft he poked himself!"

"Don't make light of it, 'Lijah, his hand is still lame."

"It's well enough to write with, obviously." He winks at Sarah. The Bishop's controversial writings on the Indians had prompted her mention of him.

President Lincoln's intervention in the machinery of justice has stoked Minnesota's thirst for revenge. Governor Ramsey, Colonel Sibley, newspaper editors like Jane Swisshelm, even Reverend Riggs have been sounding the alarm: Mobs will exact their own brand of justice if all the condemned Sioux aren't executed in short order. Citizens throughout the state have held indignation meetings and passed petitions, trying to compel Mr. Lincoln to swifter, bolder action. Brazen conspiracies are afoot to massacre the Sioux, especially those imprisoned like Ćaske at Mankato. The authorities have arrested scores of settlers.

Apart from "meddling Easterners," few voices have publicly espoused restraint. Bishop Whipple, down in Faribault, is the loudest. A few days ago, while packing her few belongings for Red Wing, she paused to read his open letter exhorting Minnesotans to seek justice "with consciousness of wrong." The government, he argued, had made "fatal errors" in its dealings with the Indians; its own poor judgment, together with the rampant corruption of the Indian system, led to the outbreak. While the guilty Sioux must "meet their doom," as demanded by the laws of God and man, no innocents must be punished, "lest God Himself hold the nation guilty."

Whipple's letter expressed much of her own opinion. But since its publication, he's being denounced as an "Indian sympathizer," both in the papers and on the streets. Every word of censure directed at him stings as if she herself were the target. Two months removed from Camp Release, her reputation is in tatters for having defended Ćaske. She's no longer the esteemed helpmeet of Dr. John Luman Wakefield, but his "errant wife." A "pariah." A "godless, hysterical woman." An "Indian lover." A "white squaw".... However widespread the talk, it had beaten her to Red Wing. Mercifully, Eli and Lu seem deaf to it.

She lifts a yawning Nellie into her lap. "I had occasion to meet Bishop Whipple at the Lower Agency, our first month on the reservation. He's a striking man."

"A fine bishop!" Eli agrees.

"I've appreciated his forthrightness," she says, "defending the Sioux."

"A hard business, as you know." Eli twists one of his bushy side-whiskers. "There were threats against Henry even before he published this last letter. I worry for him."

Lu's shuttle clicks as her thread plays out through the bobbin. "If ever there was a time for courage, this is one."

"Alas, Birdie, one man's courage is another man's treachery."

"It isn't treachery to live by scripture."

"No, but it's risky. Set your finger on this page, it says one thing. That page, it says another."

A remarkable admission, Sarah thinks, from a man who keeps his Bible closer than his well-worn *Book of Common Prayer.* "Eli, if you'll allow my asking ... as a judge, and as a Christian, what do you think should be done with the Indians?"

"'Burning for burning, wound for wound, stripe for stripe'—like it or not, that's the way of the world, and it's the scripture I live by in my courtroom. The murderers should be hanged, without question, just as soon as the President finishes his review of the trial records."

"And the rest?"

"They must be sent away. The only question is to where."

"But Minnesota is their home!"

"After what's happened, their continued presence here won't be tolerated. Their own safety demands they go." He tugs the bottom of his waist-coat over his paunch. "Once we establish them elsewhere, their lot can be improved. But much will depend on the President."

"God bless Mr. Lincoln!" Lu says, with fervor. "How does that poor man ever sleep at night?"

"My wife forgets we're Democrats in this house."

"My husband forgets I'm a Wakefield, and Wakefields are Republicans, even if they can't vote!"

"Let's not start on women's suffrage, Birdie, we're talking about Indians.... Last month, Henry carried a letter to the President asking for reforms."

"Truly?" Sarah says. "Whipple met with Mr. Lincoln? In Washington?"

"He took a letter signed by all the northern bishops—"

"—and some reputable riffraff!"

"Riffraff like me, Birdie means. Be that as it may, Henry was probably the one who convinced the President to rein in the runaway horse. Told him the nation couldn't afford to hang Sioux by the hundreds. Advised him to punish the truly wretched—those Indians who had engaged in atrocities—but then strike at the root."

"The root, I assume, being the Indian system."

"Precisely. It's corrupt beyond redemption. Henry made Lincoln feel the rascality of it down in his boots. The President promised to clean house once he's done with the South."

"But what's to happen in the meantime?" Sarah says. "All those innocents!" Ćaske, locked up in Mankato. Uŋćiśi, confined at Fort Snelling.

Eli exhales through pursed lips. "Like I said, my girl, a hard business."

5

"IT'S A FINE, fine morning, Sarah Wakefield, and here you are, lollygagging." Lu enters the bedroom with a breakfast tray and a newspaper, like a lady's maid rousing a duchess.

Sarah cuffs her pillow over her head. Through the bedclothes she listens to Lu bustling about, setting the tray on the dresser, raising the shades, tidying up clothes, humming all the while. Always humming, Lu is.

"Up with you, lay-about!" Lu swats Sarah's hip through the quilt with a newspaper. "The children have been up for hours."

Sarah rolls over to face the wall. The room is cold, the fire is out, and she'd slept badly, troubled by dreams and worries.

"Eat yourself a bite and get dressed," Lu calls over her shoulder as she breezes out of the room with the chamber pot. "Or have you forgotten our sewing?"

Sarah sighs. She eases out of the feathertick into slippers and a wool dressing gown, handsome gifts from Lu. The woman has been pampering her like a mother. Yesterday she purchased fabrics by the bolt at Smith's Mercantile, insisting that her brother's wife and children must have a proper wardrobe.

Ham, buttered toast and black coffee; a rich brew, from expensive beans. Another sip, and she picks up the *St. Paul Daily Press,* dated December 9.

Ordered that of the Indians and Half-breeds sentenced to be hanged by the Military Commission, lately sitting in Minnesota, you cause to be executed on Friday the nineteenth day of December, the following—

She rattles her cup down on the saucer. Mr. Lincoln has made up his mind. She scans the blacklist of Indians, holding her breath. It's much shorter than she expected; mere dozens of names rather than the hundreds that most Minnesotans have been clamoring for. If Captain Grant has kept his bargain, Ćaske won't be on it....
Halfway down, a tumble of dread.

No. 121. Chaskey-dan.

She stares at the name, her mind at a gallop. "Chaskey" is clearly an alternate spelling of Ćaske. Yet the Commission had tried Ćaske under his given name, Wićaŋȟpi Waśtedaŋpi. His case was No. 3, not No. 121. And they found him guilty of Gleason's murder, while they convicted this Chaskey-dan of—*God in heaven!*—"shooting and cutting open a woman who was with child." No, this Indian must be some other First Son.
Her finger slides down the remaining names to the bottom of the list.

The other condemned prisoners you will hold subject to further orders, taking care that they neither escape, nor are subjected to any unlawful violence.

Abraham Lincoln,
President of the United States.

Her eyes well up. A prison term instead of death. On Captain Grant's lips, the sentence commutation sounded so improbable. She didn't fully believe him. But now Mr. Lincoln has guaranteed it. Ćaske will live.

After Mr. Lincoln's announcement of the blacklist, some pendulum within her begins marking time until the gallows does its inevitable work. The bob swings slow as an old man's axe. Due to a lack of rope in Mankato, the military authorities postpone the execution of the Indians from December 19 to the day after Christmas.
On Christmas Eve, she keeps up appearances, fawning over Lu and

Eli's gift of a new Family Bible, meant to replace the Wakefield destroyed in the war. On Christmas morning, she and the children walk with Lu and Eli to Christ Episcopal Church for worship. So many members have ridden off to witness the execution, the pews are near empty.

On Friday, December 26, the pendulum falls to rest, gravity's work done.

It's after dinner on Sunday, December 28, when Eli hands her the *Daily Press*. "Best read this straightaway."

A special edition about the hanging. She slaps it down on the dining table. "I'm finished with all this."

"Not yet, I'm afraid."

The entire front page of the *Press* is devoted to the grim business, with even more stories inside. Despite herself, she's hooked by Confessions of the Prisoners, the last statements of the condemned Sioux, "as interpreted by Rev. S. R. Riggs, their long-time missionary." Riggs is everywhere in the newspapers these days, a snake in the grass. Perhaps embittered by the colossal failure of his life's work among the tribes, he has become not only the Indians' chief accuser and indicter but also the chief recorder of their doom.

She can't imagine any Sioux prisoner in his final hours being overcome by an urge to confess, let alone to Riggs. Indeed, many of these so-called confessions aren't admissions of personal guilt at all, but assertions of innocence. Among the dead:

Te-he-hdo-ne-cha, convicted of ravishing Mrs. Cardinal.

Tazoo, convicted of ravishing Mattie Williams.

Hay-pin-kpa, convicted of murdering Stuart Garvie with a bow and arrow. In fact, the trader died of a charge of shot to his bowels—John himself treated the Scot's mortal wounds—but apparently such discrepancies were immaterial to the Commission.

Hin-han-shoon-ko-yag-ma-ne, convicted on Marian Hunter's testimony of killing her husband Alexander.

Dowoŋsa. Ćaske's cousin. Convicted of killing five civilians around Swan Lake. In his "confession" he admitted to being at the scene but denied dealing any of the death-blows. Sarah rubs at her temples, unable to square the crime with her memories of the man.

And here is Chaskey-dan—

who says he went to the stores on the morning of Monday. There he saw
Little Crow taking away goods. He then went up to Redwood, with a
relation of his. They were there told that a white man was coming on the
road. They went out to meet him, but the first one who came along was a
half-breed. They let him pass. Then came along Mr. Gleason and Mrs.
Wakefield. His friend shot Mr. Gleason, and he attempted to fire on him, but
his gun did not go off. He saved Mrs. Wakefield and the children, and now
he dies while she lives.

"BUT THEY PROMISED HE WOULDN'T HANG! IT'S NOT HIM, IT CAN'T BE HIM!
Tell me it isn't him!"

"Oh, my dear Sarah"—Lu kneels to embrace her—"so terrible! We're so
sorry—"

"You don't understand! It has to be a mistake!"

Eli planks down a chair opposite her and tucks his starched kerchief
into her hand. "My girl, tell me what you know."

She throttles her weeping enough to tell him about Captain Grant's
promise. About the Chaskey-dan in Lincoln's blacklist, who didn't
resemble Ćaske at all. About the Chaskey-dan in the "dying confessions,"
who does. "Eli, this just can't be!"

"Don't despair."

"'Lijah," Lu says, pouring Sarah a glass of water, "don't be lighting
candles in a gale."

"There might be hope yet." He scratches at his bushy whiskers. "Two
days ago an Indian named Ćaske was hanged in Mankato. Which Ćaske,
we can't say yet, for certain." He leans in. "My girl, look at me.... *Look at
me.* Answer me this: do you want to get at the whole truth? No matter
what it is?"

Her hand molds to the water glass. She meets his gaze, straight on.

"Then, by God"—a squeeze of her shoulder—"we shall have it."

❧ 6 ☙

"Now I die while she lives." Guilt coils around her neck. Did Ćaske actually utter such words? Or was his final statement all Riggs, pure invention?

She has nothing to trust. Beyond the bare fact of the hanging, a little past ten o'clock on the morning after Christmas, the *Press* doesn't offer many hard facts. Even the total number hanged is uncertain. Put your finger down here, it says thirty-nine; over there, thirty-eight, with old Tate Mi Ma, Little Crow's camp crier, being granted a last-minute reprieve.

Two Indians, the paper says, were executed for violating white women, the rest for murdering civilians. Ćaske had done neither.

> And now, guilty and not guilty, may God have mercy upon these poor
> human creatures, and if it be possible, *save* them in the other world through
> Jesus Christ His Son. Amen.
>
> STEPHEN RETURN RIGGS

What does he mean, "guilty and not guilty?" How many innocent Indians did they wittingly send to the gallows?
Cloistered in her bedroom, she pummels her pillow with her fists. She doesn't care where Eli has gone or when he will be back, what's become of her children, whether she has eaten or slept, what hour the clock has struck. All she wants is Ćaske, alive.

He's trapped below the river ice, in a pocket of air, staring up at you. His face is pale in the dark water, his hair flared in rays. His hands press up against the ice, as against a pane of glass. The lines in his palms are distinct.

You pound at the ice with your fists to get at him. You claw with your fingernails. You kick and stamp. There's no breaking through.

His hands begin to drift, palms up, as in supplication. Bewilderment in his eyes. Or blame.

A rope, you realize suddenly, is tied around your waist. You sight its line back to Julia Paull on shore, anchoring you to the bank.

The river is tugging him away. You slither over the ice on your knees, staying above him. His eyes are still riveted to yours, but emptiness is creeping in, like light going out of the day.

You come to the end of the rope—

She wakens quick to the keening of wind in the eaves. Across the room, a lamp burns low beside a snifter of spirits and a slab of bread. Lu has laid a fire.

She rises to warm herself at the hearth. She drinks the brandy, still haunted by the face beneath the ice, part Ćaske, part her father.

It was on the third day when they carried her father through the door and laid him on the table, wrapped in sailcloth. He'd washed ashore not far from where he disappeared, tangled in seaweed, his clam hods stolen by the gods of the sea. His winter moccasins stuck out the end of the canvas; tough leather shoepacks with knee-high leggings, fur-lined for warmth. He'd fashioned them himself after a pair his father wore, obtained in trade with a sachem.

Her mother stood at the table's head, riveted on what she could no longer deny. The women who had been sitting vigil with her, the men who had delivered his remains to her, waited hushed and still, caught with her in the great divide between what once was and what would be.

That's where she died, the mother that she knew. In that divide. When she buckled, an inhuman wail poured forth from her belly, down in the region of her unborn child. Sarah clapped her hands over her ears and bolted out to her father's shop. As her mother's keening ringed the farm and choked off air, her brothers started crying from fright. She knew she should go back inside, gather them up and spirit them away from their mother's grief. But she hid beneath her father's carpentry bench. She packed her ears with sawdust.

Her father, the grown-ups said later, must have slipped off the ledge of the sandbar into deeper water. The weight of his clams, they said, must have dragged him down. His fingers, they said, must have been too numb with cold to unsheathe his knife and cut the hods free. He might never have drowned, they said, were it summertime, or had someone other than her, a poor child of seven, been clamming with him.

She'd been harvesting littlenecks from a shallow pool, discarding those already open on their hinge, just as he would do. The taste of winter clams, succulent and sweet, was spilling through her mouth. She wanted to shuck one and suck it down raw, feel its freeze slide down her throat.

Too long stooped over, she straightened and arched her back in a stretch. By habit of affection, she glanced back toward where she'd seen him last, walking on water, or so it seemed.

He wasn't there.

Her eyes swept the flat. He wasn't anywhere, and now the tide was coming in like a thief, to steal their boat from the sand.

She grabbed her basket of littlenecks and ran. Stumbled. Fell. The clams scattered and were lost. She pushed herself up, threw herself forward down the flat.

The boat was already floating free. She splashed into the incoming tide, its bitter cold barely registering through her terror.

The water was up to her chest when she nabbed the edge of the skiff. A second later, her toes couldn't touch bottom. She clung to the gunwale. Tried again and again to hoist herself over. She had no leverage.

She began to circle the boat, hand over hand. She rounded the bow from portside, continued starboard toward the stern, but the old hull was smooth. Not a toe-hold anywhere.

Down at the stern, a glint of metal, atop the gunwale. She closed in. The glint assumed shape: an eyehook, threaded through with sturdy rope. She gathered up the line floating slack in the gray-green brine. The end of it was knotted into a short loop; a stirrup of sorts, salvation for the lone fisherman gone overboard. She worked her right foot in, then boosted herself with a groan up and over the gunwale, into the bottom of the boat.

Long after the sun went down, she was still crawling in labored circles through the dark water, dipping the oars of the skiff, her palms blistering, the oarlocks creaking, the sea sucking at the hull. She rowed and rowed until she slumped over the dripping oars, to drift. That's where they found her. Even now she can hear the neighbor's voice in the night, croaking her name; she can see the glow of a boat's lantern floating toward her through haze, indistinct forms shifting about, like phantasms....

He had died, while she had lived.

She turns up the lantern wick and throws herself again into the newspaper account of Ćaske's final days, casting about for signs of life. Every sentence is a cortège.

Her mind situates Ćaske at the center of the story. Each reference to the "condemned," the "prisoners," the "savages," the "convicts," becomes singular, a reference to *him*, and him alone.

On Monday last, martial law was declared in Mankato and the vicinity. A general order was also promulgated by the commander of the Post, forbidding all persons in Mankato and the adjoining territory to a distance of ten miles, to sell or give intoxicating liquors to the enlisted men of the United States forces in this valley.

That same day, Ćaske was selected out from the hundreds of Indians being held in the Mankato jail on Front Street. He was moved next door to the Leech House, a three-story stone building, and confined in a back room on the first floor. He was chained, and closely guarded. The windows and doors were securely barricaded.

About half past two o'clock, Colonel Miller, accompanied by his staff officers, ministers, and a few others, visited Ćaske in the cell for the purpose of reading to him the President's approval of his sentence, and the order for his execution. Rev. Mr. Riggs acted as interpreter.

It would be expected that this scene would be peculiarly solemn and distressing to the doomed savage. To all appearances, however, it was not so. Ćaske received his sentence very coolly. He smoked a pipe composedly during the reading. When the time of execution was designated, he quietly knocked the ashes from the pipe and filled it afresh with kinnikinnik. He was evidently prepared for the visit and the announcement of his sentence, having overheard soldiers talking about it.

On Tuesday evening, Ćaske extemporized a dance with a wild Indian song. It was feared this was only a cover for something sinister he might attempt, and his chains were thereafter fastened to the floor. It seems, however, rather probable that he was only singing his death song.

On Wednesday, Ćaske was permitted to send for a few of his friends confined in the jail for the purpose of bidding them a final adieu, and of giving them messages to pass along to absent kin. Major Joseph Brown was present during the interview, and describes it as very sad and affecting. Ćaske sent word to his mother not to mourn for his loss, dying as he did, innocent of any white man's blood. He hoped she would consider his death but as a removal from this to a better world. A lock of hair, his coat, almost every article in his possession was given in trust for the old woman—

Your red headband. Your goose-feather, dyed red. Your wakaŋ-bag....

Ćaske was constantly attended by the missionaries, who gave great effort to bring the poor criminal to a knowledge of the merits of the Blessed Redeemer. These gentlemen are all conversant in the Dakota language and could plead with him in his own language. He exhibited no fear of the dread event. This appeared to be evidence not of Christian faith but steadfast adherence to his heathen superstitions.

On Thursday evening, we paid a brief visit to the cell. Ćaske seemed resigned to his fate. He sat perfectly motionless, more like a statue than a living man. The night passed quietly, nothing of special interest occurring.

At seven a.m. on Friday, all persons were promptly excluded from the room except those necessary to help prepare Ćaske for his doom. Under the superintendence of Major Brown, Ćaske's irons were knocked off, and he was tied by cords, his elbows being pinioned behind and the wrists in front, about six inches apart.

We visited Ćaske an hour before the execution. His face was painted with streaks of vermillion and aquamarine, and he wore a blanket over his shoulder. After shaking hands all around, though his arms and wrists were tied, he seated himself on the floor and composedly awaited the appointed hour. He seemed cheerful, occasionally smiling, or conversing. The last hour was occupied by Father Ravoux in religious service, but Ćaske did not follow him in prayer.

Around nine a.m., the hood was put upon his head. This was made of white muslin taken from the Indians when their camps were captured, part of the spoils they had taken from the murdered traders at Redwood. The hood looked like a meal sack, but, being rolled up, it only came down to the forehead, and allowed Ćaske's painted face yet to be seen.

He received the hood with evident dislike. When it had been adjusted on him, he looked around with an appearance of shame. Chains and cords had not moved him—their wear was not considered dishonorable—but this covering of his head with a white cap was humiliating. Ćaske sat in a crouched position, awaiting his doom in silence.

At precisely ten o'clock, the barricades were removed from the door. With Captain Redfield in the lead, Ćaske was marched out into the street. At once he began his death dance, and kept it up all the way to the gallows. The soldiers who were on guard in the prisoner's quarters stacked arms and followed him. They in turn were followed by the clergy and reporters.

With the weather turned mild as early autumn, the roads were muddy and the traveling bad. Nevertheless soldiers and civilians had come in from every direction. The streets, the sidewalks, the sand bar in the river, the opposite bank, windows, porches, housetops, and even trees were occupied by anxious spectators. It is estimated that not less than four thousand people, exclusive of the Military, were in attendance. Many women were dressed in their best half gowns, low neck and short skirts, to view the scene. Fathers hoisted young children onto their shoulders to give them a clear view of the gallows and admonished, "Remember this. It is a sight you'll never forget."

The Military force for the day totaled 1,419. Its display at the execution was the finest ever witnessed in the state. The soldiers had been in the service long enough to be well drilled and disciplined, they were cleanly uniformed and equipped, and presented a fine soldierly appearance.

Two lines of infantry were formed from the front door of the Leech House to the foot of the gallows, between which Ćaske passed to his doom. A line of infantry enclosed the gallows in the form of a square. The infantry was surrounded by a line of cavalry, kept in motion until Ćaske had ascended the gallows, when they were formed into lines facing the scaffold.

The gallows remains in place in hope of future use. It is constructed of heavy, square white oak timbers, cut on the hills at the back of the town. It stands in the town square, opposite the Military headquarters, close to the levee along the Minnesota River. It was erected in the form of a diamond, twenty-four feet on each angle, sufficient to execute ten on each side.

When Ćaske caught sight of the gallows, he hastened his step. Upon reaching the scaffold, he ascended the steps eagerly, almost cheerfully, as if to prove how little death can be feared. As he took his place, he was still dancing his dance and singing his death song. The noise he made was truly hideous. We are told by those familiar with the Dakota language that there was nothing defiant in his exclamations, but he was saying "I'm here! I'm here!" Indicating a readiness to meet death in partial atonement, at least, for his hellish outrages.

Though singing and dancing, pretending to die brave, a nervous clutching by Ćaske at his neck when the rope was being placed on his head was distinctly observed by those nearest the gallows.

His rope was adjusted. The white hood was pulled down over his face—

She loses him there, inside that hood. His hot breath, wetting the cold muslin. His nose, filling with the smell of cornmeal. The rope, rough around his neck. His own singing in his ears, drowning out the taunts from the crowd. Grandfather Sun, filtering through the coarse cloth. No sky to look to, except the one inside himself—

All was ready for the fatal signal. A painful and breathless suspense held the vast crowd. Though his hands were tied, Ćaske managed to point his fingers skyward—

"Nišnana yauŋ śni ye," she whispers. *You are not alone.*
Suddenly, she sees. All thirty-eight men, there on the scaffold. She hears all of them shouting, "I am here! I am here!"
She shouldn't have imagined him apart from the others. Waiting alone. Dancing alone. Singing alone. Praying alone. Preparing to die alone, on the gallows. No Sioux is ever alone.
Nišnana yauŋ śni ye.

Colonel Miller gave the command. Major Brown tapped three slow, measured and distinct beats upon the drum he held in his hand. The third tap was almost drowned by the voices of the Indians, but when it sounded, Captain William Duly, who had half his family massacred at Lake Shetek, cut at the rope with his axe. He failed to sever it. Another blow was more successful, and with a crash, down came the drop, and the 38 savage murderers were speedily sent to the happy hunting grounds—if such characters are there admissible.

A loud, prolonged huzza went up from the soldiery and citizens who were spectators. Then all were quiet and earnest witnesses of the scene.

Some fears had been entertained as to the working of the drop, but it was successful. In a second all but one were suspended by the neck. The rope broke with that one, and he fell to the ground, but his neck had been broken in the jerk and fall. He was instantly strung again—

She can't distinguish the face, this Indian who they had to hang twice. She riffles through the newspapers for a name. Lets out a sob when it isn't him.

The majority died easy, with but little suffering. The necks of nearly all were evidently dislocated by the fall, and the after-struggling was slight. A few kicked savagely.

It is unnecessary to speak of the awful sight of 38 human beings suspended in the air. Imagination will readily supply what we refrain from describing. But we will note that while the signal beat was being given, some of the doomed were seen to clasp the hands of their neighbors, which in several instances continued to be clasped until the bodies were cut down.

Drs. Seignorette and Finch were detailed to examine the bodies, and after all signs of life had disappeared, communicated the death of the prisoners to the officer of the day. The bodies were then cut down.

The scaffold fell at a quarter past ten o'clock, and in twenty minutes the bodies had been examined, and life pronounced extinct.

Four blue-painted Army wagons were now driven to the scaffold. The bodies were deposited in the wagons, and under an armed escort, conveyed to the place of burial. The great crowds of spectators, who had maintained a degree of order which had not been anticipated, quietly dispersed as the wagons bore the bodies of the murderers off to the grave. Few who witnessed the awful scene will voluntarily look upon its like again.

The burial place had been prepared near the jail, among the swamp willows on the sand bar between Front Street and the river. By appearances, it was a dreary and lonely place. All the Indians were deposited in one grave, thirty feet in length by twelve in width, and four feet deep. One layer of bodies was laid on the bottom of the trench in two rows, feet to feet. They were simply covered with their blankets, and on them two other rows were laid. Earth was then thrown over them, enough to say they were covered.

So great was the desire for relics that crucifixes, wampum, and ornaments were taken from the bodies before burial. Others took locks of hair and a few cut off pieces of clothing.

A number of physicians from different parts of the state as well as the Army surgeons were here in person or represented by agents to procure bodies for scientific use, since few were possessors of the perfect skeleton of any human being. Even a physician in Chicago proposed to pay the extravagant sum of $10 per body, once delivered to that city.

As soon as this day's night drew her sable curtain over the land, a score of resurrectionists met on the burial spot with their spades. The grave was opened, and 8-10 of the bodies were dug up. We should be surprised if any Indians still remain in the grave, as of this printing.

She abides in a dream from which she can't waken. She is insensible to her own state, to the house and its occupants, to the passage of time. She doesn't speak. She doesn't wash or brush her hair. She is dressed like a child. She is ushered out of her room, where she doesn't sleep, to the dining table, where she doesn't eat, to the parlor, where her body is a scaffold the children try to climb....

Now Lu is holding her hand, and Eli is standing over her with a tall man, clothed in black except for a white collar. *Whipple.* She peers up at their indistinct faces as through a thick pane of wavy glass. Their voices are a jumble.

"A mistake was in fact made."

"Unconscionable!"

"Oh 'Lijah, this is exactly what we feared.... Will they hold an inquiry?"

"No one sees the harm in what's happened. Like Joseph Brown said, we can't bring the Indian back."

"Joseph Brown?"

"He has charge of all the Indians in Mankato. Hanged the wrong man. Admitted as much to Henry here."

"I suspect they hanged the Indian they wanted to hang."

"But why would they hang Ćaske and let Chaskey-dan live, who carved a child from the womb?"

"They'll probably hang him, the next round."

"That gallows is built to do brisk business, Birdie. It's a hideous instrument, but ingenious.... What's vexing you, Henry? It's writ on your face."

"Major Brown said he didn't realize his mistake till Saturday, the day after the hanging. How is that possible? Forgive my saying so, Mrs. Wakefield"—Whipple's hand alights on her shoulder—"but there's been no shortage of talk about this Ćaske of yours and your defense of him at Camp Release. Even President Lincoln must have taken note of your testimony in the trial record."

"Your point, Henry?"

"Her protector was well known. Brown and his men simply couldn't have confused him with another Sioux, even one with the same name."

"For the sake of argument, suppose they did."

"Then they were confused for nearly a week! Think with me. Brown said he helped segregate the doomed Indians on Monday. Wednesday and Thursday, he witnessed their last meetings with kin. Friday, he helped prepare them for the gallows. He even gave the death signal. Yet somehow, in all that time, he never noticed he had the wrong man?"

"You're saying it was out-and-out murder."

She closes herself on the voices, feels her soul plummeting down, down, down.

SHE TESTS THE KNIFE ON HER THUMB, RAISING A TINY LINE OF BEADING BLOOD. She touches the blood to her tongue. Salty, like the sea.

How do they happen, all these moments when we find ourselves doing what we believed we could never do?

Standing before the mirror, she unties her nightcap. Lets her hair fall. Gathers her white mane into one hand behind her head, fist against scalp. Brings up the blade, begins to saw away.

Once she has shorn her head to white bristles, she rips open the front of her flannel nightgown. The dark tan from her weeks in the tipis has long ago faded to dull skin and freckles. Tentative and trembling, she nicks the side of a breast. Bites down against the sting. The wound weeps.

Now, a longer cut, not deep, across the top. She whispers to him in Dakota, unable to wail, in this house, like his woman.

❦ 7 ❧

IN THE WEEKS after her ritual of grief, she feels herself returning, wretched but recognizable, like a landscape when floodwaters start to recede. She begins tending herself again, the children too, as a woman should. "I know they need their mother," she says to Lu, "and truth be told, I need them." But sometimes, for all her love, James and Nellie seem far away as her Florie, back in Rhode Island.

It's more than work, loving and being loved. It's affliction. It can even kill.

She picks up her needle again, but she isn't as quick as she used to be at a button, and she breaks her thread between her teeth instead of snipping it with scissors. When she makes bread dough, she sometimes takes to frying it like a wiŋyaŋ before she catches herself. When she learns that Lincoln freed the slaves in the rebel states just days after hanging the Indians, she hikes to the top of Barn Bluff, braving the ice, needing to see the far dark edge of everything.

Finally she takes leave of Lu and Eli. "I have things I must tend to in St. Paul. Might the children stay with you till I'm done?"

From John, quartered at Fort Snelling, and from J.B., down in Blue Earth City, she asks no permission. She sends both brothers a curt announcement of her intentions. "I will," she writes, "be occupying your room at the American House indefinitely."

⟨∾⟩

The American House in St. Paul, at the corner of Third and Exchange, is an opulent hotel for a frontier town. Gentlemen of means and ambition meet in its dining room over drinks and fine meals. In its tearoom ladies sit for a spot of tea, sipping from hand-painted bone china teacups. Whenever the House boasts a lavish ball, the parade of the well-heeled and powerful arriving for the festivities attracts a streetful of spectators.

Sarah mounts the stairs to the top floor. At the end of the hall is Rm 313. Having frequent business in St. Paul, John and J.B. have kept this room ever since debarking in Minnesota. She swings the door open to the same solid furniture, the same sooty lamps, the same etched wall mirror, the same window with its hairline crack. In this blandly papered room, eight years ago, she'd said yes to John for the first time, agreeing to become his housekeeper.

"So"—he secured the bolt on the door and turned to confront her—"how long have you been passing, *Mr.* Jemison?"

Her stomach dropped. Through all of a hundred landscapes, all her monthlies, all her travel and toil in the company of men, she'd dreaded a moment like this.

Through his little gold spectacles his gaze swept the length of her. "You play quite a good man, on the whole. Deception is an art. I daresay its success depends at least half on the beholder. Artfully present a fiction as truth, and most men will regard it as truth, molding to their belief all evidence to the contrary."

"You have some experience with deception, then."

"Don't we all?" His face was intelligent and thin, his chin sharp under his goatee. He reached into his breast pocket with a sardonic smile and pulled out a cigar. "Care for a smoke? Or are you too much a woman?" He lit up without waiting for a reply. He pointed his cigar toward the bed, exhaling blue smoke. "Please."

She perched stiffly on the bed's edge, blood thrumming in her ears. He pinned her down with his stare.

"I can't imagine it has been easy, passing yourself off as this Jemison fellow. How long has it been?"

Her eyes traced the diagonal crack in the windowpane over his shoulder.

"If you want my help," he said, "you must speak up."

"I don't recall asking you for help."

He knocked the ash from his cigar. "Perhaps we should start again. I'm John Wakefield. A physician. Recently arrived from Connecticut after a stint in the goldfields. My brother and I—he's a lawyer—we have a property in Shakopee. You know the town, up on the Minnesota?"

"Never heard of it."

"It's not much more than a steamer landing at present, but its day is coming. Anyway, J.B. and I plan to share the house till we take hold. We need a woman to keep things in order, tend any boarders, and the like."

"I'm no maid."

"You can't be a man forever." His eyes narrowed. "You wouldn't want that, would you? To go on as a man?"

She refused him the satisfaction of an answer. He caught up his gold-handled walking stick and began to pace, tapping the floor. His long legs crossed the room in so few strides, he seemed always up against a wall.

"Here's what I think, Madam. You would gladly be done with this Jemison business, if you could." He didn't look to her for confirmation. "I'll take you by steamboat to Shakopee. You'll have your own private cabin. I'll supply dresses, petticoats, hairpieces, whatever you need to be a woman again by the time we land."

"All this, for a housekeeper?"

"For two years, I'll provide lodging, food and clothing in exchange for your labor. At the end of that period, I'll pay a hundred dollars in accumulated wages and release you from any further obligation. Any insolence, negligence or incompetence will result in a reduction of your earnings. And I'll not have you pulling another Jemison, or engaging in any sort of wickedness that might sully my name. No drunkenness, whoring, getting pregnant, consorting with Indians, or the like. If you disappoint me, by the time I finish with you, you'll have nothing left but your bloomers."

"I don't aim to be doing *anything* for you."

"Ah, but you will, unless you wish me to give away your secret." He ground out his cigar stub in an ashtray.

If the state weren't short on respectable females, Wakefield wouldn't be blackmailing a woman dressed as a man to keep his house. She sought to press her advantage. "I'll work no more than ten hours a day, with a half-day off, on Sunday. In my free time, I'll pursue gainful work of my own, with full control of my earnings."

"What kind of work?"

"I'm fair with a needle."

The slightest of nods.

"If you, sir, should marry within the two years, our business will be concluded. I'll need enough notice to find a new situation."

"Certainly."

"And I'll be fully compensated, as if I'd stayed the duration."

"Wages for time served, only." He flicked open a gold pocketwatch. "Anything more?"

"One last thing." She girded herself to speak like a man. "You may not strike me, or touch me, or mistreat the mortal part of me in any way."

He snapped his watchcase shut. Massaged it, in silence. "Very well." He went to the door, put his hand on the bolt. "I'll need your name, for the contract. Your *real* name."

"Sarah Butts," she said, upon consideration. "A widow, from back East."

WHEN JOHN VISITS HER FOR THE FIRST TIME FROM FT. SNELLING, HE SEATS HER on a corner of the bed and examines her shorn head as though she were his patient.

"How did this happen? You look like Jemison, grown old."

"They killed Ćaske." She grips the cannonball bedpost.

"So I read in the papers. A regrettable mistake."

"It wasn't a mistake. It was murder." She tells him about Eli and the Bishop making inquiries in Mankato; about Joseph Brown admitting he executed the wrong Indian.

"Christ." He burrows his fingers into the shock of her hair. "You look wretched."

"I cut it on impulse."

"Have you lost your mind? You'll be in your dotage before it grows back."

"It offends you?"

"As it would any man! What were you thinking?"

She winds a scarf around her head and knots it. "What's the latest on our claim?" Their depredation settlement is months overdue.

He removes his frock coat. "I've hired Gilfillan on contingency to expedite our case. The commission has asked for additional affidavits. They say our losses seem 'excessive.' Gilfillan's trying to locate witnesses to depose." He unties his cravat, tosses it aside. "The government is spending a fortune to keep thousands of Indians at Snelling, while we who lost everything at their hands get nothing. Where's the justice?"

❧ 8 ❧

FROM WIFELY DUTY Sarah calls on John at Fort Snelling each Monday and Thursday afternoon, as allowed by her military pass. On her outings, white refugees catch her eye in the streets. War widows and orphans, mostly. What betrays them isn't just their hand-me-down clothes or their guarded gait, but their eyes. One glimpse of their eyes and she can see the haunting, shades of the unforgettable, the untellable. They closely resemble the eyes in her own mirror.

Fort Snelling, mammoth and unassailable, has the shape of a diamond. Two sides are enclosed by a limestone wall, ten feet thick; steep bluffs overlook the river, protecting the other two. Towers command the four corners.

Below the fort, in a stockade on the flats, Sioux are dying by the dozens. Sickness has invaded the tipis: measles, pneumonia, smallpox, typhoid, scarlet fever, dysentery, mumps. Though employed as Indian physician, John shuns the "squaw pen" as much as possible. "I don't want you going down there under any circumstances," he warned, on Sarah's first visit. "It's a death trap." She didn't need him to tell her. The death wails of the wiŋyaŋ already had.

Rarely does he greet her at the main gate at the appointed hour. Sometimes she finds him engrossed in dissecting an animal carcass or doing paperwork in the office he shares with Dr. Potts, the post surgeon. More often, he's drinking and gambling with the troops. In recent days, he has been charged with negligence. A chaplain had reported him up the chain of command to Sibley himself.

This afternoon she discovers him at his desk, forehead on his arm, goatee resting on his casebook. His mouth is agape, his breathing slow and uneven. Despite appearances, he isn't passed out from drink. She doesn't even have to sniff. This is laudanum. Tincture of opium.

She eases the casebook from under his cheek; something to read until he comes around. He sighs, burbles, quiets again. Something of the boy creeps into him when he sleeps. A youthfulness around his eyes and lips. A looseness in his limbs, complete carelessness of body. His face is relaxed, without guise. In his sleeping she always sees visions of him at his best and cares for him a little beyond need.

She sits down with the casebook at Potts's desk. It falls open to a half-sheet of paper. Her initials are at the top.

S.F.W., 33 yrs.

Exhibits pathological preoccupation with savages. Intellectual faculties, moral reasoning otherwise intact.

Further symptoms: insomnia, constant use of irony, hysterical rants, over-dramatic gestures, declamatory voice, masculine willfulness. Fancies herself sensible and composed. Cut off all her hair.

Diagnosis: Monomania.

Treatment: Laudanum, other antihysterics. Educate pathology out of her, or startle out by vivid moral impression.

Prognosis: Condition in early stages. If not regulated, mania could cause stupidity or full dementia.

THE INSTANT JOHN STIRS, SHE SLAMS THE PAPER DOWN ON HIS DESK. "WHAT do you take me for?" She struts across the office, as far from him as she can get. "'Monomania?' You think me mad?"

"You ... aren't yourself." His words hesitant, slurred.

"I am entirely myself, I assure you."

"Ah ... proving your own delusion."

"I will *not* take laudanum. My *God,* John!"

"It will help restore your senses." He dodders around his desk. "You ought to be recovered by now ... it's been months."

"Recovered from what, exactly? Gleason, shot right in front of me? The loss of all my worldly possessions? Ćaske, hanged like a dog? The ruin of my good name?"

Wincing, he cups his hands over his ears. "You must quit with these rants of yours—"

"I want to see her."

"Who?"

"Uŋćiśi. Ćaske's mother. She's somewhere in the stockade."

"Sarah, I told you—" He reaches for her arm.

"Don't you touch me!"

"I don't want you going down there."

"Get me a pass."

"No." He trips back to his chair and drops onto the seat.

"Get me a pass, John, or I swear—"

"There's no point, Sarah! She isn't there."

"And just how would *you* know? One old woman, among thousands of Sioux you're loath to treat!"

"I know because she's dead." He swings his drugged head back and forth, as if trying to clear the fog. "She hanged herself, the day after they hanged *him.* I watched them cut her down."

SHE DOUBLES OVER WITH A MOAN AT SNELLING'S GATE, HAVING FLED JOHN IN horror. Snowflakes drop heavy on the back of her coat.

"Ma'am, are you well?" A sentry.

She stands herself up. Wills her feet to move. Crunches up the whitening fort road at a good clip. Once she rounds out of sight of the gatehouse, she bustles into a scraggly copse and retches.

"Of course I didn't tell you," John had said. "You haven't been yourself."

She loops back through the woods, heart beating against her ribs, skirts snagging on dead briars. At last she emerges from the tree line atop the cliff, beyond the fort's southeastern wall. She follows the dizzying rim of the precipice until she can view the stockade below. High fencing surrounds two or three acres of tipis on the flatland between the Minnesota and Mississippi Rivers. In one corner of the camp, Sioux are swarming an Army wagon as bluecoats dump barrels of hardtack on the ground.

Cannon are trained on the stockade from the bastion atop the bluff; a peculiar deployment, since the government claims to be detaining the Sioux for their own protection until their exile. And exile is now inevitable. Congress has nullified all treaties with the tribes and authorized their deportation to unoccupied land beyond the borders of the country, perhaps in Dakota Territory. The Winnebagos, who played no part in the war, will also be expelled.

"She hanged herself," John had said, "I watched them cut her down...."

Yes, there have been suicides in the camp, especially since the mass hanging in Mankato. According to the *Daily Press*, Chief Wapaśa's wife was among them. She'd simply stopped eating and wasted away. But Uŋćiśi? Even if grief were cleaving the flesh from her bones and sucking her lungs dry, she wouldn't have tied a noose around her neck. She would have fought to stay alive, she would have braved any suffering, for Ćaske's sake. Who else was there to listen for the voice of his spirit, to speak to him in prayers, to honor him with offerings? His wife and child were dead. Uŋćiśi was all he had.... No, she would never have done herself in.

A dozen or so wiŋyaŋ are rooting around in the woods, collecting fuel for their fires in the quiet of settling snow. For this chore, evidently, they're allowed to leave the stockade. Most are scavenging close to the Minnesota River, still frozen in its banks. But one wiŋyaŋ is below Sarah's perch on the bluff, hunting amidst the skeletons of trees. She must have strayed too far from the rest, because four bluecoats are advancing with rapid strides to fetch her back. When she spots them, she freezes. Lets her wood fall. Tears off on a run.

Two bluecoats soon catch her. Thrusting her facedown in brown weeds, they shove her head into the ground, smothering her screams. A third soldier, big as a moose, props his gun against a tree. Loosens his belt.

Sarah can't bear to watch. Too much of her is in that woman. Too much of that woman is in her. She stares in accusation at the dripping sky.

WHEN SHE DARES TO LOOK DOWN AGAIN, THE WOMAN IS WRITHING BENEATH A scrawny one. The moose clubs her temple with his gun. The wiŋyaŋ goes limp.

. . .

THE SCRAWNY ONE HAS FINISHED. THE MOOSE STRADDLES THE WIŊYAŊ FROM behind. With one hand he yanks up her head by the hair. With the other he swipes his knife across her throat.

The four soldiers dig a shallow hole with their knives and gunstocks. Roll the woman in. Scuff over a little dirt. The scrawny one spits, in valediction, as steady snowflakes fall.

9

"YOU'RE GOOD TO COME." Sarah pours Riggs's cup in the tearoom of the American House. "Black, I believe?"

"You remember." His eyes rest with disapproval on her close-cropped hair. She'd elected not to wear her headscarf down from RM 313.

"We are all ... much changed, are we not, Reverend?" She strokes the thatch of white at her temple.

He raises his teacup in agreement.

"How is Mrs. Riggs?" she asks. "The children?"

"They're adjusting, thanks be to God."

"They're living here in town?"

"Friends have hired us a house in St. Anthony."

"Not so far then."

"Not far." Beneath his greatcoat, spattered with dried mud, he's no longer in uniform. His service with Sibley must be done. "Dr. Wakefield tells me you're lodging here at the American." His eyes flick back to her hair. "Where are your children?"

"With John's sister in Red Wing. Like you, Reverend, we must rely on Providence, whatever form it might take."

The cleft between his eyebrows deepens.

"My husband tells me you're often at the Snelling stockade."

"Have you toured the camp?"

"No."

"You should. It's a revelation."

"I can't endure the crying of the women."

"Many in the camp are dying, regrettably."

"Up to ten a day, my husband says."

"I fear the dead aren't always treated with the respect that civilized people—Christian people—should afford them."

Her mind flits to the wiŋyaŋ in the woods. "The same could be said of the living."

"Yet despite everything, I have to say the Lord is performing a miracle in that camp. Between the Mankato hangings and all the deaths from disease, we're witnessing a great awakening of faith. Hundreds of Sioux have converted. It's a Heavenly visitation, a most amazing work of God's spirit, like the Pentecost of old! Someday, when the Lord God sees fit to supply a backer, I will have to tell it in a book."

"Mr. Riggs"—she sifts for words—"mightn't this 'awakening' be evidence of something other than faith? Fear, perhaps?"

"Nay, we've finally proven their gods weaker than ours. All these years, we've planted seeds among them, hoping for a harvest, and now, what a Godsend! How they pray! Not only for themselves and their absent kin but for the soldiers guarding them, and their White Father in Washington, and all the citizens of Minnesota who are angry at them. Sword and famine have evangelized the Sioux like schools and farms never could!"

"You believe the war ... the trials ... the hangings ... all of it has been God's will?"

"Without question! In the very same way that God permits Africans to be enslaved, that He might make Christians of them on American soil, He has allowed this harsh discipline to be inflicted upon the Sioux. Their superstition has been dashed to pieces like a potter's vessel! You really must see for yourself. I'm surprised your husband hasn't remarked on it. In fact, I asked him to approach you on my behalf.... Isn't that why you invited me today?"

"You have me at a disadvantage, I'm afraid."

"With the awakening in the camp and in the prison in Mankato, the Sioux are desperate to read and write. We're in urgent need of Dakota schoolbooks, hymnals, New Testaments...."

He wants you to join his translating efforts. Get on with it before he poses the question. "Mr. Riggs, I'm wondering if you might advise me as you would a daughter. You see, I have no father to ask."

"You *do* have a husband."

She smiles. "I don't wish to be indiscreet, but I can't be certain of my husband's goodwill. He thinks me a monomaniac, and a great many other things as well. He blames me very much for speaking as I did at Camp Release. The vile reports in circulation about me stain his reputation. He says he would have killed himself before remaining a captive in a tipi, and to my dishonor, so should have I."

Riggs runs his fingers through his disheveled hair. "What advice are you seeking?"

"How might I procure a situation by which to accompany the Sioux in their removal west? I don't care for any remuneration. I wish only to make myself useful."

"Madam, a woman's place is with her—"

"I've reason to believe the Sioux would welcome me back among them. If allowed, I'd happily devote my remaining years to them."

"Mrs. Wakefield—"

"You see, my disposition is of a peculiar kind. If someone befriends me, I would, in return, sacrifice everything but my honor to repay them."

"But you can't possibly go west without your husband!"

"Yet *he* could go west without *me*, if he chose, with your full blessing?"

"The Lord saith, 'Let not the wife depart from her husband—'"

"My husband cares not one whit about the Sioux! He considers them wolves! Yet you wouldn't bat an eye if he went west with them and abandoned me to my fate, deserted by friends, without sufficient means to support myself!"

"Madam, think of your children! Dakota Territory is no place for a civilized woman to raise her babies!"

"The Sioux have their own civilization, Reverend."

"And look what ruin it has brought them!"

"*We* have brought them to ruin!"

"Bridle your tongue! Why must you be so contrarian? Have you no decency?"

"You wish to speak of decency? Let's do…. I'd be pleased to learn from you the particulars of what happened in Mankato."

He sinks back in his chair. "Mankato?"

"I want to know how an innocent man was hanged."

"Ćaske, you mean." A slow shake of his head. "I doubt I can satisfactorily explain it."

"Kindly try."

He crosses his legs. Uncrosses them again. "Try to understand, Madam. From my youth up, I was determined never to see a fellow hanged."

"Yet you were at the prison that day. In fact, you were there throughout the final week, the papers said."

"As a matter of duty, yes, and as a favor to Colonel Sibley. Duty must always take precedence over feeling."

"And over conscience as well?"

"I hoped to be of service, and to further the ends of justice. The hangings were a terrible necessity. But they should have been carried out on the reservation instead of Mankato, away from the public's view. The desire for spectacle should never be gratified."

"I asked you about Ćaske."

"I'm coming to it." He's turning his teacup in its saucer, little by little, like the unhurried ticking of a clock. "We'd forgotten he was condemned under his given name."

"Wićaŋhpi Waśtedaŋpi."

"In the prison he was called Ćaske. And on that fatal morning—"

"The day of the execution?"

"No, on Monday, when we culled the prisoners to be hanged. It was a dreadful morning. We had to select thirty-nine Indians from hundreds of prisoners and mark them for death, without any sure means of identifying them."

"You couldn't tell one from another? Why, in Heaven's name?"

"The President listed the doomed Indians by case number. But no one could remember which case number attached to which Indian. The trial transcripts had been sent to Washington."

"Surely Sibley had retained a list of the Indians convicted."

"It came up missing from his files."

"'Missing?'"

His forehead is beading with sweat. "That's one reason he wanted me in Mankato—to help the executioners identify the right Indians in the absence of such a list. But Joseph Brown knew more of the Indians than I did. He had the final word. When we called for Ćaske, your Indian stepped forward."

"There must have been other Ćaskes among those hundreds of prisoners."

"In hindsight, at least two.... Robert Hopkins, an elder in my church—"

"I've met him." Riggs esteemed Hopkins so highly, he baptized him with the name of a dead friend. Had that Indian stepped forward, he certainly would have intervened. "And the other?"

"Ćaske-daŋ."

"The Indian on Lincoln's blacklist. The one who gutted a pregnant woman."

"Yes."

"So ... the name Ćaske was called, and my protector, of these three Ćaskes, was the only one who stepped forward."

"Yes. That's the only explanation."

"He stepped forward of his own free will?"

"He must have."

"No white man singled him out?"

"We acted with honor."

"Joseph Brown didn't recognize him as the man who had saved my life?"

"Apparently not."

"Nor you?"

"Obviously."

"And after that morning, you never once questioned whether you had selected the right Ćaske?"

"No. And neither did Brown."

She wants to believe him. But he was too familiar with Ćaske not to have realized the error. During the census at Camp Lookout, he recalled having met Ćaske before the war. He fawned over him for having protected her. Then, without explanation, he reversed himself and recommended Ćaske be put on trial. He even assisted Olin in the prosecution of the case, brushing aside her statements in Ćaske's defense and using her confidences against him.

"Could Ćaske have stepped forward because he thought you were freeing him," she says, "or thought you were separating him for some other purpose?"

"Possibly. But right after the sorting, we read the death sentence, in both English and Dakota. At that point, our meaning would have been clear. He could have saved himself."

She is quaking in her chair. *He would never have stepped back again. Not if it meant another Sioux dying in his place.... More likely, he'd stepped forward on purpose, sacrificing himself to spare a brother the white man's punishment.* "Reverend, I'm just an ignorant woman, and I'm squandering your valuable time, but I beg you to bear with me. More tea?"

He covers his cup with his hand.

She pours for herself. She adds a cube of sugar and a nip of cream, then a second sugar, stalling to regain her composure. "That final week," she says, "you took confessions from the men on the blacklist."

"Yes, I spent an entire day writing down their last words, in summary."

"I read them in the paper. But Ćaske didn't confess. He maintained his innocence."

"As did most of the scoundrels, you'll recall. Their protestations were less than convincing."

"In his declaration Ćaske recounted Hepaŋ's murder of Gleason, and his own protection of me."

"Yes."

"His story didn't ring a bell?"

"No."

"You didn't recall that Mr. Lincoln's order reprieved him? That Mr. Lincoln wanted Ćaske-daŋ to swing, for a truly despicable crime? You never noticed the contradiction in these two Indians' cases?"

His eyes bore into hers. "What are you accusing me of?"

"What are you guilty of?"

Their tones aren't fitting for a tearoom. Patrons around them have stopped talking to frown in their direction. Riggs flushes, his embarrassment plain. "It was a simple mistake, Madam. No one was to blame. In the trials we trusted that the innocent would make their innocence appear. In the hangings we did as nearly right as we knew how."

"'Nearly right?' You're a man of the cloth, and you helped send to the gallows a man meant to receive mercy. Mercy at the order of the President! Mercy deserved in full measure!"

"I won't defend what happened. I can only confess it and ask God's forgiveness." His face is a Pharisee's. No remorse, no shame, no sorrow.

"Mr. Riggs, I'll speak frankly. I myself unwittingly played a part in Ćaske's death. At Camp Release I was so afraid that you and the other authorities would think he'd abused me, I overexerted myself, trying to convince you otherwise. My anxiety to save him ended up killing him—I confess this. I'll always feel responsible for his murder. I'll never know quietness again." She feels an epic calm, admitting this aloud. "Yet I must also say, there are people whose guilt is far greater than mine. Wouldn't you agree?"

He stares at her.

"Say what you will, Mr. Riggs, but I do not believe these two Indians were confused. I do not believe Ćaske died by mistake, or accident, or oversight, or blunder. I believe somebody in Mankato wanted him dead, and killed him. I demand to know who."

"I can't oblige you."

"You mean, you *won't*."

He sniffs.

"When did you realize the wrong man had been hanged?"

"The next morning. I told your husband to forewarn you in advance of the papers, but he said he wouldn't see you in time."

The tearoom goes cold as a root cellar. "You saw *John,* in *Mankato,* after the hanging?"

"Climbing into a sleigh with two or three other men. He said you had taken the children away…. Are you all right, Madam?"

She flattens her palms on the table. "No, I'm not. Nor should I be, for more reasons than I can tell you."

Something akin to pity shows in him. "You've suffered enormously on account of this Indian."

"And Ćaske—what has *he* suffered on account of *us?*"

He rolls his little white tea napkin. "I might tell you I've written to President Lincoln, seeking pardons for Robert Hopkins, John Other Day, and Lorenzo Lawrence, who saved Mrs. DeCamp and her children. Good Christian Indians, all of them. They've been made to suffer enough."

"Had Ćaske been one of your mission Indians, you wouldn't have hanged him."

"Madam, *please….* I was going to say, perhaps I might also intercede on behalf of Ćaske's close relations. I delivered a letter once, on his behalf, to an old woman in the stockade—"

"His mother." She rises from the table. "You should go. We're done here."

"Let's not make a spectacle, I want to help—"

"There's nothing you can do, Reverend. Uŋćiśi hanged herself, the day after you hanged *him.* Put *that* in your book."

For an extraordinary moment they're two people alone in a noiseless, empty room. Then the chatter rushes in again, and the ping and tinkle of silver on china.

Riggs stands up like an invalid, steadying himself on the table. "Mrs. Wakefield, I pray you, indulge me one more minute."

They retake their chairs. He brings out a rumpled piece of paper from the pocket of his waistcoat and slides it across the tablecloth. "This is the letter I spoke of. I read it to the old woman. She didn't want to keep it … only the lock of hair wrapped inside."

All breath goes out of her. The letter lies between them like the dead. "He *wrote* her?"

"He dictated its contents to me."

"When?"

"I can't say. I wrote for so many prisoners over that span—"

"When?"

He lifts his hands helplessly, lets them fall. "Sometime in December, before the sorting. I made so many trips, carrying letters back and forth between Mankato and Fort Snelling—"

"Why did you hold onto it?"

"I don't know…. At least, I didn't till you asked to see me. Then I saw the Hand of God in it." He pushes himself up from the table and begins buttoning his coat. "I can't atone for all that's happened, Madam, but this letter might provide you some consolation."

"I can't take this. It wasn't meant for me."

"My dear woman, you *must* take it. I've no one else to give it to."

IT COULDN'T HAVE BEEN EASY FOR ĆASKE, IN CHAINS AT MANKATO, entrusting to Riggs his last words for Uŋćiśi. It isn't easy for her now, deciphering Riggs's transcription of them. She interprets the Dakota as she reads, grief an impediment to her parsing.

My mother I make this letter for you. It is so. I want you to listen. It is so. I am saddened my mother. Our people are experiencing great difficulty because of the war. We are all scattered and separated. Those of you who went north to Waterfalls At Mdote, we here remain one body with you.

Waterfalls At Mdote must be an allusion to Fort Snelling's location. Rather than name the fort where Uŋćiśi was confined, he'd referred to the waters at the heart of the Dakota world. *Ȟaȟa Mdote.* An understated attempt, it must have been, to reassure his mother and encourage her blood to be strong….

We have not seen you for a long time and it is a hard burden to bear. Now the missionaries have brought many letters. We hear the women and children at Waterfalls are pitiful and frightened and very hungry. Many of you are sick. I want you to be well. It is so. We are defeated and we suffer because of it. They say we are going to die. I think I will not be afraid. I want to die like I have lived. In the Dakota way. That is what I am thinking. In the manner soldiers die we want to die. The white people think we should all be killed because of what happened. No matter what we say to defend ourselves they will think of us as dogs. We want all our relatives imprisoned at Waterfalls to remain alive. If you ever get free you will make us glad. We are dead men. The things they tell us I do not understand very well. I trust Wakaŋtaŋka. This is for you to hear. It is so. This is all I will say. It is so. I shake your hand with my heart. It is so. And I kiss you Your son

Beneath Riggs's transcription, Ćaske had printed his name. He pressed so hard, scratching the letters, the nib dug the paper.

§ 10 ❧

SHE POSES IN THE LOOKING-GLASS. Turns left, pivots right. Practices her man-gait. Admires the perfect fit of her gray trousers, snatched from a clothes-line behind the hotel. She has never worn a finer pair.

She borrowed the shirt from the fat man two rooms down after he passed out bucknaked, with his door ajar. She paid a street waif a half-penny to poach the bowler hat from a barbershop across the street. The boots, tight but tolerable, she pinched from the porch in the officer's quarters at Snelling. No soldier worth his stripes would be so careless with his boots.

The black overcoat with fur collar and cuffs required no stealing. She'd brought it from Red Wing for John, a belated Christmas gift from Lu, but he prefers military issue. His Union greatcoat wins him goodwill from soldiers at the fort and civilians on the street.

She tests her man-smile in the glass. Arches an eyebrow. Purses her lips. Scowls.

The last time she was Thomas Jemison, here at the American House, she'd recently landed in St. Paul. She was still waiting for her man-hair to grow out when, in this very room, John unmasked her and made her his housekeeper. Steaming with him up the Minnesota River to Shakopee, she transformed herself into the widow Sarah Butts, aided by expensive hair-pieces and a serviceable woman's wardrobe. She got rid of Jemison for good, dropping his getup over the side of the boat. Or so she thought.

But now she must go to the stockade, as one bereaved must go to the wake. She can't possibly go as herself. Soldiers whose units had jeered her at Camp Release are posted there. And those few fenced-off acres are to preachers what empty fields are to farmers in the spring. Riggs, Williamson, Hinman, even Bishop Whipple have all put their shoulders to the gospel plow. Should one of them spot her, word would inevitably get back to John. He mustn't learn she has flouted him. A husband's fury, like public humiliation, can be borne by a wife, but only if it doesn't kill her first.

Then there are the Sioux, penned up like animals on Mdote, their most wakaŋ ground. She could never endure the shame of walking openly among them. They can't but revile Doctor Wife now, for what she and her people have caused them to suffer. Good Big Woman should slither away on her belly.

This morning at Snelling she stopped in the Provost Marshal's office, right before dress parade, a busy hour. "My cousin Thomas Jemison," she told the clerk, "has asked me to arrange him a tour of the Sioux camp. He wishes to donate books by which the missionaries might progress savage souls toward Heaven."

The harried clerk dashed off a pass, dated tomorrow. John will be absent from the fort, lately summoned to Shakopee by the lawyer Gilfillan in the ongoing dispute over their depredation claim. He won't be back for a couple of days.

She'd assumed that slipping back into Jemison after a lapse of years would be effortless, like slipping back into her Rhode Island accent after a couple of drinks. But somehow, even in full costume with her breasts trussed up, she can't put him on. It's as though he never existed.

She will have to add a limp, perhaps even a beard. She slants into the glass. Yes, a tuft below her bottom lip, like Sibley's; snippings of her hair, affixed to her chin with glue. A tiny badge of masculinity, white with the dignity of age.

Swinging her right leg from the hip, saddlebags slung over her shoulder, she limps into a line of civilians bearing passes. The bulky saddlebags are a ruse, should the guards notice the clerk's mention of missionary books. That part of her fiction had presented a regrettable complication. She owns only two books, the Sioux having burned the rest. So she'd stuffed the saddlebags with parcels meant to resemble books—old newspapers and cardboard cut to size, wrapped with paper and tied with string. She prays the guards will be either too lax or too busy to search. Just in case, the topmost parcel in one bag is her new Family Bible. In the other, the Williamsons' Old Testament.

The late-winter morning is milder than she expected. She sneaks a touch to her chin hair, checking the glue, as she pigeonholes the other visitors by talk and dress: a few immigrant farmers; several drunken rogues; a reporter; two gentlemen in expensive suits and top hats; a black-robed Catholic priest; the photographer Joel Whitney with an assistant, his studio name emblazoned on an equipment cart; and right in front of her, a family of five. One of the children is a shy boy, not much younger than James. He's turning in lazy circles, humming to himself.

Now she hears it—the absence of wailing from the stockade below. At least for today, there's no death. With trembling fingers she lights a cigarette pinched from Dr. Potts's desk and sucks the smoke down into her lungs.

A little hand coils around her two middle fingers. The boy. He has latched onto her by accident, as if she's his. Should she bend down and fuss over him like a mother, or grunt him off like a man? Her hand tightens, from missing James. The boy peeps up. She smiles. He pulls away and pins himself against his father's leg.

After a cursory inspection of their passes, an escort of soldiers conducts the visitors down a precipitous road cut out of the cliff. The track is slippery with mushy snow. With her false limp and saddlebags, Sarah's going is slow.

At the base of the cliff they file past a two-story warehouse-cum-commission station and arrive at the entrance to the Indian camp. A second examination of their passes, then the guards at the stockade gate unlock the great chains and admit the group into a desolation of tipis.

Sarah covers her mouth and nose with one of John's kerchiefs, to conceal her face. *Even a gentleman will guard himself against stench and disease.* She wills her boots forward through half-frozen muck and yellow slush. She has gone a hundred feet before she remembers to limp.

The prison camp is a perverse imitation of a Sioux village. The lodges are organized in dense lines along narrow alleys. Their doors are all to the east, by custom, but they have no yards. No busyness. No stories are being told by the fire, no games being played, no food being cooked or preserved, no hides being tanned, no wood being carved, no guns being cleaned. The only smells are wood smoke and dung. There's a profound absence of sound where there should be laughter, bickering, the play of children, hammering and chiseling, the clink of metal, dogs barking, the soft music of flutes, hoofbeats and whinnies and snorts.... The place feels all wrong.

"Not one step further!" cries the shy boy's mother, sunk to her ankles in an icy puddle, but her children, even the timid one, have scattered in excitement, oblivious to the filth.

The woman's husband puts an arm around her waist and helps her to more solid footing. "I'll keep you from falling, Harriet."

"You'll buy me a new dress, *that's* what you'll do! Just look at my skirt!"

Most of the tipi covers are the usual hide or canvas, but some are a patchwork of reed mats, sheets of bark, ragged quilts. The Sioux, as unprepared for captivity as they had been for war, have used whatever materials they could find for shelter and insulation. Sarah can't imagine their spending an entire winter in such wretched conditions, with furious storms ripping over the river flats.

One of the top hats has propped his cane over his shoulder like a musket. "Why, the Sioux look like Negroes on slave row," he says to no one in particular, as his well-heeled companion disappears into a tipi.

Sarah lags behind Joel Whitney, observing. His hat rests on top of his camera. He's already under the hood, lining up a shot; another "Sioux Belle" to immortalize on a 25-cent carte de visite. John, she knows, has a few such Belles locked in the bottom drawer of his desk, along with a bottle and a stash of money.

"Make her turn and face the camera!" Whitney says.

His scarecrow assistant tries without success to square the wiŋyaŋ's body. "She won't stay where I put her!"

Whitney withdraws from his box. He's working in his sleeves. "Her face, Dudley, I must have her face."

"Then *you* try her!" Dudley stalks off, leaving Sarah with a clear view of the woman.

Dinah.

The girl's body, angled left, is wrapped in a frayed plaid blanket shawl. She has nothing but rags on her feet, but she still wears beaded earrings, beads in her twin braids, beads in chains around her neck. Her hands are folded upon the table of her belly.

A baby ... not long to go. Not long at all.

The child could be anyone's. But suddenly Sarah's remembering the morning she left with Gleason; how forlorn the girl looked, sitting behind John on the stoop. She counts backwards to August.... Eight months.

She feels sick in her bones. Could it be true? Her own husband, perhaps in her own house?

Her mind runs to his curious seclusion during last winter's blizzard, when she regularly dispatched Dinah to his office with hot meals and fresh changes of clothes. Perhaps he was having his way with the girl even then....

She shudders. What if some lowdown, weaselly part of her had suspected right along? What if she occasionally noticed the girl's hair in disorder, or a mussing of her clothes, or the smell on her of his smoke, his liquor, his seed? What if she sensed the harm, and chose to say nothing, so she wouldn't have to suffer the brunt of him alone?

She can't bear the reek any longer. She was a fool, visiting this camp. She shifts the cumbersome saddlebags to her other shoulder and swings about to leave. But there at her feet, sitting on bony haunches, is a scabby white dog.

"Sadie?" Sarah says, uncertain.

The terrier cocks her ears. She stares up at Sarah with rheumy eyes. After two heavy blinks, her head sags.

Sarah stands like a prayer.

Sadie pulls up her hindquarters. Without bark, whine or whimper she hobbles down the sloppy street, lame in one leg.

Sarah casts a glance toward the stockade gate. She glares up at the pewter sky. Then she sets out after the mangy dog.

RUNNY-NOSED CHILDREN SEE THE FULL SADDLEBAGS OVER HER SHOULDER AND stretch out their palms as she limps by. Some of them wear the blotchy rash of measles. Their mattery eyes are a thousand years old.

Women hide their painted faces behind the folds of their blanket shawls. They want to trade, in murmurs—their trinkets for hardtack, their holey moccasins for jerky, their bodies for tobacco....

An iron-faced wiŋyaŋ with flashing eyes obstructs Sarah's path. She points at her tipi. Startled by the apparent overture, Sarah retreats a step, but the woman hastens to lift the flap over her door. "Wasiću see!"

Out of courtesy Sarah advances and stoops to peer in. The lodge is almost empty of possessions. An old couple hunches under a tattered crazy quilt near a smoldering fire. A younger wiŋyaŋ, racked with coughs, is nursing an infant piss-yellow with jaundice.

The woman at the door holds out her hand. "Mazaska!" *Money,* she wants, in payment for this pathetic living tableau.

The sky has fallen on this wiŋyaŋ, like all the other women in this prison camp. But however heavily the sky weighs on them, Sarah prays they stay on their feet. Even if the Big Knives hang all their men in Mankato; even if the Big Knives track down all their kin who fled after Lone Tree Lake and punish them with their big guns; even if the ancestors lose sight of them in this stockade; even if they must beg and steal and sell their bodies to survive, they must stand. They must be the people's spine. Else their little ones will not live, their old ones will go into the earth and their nation will perish forever.

"Mazaska!" the wiŋyaŋ says again, insisting with her hand. But Sarah has no money. She has nothing at all to give aside from worthless bundles of paper, and scripture.

With the toe of her boot, she nudges the woman's last sticks of kindling. Then she slings off her saddlebags. She unbuckles them and dumps their contents in a heap. The wiŋyaŋ stoops to pick up the biggest parcel. "Dena ideya," Sarah tells her.

Even Family Bibles can burn.

SADIE HAS VANISHED. SARAH LIMPS FURTHER INTO THE GRIM HEART OF THE place, blindly following her feet.

On the green at the center of the stockade huddle hundreds of Sioux. Many are barefoot and without comfort of a blanket. Gaunt as tipi poles, they cough from their chests, hack and spit. Little ones droop in their mothers' arms, without strength enough to bawl.

In the midst of the assembly, Little Paul is trying to raise a Dakota hymn, though he can't hit a pitch. "Wakaŋtaŋka taku nitawa...." Sarah remembers the song from her mission Sabbaths. *Great Spirit God, the things which are thine....* Even on a good day, the melody has something of a dirge about it. The congregants repeat each line after Little Paul in thin unison, drawing it out like misery, a few stout voices holding up the rest. This one hymn, with seven verses, might drag on until noon.

Mother Friend is seated on the cold ground near Little Paul's feet. Her head is tilted back, her eyes shut, her lips forming the words. Not far behind her sits Eagle Head. Last November, as the Military Commission was winding down its proceedings, the old man had been arrested after soldiers caught him trying to smuggle a case of knives into the Indian jail. The newspaper reports made no mention of his punishment.

From outside the square, wailing spirals up. Another death. Behind Little Paul a red shawl rises at the sound, steps around children, weaves between aunties, sets off in the direction of the grief. Something about the woman prompts Sarah to shadow her. One glimpse of her face is all she wants, but she's too far behind, and hindered by the pretense of her limp. Hurrying will attract attention. She cocks her bowler hat lower over her eyes.

Sadie appears up ahead, ears pointed forward, tail wagging. A thin hand reaches down from the shawl to grasp the dog's muzzle. Sadie licks it with affection.

Uŋčíši.

ꙮ I I ꙮ

MARCH 23, 1863

To His Excellency, Abraham Lincoln, President of the United States.

Dear Sir

I will introduce myself to your note as one of the prisoners in the late Indian War in Minnesota.

IN SARAH'S FANCY, Washington City has always been a mythical place, like King Arthur's Court. And poor Mr. Lincoln, with his dead son Willie and his awful War, is straight out of Shakespeare. Before these last months, she couldn't have imagined an ordinary citizen calling upon him at the Executive Mansion or writing him a letter in hopes of a reply.

She's no bishop like Whipple, no clergyman like Riggs, no eminent churchman like Eli. She hasn't even been baptized. She's only a woman, and her name is foul. But she has a righteous cause.

By the light of her candle, she dips her nib again.

My Husband was Physician for the Sioux at Yellow Medicine, and it was near there that I was overtaken by two Indians. I was saved from death by one called Ćaske, when Hepaŋ, the murderer of George H. Gleason, endeavored three times to shoot me. He not only saved me then but several times when I was in great danger.

Her room on the fourth story of the Mankato House overlooks the intersection of Front and Hickory. Shortly after her arrival, a thunderstorm crawled low and tar-black over the rooftops. After five hours of icy rain and bluster, it still hasn't budged. Wakiŋyaŋ and Uŋktehi are doing battle. Close thunder rattles the windows. Lightning forks down, cracking the sky, lighting the room like day. Uŋćiśi, were she here, would light a braid of sweetgrass.

She swills the air, lets it sink in, soak out. It has been far too long since she breathed like this. It feels a little like freedom.

When Col. H. H. Sibley arrived Ćaske was arrested and tried by Court Martial, no evidence appearing against him. His name was among others whose Punishment you commuted to imprisonment.

Back in the stockade, when she recognized Uŋćiśi, she was transfixed. How to follow her? How to face her? How to safeguard her, as once, with real intention, she'd sworn Ćaske she would? As Thomas Jemison, she could only stand there, weak in the knees, and watch the old woman go, blessing her inwardly, cursing herself and John and all the folly and treachery that had swept them to that place and time.

When you, Honorable Sir, sent on the list of those you wished Hanged, you named "Chaskey-dan," an Indian who murdered and cut open a Pregnant Woman.

As soon as Uŋćiśi's red shawl receded from view, she limped fast for the stockade gate. But when she got close, a substantial party of Sioux women was there, dancing in place to the throb of a hand drum. An imposing kuŋśi was striking the beat, her long white hair flowing free of braids. A wiŋyaŋ wakaŋ, she must have been, for she was singing in that spirit-tongue only Sioux understand. Louder and louder the holy woman sang to the heartbeat of the drum, and all the wiŋyaŋ were treading in rhythm, dozens of them, hundreds even, and the soldiers' trigger fingers were itching, itching to the insistent crescendo of song—

Then, all at once, those great chains dropped.

The great chains dropped off, and that immense gate swung open, as though under the influence of unseen hands. The chains dropped off, and that gate swung wide to the east, enough to reveal that Mdote was out there yet, and the wheel of life was tipping toward the thaw, when rivers and spirits would run free again—

That gate swung wide, and everything went, oh, so quiet. The drumming stopped. The singing stopped. The dancing stopped. Why, even the soldiers just stood there, wide-eyed and slack-jawed, like they were seeing Jesus.

The triumphant wiŋyaŋ let loose unearthly ululations. A few of the Big Knives, in a panic, trained their guns on the women's chests. "Get the hell back!" Sentries rushed to close the gate.

A standoff, it was, between the two sides, until the holy woman gave ground. The crowd of women gave ground with her, but much altered in spirit … or so Sarah believed, for she could feel the change in herself, as if those chains had dropped and that gate had swung open for her, too; as if that vision of Mdote, by some tender mercy, had also been allowed her, who didn't deserve it, and couldn't fathom it. A miracle, it was, like the parting of the Jordan River, by which Yahweh had assured the Israelites of His presence. With her own eyes she witnessed it, in an eternal space pried open by wakaŋ song.

"The Indian is too much a warrior," Thoreau had said. "He'll refuse to submit. Therefore, he will perish."

But Thoreau was wrong, because he didn't know the power of Mdote. And he didn't know the power of women.

Then there was made a sad mistake, whereby Ćaske who saved me and my little Family was executed in place of the guilty man. This man is now at Mankato, living, while a good honest man lies sleeping in Death.

As the wiŋyaŋ withdrew from the gate to the camp's interior, she dawdled uncertainly a short distance from the sentries, one hand on her empty saddlebags. Minutes before, she'd been anxious to get out. Now she couldn't seem to leave.

That's when a gust of wind plucked off her hat. Except, there was no wind. There hadn't been wind all morning. The hat landed at the feet of a skittish soldier who, not noticing, mashed it under his boot.

It's time, she knew then. Time to get herself free from her own sad prison. Time to regain her feet for the sake of her babies. Time to beat the drum of her life like a holy woman. Time to sing for a vision, how to live larger and truer. *Waćiŋ taŋka ye.*

She passed through that wakaŋ gate at full stride. She would never limp again. Not for anyone.

Ascending the steep wagon road, she saw in her mind what would happen next, clear as God. She would leave the next day for Red Wing. She would collect the children from Eli and Lu and take them by stage down to Galena; from there, by train to Chicago; then on to Rhode Island,

and a life where she could breathe. A life where she could be her natural self, without apology. A life lived uncommonly, in her home place, by the sea. All she had to do was start, and proceed like she couldn't fail.

She went posthaste to the post surgeon's office and jimmied the locked bottom drawer in John's desk. After thrusting his "Sioux Belles" into the stove, she took all his money. She slid past Dr. Potts on her way out the door.

Back at the American House she charged into her room, threw off her man clothes, and labored back into hers. She folded the fat man's shirt, carried it down the hall and laid it outside his door like a gift. She returned the comfortable pants to the clothesline behind the hotel; the crushed hat, to the barber across town. "My husband," she told him, "tends to confuse what's his with what isn't."

At the Minnesota Stagecoach Company she slid some of John's money across the counter. "One ticket for Red Wing," she said to the clerk.

"I'm sorry, Madam, the next coach is full. Not another till Monday."

She thought a moment, studying the timetable. She had to get gone before John came back.

"What's the fare to Mankato?"

I am extremely sorry this thing happened as it injures me greatly in the community where I live. I exerted myself very much to save him, and many have been so ungenerous as to say I was in love with him, that I was his wife & so on, all of which is absolutely false. He always treated me like a Brother would his Sister and as such I respect his memory and curse his slanderers.

All her life she has loved words. But they are too often confused with what's true. At best, they're mere approximations of truth, and must be carefully managed. Even God, in His wisdom, had introduced errors, contradictions and absurdities into His Scriptures; not to deceive, but to dispense the truth in measured doses. Too much truth too straight and fast can blind even the most faithful.

I was promised by the Court Martial that he should be saved from Death. I was content and much pleased when the list was published that you, Sir, declared guilty, and the nature of their crimes. You will imagine my astonishment shortly after the Execution to see in print the Confession of Ćaske, who saved my life and Babes. As soon as convenient I sent for Rev. S. R. Riggs, Missionary with the Sioux for many years. He said it was a sad affair and it ought to be known.

Riggs, to the contrary, would like the "sad affair" done with. Failing that, he will shovel the blame on Joseph Brown, and bury him alive, with sanctimony. But since Mr. Lincoln is familiar with Riggs through correspondence, she will stoop to using his name.

> *Where the fault lies I know not, but it would be extremely gratifying to me to have these heedless persons brought to Justice. I am abased already by the world, as I am a Friend of the Indians. This Indian's family I had known for eight years, and they were Farmers and doing well. This poor old Mother is left destitute, and broken hearted. She has the feeling if she is an Indian, surely we are Brothers, all made by one God, and we will all meet some day, and why not treat them as such here.*

Sioux and white, all children of one God, all bound for the same Heaven, and duty-bound, therefore, to treat one another as such: This is the bright strand of belief upon which she has washed up. But what of Mr. Lincoln? What manner of man is he, who executed Indians by the dozens yet emancipated slaves? Flawed, yes, but surely no tyrant, else he would have hanged all 303 condemned Sioux outright instead of whittling the blacklist to thirty-eight. Else the trial testimony of a woman could never have swayed him, and he would have signed off on Ćaske's death sentence over dinner.

> *I beg pardon for troubling you, but there is much said in reference to his Execution. The world says, If he was not convicted of Murder then why was he hanged? Then they draw their own conclusions. If this could be explained to the world, a great Stain would be lifted from my name. God knows I suffered enough with the Indians without suffering more now by white brethren & sisters.*

By and large, a woman's stains and sufferings are of little concern to a man if she isn't his kin. To gain Mr. Lincoln's sympathy, perhaps she should appeal to his fraternal feeling, by hinting at a smirch on John's honor....

> *My Husband is very anxious this thing should be made public, as he thinks the mistake was intentional on the part of a certain "Officer" at Mankato who has many children in the Sioux tribe.*

She won't mention Joseph Brown by name. She'll just touch a firebrand to the dry grass.

I pray you deem me not bold in addressing you, and grant my pardon for troubling you.

I remain

Yours Respectfully
  Sarah F. Wakefield.

P. S. It would be gratifying to me to have this guilty man "Chaskey-dan" executed, although I am in favor of the majority of the poor fellows being pardoned. I cannot deem them guilty as many persons, as they were so very kind and honorable to me while I was with them. And you, Sir, protect and save them as a people.

Somewhere on the stage from St. Paul to Mankato, she resolved to write this letter. If Reverend Riggs could appeal to the President on behalf of *his* Indians, she could inveigh against the murder of *hers.* Mr. Lincoln can't right the wrong, but by petitioning him for justice, she might yet vindicate Ćaske's name, and have her redemption. Indeed, her appeal might rouse the President to make amends somehow to Uŋćiśi, if not all the innocent Sioux. She will post the letter on Monday, before she boards the stage to Red Wing and her new life beyond.

She crosses the room to the rain-streaked window. Front Street is dark as sin. Somewhere down there waits the gallows.

SHE SIPS the mock turtle soup. The broth is weak, but she relishes the bite-sized squares of forcemeat, pleasantly spiced. In the interest of her purse strings, one bowl of soup must suffice.

Once she gets to Rhode Island, she will use her needle to support herself and her babies. But while building her clientele as a dressmaker, she might be wise to publish the story of her captivity. She could secure a backer, as Riggs means to do, and tell her story, delicately, without a third party twisting her words. Her book would almost certainly sell. New Englanders have strong ties to Minnesota. Many, like Julia, would have been following the headlines about the uprising and its aftermath—

"Pardon me." It's the fellow who was eating earlier at the corner table. His slicked-back hair is as orange as the stripes in her dress. "Don't think me forward, but it seems we're each dining alone. Might I suggest some strawberry ice cream? My treat, for suffering my company."

Her favorite flavor. She motions him to the chair across the table. He has a hideous purple scar along his neck, half hidden by his cravat.

"New to town, Mrs. —?"

"Brown." Her maiden name seems apt. "I'm here for a brief visit only."

"A wee shame." His features are freckled porcelain. "I own the hardware across the street. Name's John Meagher."

"Do I hear an accent, Mr. Meagher?"

"Thought me tongue worn off but for when I'm with me lads." Exaggerating his Irish brogue for her benefit.

He eyes her hair. She eyes his scar.

"Battle scratch," he says. "New Ulm."

"Forgive me for staring."

He reaches to stop a passing waiter. The front of his frock coat falls open, revealing his watch fob, fashioned from a braid of hair. A sweetheart's, perhaps. "Two strawberry ice creams, please."

"Thank you, Mr. Meagher."

"Say, the day's fine as can be. Have you seen the gallows yet? Lots of folks are coming to town for a look."

"There's been no time."

"Then allow me, once we've finished. It's a short walk. After, I can show you the river."

THE SCAFFOLD RISES FROM THE CENTER OF THE TOWN SQUARE, LOOKING RATHER like the frame of a small barn. Ten steep narrow steps lead up to a platform; above the platform loom four heavy crossbeams, each having ten empty notches, for ten ropes. "Built to do brisk business," Eli had said.

Three months it's been, since the hanging. She thinks of Ćaske's letter, which she carries in her corset. "I want to die," he'd said to Uŋćiśi, "like I have lived."

Meagher approaches the scaffold and slaps the end of an oaken plank. "Drove a nail myself, right here, when she was being built."

"Did you attend the execution?"

"Was on duty with my lads. Quite the day!"

A red-tailed hawk lands atop the gallows with a wild scream. She shivers.

"Cold?" Meagher starts to unbutton his coat.

"I'm warm enough, thank you. Might we walk on? To the grave, please, if it's not too far."

His eyebrows shoot up. "The hole? That ground isn't meant for a lady. Especially not after a rain."

"I'm not afraid of muddying my skirts."

"Well, then...."

He insists on her taking his arm. The two of them stroll toward the river, edging around glazed puddles and crusty mire, the frozen remains of last night's storm.

"So, Mrs. Brown, what brings you to Mankato?"

"I'm not like you, Mr. Meagher. I wasn't here that day. I wanted to see the place."

"I'm guessing the war caved in the roof on you."

"The roof and every wall."

"But see now, you're still standing."

"Like a chimney in the ruins."

"And your man?"

She swallows. "They killed him."

"Holy Mary, Mother of God."

At the end of the levee they pass into rough scrub. They proceed along a soft trace through swamp willows, talking the weather, the hardware business, the Confederacy, the Sioux. After a quarter-mile or so, Meagher veers off down the bank onto a strip of crusty sand that will soon be submerged by the spring thaw.

"My mucker George, he died in the war, the very first day. How that lad could sing...."

She's only half listening.

"The redskin that killed him, we strung him up with the rest—"

There's the hawk again, riding circles of air.

"—stacked the bodies in wagons, three or four deep, and hauled them out here. When we tossed George's redskin into the hole, I thought I'd be content. But my soul still had an itch, and when the Colonel said he wanted to post a picket around the place, I up and volunteered."

"A sandbar is an odd place for a grave."

"Easier to shovel, in winter." He stops in front of her and lights a handrolled cigarette.

"Can we keep going, Mr. Meagher?"

"Nowhere to go to, Mrs. Brown. We're here."

Ahead is the long, open grave. It's empty, of course, what with the robbing, but this is where the thirty-eight last lay, Ćaske among them.

"You've gone all white. Here—" Meagher gives her his cigarette and directs her to a boulder half-buried in sand.

She eases herself down onto the rock, her back to the hole. Glad for the tobacco, she sits blowing smoke toward the sky, where the hawk is now a pair.

"Sometime after supper," Meagher says, "a couple wagons came out. Dr. Bootilier was along, said him and his lads wanted to resurrect some 'skins."

It strikes her in a flash. She gapes at him. *"George,* you said? Killed the first day?"

"We let them have most of the bodies, but when I saw them hauling out Chaskey-dan, I said, 'Not so fast!'"

The cigarette drops from her fingers. "George *Gleason!*"

"I cut the rope off the savage's hands and feet. Sweet Mary, I even got a braid of his hair."

His watch fob. "Oh my God—"

"I meant to send the relics to George's people, but—"

"Oh God." She up and stumbles toward the grave. "These doctors ... who were they? Bootilier and who else?"

"Him and Mayo—he was with us at New Ulm. I can't say I knew the rest, but I couldn't see for sinning in the dark."

"What did they want the bodies for, did they say?"

"To cut on. Said they shouldn't go to waste—they'd wash downstream anyway, come spring."

Dissection. She sinks down on the edge of the shallow trench. *Riggs saw John the morning after the hanging, climbing into a sleigh with several other men. Doctors, they must have been.* "Leave me."

"You're het up." He kneels beside her.

"Leave me, I said!"

"Let me help you." His tobacco breath on her cheek. His glittering green eyes.

She seizes him by the collar and jerks him to her nose. "Mr. Meagher, either skedaddle your white ass back to town, or I swear, I'll bury you myself in this goddamned hole!"

THE CIGARETTE IS STILL WHERE SHE'D DROPPED IT, EXTINGUISHED BY THE DAMP. It's the only tobacco she has. Wakaŋtaŋka will have to forgive her if she doesn't use it properly. She's only a wasiću-win.

She wrestles off her coat and throws it aside. Wrapped around her shoulders is her half of Uŋčiśi's red shawl. The fringed shawl still smells faintly of the tipi, or the old woman herself. She rubs it against her cheek. Feels the coarseness of grief.

She slides down into the grave, out of the breeze, and unfurls the shawl on the sandy bottom. Then she draws Ćaske's letter from her corset. She doesn't want to give it up. Already she's losing the sound of his voice, the smell of his skin, the taste of his mouth, the feel of his touch. One day, she might lose the details of his face, and this letter will be all she has left of him. But she must try to put his spirit to rest, as best she can.

One last time she brushes the letter with her lips. Then she smooths it open upon the shawl. She taps onto it the cheap tobacco from the cigarette, saving back a little in the wrapper. After rolling it all up in a bundle, she binds it with strands of fringe.

She climbs to a copse of cottonwoods on the crest of the riverbank. Before long, under influence of spring, the swollen green buds on the trees will bloom into catkins. Sunlight glimmers on their reddish sap, Balm of Gilead, harvested as medicine by Sioux and settlers alike. The warming air is heady with its fragrance, honey tinged by camphor.

Perhaps someday, as Ćaske believed, part of his soul will live again on Earth. Perhaps somehow the violence of this generation won't be visited upon the next. Old hatreds will cease, and he will live in peace.

Here's the tree for it—a tall, graceful cottonwood, with a crook all but out of reach. She stretches on her toes to nest her bundle inside, the only grave she can provide. Then she rests the length of her body against the thick, craggy bark, as though the tree were him.

SHE EMPTIES INTO THE CUP OF HER HAND THE LAST TENDER PINCH OF TOBACCO from the cigarette wrapper. Clenching the tiny leaves in her fist, she presses the tobacco to her heart.

She'd been his accidental wiŋyaŋ, his wasiću wife, in a time of war. She doesn't know what that meant to him, exactly, or even to herself. It was wakaŋ, beyond the power of words to explain. All she knows for certain is that without him, she would have died, while without her, he might have lived. No weight can balance the uneven scales, forever tilted to the wrong.

"If I am killed," he told her once, "I will haunt My Wife forever."

This, too, she knows.

"Wićaŋȟpi Waśtedaŋpi!" she calls, in Dakota. "My Husband, I am here!"

"Two-hearted," he'd said she was, and what was true then is still true. Her white heart will always remember George Gleason, the Humphreys, Joseph DeCamp, the hundreds of settlers slain, the thousands displaced. And her Dakota heart will never forget Uŋćiśi, Eagle Head, Dowaŋ S'a, Opa, Pasu Kiyuksa, Mother Friend…. What suffering her people had caused them! Ćaske, most of all.

Her grief is impartial. Its skin has no color.

"My Husband was a good Dakota! I give thanks for his life!" Her voice ascends through the trees like a prayer song. "May the spirits lift him up and bear him home to his first wife in peace! May he greet his unborn child!"

She waits for a preternatural stirring of air, the screech of a hawk, the cooing of a mourning dove, an impossible whiff of burning sage ... any trifling sign, to reassure. But she is met with perfect indifference. The river ice, unmoving. The sun, dull and cool.

She feels as though she were drifting again in the skiff, all alone on the becalmed sea, her sail slack, no visible shore, only the winking light of old stars to tell her: something imperishable might yet be recovered from the deep. She will row in darkness until she drifts, she will drift in darkness until she rows.

"I will see you again, My Husband, when there is no more death...."

Her hand curls open. Tobacco flies loose on what's left of the wind.

I trust all who may read [my Narrative] will bear in mind that I do not pretend to be a book-writer, and will not expect to find much to please the mind's fancy.... I have written a true *statement of my captivity: what I suffered, and what I was spared from suffering, by a few Friendly or Christian Indians.... I do not publish a little work like this in the expectation of making money from it, but to vindicate myself, as I have been grievously abused by many, who are ignorant of the particulars of my captivity and release by the Indians. I trust all errors will be overlooked, and that the world will not censure me for speaking kindly of those who saved me from death and dishonor.*

Mrs. Sarah F. Wakefield
Six Weeks in the Sioux Tepees:
A Narrative of Indian Captivity (1863)

AUTHOR'S AFTERWORD

BENEATH THE SAME STARS is based on the life of Sarah Wakefield, a white doctor's wife who was caught up in the U.S.-Dakota War of 1862. That conflict, obscured in national memory by the concurrent Civil War, saw a faction of the Dakota nation (i.e., "the eastern Sioux") rise up against American traders, settlers and troops in southwestern Minnesota. Though lasting only six weeks, from August 18 to September 23, the war was pivotal in the history of this continent. It resulted, first of all, in more American casualties and refugees than any other Indian war. At least 650 Americans were killed, most of them unarmed men, women and children, and more than a fifth of Minnesota's 170,000 citizens were displaced.

The Dakota side also suffered. Perhaps 100 warriors fell in battle. Another 303 Dakota men were condemned to death by U.S. military tribunals speedily convened after the war. Forty were eventually hanged, 38 of them on December 26, 1862, at the order of President Abraham Lincoln. It was the largest judicial mass execution in American history. Of the roughly 278 men whose sentences were commuted to prison terms, at least a third would die in confinement. Meanwhile, the remaining Dakotas in Minnesota were rounded up and interned for half a year in a stockade at Fort Snelling. Hundreds in the camp perished from malnutrition, disease and murder. In May, 1863, American authorities expelled the surviving detainees to a reservation in Dakota Territory. Hundreds succumbed during and immediately after their deportation.

The 1862 uprising ignited decades of fighting between the U.S. Army and the Oćeti Šakowiŋ (the Seven Council Fires of the Dakota, Nakota and Lakota confederacy, more commonly referred to as "the Sioux"). That period of military engagement effectively ended on December 29, 1890, with the massacre at Wounded Knee. By that point, American subjugation of the West was almost complete, and the eastern Dakotas had been splintered into a diaspora people. Today, Dakota communities are found in five states and two Canadian provinces.

Generations after these nineteenth-century events, their painful repercussions are still with us. Yet a remarkable number of people remain unaware that the U.S.-Dakota War of 1862 ever happened.

SARAH WAKEFIELD'S *SIX WEEKS IN THE SIOUX TEPEES* IS THE BEST-KNOWN captivity narrative of the U.S.-Dakota War, probably the most studied, and by far the most controversial. The earliest version of her "pamphlet," as she called it, appeared in November, 1863, little more than a year after her captivity. She had hoped to publish it in Rhode Island, but I've uncovered no evidence she ever left Minnesota after the war. The Atlas Printing Company of Minneapolis issued the first edition. Copies of her book sold for a quarter each, the same cost as one of Joel Whitney's cartes de visite. She published a second edition in 1864 through the Argus Book & Job Printing Office in Shakopee.

While not entirely free of the racial prejudices of her day, Sarah's narrative is markedly different from other eyewitness accounts of the war written by white Americans. It isn't the best written in a formal sense, but it is the most passionate and the most startling in its arguments. In its pages she defends herself against accusations of immorality and scandal. She also criticizes the actions of her own people and government, castigating them for inciting the war, ineptly prosecuting it, and persecuting Ćaske and other Indians in its wake.

Beneath the Same Stars is my attempt to look deeper into the story of the war through the prism of Sarah's experience. In certain respects, the Sarah in these pages is a more reliable narrator than the Sarah of *Six Weeks*, who appears to have been suffering from post-traumatic stress stemming from both her wartime experiences and longtime spousal abuse. To some degree, my Sarah is probably also more fluent in Dakota than her historical counterpart.

This book is heavily researched. With minor exceptions, I confined my cast of characters to people who actually lived, and I was faithful to the broad contours of their lives, insofar as I was able to discern them. I based many scenes on documented events, much dialogue (including oratories) on written records and oral histories, and some correspondence on actual letters.[1] I drew all newspaper reports from original sources, though sometimes in abridged or composite form. I developed my depiction of Ćaske's trial from the sketchy court record and my research into court-martials as conducted in that period.[2]

Yet what I've written isn't history or biography, but fiction. I interpreted and shaped the facts, took liberties with them (e.g., by conflating similar events), and where they stopped, went beyond them to plausibly fill in the gaps. By confining the reader to the tight lens of Sarah's perspective, I also neglected and obscured some facts. So *Beneath the Same Stars* is ultimately a work of moral imagination, an act of earnest invention.

Sarah, James and Nellie Wakefield owed Ćaske their lives. As I understand traditional Dakota warfare, the warriors sometimes took captives, but they didn't view an enemy's women and children as noncombatants who should, by definition, be spared. Ćaske's actions on behalf of the Wakefields were therefore remarkable. Sarah attributed his heroism to his inherent goodness, his ability to discern right from wrong and his gratitude for the many kindnesses she had formerly shown his family and his band. Whatever his actual motives might have been, because he was the first Dakota man to touch her after her capture, she and her children belonged to him. Their fate passed into his hands. By allowing them to live, he essentially adopted them and assumed responsibility for protecting them and meeting their needs.

By tradition, Dakota people sometimes adopted captives as surrogates for dead relatives. Whether Ćaske regarded Sarah as a replacement for his deceased wife, I can't say. But he and many in his family honored Dakota custom by looking after the Wakefields like kin. Not all captives during the uprising were as fortunate in their treatment (e.g., Jannette DeCamp). Dakota warriors slew scores of settlers at the start of the outbreak, but they also took an unusual number of prisoners, both white and mixed blood, perhaps reflecting the ambivalence many tribal members felt about the war. Absorbing all those captives during wartime and properly caring for them proved exceedingly difficult.

The wartime relationship between Sarah and Ćaske was fraught. No one can specify with certainty its exact nature. After her release, Sarah repeatedly denied the charge that their involvement was ever romantic or sexual. Yet Dakota oral tradition, according to one of my sources, assumes they were a willing couple, a view that aligns with my own. What's beyond dispute is that Sarah deeply appreciated Ćaske, survived the war with her children because of him and his family, and sacrificed much for repeatedly saying so. Ironically, her regard for him likely contributed to his death.

Ćaske was hanged on December 26, 1862, with thirty-seven other Dakota men. He was one of two prisoners supposedly executed by accident. The other was Wasicuŋ, a sixteen-year-old white boy whom the Dakotas had adopted in childhood. The Military Commission acquitted the boy of the charges against him, but somehow the authorities still sent him to the gallows.

Sarah learned about Ćaske's hanging through newspaper coverage of the mass execution. "I am sure, in my own mind, it was done intentionally," she wrote in her narrative. "I dare not say by whom."[3]

ON MAY 4-5, 1863, IN ACCORDANCE WITH THE INDIAN REMOVAL ACT, THE 1,200 Dakotas still in the stockade at Fort Snelling were shipped out of St. Paul on the first leg of their harrowing transfer to Crow Creek, a new reservation in Dakota Territory. Uŋćiśi (whose given name I couldn't determine) and Eagle Head (Ḣuyapa) were likely among them. Also on board the steamer was the Reverend John P. Williamson, missionary son of Thomas and Margaret.

A month later, John Wakefield journeyed west with Thomas Galbraith to continue his service as Indian physician. In anticipation of Wakefield's appearance, John Williamson wrote his father: "Dr. Wakefield told me he was coming around with [Agent Galbraith], though I hope to never see him out here & all the Indians wish the same thing most heartily."[4] On June 9, Williamson informed Stephen Riggs: "These Indians have been dying very fast.... I am sorry to say Dr. Wakefield has come out with the Agent."[5] Young Samuel Brown, who served as Galbraith's interpreter at Crow Creek, later recalled that "The Doctor's *immoral* conduct was ... well known."[6]

John Wakefield apparently "got so scared he left" Crow Creek after only a month or two.[7] With his stint as Indian physician now over, the Wakefield family reassembled in Shakopee. Their homecoming was likely far from happy, but they received a significant financial boost from the settlement of their depredation claim. By 1870, John's worth had increased to ten times what it was before he and Sarah moved to the reservation. With prosperity came two more children, Julia (1866) and John, Jr. (1868).

During this time, John was gambling and drinking heavily in the town's saloons.

John died at the family residence on February 17, 1874. His death at the age of 50 was sudden and mysterious, variously attributed to minor illness,[8] "congestion of the brain"[9] and "an over dose [sic] of an opiate."[10] His death saddled Sarah with considerable debt. She might have felt some justice in burying him in an unmarked grave.

Within two years of John's death, Sarah moved the children from Shakopee to St. Paul, purportedly to advance their education. How she supported her family is unknown. The 1880 census listed her as the 51-year-old wife of 28-year-old Louis (or Lewis) Henderson, a farmer and tinner, living in New Canada, a French-Canadian suburb of St. Paul. That marriage was short-lived.

Sarah eventually purchased a new house in fashionable Merriam Park on the west side of St. Paul. She died there from "blood poisoning" resulting from "other ailments" on May 27, 1899, aged 69. She was preceded in death by her son James. Her obituary's subtitle reminded the public: "SHE WAS PRISONER OF THE SIOUX FOR SIX WEEKS DURING THEIR OUTBREAK."[11]

Upon Sarah's death, daughter Lucy (Nellie) burned all her parents' papers.

I WROTE *BENEATH THE SAME STARS* BECAUSE I WAS FASCINATED BY THE PEOPLE on whose lives it is based and their shared history. I wanted to bear witness to them, create empathy for them, and facilitate greater under-standing of the complex world they inhabited. But I also wrote because I'm troubled by how the uglier dynamics of their nineteenth-century world still contribute to much suffering today. Those dynamics include government corruption, clash of worldviews, religious arrogance, cultural and racial hegemony, demonization of "the Other," violation of basic human rights and treaty obligations, environmental degradation, competi-tion for natural resources, and gender-based violence. I wanted to shine a light on them, spark discussion of them, and help promote wise changes in the status quo.

Stories can be good medicine for what ails us. That's why we bother to tell them. They delve beneath jockeying facts and opinions to help us fathom one another and ourselves. They can nudge us toward the difficult reparation of wrongs, long recovery from woundedness and trauma, and the prevention of additional injury.

I offer this work with a good heart for the healing of the peoples. In the hard work of repair, there is much yet to be done.

NOTES

1. I used excerpts from Henry Sibley's letters to his wife Sarah, dated September 27 and 28, 1863. I presented Sarah's letter to President Lincoln verbatim, with some changes to punctuation and spelling. (There is no evidence that Lincoln ever replied.) Ćaske's letter to his mother, though a fiction, is comprised largely of phrases and sentences I culled from letters written or dictated by Dakota men while imprisoned after the war. Those letters were made available in *The Dakota Prisoner of War Letters: Dakota Kaśkapi Okicize Wowapi*, edited by Clifford Canku and Michael Simon (Minnesota Historical Society Press, 2012).

2. Not that Sibley's Military Commission bothered with proper procedures. For an excellent discussion of the legal aspects of the trials, see Carol Chomsky, "The United States-Dakota War Trials: A Study in Military Injustice," *Stanford Law Review* 43:1 (1990) 13-98. Ćaske's trial "transcript" consists of roughly five pages of longhand notes on legal-sized paper, about two-thirds being "testimony." This record, though scant, is still around seven times longer than the transcripts of most other defendants. The Dakota Trials Records are housed in the Senate records at the National Archives in Washington, DC. They have been transcribed by Walt Bachman and also published in unedited form as *The Dakota Trials* by John Isch.

3. Wakefield (1864) 122.

4. Letter to Thomas S. Williamson, undated [late May] 1863.

5. Letter to Stephen R. Riggs, 9 June 1863.

6. Samuel J. Brown, letter to William Watts Folwell, 25 July 1918.

7. John P. Williamson, letter to either Thomas S. Williamson or Stephen R. Riggs [late June or July] 1863.

8. *Shakopee Argus*, "Death of Dr. Wakefield," 19 Feb. 1874.

9. Yale's *Obituary Record*.

10. *St. Paul Daily Pioneer*, 19 Feb. 1874.

11. *St. Paul Pioneer Press*, "Death of Mrs. Wakefield," 29 May 1899.

DAKOTA GLOSSARY

Below are some of the Dakota words that appear in this novel. I've based their entries on the dictionary of Stephen Riggs, which Sarah Wakefield owned, and the linguistic and cultural knowledge of Darlene Renville Pipeboy, a Dakota-speaking Sisituŋwaŋ elder. Where I have misunderstood or strayed too far from these sources, the error is mine.

Dakota is the language of an oral society. Due to longstanding policies that prohibited its use, it is also an endangered language. It has no universally accepted orthography. Pronunciation varies according to dialect and other factors. English spelling and definitions are approximations.

QUICK PRONUNCIATION GUIDE

Vowels. Each of the five Dakota vowels has one distinctive sound: *a,* as in *father (ah),* sometimes tending toward *(uh),* as in *fudge; e,* as in *bet (eh),* sometimes tending toward *(ay),* as in *(bay); i,* as in *magazine (ee); o,* as in *hope (oh);* and *u,* as in *rule (oo).* Vowels are nasalized when followed by the symbol *ŋ.* In the word *wakaŋ,* for instance, the first *a* is pronounced *ah* while the second *a* is nasalized, yielding *wah-KAW.*

Consonants. Dakota uses a number of consonants not found in English. The following are employed in this word list: *ć,* as in *chin; h̃,* as in the guttural German pronunciation of *Bach* (represented by *kh* in the pronunciations below); *ś,* as in *shine;* and *ż, as in pleasure.*

Upper-case letters indicate accented syllables. An apostrophe (') represents a hiatus or pause between sounds.

At-e *(ah-TEH)*: father. (*Note:* I've inserted a hyphen between the syllables to distinguish this word from the English word "ate.")

Ćaske *(chahz-KEH)*: birth-order name of a firstborn son. Sarah Wakefield's captor and protector, a Mdewakaŋtuŋwaŋ.

Dakota *(dah-KOH-tah)*: friends, or allies. The Dakota nation's aboriginal name, as opposed to the more commonly used *Sioux*, a name assigned them by the Anishinaabe, a traditional enemy. *Sioux* appears to derive from *Nadouëssioux*, meaning "little snakes."

Dowaŋ S'a *(doh-WAW s'uh)*: The Singer, a cousin of Ćaske.

haŋ *(haw)*: male greeting or expression of agreement. Sometimes translated "It is so."

Hapstiŋna *(HAHP-stee-nah)*: birth-order name of a thirdborn daughter. The fictional name of *Śina Zi*, the servant of the Wakefields.

Hepaŋ *(heh-PAW)*: birth-order name of a second-born son. Captor of Sarah Wakefield.

Isaŋ Taŋka *(ee-SAH TAW-kah)*: Big Knives. American soldiers.

kinnikinnik *(kee-NEEK kee-neek)*: traditional herbal smoking mixture.

kuŋśi *(KOO-shee)*: grandmother(s).

Maza Kute Mani *(mah-zah koo-teh MAH-nee)*: He Who Shoots As He Walks, a Waȟpetuŋwaŋ leader of the peace party. Known by Euro-Americans as Little Paul.

Maza Śa *(mah-zah SHAH)*: Red Iron, a Waȟpetuŋwaŋ chief.

Mdewakaŋtuŋwaŋ *(meh-DAY-wah-KAW-too-waw)*: People Of The Sacred Lake; Mdewakantonwans, in English. One of the four divisions of the eastern (Santee, or Isaŋti) Dakotas, along with the Waȟpekute (Wahpekutes), Sisituŋwaŋ (Sissetons) and Waȟpetuŋwaŋ (Wahpetons). Also known as *Bdewakaŋtuŋwaŋ*.

Mdote *(meh-DOH-teh)*: area around the conjunction of the Minnesota and Mississippi Rivers. Considered by some eastern (Santee, or Isaŋti) Dakotas to be the center of the world, where their people emerged from the earth. Also known as *Bdote*.

mni *(meh-NEE)*: water.

Oćeti Śakowiŋ *(oh-CHEH-tee shock-OH-wee)*: the Seven Council Fires of the Dakota, Nakota and Lakota confederacy, more commonly referred to as "the Great Sioux Nation."

Opa *(OH-pah)*: She Who Is Part Of Everything. With her husband Pasu Kiyuksa, a friend of Sarah Wakefield.

Pasu Kiyuksa *(PAH-soo KEE-yook-sah):* Cut Nose. With his wife Opa, a friend of Sarah Wakefield. (*Note:* This man should not to be confused with the warrior known as Cut Nose who was hanged in Mankato.)

Pežihuta Wićaśa Tawićhu *(peh-ZHOO-tah wee-CHAH-shah tah-WEE-choo):* Doctor Wife, the name given to Sarah Wakefield by Śakpe's band of Mdewakaŋtuŋwaŋ.

Śakpe *(SHAHK-pay):* Six, a Mdewakaŋtuŋwaŋ chief. The town of Shakopee, Minnesota, was founded near his village and named for him.

Śakpe Daŋ *(shahk-PAY daw):* Little Six, son of Śakpe. A Mdewakaŋtuŋwaŋ chief and staunch ally of Taoyate Duta during the war.

Śina Zi *(shee-NAH ZEE):* Yellow Shawl, or Hapstiŋna, the name of Sarah Wakefield's fictional Dakota servant.

Sisituŋwaŋ *(see-SEE-too-waw):* People Who Dwell Where The Waters Meet; Sissetons, in English. One of the four divisions of the eastern (Santee, or Isaŋti) Dakotas, along with the Mdewakaŋtuŋwaŋ (Mdewakantonwans), Waȟpekute (Wahpekutes) and Waȟpetuŋwaŋ (Wahpetons).

Ta Makoće *(tah mah-KOH-chee):* His Land, the Dakota name of Reverend Stephen Riggs.

Taoyate Duta *(tah-oh-yah-teh DOO-tah):* His Red Nation. Better known in the period as Little Crow, especially among Euro-Americans. A Mdewakaŋtuŋwaŋ chief and principal Dakota leader against the Americans in the 1862 conflict.

Tate Mi Ma *(tah-TEH mee mah):* Round Wind, the chief crier in Taoyate Duta's camp.

Tiŋta Otoŋwe *(TEE-tah oh-TOH-weh):* chief Śakpe's village of Mdewakaŋtuŋwaŋ, near which the town of Shakopee, Minnesota, was founded.

tiośpaye *(tee-OHSH-pah-yeh):* extended family.

tipi *(tee-pee):* the portable house of the Dakotas, built of poles and a cloth of either buffalo hides or canvas.

Uŋćiśi *(oo-CHEE-shee):* My Mother-In-Law. What the fictional Sarah Wakefield called the mother of Ćaske.

Uŋkteȟi *(oo-kuh-TAY-khee):* legendary water monster who did battle with Wakiŋyaŋ, the Thunder Beings.

Waćiŋ taŋka ye *(wah-CHEE taw-ka yeh):* A traditional Dakota expression, meaning something like "act with deep purpose, according to the guidance of your spirit." A male speaker would replace *ye* with *do [doh].*

Waȟpekute *(wakh-PEH-koo-TAY):* People Who Fight Camouflaged In The Trees; Wahpekutes, in English. One of the four divisions of the eastern (Santee, or Isaŋti) Dakotas, along with the Mdewakaŋtuŋwaŋ

(Mdewakantonwans), Sisituŋwaŋ (Sissetons) and Waȟpetuŋwaŋ (Wahpetons).

Waȟpetuŋwaŋ *(wakh-PAY-too-waw):* Wahpetons, in English. The literal meaning is something like People Who Camped By The Tea. One of the four divisions of the eastern (Santee, or Isaŋti) Dakotas, along with the Mdewakaŋtuŋwaŋ (Mdewakantonwans), Sisituŋwaŋ (Sissetons) and Waȟpekute (Wahpekutes).

wakaŋ *(wah-KAW):* sacred, mysterious, beyond explanation.

Wakaŋtaŋka *(wah-KAW-taw-kah):* Great Mystery or Spirit.

Wakiŋyaŋ *(wah-KEE-yaw):* Thunder Beings, whose legendary opponent was the water monster Uŋktehi.

Wakiŋya Tawa *(wah-KEE-yah tah-wah):* His Thunder, the warrior who saved the trader George Spencer and was spared punishment after the uprising. His birth-order name was Ćaske.

Wakute *(wah-KOO-teh):* The Shooter, a Mdewakaŋtuŋwaŋ chief who joined the peace party.

Wapaśa *(wah-PAH-shah):* Red Leaf, a Mdewakaŋtuŋwaŋ chief who joined the peace party.

wasićú *(wah-SEE-choo):* non-Indian man (men), usually white. Sometimes a pejorative, meaning One Who Takes More Than One Needs, or a greedy person. The feminine form is *wasićú-win (-ween). (Note:* I've inserted a hyphen in the feminine form to distinguish the latter syllable from the English word "win.")

waśte *(WASH-teh):* good.

Wićaŋȟpi Waśtedaŋpi *(wee-CHAWKH-pee wash-TEH-daw-pee):* He Who Is Liked By The Stars, the given name of Ćaske, the protector of Sarah Wakefield.

wićaśa wakaŋ *(wee-CHAH-shah wah-KAW):* holy man (men).

wiŋyaŋ *(WEE-yaw):* woman (women).

Wiŋyaŋ Taŋka Waśte *(WEE-yaw TAW-kah wash-TAY):* Good Big Woman, a fictional name given by the Upper Dakotas to Sarah Wakefield, based on their historical description of her.

wiŋyaŋ wakaŋ *(WEE-yaw wah-KAW):* holy woman (women).

Winuna *(wee-NOO-nah):* birth-order name of a firstborn daughter. Ćaske's half-sister.

ABOUT THE AUTHOR

Phyllis Cole-Dai seeks in her writing to cross deep divides to promote understanding and respect. She has edited or authored works in multiple genres, including historical fiction, spiritual nonfiction and poetry. She resides in Brookings, South Dakota, with her husband, teenage son and two cats in a cozy 120-year-old house. Visit www.phylliscoledai.com to join her e-mail list and receive a free sampler of her work.

Connect with Phyllis:

WWW.PHYLLISCOLEDAI.COM

PHYLLIS@PHYLLISCOLEDAI.COM

FREE BOOKS FOR YOU

ALSO BY PHYLLIS COLE-DAI

(RECENT WORKS)

NONFICTION

The Emptiness of Our Hands: 47 Days on the Streets (3rd edition, 2018). Join Phyllis and her co-author James Murray as they give up their homes for forty-seven days to live on the streets of Columbus, Ohio. They set out with one primary intention: *to be as present as possible to everyone they meet.* This chronological account of their experiences, perfect for use in daily meditation, includes nearly thirty black and white photographs, most shot by James on the streets using crude pinhole cameras he constructed from trash. The book has been called an "eye-opening" and "life-changing" read! Available on Amazon in e-book and print formats.

Practicing Presence: Insights from the Streets. Deepen your understanding of the practice of being present while learning more about Phyllis's time on the streets. She wrote this series of forty-seven blog posts in 2009 on the tenth anniversary of her streets experience. A companion reader to *The Emptiness of Our Hands,* each of its brief chapters is based on an excerpt from that book. Also included are photographs that until now have never appeared in print. Available on Amazon as a free e-book.

The Book of the World: A Contemporary Scripture (edited on behalf of an unknown author). Enter the mystery of this contemporary scripture, whose origins and author are unknown. Speaking on behalf of no religion, it offers alongside other holy books its own poignant witness to compassion, love for the neighbor, love for the enemy, care for the earth, and more. A book of truths to be read and tested in everyday life. Perfect for daily meditation or group study. Available as a free e-book at www.phylliscoledai.com.

POETRY

Poetry of Presence: An Anthology of Mindfulness Poems (co-edited with Ruby R. Wilson). Find "good medicine" in this award-winning collection of more than 150 mindfulness poems, mostly by contemporary or recent poets. Mindfulness poems invite us to bring our whole self to whatever moment we're in, and truly live it. They encourage us to be more present, more attentive and compassionate, in the living of our days. They grant us a taste of being good enough, just as we are, in this world, just as it is. Anthologized poets include Margaret Atwood, Wendell Berry, Billy Collins, Thich Nhat Hanh, Joy Harjo, Seamus Heaney, Galway Kinnell,

Ted Kooser, Mary Oliver, Rainer Maria Rilke, Rumi, William Stafford, Alice Walker and many more. Available in paperback from all major retailers. Learn more at www.poetryofpresencebook.com.

Made in the USA
Monee, IL
05 May 2020